ALSO BY F. PAUL WILSON

Repairman Jack Novels:
The Tomb
Legacies
Conspiracies
All the Rage
Hosts
The Haunted Air
Gateways
Crisscross
Infernal

Healer
Wheels Within Wheels
An Enemy of the State
Black Wind
Soft & Others
Dydeetown World
The Tery
Sibs
The Select
Implant
Deep as the Marrow
Mirage (with Matthew J. Costello)
Nightkill (with Steven Spruill)
Masque (with Matthew J. Costello)
The Barrens & Others
The Christmas Thingy
Sims
Midnight Mass

The Adversary Cycle:
The Keep
The Tomb
The Touch
Reborn
Reprisal
Nightworld

Editor:
Freak Show
Diagnosis: Terminal

F. PAUL WILSON

GATEWAYS

A Repairman Jack Novel

TOR®

A TOM DOHERTY ASSOCIATES BOOK
NEW YORK

This is a work of fiction. All the characters and events portrayed in this book are either products of the author's imagination or are used fictitiously.

GATEWAYS

Copyright © 2003 by F. Paul Wilson

Edited by David G. Hartwell

A Tor Book
Published by Tom Doherty Associates, LLC
175 Fifth Avenue
New York, NY 10010

www.tor.com

Tor® is a registered trademark of Tom Doherty Associates, LLC.

ISBN 0-765-34605-2
EAN 978-0-765-34605-6

First edition: November 2003
First mass market edition: February 2006

Printed in the United States of America

0 9 8 7 6 5 4 3 2 1

for Daniel and Quinn

AUTHOR'S NOTE

Thanks to the usual crew for their editorial help with the manuscript: my wife, Mary; my editor, David Hartwell; his assistant, Moshe Feder; Elizabeth Monteleone; Steven Spruill (who also allowed me to tap into his store of knowledge about the Korean War); and my agent, Albert Zuckerman.

Thanks, too, to the many friendly South Florida folk and air-boat pilots who helped me along the way, especially the rangers at the Royal Palm and Shark Valley Visitor Centers in Everglades National Park who introduced me to the amazing diversity of wildlife in the Glades.

Special thanks to Stuart Schiff for being so generous with his fabulous single malts, and to Blake Dollens for his keen eye.

Finally, thanks to NY Joe (Joe Schmidt) and Angel (Janada Oakley) for advice on the weaponry. I did a little improvising along the way, so any errors in that area are my own.

GATEWAYS

TUESDAY

1

Blessed be the blackmailers, Jack thought as he pawed through the filing cabinet.

He had a penlight clamped in his teeth and kept it trained on the labels of the hanging folders while his latex-gloved fingers fanned through them.

What a trove. If someone could be called a professional blackmailer, Richie Cordova fit the bill. Private investigation was his legitimate line, if such a line could be legit. But apparently he dug up lots of additional dirt during the course of his investigations, and put that to work for him. Never against his clients, Jack had learned. Did his blackmailing anonymously. That kept his professional rep clean, kept that stream of referrals from satisfied clients flowing. But Jack had picked him up on a money drop Cordova had set up for his latest fish and took an instant dislike to the fat slob. Nine days of shadowing him hadn't mellowed that initial impression. The guy was a jerk.

Cordova's PI office occupied a second floor space over an Oriental deli on the other side of Bronx Park. But his other line of work, probably the more profitable one, was here on the third floor of his house. Small and stuffy, furnished with the filing cabinet, a computer, a high-end color printer, and a rickety desk, it appeared to be a converted attic.

Where was the letter? Jack was counting on it being in this cabinet. If not—

There . . . *Jank*. Could that stand for Jankowski? He

pulled out the file and opened it. Yep. This was it. Here was the handwritten letter at the root of Stanley Jankowski's problems. Cordova had found it and was using it to squeeze the banker for all he was worth.

Jack tucked it in his pocket.

Yes, blessed be those blackmailers, he thought as he began emptying the folders from both drawers of the cabinet and dropping their contents—letters, photos, negatives— onto the floor, for they help keepeth me in business.

Blackmail was the reason a fair percentage of Jack's customers came to him. Stood to reason: They were being blackmailed because they had something they wanted kept secret; couldn't go to officialdom because then it would no longer be a secret. So they were left with two options: pay the blackmailer again, and again, and again, or go outside the system and pay Jack once to find the offending photos or documents and either return them or destroy them.

Destroying was better and safer, Jack thought. But untrusting customers feared Jack might simply use the material to start blackmailing them on his own. Jankowski had been burned and wasn't about to trust no one no how no more. He wanted to see the letter before he paid the second half of Jack's fee.

Jack spread the two drawers' worth of photos and documents on the floor. A small, voyeuristic part of him wanted to sit and sift through them, looking for names or faces he recognized, but he resisted. No time. Cordova would be back in an hour.

He pulled a pair of glass Snapple bottles out of his backpack and unwrapped the duct tape from around their tops. He was about to do a big favor for some of the people in that pile. Not all. Cordova had probably scanned all this stuff into a computer and had digital copies stashed away somewhere. But a scan couldn't sub for a handwritten letter. Cordova needed the original, with its ink and fingerprints and all, to have any real leverage. A copy, no matter how close to the original, was not the real deal and could be dismissed as a clever fake.

He looked down at the pile of damning evidence. Some of these folks were about to get a freebie. Not because Jack particularly cared about them—for all he knew, some of them might deserve to be blackmailed—but because if he took just the Jankowski letter, Cordova would know who was behind this little visit. Jack didn't want that. With everything destroyed or damaged beyond repair, Cordova could only guess.

Burning the pile would have been best but the guy lived in a tight little Williamsbridge neighborhood in the upper Bronx. Lots of nice, old, post-war middle-class homes stacked cheek by jowl in a neat grid. If Cordova's place burned, it wouldn't burn alone. So Jack had come up with another way.

He held one of the Snapple bottles at arm's length as he unscrewed the cap. Even then the sharp odor stung his nose. Sulfuric acid. Very carefully—this stuff would burn right through his latex gloves—he began to sprinkle it on the pile, watching the glossy surfaces of the photos smoke and bubble, the papers turn brown and shrivel.

He'd used up most of the first bottle and the room was filling with acrid smoke when he heard the front door slam three floors below.

Cordova?

Checked his watch: about a quarter past midnight. In the past week or so that Jack had been shadowing him, Cordova had hit a neighborhood bar over on White Plains Road three times, and on each night he'd hung till 1 A.M. or later. If that was Cordova downstairs, he was home at least an hour early. Damn him.

Dumped the rest of the acid from the first bottle and sloshed the contents of the second over the pile, then left them atop the filing cabinet. Now to get out of here. Wouldn't be long before Cordova detected the stink.

Opened the window and slid out onto the roof. Looked around. He'd planned on leaving as he'd entered—through the back door. Now he was going to have to improvise.

Jack hated to improvise.

Looked over at the neighboring roof. Pretty close, but close enough to . . . ?

Through the open window behind him he heard Cordova's heavy feet pounding up the stairs. Another glance at the neighboring roof. Guessed it was going to have to be close enough.

Hauling in a deep breath, Jack took three running steps down the shingled slope and leaped. One sneakered foot, then the other, landed on the opposing roof and found traction. Without pausing to congratulate himself, Jack used his forward momentum to keep going, his rubber soles slipping and scraping up the incline toward the peak.

A loud, whiny "Noooooo!" followed by a bellow of rage and dismay echoed from Cordova's house, but Jack didn't turn to look—didn't want Cordova to see his face. Then he heard a shot and almost simultaneously felt the slug *zing* past his ear.

Cordova had a gun! Jack had figured he'd have one somewhere, but hadn't expected him to shoot up his own neighborhood. Two miscalculations tonight. He hoped he hadn't miscalculated on getting home alive.

Dove over the peak of the roof and slid down toward the gutter, the shingles shredding the palms of his latex gloves and wearing away the front of his nylon windbreaker like an electric sander. Halfway to the gutter he slowed his slide and angled his body ninety degrees. That slowed him a little more. Further angling around allowed him to get his foot in the gutter and stop altogether.

Not home free yet. Still two stories up with Cordova no

doubt pelting down his stairs and heading for the street. Plus this house was occupied, probably with two families, since that seemed the rule around here. He could see the glow of lights turning on inside. He was sure the owners were dialing 9-1-1 right now to report the racket on their roof. Probably thought he was a clumsy second-story burglar.

Jack peeked over the gutter and positioned himself over a dark window. Slid off the roof feet first and belly down, easing his weight onto the gutter. It groaned and creaked and sagged as he hung by his fingers. Before it could give way he managed to place his feet on the windowsill and let that take his weight. Eased himself into a crouch to where he could grip the sill with his hands, then dropped again. He clung to the sill only a second or two, poising his feet a mere six feet off the ground, then let go. He twisted in the air and hit the ground running.

His sneakers made no sound as he sprinted along the sidewalk. He bent as low as he could without compromising his speed and waited for a second shot. But none came. Took a left at the first corner and a right at the next and kept running. At least now he was out of the line of fire—if Cordova stayed on foot. But if he got into a car and started cruising . . .

Plus, cops should be on their way.

What a mess. This was supposed to be a simple in-and-out job with no one the wiser until later.

Kept moving in a crouch, watching the passing cars, on alert for flashing lights. Slipped out of his partially shredded windbreaker—he was wearing a WWE Lance Storm T-shirt beneath—and pulled the Mets cap from the pocket. Jammed the cap on his head and bunched the jacket into a nylon lump the size of a softball. Palmed that and slowed to a speedy walk.

Slowed further when he hit 232nd Street. Stuffed the windbreaker down into a trash receptacle as he walked to the elevated subway station on 233rd. Caught the 2 train and settled down for a long ride back to Manhattan.

He patted the letter folded in his jeans pocket. Another problem fixed. Jankowski would be happy, and Cordova . . .

Jack smiled. Fat Richie Cordova had to be fuming as much as the sulfuric acid on his photos and papers.

A man who was something more than a man crouched among the foundation plantings of a two-story house in a quiet Connecticut community. He moved through the world under different guises, using different names, but never his own, never his True Name. And as he traveled, doing what must be done to prepare the way, he searched out places such as this family home.

He sat with his spine and the back of his head pressed against the house's concrete foundation. Someone coming upon him might have thought he was an indigent sleeping off a bender. But he hadn't been sleeping. He required very little rest. He could go for days without closing his eyes.

And even if this had been one of those rare occasions when he needed rest, he would have found sleep impossible while basking in the exhilarating emanations from the basement of this house.

On the other side of the wall . . . systematic torture, mutilation, and defilement. The victim wasn't the first so abused by this family of three, and would not be the last. Or so the man who was something more than a man hoped.

What the two adults within had done to the ones they'd captured and imprisoned over the years would have been sustenance enough for this man. But the fact that they had debased their own child and made him a willing participant in the systematic defilement of another human being . . . this was exquisite.

He flattened his back more firmly against the wall, drinking, feasting . . .

After stopping at Julio's for a couple, Jack fell into bed when he got home. Jankowski could wait till morning for the good news.

Somewhere around 3 A.M. the ringing of the front-room phone dragged him from slumberland. The answering machine clicked on and out came a voice he hadn't heard in fifteen years.

"Jackie. This is your brother Tom. Long time no see. I assume you're still alive, though it's hard to tell. Well, anyway, Dad was in a car accident earlier tonight. He's in pretty bad shape, in a coma, they tell me. So give me a call, prontissimo. We need to talk."

He rattled off a number with a 215 area code.

Jack had been up and moving at the mention of his father's accident, but didn't reach the receiver in time to pick up. He stood over the phone in the dark.

Dad? In an accident? In a coma? How the hell—?

Unease trickled through his gut. The past he'd cut himself off from was worming its way back into his life. First he runs into his sister Kate last June, and a week later she's dead. Now, three months after that, he hears from big brother Tom that his father's in a coma. Was he detecting a scary symmetry here? A pattern?

Deal with that later, he told himself. First find out what happened to Dad.

Jack replayed the message, writing down the phone number. He used his Tracfone to return the call. That same voice answered.

"Tom? Jack."

"Well, I'll be. The long lost brother. The prodigal son. He lives. He returns a call."

Jack didn't have time for this. "What's the story with Dad?"

Jack had never particularly liked his brother. Hadn't disliked him either. They'd never had any sort of a relationship growing up. Tom—Tom, Jr., officially—was ten years older and seemed to have viewed his little brother as an inconvenient pet, one that belonged to his parents and his sister but had nothing to do with him. He'd always been self-involved to a fault. Kate had said he was on his third wife and hinted that the latest marriage was headed for the same fate as his others. Jack hadn't been surprised.

Tom had been a Philadelphia lawyer for a couple of decades and was now a Philadelphia judge. Which meant he was an officer of the court, a cog in the wheels of officialdom. All the more reason for Jack to keep his distance. Courts gave him the creeps.

"Pretty much what I told you. I got a call from this nurse at the Novaton Community Hospital that Dad was involved in an MVA and—"

"M-V—?"

"Motor vehicle accident—and that he's in bad shape."

"Yeah. A coma, right? Jeez, what do we do?"

"Not we, Jackie. You."

Jack didn't like the sound of this. "I don't get you."

"One of us has to go down there. I can't, and since Kate's not exactly available, that leaves you."

"What do you mean, you can't?"

"I—I'm in the middle of a bunch of legal business . . . judicial matters that have me tied up."

"You can't get away to see a comatose father?"

"It's complicated, Jackie. Too complicated to go into on the phone at this hour of the morning. Suffice it to say that I can't leave the city now."

Jack sensed a lot more going on here than Tom was telling.

"Are you in some sort of trouble?"

"Me? Christ, why would you ask something like that?"

"Because you sound funny."

Tom's tone took on a sharp edge. "How would you know what I sound like? We haven't spoken in, what, ten years, and you're going to tell me how I sound?"

"It's been fifteen years"—not quite long enough, Jack thought—"and yeah, I'm telling you you sound funny."

"Yeah, well, don't worry about me. Worry about Dad. He gave me your number before he moved to Florida. 'Just in case,' he said. Well, 'just in case' just happened. Tag, you're it."

Jack sighed. "All right. I guess I'll go."

"Don't sound so enthusiastic."

Jack shook his head. First off, he hated to leave New York for any reason, period. Plus, this wasn't a good time for him to be heading for Florida or anywhere else. He had another fix-it in the early stages of development, but he'd have to let it wait. Worse, an emergency trip like this meant that driving and Amtrak were out. He'd have to take a plane. He didn't mind flying itself, but all the extra security since 9-11 made an airport a scary place for a guy with no official identity.

But then, it was his father down there.

Tom said, "In a way you're lucky he's in a coma."

Strange thing to say. "How's that?"

"Because he's pissed at you for not showing up for Kate's funeral. Come to think of it, so am I. Where the hell were you?"

As if he'd tell a judge, even if that judge happened to be his big brother.

Big Brother . . . judge. How Orwellian.

"Suffice it to say," he said, deciding to give Tom a dose of his own medicine, "that it's too complicated to go into on the phone at this hour of the morning."

"Very funny. I tell you, though, I can't say I was unhappy about him taking a turn on you. All we heard for years from him was how he wanted to reach you and bring you back into the fold. That was how he put it: 'Bring Jack back into the fold.' It became his mantra. He obsessed on it. But he's not obsessing anymore."

Jack felt he should be glad to hear that—he'd had no intention of ever returning to any fold anywhere—but he wasn't. Instead he felt a pang of regret, as if he'd lost something.

A decade and a half ago, when Jack had dropped out of college, out of his family, and out of society in general, his father spent years tracking him down. Somehow he found someone who had Jack's number. He started calling. Eventually he wore Jack down to the point where he agreed to meet him in the city for dinner. After that they got together maybe once a year for a meal or a set of tennis.

A tenuous relationship at best. The get-togethers were always uncomfortable for Jack. Though his father had never said it, Jack knew he was disappointed in his younger son. Thought he was an appliance repairman and was always pushing him to better himself—finish college, get a pension plan, think about the future, retirement will be here before you know it, blah-blah-blah.

Dad didn't have a clue about what his younger son was about, the crimes he'd committed, the people he'd had to kill while earning his living, and Jack never would tell him. The old guy would be devastated.

"Where'd you say he was?"

"Novaton Community Hospital, and don't ask me where that is because I don't know. Someplace in Dade County, I'd imagine. That's where he had his place."

"Where's—?"

"South of Miami. Look, the best thing to do is call the hospital—no, I don't have the number—and ask for directions from Miami International. That's where you'll have to fly into."

"Swell."

"If he wakes up, explain to him that I'd be there if I could."

Sure you would, Jack thought. And then it hit him.

" '*If* he wakes up'?"

"Yeah. If. They say he's banged up pretty bad."

Jack's chest ached. "I'll leave as soon as I tie up a few loose ends here," he said, suddenly tired.

He hung up. He had nothing more to say to his brother.

4

Semelee awoke alone in the dark. She opened her eyes and lay perfect still, listenin. She heard the breathin sounds of her clansmen around her, some soft, some rough. She heard the creak of the old houseboat timbers as it rocked gentle like, the soft lap of the lagoon water against the hull, the croakin of frogs and the chirpin of crickets among the night sounds of the other Everglades critters. She jumped as someone nearby—Luke, most likely—made a coughin sound that turned into a snore.

The thick hot air lay like a damp sheet on the exposed skin of her arms and legs, but she was used to it. This September was provin to be a hot one, but not like August. *That* had been a hot one, hottest she could remember.

Why was she awake? She usually slept straight through the night. And then she remembered the dream—not the details, for they had vanished into the night like mornin mist before a storm, but the overall feel of movement . . . movement toward her.

"Someone's comin," she whispered aloud.

She didn't know how she knew, she just did. This weren't the first time she'd had a second sight. Every so often, without warnin, she'd get a sense of somethin about to happen, and then it did, it always did.

Someone was comin her way. A him, a man, was on his way. She didn't know if that was a good thing or a bad thing. Didn't matter. Either way, Semelee would be ready.

5

"Such bounty," Abe Grossman said, staring down at the half dozen donuts laid out in the box before him. "I've done what to deserve this?"

Jack said, "Nothing . . . everything."

Abe's raised eyebrows sent wrinkles like sets of surfing waves up his brow and into the balding bay of his scalp to crash on the receding gray shore of his hairline. "But Krispy Kremes? For me?"

"For *us*."

Jack dipped into the box and extracted one of the crustier, sour-cream models, heavy with grease and glazed to within an inch of its life. He took a big bite and closed his eyes. Damn, these were good.

Abe made a face. "But they're full of fat, those things." He rubbed his bulging waistline as if he had a belly ache. "Like ladling concrete into the arteries."

"Probably."

"And to me you brought them?"

The two of them flanked the scarred rear counter of Abe's store, the Isher Sports Shop, Jack on the customer side, Abe across from him, perched like Humpty Dumpty on a stool. Jack made a show of looking around at the dusty cans of tennis balls, the racquets, the basketballs and hoops, footballs and Rollerblades along with their attendant padding shoved helter skelter onto sagging shelves lining narrow aisles. Bikes and SCUBA gear hung from the ceiling. If the Collyer brothers had been into sporting goods instead of newspapers, this is what their place might have looked like.

"You see anyone else around?"

"We're not open yet. I should see no one."

"There you go." Jack pointed to the donuts. "Come on. What are you waiting for?"

"This is a trick, right? You're trying to pull one over on your old friend. You brought them for Parabellum."

As if in response to his name, Abe's little blue parakeet peeked out from behind a neon-yellow bicycle safety helmet, spotted the donut box, and hopped across the counter to it.

Jack spoke around a mouthful of donut. "Absolutely not."

Parabellum cocked his head at the donuts, then looked up at Jack.

"Better not deny him," Abe warned. "He's a fierce predator, that Parabellum. A raptor in disguise, even."

"Oh, right." Jack tore off a tiny piece and tossed it to the bird, who leaped on it.

"What happened to the fat-free Entenmann's and the low-fat cream cheese?"

"We're taking a vacation from all that."

Abe rubbed his belly again. "*Nu*? I shouldn't be worried about my heart? You want I should die before my time?"

"Jesus, Abe. Can we have one breakfast without you complaining? If I bring in low-cal stuff, you bitch. So here I bring the kind of stuff you always say you wish you were eating instead, and you accuse me of trying to kill you."

Abe was past sixty and his weight ran in the eighth-of-a-ton range, which wouldn't have been so bad if he were six-eight; but he missed that by a foot, maybe more. Jack had become concerned last year about his oldest and dearest friend's potential lack of longevity and had been trying to get him to lose weight. His efforts had not engendered an enthusiastic response.

"Such a crank he is this morning."

Abe was right. Maybe he was feeling a little short. Well, he had his reasons.

"Sorry," Jack said. "Look at it this way: Think of them as a going away present."

"Going? I'm going somewhere?"

"No, I am. To Florida. Don't know how long I'll be there so I figured I'd pre-load you with some calories to tide you over."

"Florida? You want to go to Florida? In September? In the middle of the worst drought they've had in decades?"

"It's not a pleasure trip."

"And the humidity. It seeps into your pores, heads for

the brain, makes you *meshugge*. Water on the brain—it's not healthy."

"Swell." Jack drummed his fingers on the counter. "Eat a damn donut, will you."

"All right," Abe said. "If you insist. A *bisel*."

He picked one, took a bite, and rolled his eyes. "Things should not be allowed to taste this good."

Jack had a second donut while he told Abe about his brother's call.

"I'm sorry to hear this," Abe said. "This is why you're so cranky? Because you don't want to see him?"

"I don't want to see him like that . . . in a coma."

Abe shook his head. "First your sister, and now . . ." He looked up at Jack. "You don't think . . . ?"

"The Otherness? I hope not. But with the way things have been going lately, I wouldn't be surprised."

After hanging up with Tom last night he'd called the hospital and learned that his father was stable but still on the critical list. He got directions from the airport, then tried to watch a movie. He'd started a Val Lewton festival, watching *The Cat People* Sunday night. He'd been looking forward to seeing *I Walked with a Zombie*, but after starting it he couldn't get into it. Thoughts about his father in a coma and getting through airport security proved too distracting. He'd shut if off and lain in the dark, trying to sleep, but thoughts about an indefinable something pulling the strings of his life kept him awake.

So this morning he was tired and irritable. The chance that the accident might not have been so accidental put him on edge. Learning that both the Ashe brothers were out on charters and he'd have to fly commercial made it worse. Much worse.

"You have any details on what happened?"

"Car accident is all I know."

"That doesn't sound too sinister. How old is he?"

"Seventy-one. But he's in great shape. Still plays tennis. Or at least he did."

Abe nodded. "I remember when he roped you into a father-son doubles match last summer."

"Right. Just before all hell broke loose up here."

"Another summer like that I don't need." Abe shook himself, as if warding off a chill. "Oh, I may have something for you on that citizenship matter."

"Yeah? What?"

Since he'd found out last month that he was going to be a father, Jack had been looking for a way to sneak up from underground without having to answer the inevitable questions from various agencies of the government as to where he'd been and what he'd been doing for the last fifteen years, and why he'd never applied for a Social Security Number and never filed a 1040 or paid a cent in taxes in all that time.

He'd thought of simply telling them he'd been ill—disoriented, possibly drug addled—wandering the country, depending on the kindness of strangers, and now he was better and ready to become a productive citizen. That would work, but in these suspicious times it meant he'd be put under extra scrutiny. He didn't want to live the rest of his life on the Department of Homeland Security's watch list.

"A contact in Eastern Europe called and said he thought maybe he had a way. Maybe. It's going to take a little more research."

This bit of good news felt like a spotlight through the gloom that had descended since Tom's call.

"Didn't he give you even a hint?"

Abe frowned. "Over an international phone line? From his country? He should be so foolish. When he works out the details—if he can—he will let me know."

Well, maybe it wasn't such good news. But at least it was potentially good news.

Abe was staring at him. "*Nu*? You're leaving for Florida when?"

"Today. Haven't booked a flight yet though. Want to talk to Gia first, see if I can convince her to come along."

"Think she'll go?"

Jack smiled. "I'm going to make her an offer she can't refuse."

6

"Sorry, Jack," Gia said, shaking her head. "It won't work."

They sat in the old-fashioned kitchen of number eight Sutton Square, one of the toniest neighborhoods in the city, he nursing a cup of coffee, she sipping green tea. Gia had been letting her corn-silk-colored hair grow out a little; it wasn't so close to her head anymore, but still short by most standards. She wore low-cut jeans and a white scoop-neck top that clung to her slim torso. Although into her third month of pregnancy, she had yet to show even the slightest bulge.

Gia's discovery last month that she was pregnant had thrown them both for a loop. It had not been on the radar, and they hadn't been prepared for it. It meant changes for both of them, most drastically for Jack, but they were dealing with it.

Jack had told her about his father as soon as he stepped through her door this morning. Gia had never met him but had been upset by the news and urged Jack to hurry down to Florida. Jack didn't share her sense of urgency. All he could do down there was stand next to his unconscious father's bed and feel helpless; he could think of few things in the world he hated more than feeling helpless. And if and when his father awoke, how long before he started in on why Jack had missed Kate's funeral.

So Jack had sprung his plan on Gia and she had shot him down.

He tried to hide his disappointment. He'd thought it was a sure thing. He'd offered to fly her and Vicky down to Orlando and put them up in Disney World. He'd shuttle back and forth between his father and Orlando.

"How can you say no?" he said. "Think of Vicky. She's never been to Disney World."

"Yes, she has. We went with Nellie and Grace when she was five."

Jack saw a cloud pass through her sky-blue eyes at the mention of Vicky's two dead aunts.

"That was three years ago. She needs another trip."

"Did you forget school?"

"Let her play hooky for a week. She's a bright kid. How much of a challenge can third grade be for her?"

Gia shook her head. "Uh-uh. New year, new class, new teacher. She just started two weeks ago. I can't pull her out for a week this early in the year. If it was November, maybe, but then"—she patted her tummy—"I'd be far enough along to where I wouldn't want to fly."

"Swell," Jack said. He took a turn patting her tummy. "How's Little Jack coming along?"

"She's doing just fine."

This had been their tug-of-war since learning she was pregnant. Jack was sure it was a boy—had to be—while Gia insisted it was a girl. So far the fetal doppler had been inconclusive as to sex.

"Hey, I just had an idea. What do you think about hiring Vicky a nanny for a week and . . ."

Gia's azure stare stopped him. "You're kidding, right?"

He sighed. "Yeah, I guess so."

What had he been thinking? Obviously he hadn't. Gia going off to Disney World without her daughter? Never. It would crush Vicky. And Jack would be as uncomfortable as Gia about leaving her with anyone else for a week.

He leaned back and watched her take tiny sips of her tea. He loved the way she drank tea, loved the way her whole face crinkled up when she laughed. Loved the way she did everything. They'd met a little over two years ago—twenty-six months, to be exact—but it seemed as if he'd known her all his life. All the women before her, and there'd been more than a few, had faded to shadows the first time he saw her smile. No one had a smile like Gia's. They'd hit a few speed bumps along the way—her discovery of how he earned his living had almost derailed them—and still didn't see eye to eye on everything, but the deep regard and trust they'd developed for each other allowed them to live with their differences.

Jack couldn't remember feeling about anyone as he felt about Gia. Every time he saw her he wanted to touch her— *had* to touch her, even if only for an instant brush of his fingertips against her arm. The only other person who approached Gia in his affections was her daughter Vicky. Jack and Vicks had bonded from the get-go. He couldn't think of too many people or things worth dying for, but two of them lived in this house.

"Aww," Gia said, smiling that smile and patting his knee. "Feeling shot down?"

"In flames. Looks like I'll be going alone. Usually you're the one getting on a plane and leaving." Gia made regular trips back to Iowa to keep Vicky in touch with her grandparents. Those weeks were like holes in his life. This one would be worse. "Now it's me."

"I've got a cure for those hurt feelings." She put her cup down, rose, and took his hand. "Come on."

"Where?"

"Upstairs. It's going to be a week. Let's give you a bon voyage party."

"Do we get to wear dopey hats?"

"No hats allowed. No clothes allowed either."

"My kind of party."

7

Jack was feeling a little cross-eyed and weak in the knees when they left Gia's. She had that effect on him.

On their way to his apartment on the West Side—she'd volunteered to help him pack—he stopped at a mailing service and picked up a couple of FedEx overnight boxes, along with some bubble wrap.

"What are those for?"

"Oh . . . just have to mail a couple of things before I go."

He didn't want to tell her more than that.

When they reached his third-floor apartment in a West-Eighties brownstone, he opened the windows to let in some air. The breeze carried a tang of carbon monoxide and the throbbing bass of a hip-hop song with the volume turned up to 11.

Gia said, "How are you going to work this?"

"What do you mean?"

"Buying the ticket."

They stood in the cluttered front room filled with Victorian wavy-grained golden oak furniture laden with gingerbread carving.

"How else? Buy a ticket and go."

"Who are you going to be this time?"

"John L. Tyleski."

After careful consideration, Jack had settled on Tyleski as his identity for the trip. Tyleski's Visa card, secured with a dead kid's Social Security Number, was barely six months old, and so far he'd made all his payments on time. Tyleski had a New Jersey driver license with his photo on it, courtesy of Ernie's ID. It was as bogus as everything else Ernie sold, but the quality was Sterling.

"Isn't that risky?" she said. "You get caught buying a ticket under an assumed identity these days and you're in trouble. Big, Federal trouble."

"I know. But the only way I can get caught is if someone checks the number on the driver license with the Jersey state DMV. Then I'm screwed. But they don't do that at airports."

"Not yet."

He looked at her. "You're not making this any easier, Gia."

She dropped into a wing-back chair, looking worried. "I just don't want to turn on the news tonight and hear that they're investigating some man with no identity who tried to board a plane, and see a picture of you."

"Neither do I."

Jack shivered. What a nightmare. The end of his life in the interstices. But even worse would be having his picture in the papers and on TV. He'd made a fair number of people very unhappy during the course of his fix-it career. The only reason he was still alive was because they didn't know who he was or where to find him. A very public arrest would change all that. Might as well paint a bull's-eye on his chest.

While Gia checked the Miami weather on the computer in the second bedroom, Jack seated himself at the claw-foot oak table and took out a spare wallet. He removed all traces of other identities, leaving only the Tyleski license and credit card, then added about a thousand in cash.

Gia returned from the other room. "The three-day forecast for Miami is in the nineties, so I'd better pack you light clothes."

"Fine. Throw in some running shorts while you're at it." He was dressed in jeans, sneakers, and a T-shirt now, but he needed something more for the trip. "While you're in there, pull me out a long-sleeved shirt, will you?"

She made a face. "Long-sleeved? It's hot."

"I have my reasons."

She shrugged and disappeared into his bedroom.

While she was digging through his drawers, Jack swathed his 9mm Glock 19 in bubble wrap, then wrapped that in aluminum foil, and shoved it into the FedEx box; he did the same with his .38 AMT Backup and its ankle holster, then packed in more wrap to keep them from shifting around in the box. That done he wrapped duct tape around the box wherever the FedEx logo appeared.

"How many days should I pack for?" Gia called from the other room.

"Three or four. If I stay longer I'll have them washed."

Gia popped back into the front room holding a lightweight cotton shirt with a tight red-and-blue check.

"You sure you want long sleeves?"

He nodded. "Need them to hide this."

He held up a plastic dagger. It was dark green, almost black, with a three-inch blade and a four-inch handle, all molded from a single piece of super-hard plastic fiber compound that Abe guaranteed would breeze past any metal detector on earth. The blade had no cutting edge to speak of, but the point was sharp enough to pierce plywood.

No one was hijacking *his* flight.

Gia's eyes widened. "Oh, Jack! You're not really thinking of—"

"I'll have it taped to the inside of my arm. No one will find it."

"This is insane! Do you know what will happen to you if you're caught?"

"I won't be." He held up a roll of adhesive tape. "Help me tape it on?"

"Absolutely not! I'll have no part in this craziness. It's irresponsible. You have a child on the way! Do you want to be in jail when she's born?"

"Of course not. But Gia, you should understand by now, this is the way I am, this is the way I have to do it."

"You're afraid of giving up control is what it is."

"Maybe so. Getting on a plane piloted by someone I don't know puts a crimp in my comfort zone. But I can handle that. What I can't handle is handing some out-to-lunch airline full responsibility for making sure that all the other passengers are going to behave."

"You've got to learn to trust, Jack."

"I do. I trust me, I trust you, I trust Abe, I trust Julio. Beyond that . . ." He shrugged. "Sorry. It's the way I'm wired." He held up the tape again. "Please?"

She helped, but he could tell her heart wasn't in it.

He blunted the point with a small piece of tape, then held it in place against the inside of his left upper arm, the butt of the handle almost in his armpit, while she secured it with three long strips that encircled his arm. Not the most comfortable arrangement, but he'd remove it in the restroom once they were in the air and transfer the knife to the inside of one of his socks for the rest of the flight.

When she finished taping she stepped back and looked at her work.

"That should hold. I . . ." She shook her head.

"What?"

"I can't help thinking that if there'd been someone like you on those 9-11 planes, the Trade Towers might still be standing."

"Maybe. Maybe not. I'm not Superman. I can't take on five alone. But along with guys like the ones on Flight 93, who knows?"

He pulled on the shirt, rolled the cuffs halfway up his forearms, and struck a pose.

"How do I look?"

"Suspicious," she said.

"Really?"

She sighed. "No. You look like you always look: Mister Everyday People."

That was what he wanted to hear. "Great. Am I packed?"

"I put it all on the bed. Where's your suitcase?"

"Suitcase? I don't have one. I've never needed one."

"That's right. You don't travel. How about a gym bag or something along that line?"

"Yeah, but it's filled with tools." His kind of tools.

"Well, if it's not too dirty inside, empty it out and we'll see if it'll do the job."

Jack pulled the bag out of a closet and emptied its contents on the kitchen counter: glass cutter, suction cup, rubber mallet, pry bar, slim jim for car doors, lock picks, an assortment of screwdrivers and clamps in various sizes and configurations.

"What is all this?" Gia asked as she watched the growing pile.

"Tools of the trade, m'dear. Tools of the trade."

"If you're a burglar, maybe."

He wiped out the inside of the bag with a damp paper towel and handed it to her. "Will this do?"

It did. His wardrobe down south would consist of shorts, T-shirts, socks, and boxers. They managed to stuff it all into the bag.

"You're going to look wrinkled," she warned.

"I'm going to Florida, remember? Wrinkle City."

"Touché."

He hefted the bag. "Do I check this or will they let me carry it on board?"

"That looks plenty small enough for the overhead."

"Overhead . . . ? Oh, right. I know what you mean."

She looked up at him. "When was the last time you were on a plane?"

Jack had to think about that. The answer was a little embarrassing. "I think it was sophomore year of college. Spring break in Lauderdale."

He barely remembered it. Seemed like a lifetime ago. In a way it was. A different life.

"Not once since?"

He shrugged. "No place I want to go."

She stared at him. "Is that the truth?"

"Of course. Anything I could ever want is right here in this city."

"You don't think the fact that flying is so much of a hassle, a *risky* hassle for you, has anything to do with it?"

"Maybe some." Where was this going?

Gia slipped her arms around him and squeezed, pressing herself against him.

"Don't you see?" she said. "Don't you see? You've built this anonymous, autonomous life for yourself, but it's become a trap. Sure, no one knows you exist and you don't spend the first four or five months of every year working for the government like the rest of us, and that's great in its way, but it's also a trap. Everywhere you go you've got to pretend to be someone else and run the risk of being found out. I go anywhere I want without a second thought. If I go to an airport and someone scrutinizes my ID, I'm not worried. But you've got the anxiety that someone will spot a flaw."

She released him and fixed him with her blue stare.

"Who's freer, Jack? Really."

She didn't understand. Jack figured she'd never fully understand. But that was okay. It didn't make him love her any less, because he knew where she was coming from. She'd been on her own for years, a single mother trying to make a career for herself and a life for her child. She had responsibilities beyond herself. Her days, spent dealing with the nuts and bolts of everyday life, were hectic and exhausting enough without adding multiple layers of complexity.

"It's not subject to comparison, Gia. I've lived the way I felt I had to live. By my rules, my code. My not paying taxes has nothing to do with money, it has to do with life, and who owns mine, or who owns yours, or Vicky's, or anyone's."

"I understand that, and philosophically I'm with you all the way. But in the practical, workaday world, how does that work for a man with a family? 'Oh, I'm sorry, honey. Daddy's not traveling with us because he's using a false identity and doesn't want us involved if he's picked up. But don't worry, he'll meet us there. I hope.' That's no way to bring up a child."

"We could *all* have false identities. We could be an under-the-radar family." He quickly held up his hands. "Only kidding."

"I hope so. What a nightmare that would be."

This time he pulled her close. "I'm working on it, Gi. I'll find a way."

She kissed him. "I know you will. You're Repairman Jack. You can fix anything."

"I'm glad you think so."

But coming back from underground with his freedom intact . . . that was a tall order.

You'd better come through for me, Abe, he thought, because I've hit a wall.

He didn't want the hassle of parking at the airport so he called a cab to take him to LaGuardia. Since Gia lived in the shadow of the Fifty-ninth Street Bridge, a minimal detour would allow him to drop her off at home along the way.

"Be careful," she whispered after a long good-bye kiss. "Come back to me, and don't get into any trouble down there."

"I'm visiting my comatose father. How on earth could I possibly get into any trouble?"

8

Jack reached the OmniShuttle Airways counter an hour before the next scheduled flight.

Before dropping Gia off, he'd had the cab take him over to Abe's where he left the package to be overnighted to his father's place. Abe used a small, exclusive, expensive shipping company that didn't ask questions. The cab ride had been uneventful, but it felt so odd to be moving about the city without a gun either tucked into the small of his back or strapped to his ankle. He didn't dare risk trying to sneak one onto the plane, though, even in checked luggage, now that they were x-raying every piece.

The ticket purchase went smoothly: A mocha-skinned woman with an indeterminate accent took the Tyleski Visa card and the Tyleski driver license, punched a lot of keys—an awful lot of keys—then handed them back along with a ticket and a boarding pass. Jack had chosen OmniShuttle because he didn't want any round-trip-ticket hassles. The airline sold one-way tickets without regard to Saturday stayovers or any of that other nonsense: When you want to go, buy a ticket; when you want to come back, buy another.

Jack's kind of company.

He asked for an aisle seat but they were all already taken. But he did manage to snag an exit row, giving him more leg room.

He had some time so he treated himself to a container of coffee with a trendoid name like mocha-latte-java-kaka-kookoo or something like that; it tasted pretty good. He bought some gum and then, steeling himself, headed for the metal detectors with their attendant body inspectors.

He made sure to get on the end of the longest line, to give him a chance to see how they conducted the screening process. He noticed that a much higher percentage of the people who set off the metal alarm were taken aside for more thorough screening than the ones who didn't. Jack wanted to be in the latter category.

This is how a terrorist must feel, he realized. Standing on line, sweating, praying that no one sees through his bogus identity. Except I'm not looking to hurt anyone. I'm just looking to get to Florida.

When it came his time, he placed his bag on the belt and watched as it was swallowed by the maw of the fluoroscope. Then it was his turn to step through the metal detector. He put his watch, change, and keys into a little bowl that was passed around the detector, then stepped through.

His heart skipped a beat and jumped into high gear when a loud beep sounded. Damn!

"Sir, have you emptied your pockets?" said a busty bottle-blonde woman in a white shirt with epaulettes, a gold badge, and a name tag that read "Delores." She was armed with a metal detecting wand. A dozen feet behind her, two security guards stood with carbines slung over their shoulders.

"I thought I did. Let me check again." He patted his pants pockets front and rear but, except for his wallet, they were empty. He pulled out the wallet. "Could this be the culprit?"

She waved her wand past it without a beep. "No, sir. Step over here, please."

"What for?"

"I have to wand you."

When had "wand" become a verb?

"Is something wrong?"

"Probably just your belt buckle or jewelry. Stand here, back to the table. Good. Now spread your legs and raise your arms out from your body."

Jack assumed the position. The moisture deserting his mouth seemed to be migrating to his palms. She waved the wand up and down the inside and outside of his legs, then across his waist where she got a beep from his belt buckle— no problem—and then she started on his arms. Right one first—inside and outside, okay; then the left—outside okay, but a loud beep as the wand approached his armpit.

Oh shit, oh hell, oh Christ. Abe you promised me, you swore to me the knife would pass the detectors. What's happening?

Without moving his head, Jack checked out the two security guards from the corner of his right eye. They looked bored, and certainly weren't paying attention to him. To his left a handful of unarmed security personnel were busy screening—wanding—other travelers. He could barrel past them and dash back out into the terminal, but where to go from there? His chances of escaping were nil, he knew, but he damn well wasn't simply going to stand here and put his hands out for the cuffs. If they wanted him, they were going to have to catch him.

"Sir?"

"Hmmm? What?" Jack could feel the sweat breaking out on his forehead. Had she noticed?

"I said, do you have anything in your breast pocket?"

"My—?"

He jammed his hand into the pocket and came out with

his package of Dentyne Ice. Gum in a blister pack . . . sealed with foil . . .

She ran her wand over it and was rewarded with a beep. She took the pack, opened it to make sure it was only gum, then dropped it on the table. The rest of the wanding was beepless.

The future that had been telescoping closed at warp-10 now opened wide again. Feeling as giddy as a man with a reprieve from death row, Jack retrieved his watch, keys, and chain, but he left the damn gum. It had put him on a train to heart attack city. Let Delores have it.

As he hefted his gym bag strap onto his shoulder he fought an urge to ask Delores if she wanted to inspect that too. Inspect anything you want! The mad inspectee strikes again!

But he said nothing, contenting himself with a friendly nod as he started toward his gate. He reached it with just enough time to put in a quick to call Gia.

"I made it," he said when she answered. "I board the plane in a couple of minutes."

"Thank God! Now I won't have to figure out how to bake a cake with a file inside."

"Well, there's still the flight home."

"Let's not think about that yet. Call me when you've seen your father, and let me know how he is."

"Will do. Love ya."

"Love you too, Jack. Very much. Just be careful. Don't talk to strangers or go riding in strange cars, or take candy from—"

"Gotta run."

He wound up in a window seat in the left emergency row with the perfect traveling companion: The guy fell asleep before takeoff and didn't wake up until they were on the Miami tarmac. No small talk and Jack got to eat the guy's complimentary bag of peanuts.

The only glitch in the trip was a slight westward alteration of the usual flight path due to tropical storm Elvis. Elvis . . . when Jack had heard the name announced on TV the other night he'd done a double take that would have put Lou Costello to shame.

He wondered now if there'd ever been a tropical storm named Eliot. If so, had it been designated on the maps as T. S. Eliot?

Elvis was not expected to graduate to hurricane status, but was presently off the coast near Jacksonville, cruising landward and stirring things up, just as its namesake had in the fifties. Though the plane swung westward to avoid the turbulence, Jack could see the storm churning away to the east. From his high perch he looked out over the rugged terrain of cloud tops broken dramatically here and there by fluffy white buttes from violent updrafts. Elvis was entering the building.

"Don't let her bite me, Semelee!" Corley cried.

Semelee lifted the shells away from her eyes and looked at Corley.

Corley's good eye, the one he could open, rolled in its socket under his bulging forehead as he looked up at her from where he stood waist deep in the lagoon. Normally at that spot in the lagoon the water'd be up to his neck. But with this drought . . .

Corley was hard on the eyes, that was for sure, but that made him good for beggin. They'd take him to town, sit him in a shady spot on the sidewalk, put a beat-up old hat in front of him, and wait. That hat wouldn't stay empty for long. People'd take one look at that face and empty their pockets of all their spare change, even toss in a few bills now and then.

But Tuesdays weren't no good for beggin—not as bad as Mondays, but bad. So Mondays and Tuesdays became fishin days.

"Tell her not to bite!" Corley wailed.

"Hesh up and hold the net," Luke told him.

Semelee smiled as she watched the two clansmen from the deck of the second, smaller houseboat, the *Horse-ship*. They stood in the water beside the boat, each holdin a four-foot pole with a net of half-inch nylon mesh stretched between them. Twisted trees with tortured trunks on the bank leaned over the water.

Luke was Corley's half brother, and he was special too. Not in ways you could see so plain like Corley's, and not in ways that was much good on the beggin front. So he mostly just ferried the beggin folk around. But Luke was special in his own way. Maybe too special. He'd tried the beggin thing, takin off his shirt to show the little fins runnin down his spine and all the big scales that covered his back, but he was a flop. Didn't collect a dime. People was heard to say it looked fake, that no one could really have a back that ugly, and wouldn't drop a dime. The cops tried to arrest him for public disgustation or somethin like that, but he run off before they could catch him.

Semelee was glad she wasn't misshapen like Corley or Luke or the other members of the clan. But she was special too. She had a weird look that had been enough to bring her a lot of pain, but not weird enough to bring in loose change. She was special in another way. In her own way. Special on the inside.

"Ain't like this is the first time you ever done this," she told Corley.

"I know, but I hate it. If'n I do it a million times I'm still gonna hate it. That thing could take my leg off with one bite if it got a mind to."

"Not just one leg, Corley," Luke said with a grin. "When you think about it, she could take both off at once—if she got a mind to, that is."

"Or if I got tired of your whining and told her to," Semelee added.

"That ain't funny!" Corley said, dancing in place like a little boy who had to take a wizz.

"Stand still!" Luke said. "We're tryin to catch fish, not scare 'em away! Just be glad it ain't Devil doin the herdin."

Corley's hands shook. "If'n it was Devil, I wouldn't be in the water! Hell, I wouldn't even be on the bank!"

Semelee spotted a dark shape, maybe a foot or two deep, slidin through the water toward them, rippling the surface above as it moved.

Dora was comin, drivin the fish before her.

"Get ready," she told them. "Here we go."

Corley let out a soft, high-pitched moan of fear but held his ground and his end of the net.

The shape glided closer and closer to Luke and Corley, and then suddenly the net bowed backward and the water between them was alive with fish, frothing the surface as they thrashed against the net. The two men pushed their poles together and lifted the net out of the water. A coupla dozen or more good-size mollies and even a few bass wiggled in the mesh.

"Fish fry tonight!" Luke cried.

"She touched me!" Corley said, looking this way and that. If his neck would've allowed it, it'd be swivelin round in circles. "She tried to bite me!"

"That was just her flipper," Luke said.

"I don't care! Let's get these things ashore!"

"Don't forget to leave me some," Semelee said. "Dora'll be very unhappy if you don't."

"Oh, right! Right!" Corley said. He reached into the net and pulled out a wriggling six-inch molly. "The usual?"

"A couple should do."

He flipped one and then another onto the deck, then headed for shore.

Semelee picked up one of the flopping, gasping fish and held it by its slick, slippery tail over the water.

"Dora," she sing-songed. "Dora, dear. Where are you, baby?"

Dora must have been waitin on the bottom because she popped to the surface right away. The snapping turtle's mountainous shell with its algae-and-grass-covered peaks and valleys appeared first, runnin a good three-four feet stem to stern. Then her heads broke the surface, all four beady little eyes fixed on her, both hooked jaws open and waitin. Semelee could see the little wormlike growth on each of her tongues that Dora used like fishin lures when she sat on the bottom during the daytime and waited for lunch. Finally the long tail broke the surface and floated behind her like a big fat water moccasin.

Semelee was sure scientists would give anything for a look at Dora, the biggest, damnedest, weirdest-looking alligator snapper anyone had ever seen, but she was Semelee's, and no one else was gettin near her.

She tossed a fish at the left head. The sharp, powerful jaws snapped closed across the center, severing the head and tail. The right head snatched those up as they hit the water. A pair of convulsive swallows and the mouths were open again.

Semelee gave the right head first crack at the second

fish, with similar results, then she stretched her hands out over the water. Dora reared up so that her heads came in reach.

"Good girl, Dora," she cooed, stroking the tops of the heads. Dora's long tail thrashed back and forth with pleasure. "Thanks for your help. Better get outta sight now before the dredgers come."

Dora gave her one last look before sinkin from sight.

As Semelee straightened she caught a glimpse of her reflection in the churned-up water and took another peek. She didn't hold much with mirror gazin, but every once in a while she took a look at herself and wondered how different things mighta been for her if she'd had a head of normal hair—black or brown or red or blond, didn't matter, just so long as it wasn't what she'd been born with.

The surface of the water showed someone in her mid-twenties with a face that wasn't no head turner but not ugly neither. If heads did turn, it was cause of her hair, a tangled silver-white mane that trailed after her like a cloud—a very tangled, twisted stormy cloud that no amount of combin or brushin could straighten. No amount at all. She should know. She'd spent enough hours as a kid workin on it.

That hair had been a curse for as long as she could recall. She didn't remember bein born here, right here on the lagoon, and didn't remember her momma leavin the lagoon and takin her to Tallahassee. But she did remember grammar school in Tallahassee. Did she ever.

Her earliest memories there was of kids pointin to her hair and callin her "Old Lady." Nobody wanted Old Lady Semelee on their team no matter what they was playin, so she used to spend recesses and after school mostly alone. Mostly. Being left out would have been bad enough, but the other girls couldn't let it go at that. No,

they had to crowd around her and pull off the hat she
wore to hide her hair, then they'd yank on that hair and
make fun of it. The days she came home from school
cryin to her momma were beyond countin. Home was her
safe place, the only safe place, and her momma was her
only friend.

Semelee remembered how she'd cursed her hair. If not
for that hair she wouldn't be teased, she'd be allowed into
the other kids' games, she'd have friends—more than anything else in the world little Semelee wanted a friend, just
one lousy friend. Was that too much to ask? If not for that
hair she'd *belong*. And little Semelee so wanted to belong.

Since hats wasn't helpin, she decided one day at age
seven to cut it all off. She took out her momma's sewin
scissors and started choppin. Semelee smiled now at the
memory of the mess she'd made of it, but it hadn't been
funny then. Her momma'd screamed when she seen it. She
was fit to be tied and that scared Semelee, scared her bad.
Her only friend was mad.

Momma took the scissors and tried to make somethin
outta the chopped-up thatch but she couldn't do much.

And the kids at school only laughed all the harder when
they saw it.

But they ain't laughin now, Semelee thought with grim
satisfaction as she threaded the holes in the eye-shells
through the slim leather thong she wore around her neck.
At least some of them ain't. Some of them'll never laugh
again.

She watched the ripples and eddies that remained behind on the surface in Dora's wake. Something about their
crisscrossing pattern reminded her of her dream last night,
the one about someone coming from someplace far away.
As she watched the water she had a flash of insight. Suddenly she knew.

"He's here."

10

Miami International was a mob scene, far more hectic and crowded than LaGuardia. Jack wound his way through the horde of arrivees and departees toward the ground transportation area. There he caught a shuttle bus to Rent-a-Car Land. In order to help them out of second place, Jack decided to rent from Avis. He settled on an "intermediate" car and chose the most anonymous looking vehicle they had: a beige Buick Century.

The hospital had given him directions from the Florida Turnpike but Jack chose US 1 instead. He figured it would take longer. The red-vested guy at the Avis desk gave him a map and highlighted the way to Route 1.

He was on his way.

All around him South Florida lay flat as a tabletop under a merciless sun, bright in a cloud-dappled sky, blazing through a haze of humidity that hugged the land. Someone somewhere had called Florida an oversized sandbar hanging off the continent like a vestigial limb. Jack couldn't see anything to contradict that.

He'd expected more lushness, but the fronds of the palms along the side of the road hung limp and dull atop their trunks, their tips a dirty gray-brown. The grass and brush around them looked burned out. No doubt the result of the drought Abe had mentioned.

He reached Route 1—also known as Dixie Highway according to the signs—and ran into some traffic at the southbound merge. People rubbernecking an accident on the northbound side slowed him for a while. He saw the strobing police and ambulance lights and felt a flash of resentment, wondering if people had rubbernecked his father's accident like these yokels.

As soon as they passed the crash, the road speeded up again.

For a while the view along US 1 threatened to devolve into Anytown, USA—at least an Anytown warm enough for palm trees—with a parade of Denny's and Wendy's and McDonalds, and Blockbusters and Chevrons and Texacos. Further proof of the depressing homogenization of America, its terror of the untried, its angst of the unique.

But then he started noticing taquerias and tapas joints, and billboards in Spanish. The Cubano and Mexican influence. He passed a place offering "fishes." Okay, this wasn't Anytown. This had a flavor all its own.

The colors of the buildings struck him between the eyes. Standard granite gray had been banished. The palette here was way heavy on the pastels, especially turquoise and coral. The buildings looked like molded sherbet—orange, raspberry, key lime, lemon, watermelon, casaba, and maybe a few as yet untried flavors. He spotted a mall done up in what might be called rotten-lemon-rind yellow.

Further south he passed one car dealership after another, every make from every nation that exported cars, all interspersed with AutoZones and Midas Mufflers, Goodyear Tire Centers, and dozens of no-name auto parts shops. People must be nuts about cars down here.

He realized he was hungry. He saw a place called Joanie's Blue Crab Café and pulled off the road. The place was pretty much empty—this was off-season, after all—and decorated with local crafts. Paintings by local artists studded the wall. The other three patrons were glued to the TV where the Weather Channel was showing green, yellow, and orange swirls that were supposed to be tropical

storm Elvis. They were asking when the hell they were going to get rain.

An air conditioner or two might have expanded the comfort zone in Joanie's, but that would have detracted from
the funky Florida ambiance. Jack hung in there under the
twirling ceiling fans and asked the waitress for a local
brew. She brought him something called Ybor Gold and it
tasted so damn good he had another along with a crabcake
sandwich that was out of this world. This lady could open
on the Upper East Side and clean up.

Belly full, Jack stepped outside. Elvis might be dumping
tons of water on Jacksonville and the rest of north Florida,
but down here, though the sky was speckled with clouds,
none of them looked like the raining kind. The forecast
was bone dry. Dry at least as far as precipitation went, but
the air itself lay thick with humidity and clung to his skin
like a sloppy wet kiss from a least-favorite aunt.

Back in the car he searched around the radio dial for
some music—rock, preferably—but all he found was country or folks speaking Spanish or sweaty-voiced preachers
shouting about *Jay-sus*.

If you want to believe in *Jay-sus*, he thought, fine. If you
want me to believe in *Jay-sus*, fine too; you can want anything you wish. But do you have to shout?

He finally found a rock station but it was playing Lou
Reed. He quick-hit SCAN. Through the years Jack had
come to the conclusion that Lou Reed was a brilliant per-
formance artist whose act was a lifelong portrayal of a
singer-songwriter who couldn't carry a tune or write a
melody.

The tuner stopped on a dance station. Jack didn't
dance, the beat was monotonous, and he'd arrived in the
middle of a woman doing a double-time version of "Boys
of Summer." He bailed when a cheesy organ attempted to
duplicate Kootch Kortchmar's riffs from the original.

What had Don Henley ever done to deserve that?

Next stop, one of the country stations—"Gator Country One-Oh-One Point Nine!" He liked some country, mostly the Hank Williams—Senior, preferably—Buck Owens, Mel Tillis brand of mournful nobody-loves-me-but-my-dog-and-he's-got-fleas-so-pass-that-whiskey-bottle-over-here-if-you-please ballad. He lasted maybe fifteen minutes on 101.9. Three songs, three singers, and they all sounded exactly the same. Was that the awful truth about modern country music? The one they'd kill to keep? One lead singer performing under a gazillion different names? Jack wasn't sure about that part, but he had no doubt that the same guy had been singing backup harmony on all three songs.

Okay. Can the radio.

He saw a sign for Novaton and hung a right off US 1 onto a road that ran due west, straight as a latitude line. Looked like someone had given a guy a compass and a paver filled with asphalt and said, "Go west, young man! Go west!" It made sense. No hills or valleys to skirt. The only rises in the road he'd seen since leaving the airport had been overpasses.

He checked out the sickly palms and pines flanking the road. He'd worked with a landscaper as a teen and knew northeast greenery, but even healthy these trees would be a mystery to him. Dead gray fronds lay on the shoulder like roadkill while some skittered onto the pavement when the breeze caught them.

All the houses along the road were squat little ranches in overgrown yards, with carports instead of garages; they hunkered against the earth as if hiding from something. Every once in a while a warehouse would soar to one-and-a-half stories, but that was an aberration. The favored exterior shade seemed to be a sick green like oxidized copper, and here and there a pizza-size DTV dish would poke up from a roof. He'd been expecting lots of red-tile roofs but they seemed a rarity; most were standard asbestos shingles, pretty threadbare in many cases. Oddly, the shabbiest houses seemed to sport the most magnificent palms in their front yards.

Even if he didn't know much about tropical or subtropical trees, he did know banyans; their distinctive aerial roots gave them away. The road to Novaton was loaded with them. In some stretches banyan phalanxes lined each side of the street and interwove their branches above the pavement, transforming a bumpy secondary road into a wondrous, leafy green tunnel.

He recognized a couple of coconut palms, only because of the yellowing nuts hanging among the fronds. Plants that in New York grew only indoors in carefully watered and fertilized pots flourished like weeds down here.

He passed a tall white water tower emblazoned with the town name and shaped like one of those old WWI potato-masher hand grenades the Germans used to toss at the Allies. At its base lay a dusty soccer field flanked by a high school, a middle school, and a senior center.

He passed a feed store. Feed what? He hadn't seen any cattle.

Abruptly he was in Novaton and quickly found the center of town—the whole four square blocks of it. The directions from the hospital told him how to find it from there. Two right turns off Main Street and he came to a three-story cantaloupe-colored brick building of reasonable vintage. The sign out front told him he'd reached his destination.

NOVATON COMMUNITY HOSPITAL
A MEMBER OF DADE COUNTY MEDICAL
SYSTEMS

He parked in a corner of the visitor lot next to some sad looking cacti and headed through the stifling late-afternoon heat toward the front door. An arthritic old man in the information kiosk gave him his father's room number on the third floor.

Minutes later Jack was standing outside room 375. The door stood open. He could see the foot of the bed, the twin tents of the patient's feet under the sheet. The rest was obscured by a privacy curtain. He sensed no movement in the room, no one there besides the patient.

The patient . . . his father . . . Dad.

Jack hesitated, advancing one foot across the threshold, then drawing it back.

What am I afraid of?

He knew. He'd been putting this off—not only his arrival, but thinking about this moment as well—since he'd started the trip. He didn't want to see his father, his only surviving parent, laid out like a corpse. Alive sure, but only in the bodily sense. The man inside, the sharp-though-nerdy-middle-class mind, the lover of gin, sticky-sweet desserts, bad puns, and ugly Hawaiian shirts, was unavailable, walled off, on hold, maybe forever. He didn't want to see him like that.

Yeah, well that's just too damn bad for me, isn't it, he thought as he stepped into the room and marched to the foot of the bed. And stared.

Jeez, what happened to him? Did he shrink?

He'd expected bruises and they were there in abundance: a bandage on the left side of his head, a purple goose egg on his forehead, and a pair of black eyes. What shocked him was how small his father looked in that bed. He'd never been a big man, maintaining a lean and rangy build even through middle age, but now he looked so flat and frail, like a miniature, two-dimensional caricature tucked into a bed-shaped envelope.

Besides the IV bag hanging over the bed, running into him, another bag hung below the mattress, catching the urine coming out of him. Spikes marched in an even progression along the glowing line on the cardiac monitor.

Maybe this wasn't him. Jack looked for familiar features. He couldn't see much of the mouth as it hung open behind the transparent green plastic of the oxygen mask. The skin was tanned more deeply than he'd ever remembered, but he recognized the age spots on his forehead, and the retreating gray hairline. His blue eyes were hidden behind closed lids, and his steel-rimmed glasses—the only time his father took off his glasses was to sleep, shower, or trade them for prescription sunglasses—were gone.

But yeah, this was him.

Jack felt acutely uncomfortable standing here, staring at his father. So helpless . . .

They'd seen very little of each other in the past fifteen years, and when they had, it was all Dad's doing. His earliest memories of home were ones of playing catch in the backyard when he'd been all of five years old and the mitt was half the size of his torso, standing in a circle with his father and sister Kate and brother Tom, tossing the ball back and forth. Dad and Kate would underhand it to him so he could catch it; Tom always tried to make him miss.

His lasting, growing-up impressions were of a slim, quiet man who rarely raised his voice, but when he did, you listened; who rarely raised his hand, but when he did, a single, quick whack on the butt made you see the error of your ways. He'd worked as a CPA for Arthur Anderson, then moved—decades before the Enron scandal—to Price Waterhouse where he stayed until retirement.

He wasn't a showy sort, never the life of the party, never had a flashy car—he liked Chevys—and never moved from the west Jersey house he and Mom had bought in the mid-fifties. Then, without warning, he'd up and sold it last fall and moved to Florida. He was a middle-class man with a middle-class income and middle-class mores. He hadn't changed history and no one but the surviving members of his family and steadily diminishing circle of old friends would note or mourn his passing, yet Jack would remember him as a man who always could, as Joel McCrea had put it in *Ride the High Country*, enter his house justified.

Jack stepped around to the left side of the bed, the one opposite the IV pole. He pulled up a chair, sat, and took his father's hand. He listened to his breathing, slow and even. He felt he should say something but didn't know what. He'd heard that some people in comas can hear what's going on around them. It didn't make much sense, but it couldn't hurt to try.

"Hey, Dad. It's me. Jack. If you can hear me, squeeze my hand, or move a finger. I—"

His father said something that sounded like "Brashee!" The word startled Jack.

"What'd you say, Dad? What'd you say?"

He caught movement out of the corner of his eye and saw a heavyset young woman in a white coat enter with a clipboard in her hand. She had a squat body, café au lait skin, short dark hair; a stethoscope was draped around her neck.

"Are you a relative?" she said.

"I'm his son. Are you his nurse?"

She smiled briefly—very briefly. "No, I'm his doctor." She put out her hand. "Dr. Huerta. I was the neurologist on call when your father was brought to the ED last night."

Jack shook her hand. "Jack. Just call me Jack." He pointed to his father. "He just spoke!"

"Really? What did he say?"

"Sounded like 'brashee.' "

"Does that mean anything to you?"

"No."

And then he thought, Maybe he heard my voice and was

trying to say, *Black sheep.*

"He's been vocalizing gibberish. It's not unusual in his state."

He studied Dr. Huerta for a few seconds. She didn't look old enough to be in med school, let alone a specialist.

"What *is* his state? How's he doing?"

"Not as well as we'd like. His coma score is seven."

"Out of ten?"

She shook her head. "We use the Glasgow Coma Score here. The lowest, or worst score, is three. That's deep coma. The best is fifteen. We go by eyes, verbalization, and movement. Your father scores a one on his eyes—they remain closed at all times—and a two on vocalization, which means he makes meaningless sounds like you just heard now and then."

"That's a total of three," Jack said.

This wasn't sounding too good.

"But his motor response is a four, meaning he withdraws from painful stimuli."

"What kind of painful stimuli? I won't be finding cigarette burns on his soles, will I?"

Dr. Huerta's eyes widened. "Good heavens, no! What on earth do you think—?"

"Sorry, sorry." Jeez, lady. Chill. "Just kidding."

"I should hope so," she said with an annoyed look. "We use a special pin to test motor responses. Your father's score of four brings his total to seven. Not great, but it could be worse." She checked her clip board. "His reflexes, however, are intact, his vitals are good, so are his labs. His brain MRI showed no stroke or subdural hemorrhage, and his LP was negative for blood."

"LP?"

"Lumbar puncture. Spinal tap."

"No blood. That's good, right?"

She nodded. "No signs of intracranial bleeding. His

heart's been acting up, though."

"Whoa," Jack said, jolted by the remark. "His heart? He's always had a good heart."

"Well, he went into atrial fibrillation last night—that's a chaotically irregular heartbeat—and again this morning. I called for a cardiology consult and Dr. Reston saw him. Both times your father converted back to normal rhythm spontaneously, but it does indicate some level of heart disease."

"How bad is this atrial fibrillation?"

"The main worry is a clot forming in the left atrium and shooting up to the brain and causing a stroke."

"Swell," Jack said. "As if a coma isn't bad enough."

"Dr. Reston started him on a blood thinner to prevent that. But tell me about his medical history. I've been working in the dark, knowing nothing about him beyond the address and date of birth we got off his license. Has he been treated for any illnesses or heart problems in the past? Does he take any medications?"

"I think he once mentioned taking an aspirin a day, but beyond that . . ."

"Do you know if he's been seeing a doctor down here, for checkups and the like?"

Jack was embarrassed. He knew no more about what his father had been doing down here than what he'd been doing in Jersey before the move. He knew his father's new address but had never seen the place. Truth was, he knew nothing about his father's life down here or anywhere else, and even less about his health.

But he was getting a crash course this afternoon.

How to put this . . .

"He wasn't much for talking to me about his health."

Dr. Huerta smiled. "That's a switch. Most people his age talk about nothing but."

"Is he going to be okay?"

"I wish I could say. If his cardiac rhythm stabilizes, I believe he'll come out of this with little permanent damage. He won't remember a thing about the accident, but—"

"What about the accident?" Jack said. "What happened?"

She shrugged. "I have no idea. All I know is that he was brought in unconscious from head trauma. You'll have to ask the police."

The police . . . swell. The last people Jack wanted to talk to.

She fished in her pocket. "I'll be looking in on him again in the morning. If you learn anything about his medical history, give me a call." She handed him a card.

Jack slipped it into his pocket.

11

After the doctor bustled out of the room, Jack turned back to his father. As he stepped toward the bed—

"So, you're one of Thomas's sons."

Jack jumped at the sound of the voice, raspy, like someone who'd been gargling with kerosene. Startled because he hadn't heard anyone come in, he looked around and found the room empty.

"Who—?"

"Over here, honey."

The voice came from behind the curtain. Jack reached out and pulled it back. A thin, flat-chested old woman sat in a chair in a shadowed corner. Her black hair was pulled back in a tight bun and her skin was dark, made even darker by the sleeveless canary yellow blouse and bright pink Bermuda shorts she wore, but in the shadows he couldn't tell her race. A large straw shopping bag sat on the floor beside her.

"When did you come in?"

"I've been here the whole time." She pronounced it "Oy've been here the whole toym." The accent was from somewhere on Long Island—Lynn Samuels to the Nth degree. But that cinderblock-dragging-behind-a-truck voice . . . how many packs of cigarettes had it taken to achieve that tone?

"Since before I came in?"

She nodded.

That bothered Jack. He wasn't usually so careless. He'd have sworn the room was empty.

"You know my father?"

"Thomas and I are next-door neighbors. We moved in the same time and became friends. He's never mentioned me?"

"We, um, don't talk a lot."

"He's mentioned you, many times."

"You must be thinking of Tom."

She shook her head and spoke at jackhammer speed. "You don't look old enough to be Tom, Jr. You must be Jack. And he did talk about you. Hell, sometimes I couldn't get him to shut up about you." She rose and stepped forward, extending a gnarled hand. "I'm Anya."

Jack took her hand. He saw now that she was white—or maybe Caucasian was a better term, because she was anything but white. Her skin was deeply tanned and had that leathery quality that only decades of dedicated sunbathing can give. Her skinny arms and legs had the shape and texture of Slim Jims. Her hair was mostly jet black except for a mist of gray roots hugging her scalp.

Jack heard a faint yip from behind her. He looked and saw a tiny dog head with huge dark eyes poking over the edge of the straw shopping bag.

"That's Oyving," she said. "Say hello, Oyv."

The Chihuahua yipped again.

"Oyving? How do you spell that?" Jack said.

She looked at him. "I-R-V-I-N-G. How else would you spell it?"

He released her hand. "Oyving it is. I didn't know they allowed dogs in hospitals."

"They don't. But Oyv's a good dog. He knows how to behave. What they don't know won't hurt them. And if they find out, fuck 'em."

Jack laughed at the unexpected expletive. This didn't seem like the kind of woman his father would hang out with—she couldn't be more unlike his mother—but he liked her.

He told her so.

Her bright dark eyes fixed on him as she smiled, revealing too-bright teeth that were obviously caps.

"Yeah, well, I'll probably like you too if you hang around long enough for me to get to know you." She turned back to the bed. "I do like your father. I've been sitting with him for most of the day."

Jack was touched. "That's very kind of you."

"That's what friends are for, hon. The benison of a neighbor like your father you don't take for granted."

Benison? He'd have to look that up.

He cleared his throat. "So . . . he's mentioned me?"

Jack was curious how his father had depicted him but didn't want to ask.

He didn't have to.

"He speaks of all his children. He loves you all. I remember how he cried when he heard about your sister. A terrible thing, to outlive a child. But he speaks of you the most."

"Really?" That surprised Jack.

She smiled. "Perhaps because you so vex him."

Vex . . . another word you don't hear every day.

"Yeah, I guess I do that." In spades.

"I don't think he understands you. He wants to know you but he can't get near enough to find out who you are."

"Yeah, well . . ."

Jack didn't know what to say. This conversation was sidling into uncomfortable territory.

"But he loves you anyway and worries about you." Her eyes bored into his. "Sad, isn't it: The father doesn't know his son, and the son doesn't know his father."

"Oh, I know my father."

"You may think you do, hon," she said with a slow shake of her head, "but you don't."

Jack opened his mouth to correct her—no way this woman who'd met Dad less than a year ago could know more about the man he'd grown up with—but she held up a hand to cut him off.

"Trust me, kiddo, there's more to your father than you ever dreamed. While you're here, maybe you should try to get to know him better. Don't miss this opportunity."

Jack glanced at the still form pressed between the hospital sheets. "Maybe I already have."

She waved a dismissive hand at the bed. "Thomas will be fine. He's too tough for a little bump on the head to put him down."

More than a little bump on the head, Jack thought.

"The doctors don't seem to think so."

"Doctors." Another dismissive flip of her hand. "What do they know? Most of them have their heads up their *tuchuses*. Listen to Anya. Anya knows. And Anya says your father's going to be fine."

Foyn? Jack thought, taking on her accent. He's gonna be *foyn* because you say so, lady? Let's hope so.

She looked up at him. "Where are you staying tonight?"

"Not sure. Passed a Motel 6 on the way—"

"Nonsense. You'll stay at your father's place."

"I . . . I don't think so."

"Don't argue with Anya. He'd want you to. He'd be very upset if you didn't."

"I don't have a key. I don't even know how to get there."

"I'll show you."

She walked over to the bed and took his father's hand. "Jack and I are going now, Thomas. You rest. We'll be back tomorrow." Then she turned to Jack and said, "Let's go. Where's your car?"

"In the lot. Where's yours?"

"Oh, I don't drive. Trust me, hon, you wouldn't want to be on the same road as me. You're taking me and Oyv home."

12

As soon as Anya got in the car she placed Oyv on her lap and lit up an unfiltered Pall Mall.

"Mind if I smoke?"

A little late to object now, Jack thought.

"Nah. Go ahead." He lowered all the windows.

"Want one?"

"Thanks, no. Tried it a few times but never picked up the habit."

"Too bad," Anya said, blowing a stream out the window. "And if you're going to tell me to stop, save your breath."

"Wouldn't think of it. It's your life."

"Damn right. Over the years I've had five doctors tell me to stop. I've outlived every one of them."

"Now I definitely won't say a word."

She smiled and nodded and directed Jack onto a road leading west of town.

The sinking sun knifed through his dark glasses and stabbed at his eyes as he drove westward. He watched what passed for civilization in these parts fall away behind them. The land became progressively swampier, yet somehow managed to retain that burnt-out look.

They passed a freshly tilled field of rich brown earth and wondered what had been growing there all summer. Most of the cultivation seemed given over to palm tree nurseries. Odd to pass successive acre plots, each packed with successively larger palms, all of equal height within their own acre.

Anya pointed a crooked finger at a twin-engine outboard motorboat in someone's front yard.

" 'For Sale By Owner'?" she said. "I should hope so. Who else would be selling it? Do they make 'For Sale By Thief' signs?"

A few turns later, past stands of scrub pines, they came to a block of concrete with a blue-and-white-tiled mosaic across its front.

GATEWAYS SOUTH
GATEWAY TO THE FINEST IN MATURE
LIFESTYLES

The droopy plants and palms framing the sign looked like they were on their last legs.

"Here we are," Anya said. "Home sweet home."

"This is it? This is where he lives?"

"Where I live too. Turn already or you'll miss it."

Jack complied and followed a winding path past a muddy pit with a metal pipe standing in its center.

"That used to be a pond with a fountain," Anya said. "It

was beautiful."

All of Gateways South must have been beautiful when it was green, but it looked like it had been particularly hard hit by the drought. All the grass lining the road had been burned to a uniform beige. Only the pines—which probably pre-dated the community—seemed to be holding their own.

They came to a checkpoint divided into VISITORS and RESIDENT arches, each blocked with a red-and-white-striped crossarm. Jack began to angle left toward the visitor gate where a guard sat in an air-conditioned kiosk.

"No," Anya said, handing him a plastic card. "Use this at the other gate. Just wave it in front of the whatchamacallit."

The whatchamacallit turned out to be a little metal box atop a curved pole. Jack waved the card before the sensor and the striped crossarm went up.

"I feel like I'm entering some sort of CIA installation," he said. "Or crossing a border."

"Welcome to one of the retirement Balkans. Seriously though, as we all get on in our years, and become more frail than we like to admit, sometimes this is what it takes to let us feel secure when we turn out the lights."

"Well, as the song says, whatever gets you through the night. But I can't see this place as much of a crime risk. It's in the middle of nowhere."

"Which is exactly why we like a security force guarding the gate and patrolling the grounds." She pointed straight ahead. "Just take this road to its end."

Jack shook his head as he followed the asphalt path that wound past what looked like a par-three golf course. The grass was sparse and brown and the ground looked rock hard. That wasn't deterring the hardcore hackers; he spotted half a dozen golf carts bouncing along the fairways.

"Can't they even water the greens?"

Anya shook her head. "Drought emergency restrictions. No watering at all in South Florida now, even if you have your own well."

He drove on, passing tennis courts—at least their Har-Tru surfaces were still green—and shuffleboard areas, all busy.

"There's the assisted living facility," she said, pointing to a three-story building done up in coral shades. Then she pointed to a one-story structure. "That's the nursing home."

"I don't get it."

"The drought?"

"No. Why my father moved down here."

"Warmth is a factor. You get old, you feel the cold. But the main reason people come to Gateways and other places like it is so they'll never be a burden on their children."

"You talk like you're not one of them."

"I don't have anybody to burden, hon. I'm here for the sun." She held up an arm to show off her wafer-thin, beef-jerky skin. "As you can tell, I love to sit and soak up the rays. I used to sunbathe in the nude when I was younger. If I didn't know how the community board would squawk, I'd do it now."

Jack tried not to picture that.

"But I can't see my father being a burden on anyone."

"Maybe you don't, kiddo, but *he* can. That's why he's here instead of in some West Palm condo."

"I'm not following you."

"Gateways South—and North and East, for that matter—is a graduated care community that provides for us through the final stages of our lives. We start off in our own little bungalows; when we become more frail we move to assisted living where we have a suite and they provide meals and housekeeping services; and when we can no longer care for ourselves, we move into the nursing home."

"All it takes is money, I suppose."

She snorted a puff of smoke out her nose. "It's not cheap, I can tell you that. You buy your house, you buy a bond, you pay monthly maintenance fees, but your future care is assured. That's important."

"Important enough to hide yourself away down here?"

She shrugged and lit another cigarette—her third since leaving the hospital. "I'm just telling you what I've heard my neighbors say. Me, I'm here because I've got no one to care for me when I start losing it. But the rest, they're all terrified of ending up in diapers in a son or daughter's home."

"Some children might not see that as a burden."

"But what of the parents? They don't want to be remembered like that. Would you?"

"No, I guess not. I *know* not."

He didn't even want to remember his father as that flattened man pressed between the hospital sheets today. He wanted even less to remember him as an empty-eyed drooler in diapers, a lifetime's store of dignity vanishing like a gambler's paycheck.

He said, "Getting old sucks, doesn't it."

"For some, yes, but not all. The body begins to remind you in ways big and small that you ain't the *maidel* or *boychick* you used to be, but you find ways to adjust. It's largely a matter of acceptance." She pointed to the right. "Turn here."

Jack saw a sign for White Ibis Lane as he made the turn. At the end of the short road stood two small, identical houses. The four parking spots in the little cul-de-sac were empty. Jack pulled into one and stepped out of the car. Anya opened her door and let Oyv hop to the ground. The Chihuahua immediately trotted to the nearest palm and let loose a tiny yellow stream against its trunk.

Jack smiled. "That tree looks so dry, I bet it's grateful

even for that."

Anya laughed as she straightened slowly from the passenger seat to a standing position. "You'd win. Take a look around while I go in and get the key to your father's place."

Jack felt his eyebrows jump. "He gave you a key?"

She waved a hand at him and laughed. "Nothing like that, kiddo. We traded keys as a precaution. In case of, you know, an emergency."

Jack couldn't resist. He winked at her. "You're sure that's all?"

"What? Thomas with an old skinny-assed crone like me when he has all those other women chasing him? Don't be silly."

Jack held up a hand. "Whoa. Rewind that. My father's got women chasing him?"

"Like vultures, they circle. Let me tell you, Thomas could have his pick of scores—*scores.*"

Jack had to laugh. "I don't believe this. My father, the stud."

"It's not that. It's just that there's four widows for every widower down here. Thomas is an able-bodied man with a good mind and a nice personality. And best of all, he can drive himself. Such a catch, you wouldn't believe."

She reminded him a little of Abe. "Speaking of catches, Anya, if you ever decide to move back north, have I got a guy for you."

She waved her cigarette at him. "Forget about it. My balling days are over."

Jack shook his head. "My father, the catch. Wow." He smiled at her. "So if you're not one of the circling vultures you mentioned, can I ask how you two spend your time together?"

"It's none of your beeswax, hon, but I'll tell you anyway: Mostly we play mahjongg."

Another shock. "My father plays mahjongg?"

"See? I told you there were things you didn't know about him. I'm teaching him and he's getting very good." She tapped her temple. "That accountant's mind, you know."

"My father, the mahjongg maven. I think I need a drink."

"So do I. Come over after you've settled in. We'll knock back a few and I'll give you your first mahjongg lesson."

"I don't know . . ."

"You have to give it a try. And once you learn, it'll give you and your father something to do together."

When there's frost on hell's pumpkins, Jack thought.

"Anyway," Anya said, pointing to the house on the right, "this one's your father's. Look around. I'll be back in a minute."

She headed toward the house on the left with Oyv trotting behind. Her place was painted . . . what would they call that color? He'd never heard of white zinfandel pink as a paint shade, but if there were such a thing, that would be the color of Anya's house. Dad's was a more masculine sky blue.

Jack realized he was facing the rear of the house. He tried the door to the jalousied back porch but it was locked. It would have taken all of twenty seconds for him to open it but why bother if Anya had a key.

He strolled the slate walk between the houses. The grass around the stones was as dead and brown as the rest of Gateways South; the foundation plantings along the base of the smooth stucco exterior of his father's place looked thirsty but not as wilted as what he'd seen along the way. Jack suspected him of sneaking them a little water during the night.

Then again, maybe not. His father was such a stickler for rules that he just might watch all his plants die before breaking one.

Jack tried to peek through the windows but the shades were drawn. As he backed away from a window he glanced over at Anya's and stopped dead in his tracks.

Her place looked like a rain forest. Lush greens and reds and yellows of every imaginable tropical plant concealed most of the side of her house, not merely surviving, but thriving. A grapefruit tree, heavy with fruit, stood at a corner. And her grass . . . a rich, thick, pool-table green.

A little surreptitious sprinkling was one thing, but Anya seemed to be thumbing her nose at the water restrictions.

He noticed a small forest of ornaments dotting her lawn: the usual elves and pink flamingos and pinwheels of various models, but in among them were strange little things that looked homemade, like painted tin cans and bits of cloth on slim tree branches that had been stuck into the ground.

He spotted a name plaque on the side of the house. He stepped closer until he could read it. MUNDY.

He walked on to the front of his father's place. The front yards of the two bungalows sloped down to a pond, roughly round, maybe fifty feet in diameter. As he approached for a look he heard a number of splashes as frogs leaped off the bank for the safety of the water. A black bird stood on the far bank, its chevroned wings spread and held toward the sun as if storing up solar power. The pond stood full and clear, its perimeter rimmed with healthy looking grass and reeds. Beyond it lay a grassy marsh that seemed to stretch forever north and south, but ended at a stand of tall cypresses about a mile due west. Jack knew it was west because the sun was dipping behind the treetops.

He turned and checked out the front of his dad's place. A front porch, covered but open, held a small round table and a pair of chairs, all white. Some sort of flowering vine was trying to crawl up the supporting columns. The floor of the front porch was bluestone slate. A picture window dominated the wall to the left of the door, but vertical blinds hid the interior. He pulled open the screen and tried the front door. Locked, just like the rear.

"Here's the key," Anya said.

Jack turned to find her bustling from her green lawn across his father's brown one, a key held up in her left hand, a cigarette in her right. Oyv paced her.

"Your last name's Mundy?" Jack said. "Any relation to Talbot?"

"The author? Possibly."

"*King of the Khyber Rifles* was one of my favorite books as a kid."

"Never read it. Here's the key." She pressed it into his palm.

He waved his arm at the vista. "Looks like you two landed prime locations."

"Yes, quite a view. Of course, I was one of the earliest residents so I had my pick. I'm such a part of the scenery they hire me for temp work when they need help. Mostly it's just stuffing envelopes or applying address stickers to advertising brochures. At minimum wage, I won't get rich, but it gets me out of the house. It lets me pull a few strings, too. I helped Tom get this place when it went up for sale."

"Really?" He wanted to ask her why she'd do that for a stranger but didn't know quite how to put it. "I guess he owes you for that."

"He owes me more than he knows." She pointed to the jeweled watch on her wrist. "Don't forget, hon: drinks at my place in an hour."

"I'll have to take a rain check on that," Jack said.

"So, you don't want to drink with an old lady? I understand."

"Hey, come on. That's not it at all. I just want to check with the police on my dad's accident. You know, find out how it happened, if it was his fault, that sort of thing."

She frowned. "Why?"

"Because I want to know."

"Go tomorrow."

He shook his head. "I want to know now."

"Why?"

"Because that's the way I am."

She shrugged and began to turn away. "Suit yourself."

"Can I ask you a question?" Jack said. "Two questions, actually."

"Ask away, hon. Doesn't mean I'll answer."

"Okay. First thing is, how come that pond's full and all the rest are empty?"

"That one's fed by an underground channel from the Everglades."

"The Everglades?"

She gestured to the grassy marsh and the distant cypresses. "There it is. Thomas's place and mine are just about as close as you can legally build to the Everglades. Next question? I don't mean to hurry you, hon, but there's a bottle of wine chilling on my kitchen counter and it's calling my name."

"Sorry. I just want to know how you keep your grass so green in this drought."

"Just a knack, I guess. You could say I've got what they call a green thumb."

"Sure it's not just a wet thumb?"

She frowned and jabbed an index finger at him. "And if I do, so what?"

"Nothing, nothing." Jack held up his hands in a defensive gesture. "I just don't want to see a good friend of my dad's getting in trouble."

She relaxed and puffed her cigarette. "Well, okay. I guess it's natural to think I'm watering. I'm not, but no one'll believe me. Would you believe a couple of members of the board came by and threatened to turn me in if I didn't stop watering."

"What did you tell them?"

"Honey, I said if they catch me with a hose in my hand, they can slap the cuffs on. But until then, they can kiss my wrinkled *tuchus*!"

Oyv yipped in seeming agreement as Anya turned and marched off.

My kind of gal, Jack thought as he watched her go.

13

Jack unlocked his father's front door and stepped into the cool, dark interior. The shades were pulled, probably to keep it cooler during the day and cut down on the electric bill. His father had never been cheap, but he hated waste.

He closed the door behind him and stood in the darkness, listening, feeling the house. Somewhere ahead and to the left a refrigerator kicked on. He sniffed. Onions . . . a hint of sautéed onions lingered in the air. Dad's doing? He'd always been something of a chef, probably more so out of necessity after Mom's death, and had this thing for onions; liked them on just about everything. Jack remembered one Sunday morning as a kid when he'd sautéed a bunch and put them on pancakes. Everyone had started out complaining but they turned out to taste pretty good.

Jack stepped over to the picture window and pulled the blinds, letting in the fading sunlight. Dust motes gleamed in the air. He pulled up the rest of the shades and started exploring.

The front area was a large multipurpose living

room/dining room angling into a small kitchen. That was what Jack wanted. He opened the fridge and found a six-pack and a half of Havana Red Ale. He checked the label: brewed in Key West. Another local brand. Why not? He popped the top and took a pull. A little bitter, not as good as Ybor Gold, but it would do.

He spotted a bottle of Rose's lime juice on a door shelf. On a hunch he opened the freezer and there it was: a frosty bottle of Bombay Sapphire. Looked like Dad still liked a gimlet now and then.

He wandered through the front room and recognized some of the paintings from the family home in Jersey. He noticed a trophy shelf on the south wall and moved in for a closer look. First place in the men's doubles in tennis—no surprise there—but what was this? A plaque for second place in the men's bocce tournament?

My father, the bocce champ. Jeez.

He called Gia to give her the medical report on his father. She said how sorry she was that the news wasn't better. Jack said hello to Vicks, then told them he'd call back later.

After he hung up he stepped into one of the bedrooms. This looked like a guest room/office: a bed, a dresser, and a desk with a computer and a printer. Jack saw a list of buy-sell confirmations in the printer tray. Looked like Dad was still day trading. He'd started it way before it became the rage in the nineties and had made enough to retire on. He'd tried to get Jack into it once, saying that if you were vigilant and knew the ropes, it didn't matter if the market was up or down, you could make money every day.

Not if you don't have a real Social Security Number, Dad.

He moved on to the other bedroom, more cluttered and obviously Dad's. He stopped in the doorway, taken aback by the photos filling the walls. Mostly Mom, Tom, and Kate at various ages, salted with a few of Jack as a kid.

Here were the five of them as they embarked on their one and only family camp-out . . . what a disaster that had been.

Memories flooded back, especially of Kate—as his teenaged big sister, looking out for him . . . as an adult, dying in front of him.

He quickly turned away and checked the closet. There they were: Dad's ugly Hawaiian shirts. He pulled one out and looked at it: huge bulge-eyed goldfish swimming in a green fluid that could only be bile. Jack tried to imagine himself wearing this and failed. People would . . . notice him.

As he replaced the shirt he noticed a gray metal box on the shelf above the rod. He reached for it, hesitated, then took it down. He thumbed the latch but it was locked. He shook it. Papers and other things shuffled and rattled inside.

Locked . . . that piqued his curiosity. But this was his father's, not his, and probably locked for a good reason. He should put it back, he knew he should, but . . .

What would his father keep locked up when he was the only one in the house?

Jack looked at the little keyhole. Eminently pickable. All it would take was—

No. Mind your own business.

He put it back on the shelf and returned to the main room. He repressed a shudder. Time to visit the cops.

Jack found the phone book and looked up the address of the local police station. He'd planned to call them for directions, but why not see if he could learn what he wanted over the phone. Anything to avoid setting foot in a police station.

He dialed the number and was shuffled around until he wound up with Anita Nesbitt, a pleasant-sounding secretary who said she'd see what she could do for him.

"I'm assuming I'll need a copy of the accident report for the insurance," he told her. "You know, to get the car fixed."

"Okay. Here it is. I'll put a copy aside and you can pick

it up."

"Any way you can mail it?"

"I suppose. We have his address on the report. How is your father, by the way? I heard he was pretty banged up."

"Still in a coma." A thought struck him. "Was anyone else injured?"

"Not that we know of," she said. "It was hit and run."

Jack swallowed. Those last three words sent a wave of unease through his gut.

"Hit and run?"

"Yes. It's under investigation."

"Save your stamp and envelope," Jack told her. "I'm coming down to pick up that report."

14

Dusk had arrived and the air was cooling enough to bring out the mosquitoes as Jack reached the mustard-yellow building with a two-story center flanked by single-story wings that served as Novaton City Hall. A skeletal clock tower, too modern for the rest of the building, loomed over the high-columned entrance. A green roof, front portico, and awnings completed the picture. A sign said the police station was toward the rear on the left side.

Steeling himself, he stepped inside and asked for Ms. Nesbitt. The desk sergeant directed him to her office. Walking down the hall, passing cops moving this way and that, he felt like Pee Wee Herman at a Klan rally. If anyone peeked under the sheet . . .

He hoped no one asked for ID to prove his relationship.

His father's last name was not Tyleski.

Ms. Nesbitt turned out to be a plump and pleasant little woman with glossy black skin, short curly hair tight against her scalp, and a radiant smile.

"Here's the accident report," she said, handing him a sheet of paper.

Jack took a quick look at it; he meant to read it later but his eyes were drawn to the diagram of the accident site.

"Where's this intersection?" he said, pointing to the sheet. "Pemberton Road and South Road?"

She frowned. "They cross in the swamps on the fringe of the Everglades, way out in the middle of nowhere."

"What was my father doing out in the middle of nowhere?"

"That's what we're hoping you could tell us," said a voice behind him.

Jack turned to see a young, beefy cop with buzz-cut hair. His massive biceps stretched the seams of the short sleeves of his uniform shirt. His expression was neutral.

"This is Officer Hernandez," Anita said. "He took the call and found your father."

Jack stuck out a hand he hoped wasn't too sweaty. "Thanks. I guess you saved my father's life."

He shrugged. "If I did, great. But I hear he's not out of the woods yet."

"You've been keeping track?"

"We'd like to talk to him, get some details on the accident. Any idea what he was doing out there at that hour?"

Jack glanced down at the report. "What hour?"

"Around midnight."

Jack shook his head. "I can't imagine."

"Could your father have been mixed up in something he shouldn't have been?"

"My dad? Into something shady? He's like . . ."

Like who? Jack tried to think of a public figure who was a true straight shooter, whose integrity was beyond reproach, but came up blank. There had to be somebody. But no one came to mind. He almost said Mr. Deeds but Adam Sandler had screwed up that reference.

"He's like Casper Milquetoast." Jack saw no hint of recognition in Hernandez's face. "He's a regular everyday Joe who minds his own business and doesn't take chances. My dad is *not* a risk taker." Jack didn't want to call him timid, because he wasn't. Once he took a position he could be a bulldog about defending it. "He lived in Jersey most of his life, not fifty miles from Atlantic City, and in all that time I don't think he once visited the casinos. So the idea of him being involved in something even remotely criminal is, well, crazy."

Hernandez shrugged. "Doesn't have to be criminal. He could have been fooling around with the wrong guy's wife or—"

Jack held up his hands. "Wait. Stop. Not him. I promise you. No way."

Hernandez was studying him.

Uh-oh. Here it comes.

"Do you live around here?"

"No. I'm still in Jersey." Where did Tyleski live? All these identities . . . after a while they ran together in his head. "In Hoboken."

"How often do you see your father? How many times a year do you visit him?"

"He hasn't been here that long. Less than a year."

"And?"

"And this is my first visit."

"Do you talk often?"

"Uh, no."

"Then you really don't know that much about your father's life down here."

Jack sighed. There it was again. "I guess not. But I know

what kind of man he is, and he's not a sneak or a liar, and people who are have no place in his life."

But how much more do I know? he wondered. What do you know about anyone, even someone who raised you, beyond how they act and what they've told you about themselves?

Anya's comment from this afternoon stole back to him: *Trust me, kiddo, there's more to your father than you ever dreamed.*

He hadn't paid much attention to it then, but now with Dad the victim of a hit-and-run accident in the middle . . .

"Say, if he got hit in the middle of nowhere . . ." He turned to Anita. "Didn't you say a call came in?"

She nodded. "It's in the report."

"But that means someone must have witnessed it."

"That's the obvious conclusion but . . ." Hernandez's macho cop persona wavered. Just a little.

"But what?"

"Well, it took me about twenty minutes to reach the intersection, and when I got there, your father's car was the only vehicle at the scene and it looked like the accident had just happened. The car was sitting across Pemberton Road. From the debris spray I reckoned your father had been proceeding west on Pemberton. He had a stop sign at South. Looked like he was almost halfway across when he got hit. Maybe he hadn't been paying attention, maybe he ran the stop sign, maybe he was having a little stroke. All I know is that something hit him hard enough to spin the car ninety degrees, and there was no one else in sight when I got there."

"Then who called in?" Jack said. "Man or woman?"

"Tony, the desk sergeant took it. I asked him but he couldn't tell. Said the person was whispering, real quick like. Said, 'Bad accident at Pemberton and South. Hurry.' That was it."

"Did they ID the number?"

Hernandez glanced at Anita. "That's another thing we can't figure out. The call came from a pay phone outside the Publix."

"Publix? What's a Publix?"

"Like a Winn-Dixie."

"I'm sorry." Was this another language they were speaking? "I'm from up north and I still don't—"

"Publix is a chain of grocery stores down here," Anita said. "It's like . . ." She snapped her fingers. "I've been up your way. What's it called . . . ? A&P. That's right. Like an A&P."

"Okay. And where's this Publix?"

"About three blocks from here."

"What? But how? That's . . ."

"Impossible?" Hernandez said. "Not really. The hit-and-run driver might have been into something illegal and that's why he didn't stop. But he might have had an attack of conscience and called a friend and told him to call it in from a public phone so we couldn't ID him."

"Thank God for attacks of conscience," Anita said.

Hernandez nodded. "Amen to that. All I can say is it's a good thing we got the call when we did, otherwise your father might have been DOA."

15

Jack's mind raced as he drove toward the south end of Novaton.

After telling Hernandez where he was staying and promising not to leave without checking in with him—in case the cops had more questions—he'd left the police station in something of a daze. But not before getting directions to the impound lot where his dad's car had been towed.

A hit-and-run driver damn near kills his father but has enough Good Samaritan in him to arrange for the cops to be notified. A mixture of bad luck and good.

But the big question still remained: What the hell was Dad doing out there in the swamp at that hour?

The light had pretty well faded by the time Jack reached the south end of town. As Hernandez had told him, he passed an old limestone quarry, then a trailer park, then came to the impound lot.

It turned out to be a combination junkyard/used-car lot called Jason's. The place was closed. Jack could have climbed the chain-link fence but didn't want to risk an encounter with a guard dog, so he wandered the perimeter, squinting at the wrecked cars within.

The accident report said the make was—what else?—a silver Mercury Grand Marquis, the unofficial state car of Florida, and gave the plate number. Jack found it near the gate. He clutched the fence and gaped at the front end. The bumper was gone, the right front fender was a memory, the windshield was a caved-in, spider-webbed mess, the engine block was tilted and canted and twisted to the left.

Had he run into a tank?

Jack's fingers squeezed the chain-linked wire, making it squeak. Who'd done this and run off? Maybe Dad had been thinking of something else and hadn't seen the stop sign. Okay. His bad, not the other driver's. But still . . . what the hell had the other guy been driving?

16

Jack's stomach started to growl as he left Jason's. He realized he hadn't eaten anything since the crabcake sandwich at Joanie's. He'd seen a Taco Bell on the way in and couldn't help thinking of little Oyv. He stopped for a couple of burritos and a Mountain Dew to go.

As he ate and drove, he decided to swing by the hospital on his way back to Gateways South and have another look at his dad.

On the third floor, Jack met Dr. Huerta coming out of the room, followed by a red-haired nurse. Her picture ID badge read C. MORTENSON, RN.

"How is he? Any change?"

Dr. Huerta shook her head and brushed back a vagrant strand of hair. She looked tired.

"The same. Still a score of seven. No better but, thankfully, no worse."

Jack supposed that was good. But he hadn't come here tonight just to see his father.

"Where are his personal effects?"

"Effects?"

"You know, his clothes, his wallet, any papers he had on him."

Dr. Huerta glanced at Nurse Mortenson who said, "They're in a locker by the nurses' station. I'll get them for you."

Dr. Huerta moved on and Jack stepped into his father's room. He stood by the bed, watching him breathe, feeling

helpless and confused. This wasn't right. His father should
be at Anya's place, drinking gimlets and playing mahjongg
instead of lying here unconscious with tubes running in
and out of him.

Mortenson came in with a clipboard and clear plastic bag.

"You'll have to sign for this," she said. As Jack made an
illegible scrawl across the sheet, she added, "We couldn't
keep his clothes. The blood, you know."

"But you emptied his pockets first, right?"

"I assume so. That's done in the ER, long before he gets
to us."

Jack handed back the clipboard and took the bag. Not
much in it: a wallet, a watch, some keys, and maybe a
buck's worth of change.

When the nurse was gone, Jack checked the wallet: an
AmEx and a MasterCard, AARP and AAA cards, a Costco
card, seventy-some dollars in cash, and a couple of restaurant receipts.

Jack dropped it back into the bag. What had he been
hoping for? A note with a cryptic message? A scrap of paper with a hastily scribbled address he could check out?

Watching too many mystery movies, he told himself.

Maybe there *is* no mystery. Maybe it was just an accident. Maybe Dad was simply out for a drive and wound up
in the wrong place at the wrong time . . . got clocked by
accident by someone who wasn't quite legit and couldn't
hang around to explain himself to the police.

Jack understood that. Perfectly.

Just an accident . . . a random collision . . .

But his gut wasn't buying. Not yet at least.

Jack looked down at his father.

"Have you been holding out on me, Dad?"

No response, of course. He patted his father's knee
through the sheet.

"See you tomorrow."

17

Fortunately Anya had left her gate passcard in Jack's car. He used it to breeze through the resident's arch. The old lady's lights were out by the time Jack reached the house. Her lawn ornaments clinked and clanked and whirred in the dark.

Once inside, he went straight to his father's room and took out the metal lockbox.

"Sorry, Dad," he muttered as he carried it to the kitchen.

He hated invading his father's privacy, but this box might hold an explanation as to why he'd been out in the swamps after midnight instead of home in bed.

First, a beer. He grabbed another Havana Red from the fridge, then searched the bathroom for a pair of tweezers. He found one, and twenty seconds later the lid popped open. Jack hesitated. Maybe there were things in here his father didn't want anyone to know about. And maybe Jack wouldn't want to know about them once he saw them. Maybe parents should be able to keep their secrets.

All fine and good when they weren't the comatose victim of a hit and run.

Jack lifted the lid.

Not much there. A handful of black-and-white photos, now sepiaed with age, and something that looked like a small jewelry case. He checked the photos first. Mostly soldiers. He recognized his dad in a few of them—he didn't recall him ever having that much hair—but most were of other uniformed guys in their late teens or early twenties posing awkwardly for the camera against unfamiliar landscapes. Jack spotted a pagoda-like building in the background of one.

Korea. Had to be. He knew his dad had been in the war, in the Army, but he'd never wanted to talk about it. Jack remembered pressing him for war stories but getting nowhere. "It's not something I care to remember," he'd always say.

The last photo was a posed shot of eight men in fatigues, four kneeling in front, four standing behind, grinning at the camera. His father was second from the left, standing. It looked like a plaque had been set up in the right foreground but that corner of the photo was missing. It appeared to have been torn off.

Jack studied the other seven men, looking for a connection to his father. Who were they? They all looked so young. Like a high school varsity basketball team. It looked like a graduation photo. But from what?

Maybe he'd never know.

He put down the photos and picked up the jewelry case. Something rattled within. He snapped it open and found two medals. He didn't know much about military decorations but one he immediately recognized.

A Purple Heart.

His father's? That meant he'd been wounded. But where? The only scar he'd ever seen on his father was from his appendectomy. Maybe this belonged to someone else . . . a dead war buddy that his father wanted to remember?

Nah. Purple Hearts tended to be kept by the loved one's family.

Which meant this was probably his father's.

He checked the other medal: a gold star hanging on a red-white-and-blue ribbon; a smaller silver star was set at its center. This could be a Silver Star. Wasn't that for extraordinary bravery in battle?

Trust me, kiddo, there's more to your father than you ever dreamed.

I guess you got that right, lady. Maybe I should have stayed in touch more.

Funny . . . just a few months ago he wouldn't have felt this way. But after reconnecting with Kate . . .

With frustration wriggling under his skin like an itch he couldn't scratch, Jack replaced the contents to the box in roughly the same order that he'd found them. He'd wanted answers, but all this damn box had provided was more questions.

He returned it to the closet shelf, then headed back to the kitchen for another beer. Along the way he spotted his father's watch on the table. He hadn't noticed the cracked crystal when he'd brought it home from the hospital. He checked it out. An old Timex. No, not old—ancient. The wind-up type. Typical of him: If the old one still works, why get a new one? This Timex had taken a licking but hadn't kept on ticking. It had stopped at 12:08.

Wait a sec . . .

Jack pulled the accident report out of his pocket and unfolded it. He'd scanned through Officer Hernandez's report. He'd mentioned a call coming in to the station at . . . where was it? Here.

11:49 P.M.

But that would mean the accident had been reported before it happened. No way. His father's watch must have been set ahead. Some people did that. Or maybe he'd forgotten to wind it.

But not his father. He'd always been a stickler for the correct time, down to the minute. And he'd always wound his watch at breakfast. Jack had seen him do it a million times.

Hernandez was mistaken about the time of the call. Had to be. But for all his brawn the cop had seemed like a pretty tight, spit-shine type. And hadn't he said that even though it took him twenty minutes to reach the accident, it looked like it had just happened?

Shaking his head, Jack went to the fridge. He decided against another beer. Right now he needed a gimlet.

WEDNESDAY

1

Jack awoke with a buzzing in his ears. At first he thought it was a mosquito, but this was lower pitched. Then he thought it might be gimlet-related, but he'd had only two. Finally he realized it was coming from outside the window. He lifted his head and looked around, momentarily disoriented by the unfamiliar room.

Oh, yeah. He was at Dad's place. In the front room. Must have fallen asleep on the couch. He'd found *Rio Bravo* playing on TNT or some such station and had watched it for about the thirtieth time—not for John Wayne or Dean Martin, and certainly not for Ricky Nelson, but for Walter Brennan. Hands down, Stumpy was his best part, best job, ever—except maybe for his Old Man Clanton in *My Darling Clementine*. Old Walt made the movie for Jack.

But where was that buzzing coming from?

He rolled off the couch, padded to the kitchen, and squinted through the window.

A groundskeeper was running a weed whacker along the edge of the dead grass bordering the foundation plantings. Was that a long-sleeved flannel shirt he was wearing? In this weather? Where Jack came from a long-sleeved shirt in the summer meant one thing: junkie.

But the weed whacker . . . he blinked and shook his head . . . it looked like it was coming out of the guy's right sleeve.

The rest of Jack's clothes were still in the car so he had

to go out anyway. Maybe he could get a closer look along the way.

The heat and humidity hit him like a wave as he stepped outside. Barely 8:30 and already it was cooking. As he rounded the corner, the groundsman stopped working and stared at him, then turned off his weed whacker.

"You ain't Tom. Whatta *you* doin here?"

"I'm his son."

And yes, that was a flannel shirt he had on. He wore green work pants and a tattered olive drab boonie cap. His eyes were a piercing blue, but the left angled to the outside—the kind of eye known on the street as a bent lamp. Yet even this close Jack couldn't see his right hand. The weed whacker seemed to be growing out of the sleeve. Jack thrust out his own right hand in hopes of getting a look.

"My name's Jack."

The groundsman used his left hand to give Jack's a squeeze. "Carl."

So much for that strategy.

"How come you're out here so early?" Jack said. "You can't have much to do with this drought."

"Be surprised," Carl said. "Grass won't grow, tropical plants get all curly and dried up, but the weeds . . . the weeds do just fine. Never able to figure that out."

"Maybe they should all cultivate weeds," Jack said.

Carl nodded. "Fine with me. Green is green." He glanced at Jack. "Miss Mundy told me about your daddy. How's the old guy doin?"

"Still in a coma."

Jack fought the urge to sidle to his right to put himself in line with Carl's left eye.

"Yeah?" He shook his head. "Too bad, too bad. Nice guy, your daddy. He was one of the good uns."

" 'Was'? Hey, he's not gone *yet*."

"Oh, yeah. Right, right. Well, let's hope he pulls through. But bein so close to the Glades and all . . ."

"The Everglades? What's wrong with that?"

Carl looked away. "Nothin. Forget I said it."

"Hey, don't leave me hanging. If you're going to start a thought, finish it."

He kept his gaze averted. "You'll think I'm loco."

You don't know loco like I know loco, Jack thought.

"Try me."

"Well, all right. Gateways here is too close to the Glades. It's been mistreated for years and years now. All the freshwater runoff it's supposed to get from upstate, you know, from Lake Okeechobee, it's mostly been channeled away to farms and funeral-parlor waitin rooms like Gateways. Everywhere you look someone's filling in acres of lowlands and paving it over to build a bunch of houses or condos. The Glades been hurtin for years and years, but this year's the worst because of the drought. Summer's upposed to be our rainy season but we ain't had barely a lick."

"There's still water out there, though, isn't there?"

"Yep, there's water, but it's low. Lower than it's ever been in anyone's memory. And that could be bad. Bad for all of us."

"Bad how?"

"Well, maybe things that always used to be underwater ain't under no more."

Where was this going? *Was* it going anywhere?

"Carl—"

He stared toward the Everglades. "The good thing bout your daddy's and Miss Anya's places here on the pond is you never have to look into someone else's backyard . . ."

Jack glanced out at the endless expanse of grass. "Yeah. A panoramic view."

"Pan-o-ramic?" Carl said carefully. "What's that?"

Jack wondered how to explain it. He spread his arms. "It means wide angle . . . a wide view."

"Pan-o-ramic . . . I like that."

"Fine. The panoramic view is the good thing, but I've got a feeling you were about to tell me a down side."

"I was. The bad part is . . . they's real close to the Glades and the Glades ain't happy these days. You might even say it's kinda pissed. And if it is, we'd all better watch out."

Jack stared across the mile or so of grass at the line of trees. He'd seen a bunch of weird things lately, but an angry swamp . . . ?

You were right, Carl, he thought. I do think you're loco.

Semelee stood on the lagoon bank with Luke and watched the small dredgin barge suck wet sand out of the sinkhole and deposit it into one of the even smaller, flat-bottomed boats it had towed along behind it. Excess water ran out the gunwales and into the lagoon. The clan had moved the houseboats aside to give the barge access to the hole.

"I still can't believe you done this, Semelee," Luke said. "You of all people."

Semelee had been surprised herself. She didn't like outsiders gettin anywheres near the clan's lagoon, and especially near the sinkhole, but these folks had offered too much money to turn down.

"You been sayin that for two weeks now, Luke. Every time the barge shows up you say the same thing. And every time I give you the same answer: We can use the money. People're pretty tight with their spare change these days, in case you ain't noticed."

"Oh, I noticed, all right. Probably cause they ain't got all that much to spare. But I still don't like it, specially this time of year."

"Don't worry. They'll be outta here before the lights come. The deal I made with them was they had to finish up their business before this weekend. The lights'll start comin Friday night. Told them Friday was a stone-solid deadline. Didn't care how much they offered me, by sundown on Friday, they're gone."

"Still don't like it. This is our home. This is where we was born."

"I know, Luke," she said, rubbing his back and feeling the sharp tips of the fins through the cloth. "But just think. The top of the sinkhole is above water for the first time anyone remembers. Maybe for the first time ever. When the lights come this time, they won't have to shine through the water. They'll shine straight out into the night. That's never happened before, at least not in anyone's memory."

"I ain't so crazy about that neither." He rubbed a hand over his face. "My daddy said them lights made us the way we is, twisted us up, just like it's twisted the trees and the fish and the bugs around here. And that's from when they was just shining up through the water. What happens this year when there ain't no water?"

Semelee felt a thrill at the prospect. "That's what I want to see."

The lights had been comin twice a year—at the spring and fall equinoxes—for as long as anyone could remember. Her momma had told her they'd kept that schedule every year since she'd been born, and *her* momma had told her the same thing.

But Semelee's momma'd said that years back the lights

started gettin stronger and brighter. And it wasn't long after that, maybe a few years, that the people livin around the lagoon started noticin changes in the plants and the fish and things around the sinkhole. It started with the frogs missin legs or growin extra ones. Then the fish started lookin weird and the plants started gettin twisted up.

All that was bad enough, but when the lagooners' kids started bein born dead or strange lookin, the lagooners moved out. Not as a group to the same place, but piecemeal like, in all different directions. Some stayed as close as Homestead, some as far as Louisiana and Texas. After they moved away, they stopped havin strange kids and they was happy about that.

But the strange kids they already had wasn't happy. Not one bit. Not because they was all mistreated by people as they was growin up—Semelee hadn't been alone in that—but because when they all finally growed up they felt like somethin was missin in their lives.

One by one they all—all the misshapen ones—found their way back here to the lagoon and learned that this was where the itch stopped, this was where they felt whole, where they belonged. This was home.

And home was where your family lived. They came to call themselves a clan, and all decided to stay here on the lagoon.

Yet even with this big family-type gang around her, Semelee still felt a yearning emptiness within. She wanted more, *needed* more.

"Why do they hafta take *our* sand? There's plenty of sand around. Why they want ours?"

"Don't rightly know," Semelee said.

"Who is they, anyway?"

"Blagden and Sons. You know that."

"Yeah, I know the name, but that's all it is: a name. Who *are* they? Where do they come from?"

"Don't know, Luke, but their money's good. Cash up front. That's bout as good as it gets."

"Do they know about the lights?"

"That one I can answer: Yeah, they know about the lights."

Some guy named William somethin from this company called Blagden and Sons come around in a canoe a few weeks ago askin if anyone'd been seein funny lights about this time of the year. The clan folk he talked to sent him to Semelee since she was sorta the leader round here. Not that she'd ever looked to be the leader, but it seemed whenever somethin needed decidin, she wound up the one who did it.

Semelee played it cagey with this William fellow until she was pretty sure he wasn't no tour-guide type or scientist or anything like that, and wouldn't be bringing boat-loads of strangers or teams of pointy heads to peek or poke at the clan and the sinkhole. Nope, all William wanted was to haul off the dirt and sand from around where they'd seen the lights.

When Semelee had told him they'd been comin up through this sinkhole that used to be underwater but was now gettin dry, he got all excited and wanted to know where it was. Semelee pretended she wasn't gonna tell him, and held off even when he offered money. So he offered more money and more money until Semelee had to say yes. Maybe she could've held out for even more, but there weren't no sense in gettin all greedy about it.

When she'd took him to the sinkhole she thought he was gonna pee his pants. He danced around it, callin it a sennoaty or somethin like that. When she asked him what he was talkin about he spelled it for her: C-E-N-O-T-E. Told her it was a Mex word and you said it like coyote. Semelee liked sinkhole better.

The dredgin was all hush-hush, of course. The clan

wasn't upposed to be livin here on the lagoon, this bein a National Park and all, and Blagden and Sons wasn't upposed to be takin the sand.

"Matter of fact," she told Luke, "I'm pretty sure they want the sand *because* of the lights."

"That's kinda scary, dontcha think? Them lights ain't natural. They changed us and everythin around them. Probably even changed the sand in that hole."

"Probably did."

Luke looked uneasy. "What on earth could they want it for? I mean, what're they gonna do with it?"

"Can't rightly say, Luke. And I don't rightly care. That ain't our worry. What I do know is that our little sinkhole is gonna be a lot deeper without all that sand. And that just may mean that the lights'll be brighter than ever. When the time comes maybe someone can even look down into that hole and see where they're comin from."

"Who's gonna do that?" Luke said.

Semelee kept her eyes on the rim of the deepening hole. "Me."

Luke grabbed her arm. "Uh-uh! You ain't! That's crazy! I won't let you!"

She let Luke have sex with her once in a while when she felt the need, and that probably was a mistake. She'd told him flat out from the git-go that it didn't mean nothin, that they was just now-and-again fuck buddies and that was all there was to it, but she'd probably made a mistake lettin it get started. Still, every so often she needed to get laid and Luke was the least ugly of anyone else in the clan. Trouble was, it let him feel like he owed her, like he had to protect her or somethin.

If anyone needed protectin, it wasn't her.

"You got nothin to say about it, Luke," Semelee told him as she wrenched her arm free of his grasp. "Now lemme be. I gotta get to town."

"What for?"

She flashed him a sly smile. "I'm joinin the nursin profession."

He shook his head. "What? Why?"

Semelee felt the smile melt away in a blaze of anger. "To finish your half-assed job from the other night!"

3

As Jack stepped out of the elevator on the hospital's third floor, he spied Dr. Huerta waiting to get in.

"Any change in my father?"

She shook her head. "Stable, but still level seven."

"How long can this go on?" he said. "I mean, before we start thinking about feeding tubes and all that?"

She stepped into the elevator. "That's a bit premature. I know it must seem like a long time to you, but it's been less than seventy-two hours. The IVs are perfectly adequate for now."

"But—"

The elevator doors slid shut.

Jack walked down the hall to his father's room, wondering if Anya would be there. He'd stopped by her place before leaving this morning, threading his way through the gizmos crowding her lawn, to offer her a ride to the hospital if she needed it. But she hadn't answered his knocks.

Normally that wouldn't have bothered him, but with old folks . . . well, you never knew. She could have had a stroke or something. Jack had peered through the front door glass but hadn't seen anyone on the floor or slumped in a chair. Then he'd remembered Oyv. The little dog would have been barking up a storm by then if he'd been around.

But Anya wasn't in his father's room either—he checked the corners and behind the curtains, just to be sure. Empty except for the patient.

He stepped to the side of the bed and gripped the limp right hand. "I'm back, Dad. Are you in there? Can you hear me? Give a squeeze, just a little one, if you can. Or move just one finger so I know."

Nothing. Just like yesterday.

Jack pulled up a chair and sat at the bedside, talking to his father as if the old guy could hear him. He kept his voice low—pausing when the nurses buzzed in and out—and discussed what he'd learned about the accident and the conflicting information, dwelling on the time discrepancies between the report and his father's watch. He'd hoped talking it out would clarify the incident for him, but he was as confused afterward as before.

"If only you could tell me what you were doing out there at that hour, it would clear up a whole lot of questions."

Once off the subject of the accident, he thought he'd run out of things to say. Then he remembered the pictures in his father's room and decided to use them as launch pads.

"Remember the family camping trip? How it never stopped raining . . . ?"

4

After an hour or so of talking, Jack's mouth was dry and his vocal cords felt on fire. He stepped into the bathroom to get a drink of water. As he was finishing his second cupful his peripheral vision caught a flash of white. He turned to see a nurse approaching his dad's bed. She hadn't been around before; he was sure he would have noticed her if she had. She was pretty in an odd way. Very slim, almost to the point of boyishness, and with her dark skin—made all the darker by the contrast of her white uniform—prominent nose, and glossy black hair trailing most of the way down her back in a single braid, Jack thought she might be part Indian—not the Bombay kind, the American kind.

She had her hand in the pocket of her uniform—little more than a white shift, really—and seemed to be gripping something.

Jack was about to step out of the bathroom and say hello when he noticed something strange about her. Her movements were odd, jerky. She'd slowed her progress toward the bed and seemed to be straining to move forward, as if the air was holding her back. He saw sweat break out on her forehead, watched her face flush and then go pale as she forced herself forward another step. He watched her throat working, as if she was trying to keep from vomiting.

Jack stepped out and approached her.

"Miss, are you all—?"

She jumped, twisted toward him, staring with wide, confused, onyx eyes. Her hand darted from her pocket to a thong tied around her neck, and Jack thought he saw something move in the pocket.

She shook her head, pulling on the slim leather thong around her neck. It snapped but she barely seemed to notice. She was drenched in sweat.

"Who—?"

Before Jack could reply she turned and staggered out of the room. He started to go after her but heard a groan from the bed.

"Dad?" He rushed over to the bed and grabbed his father's hand again. "Dad, was that you?"

He squeezed the fingers—gently at first, then harder. His father winced, but Dr. Huerta had said he was responsive to pain. After shaking his father's shoulder and calling to him, all with no response, he backed off. Nothing happening here.

He went out to check on that nurse. Something wrong about her . . . besides looking sick.

At the nursing station he found a big, brawny, gray-haired nurse who seemed to be in charge. Her photo ID badge read R. SCHOCH, RN.

"Excuse me," he said. "A nurse just came into my father's room, then turned and ran out. She looked kind of sick and I was wondering if she was okay."

Nurse Schoch frowned—or rather, her frown deepened. It seemed to be her only expression. "Sick? No one said anything." She looked around at the assignment board. "Three-seventy-five, right? What was her name?"

"I didn't get a look at her badge. Come to think of it, I don't think she was wearing one."

"Oh, she had to be. What did she look like?"

"Slim, dark, maybe five-three or so."

Schoch shook her head. "No one like that here. Not on my shift, anyway. You sure she was a nurse?"

"I'm not sure of a lot of things," Jack muttered, "and that's just been added to my list."

"She could have been from housecleaning, but then she would have been in gray instead of white—and she'd still have to have a badge." She picked up a phone. "I'll call security."

Jack wished she wouldn't—he didn't want rent-a-cops messing into this—but couldn't think of a reason he could tell Schoch.

"Yeah, okay. I'll be back in my father's room."

He'd been keeping an eye on the door, making sure no one else went in there. When he returned, he checked his father to see if he'd moved—he hadn't—then went to the window and looked out at the parking lot. He saw a slim woman in white walking away through the lot. Heat from the late-morning sun made her shimmer like a mirage.

It was her. Couldn't mistake that long braid. And now she was climbing into the passenger side of a battered old red pickup.

Jack dashed into the hall in time to see the elevator doors closing. Too slow anyway. He found the stairs and raced down to the first floor. By the time he hit the parking lot, the pickup was gone. But he kept moving, running to his Buick and gunning out to the street. He flipped a mental coin and turned right, telling himself he'd give this ten minutes and then call it quits.

He'd traveled about half a mile when he spotted the truck, stopped at a red light two blocks ahead.

"Gotcha," he said.

When the light changed he followed the truck out of town and into the swamps. Somewhere along the way the pavement ended, replaced by a couple of sandy ruts flanked by tall, waving reeds. He lost sight of the truck for a while but wasn't going to worry about that unless he came to a fork. Better to stay out of sight. Luckily there

were no forks, and before too long he was pulling into a
clearing at the edge of a small, slow-moving stream.

The red pickup sat there, idling, while the woman in
white rode downstream in a small, flat-bottomed motor
boat piloted by a hulking man in a red, long-sleeved shirt.
Jack jumped out of his car and ran to the bank, waving his
arms, calling after them.

"Hey! Come back! I want to ask you something!"

The woman and the man turned and stared at him, surprise evident on their faces. The woman said something to
the man, who nodded, then they both turned away and kept
moving. He saw the name on the stern: *Chicken-ship*.

"Hey!" Jack shouted.

"Whatchoo wanner for?" said a voice from behind.

Jack turned and saw a man with a misshapen head leaning out the driver window of the pickup. With his bulbous
forehead, off-center eyes, and almost non-existent nose he
reminded Jack of Leo G. Carroll from the opening scenes
of *Tarantula*. This guy made Rondo Hatton look handsome.

"I want to talk to her, ask her a few questions."

"Looks to me like she don't wanna talk to you." His
voice was high and nasal.

"Where does she live?"

"In the Glades."

"How do I find her?"

"You don't. Whatever it is, mister, leave it be."

Suddenly another guy, thinner and only marginally better looking, jumped into the pickup's passenger seat.

Where'd he come from?

The new guy slapped the driver on the shoulder and
nodded. Neither looked too bright. If someone suggested
playing Russian roulette with a semi-automatic, they'd
probably say, "Cool!"

The driver gave Jack a little two-finger salute. "Welp,
nice talkin to ya. Gotta go now."

Before Jack could say anything the guy threw the truck into gear and roared off. Jack raced back to his car. If he couldn't follow the girl, then he'd tail these two. Sooner or later they had to—

He skidded to a halt when he saw the Buick's flat front tire, and the gash in its side wall.

"Swell," he muttered. "Just swell."

5

"I don't get it," Luke said as he piloted the *Chicken-ship* deeper into the swamp. "Who was that guy?"

Semelee pulled off the black wig and shook out her silver white hair. She didn't feel like talkin. Her stomach still wasn't right.

"He saw me in the room. I think he might be the old guy's kin."

"That why he was trailin you?"

"Maybe. I don't know. All I know is I felt so strange in that room. It started as soon as I stepped through the door and got worse and worse the closer I got to the old man's bed. I started feeling sick and weak, and the air got so thick I could barely breathe. I tell you, Luke, all I wanted to do was get out of there and get far, far away as fast I could."

"Think it was the guy?"

"Could've been, but I don't think so."

This man wasn't just a guy, wasn't just one of the old man's kin. This man was the one she'd sensed coming for the past two days, and he was special. She sensed something about him . . . a destiny, maybe. She didn't know exactly what, she just knew he was special.

So am I, she thought. But in a different way.

Maybe she and this new man was destined to be together. That would be wonderful. She liked the way he looked, liked his hair, his build—not too beefy, not too slight—liked his brown eyes and hair. She especially liked his face, his regular, normal face. Hangin round the clan like she did, she didn't see too many of those.

Maybe he'd been sent to her. Maybe he was here *for* her. Maybe they was meant to share their destinies. She sure hoped so. She needed someone.

"Well, if you don't think it's him made you sick," Luke said, "what was it?"

Semelee pulled the white dress off over her head, leaving her wearing nothin but a pair of white panties. She looked down at her small, dark-nippled breasts. Losers in the size sweepstakes, maybe, but at least they didn't sag. One of the guys she'd screwed in high school had called them "perky." They were that, she guessed.

Keepin her back to Luke—she didn't want him gettin all hot and bothered out here on the water—she slipped into her cut-offs and a green T-shirt.

"I don't know. It was like . . ." She shuddered as she remembered that awful sick feelin runnin through her body, like she was being turned inside out . . . "like nothin I ever felt before. And I hope I don't never feel it again."

She turned and whacked Luke on the leg as hard as she could.

He jumped. "Hey, what—?"

"And I wouldna had to feel it in the first place if you and Corley had done the job you was supposed to!"

"Hey, we did just what we was supposed to. You was there."

"I wasn't there."

"Well, you was watchin. You saw what happened. The sacrifice was goin exactly accordin to plan when that cop showed up outta nowhere. I said all along we shoulda just flattened the old guy inside his car and have done with it."

She hit him again. "Don't you never learn? The old man had to be done in by somethin from the swamp or else it ain't a sacrifice, it's just a killin. And we ain't about just killin. We got a purpose to what we're doin, a duty. You know that."

"Awright, awright. I know that. But I still can't figure why that cop had to come along just then. We never seen him out there before."

"Maybe he was sent," Semelee said as the thought struck her.

"Whatchoo mean?"

"I mean maybe whoever was protectin the old man today was protectin him the other night as well."

"How can that be? We was the only ones who knew we'd be out there."

"I don't know how and I don't know why, but someone's protectin that old man."

"You mean like with magic?"

"Maybe."

Lotsa people'd see what Semelee could do as magic, so why couldn't there be someone else out there who could do somethin different but just as magical? Might be all sorts of magical people out there no one ever dreamed of.

"I ain't got no idea who right now, but I'm gonna find out. And when I do . . ."

She reached down and removed a palm-sized toad from the pocket of the discarded white dress. She held it up and stroked its back. This little feller was a relative to the big African marine toads some fool had brought into Florida sometime in the last century. It had only three legs—its left arm was nothing but a nubbin—but it had these swollen glands startin behind each eye and runnin down its back in a pair of lines. Those glands was full of poison. Every so often a dog would lick or bite one of its bigger cousins and die. This little guy came from the clan's lagoon where his family had bathed in the glow of the lights for generations, and he was even more poisonous. Just a little drop on a tongue was enough to stop a grown man's heart.

That had been Semelee's plan: sneak into the room, press the toad's back against the old man's lips, then get out. A minute or so later he'd be on his way to his maker and the job would be done.

She'd have to think of another plan now.

After she set the toad on the front seat of the boat, where it squatted and watched her with its big black eyes, her hand instinctively went to her breastbone to touch—

She stiffened. What? Where is it?

Then she remembered—the thong had broken in the hospital room. As she'd fled the terrible feelin, she recalled stuffin it into a pocket.

She rummaged in the uniform's other pocket and heaved a sigh of relief when she felt the slim thong. She pulled it out, expecting to see the pair of black freshwater clam shells she wore around her neck. She gasped when she saw only one.

"What's wrong?" Luke said.

Semelee didn't answer him. Instead she lifted the uniform and pawed through one pocket then the other.

"Oh, no! It's gone!"

"What's gone?"

"One of my eye-shells is missin!"

"Check around your feet. Maybe it fell out when you was gettin changed."

She checked, running her fingers along the slimy bottom through the inch or so of water.

"It's gone!" she cried, feeling panic rising like a tide. "Oh, Luke, what am I gonna do? I need them!"

She'd had the eye-shells ever since she was twelve. She'd never forget that moment. Her mother'd taken her to her daddy's funeral. That was the first time she'd ever seen him . . . or at least remembered seein him. He'd up and left Momma when Semelee was just a baby, soon after they moved to Tallahassee. He was Miccosukee Indian, banished from the tribe for somethin Momma never knew. She'd hooked up with him at the lagoon—lotsa people livin round the lagoon back then was on the run from somethin or other—and the three of them moved outta there along with everyone else shortly after Semelee was born.

Her daddy—or rather the man who'd knocked up her momma—had been killed in a bar fight. Some of his Miccosukee kin had decided to give him a proper Indian send-off and his wife and child was invited.

She'd been scared of the whole idea of lookin at a dead man, so she'd hung back, as far away from the body as she could. Just getting her first period the day before and feelin sick and tired didn't help none. That was when she spotted the old Indian woman in a beaded one-piece dress starin at her from across the room. She had eyes black as a bird's and hair like Semelee's, but also the wrinkles to go with it. She remembered how the old lady'd come close and sniffed her. Semelee'd shrunk back, scared, embarrassed. Did her period smell?

The old woman'd nodded and showed her gums in a toothless smile. "You wait right here, child," she'd whispered. "I've got something for you."

And then she'd gone away. Semelee'd hoped she wouldn't come back but she did. And when she did she came carryin two black freshwater clam shells. They'd been drilled through near their hinges and was strung on a leather thong.

She took Semelee's hand, pried open her tight-clenched

fingers, and pressed the shells into her palms. "You got the sight, child. But it's no good without these. You take them and keep them close. Always keep them close. You'll need them when you're ready, and you'll be ready soon."

Then she'd walked away.

Semelee's first thought had been to throw them away, but she changed her mind. Nobody hardly ever gave her anything, so she kept them. She didn't know what the old lady had been talkin about—"You got the sight," and all that—but it made her feel special. Till that time in her life she'd never run into nothin that had made her feel special. As for "the sight" . . . maybe someday she'd find out what that meant.

And one day she did find out. And it had changed her life.

"Now just relax, Semelee," Luke was sayin. "It's got to be somewheres. Probably fell out while you was sittin in the truck. We'll find it."

"We got to!"

She needed those eye-shells to do her magic. She'd kept them slung around her neck so's they'd never be away from her. But now . . .

Those eye-shells'd saved her life . . . or rather, stopped her from killing herself.

It had been a day, a Tuesday in May in her sixteenth year, when everything that could go wrong did. She'd tried new hair dye the night before. Every other one she'd ever tried in the past—and she'd tried them all—didn't take. The dye just ran off her hair like water off wax. This one was touted as different, and promised to turn her hair a luxurious chestnut brown. And it looked like it might work. It didn't run off like the others.

But when Semelee looked in the bathroom mirror that morning she saw that instead of chestnut brown her hair had turned fire-engine red. Worse, it wouldn't wash out.

Maybe the color woulda been okay for the dopers and weirdoes who just wanted attention or wanted to show how they were rejecting their parents or society or whatever, but it was awful for Semelee. She'd spent her whole life bein rejected. She wanted to *belong*.

After crying for a few minutes—she would have liked to scream but Momma and her new boyfriend Freddy were in the bedroom down the other end of the trailer—she tried to figure what to do. She would've liked to call out sick and spend the day washin her hair, but that would leave her alone with Freddy, and the way she kept catchin him lookin at her gave her the creeps. Not that she was a virgin or nothin—she was havin plenty of sex—but Freddy . . . yuck.

So she dried her bright red hair, jammed a cap over it, and headed for school. Not a good start to the day but it got worse as soon as Suzie Lefferts spotted her. She'd had it in for Semelee since grammar school and never passed up a chance to torment her. She yanked off Semelee's cap just for sport, but when she saw the color of her hair she raised a holler and called all the other girls over, sayin look who's here: Lucy Ricardo!

Their laughter and cries of "Luuuuceeeeee!" chased her down the hall, right into the arms of Jesse Buckler. She was Jesse's latest squeeze—or rather, he was hers. Depended on how you looked at it. Semelee had discovered that the way to a boy's heart was through his fly. Dates for her had been as few as turtle teeth until she turned fifteen and started puttin out. After that it was a different story. She knew she had a rep but so what? She liked screwin, and durin sex was the only time she was sure she had a boy's undivided attention.

Jesse pulled her into the boy's room and for a minute she thought they was gonna have sex there—screw in school, how cool. But when she saw Joey Santos and Lee Rivers standin there with their flies open and their peckers at attention, she got scared. She tried to run but Lee grabbed her and said Jesse told them how she gave the best blow job in school and they wanted a sample. She said no and how she'd report them and they laughed and said who'd believe the school slut? They called her "Granny" and Jesse said how he got off doin it to an old lady.

The words shocked Semelee. She'd thought of herself as somethin of a goodtime gal, of easy virtue maybe, but not the school slut. And it wasn't like Semelee loved Jesse or nothin, or ever even entertained the idea that he loved her, but . . . he'd been talkin about her like she was a pull of chewin tobacco that he was gonna pass around between his friends.

With some kickin and clawin she broke free and ran out—not just out of the boys room, but out of the school as well. She could've gone to the principal, but it would be the word of three of the football stars against the school slut, and besides, nothin had happened.

So she'd run home. And there was Freddy. Alone. Drinkin a beer. And horny. He offered her a brew, then started touchin her. Semelee just snapped. She started screamin and throwin things and the next thing she knew Freddy was out the door and headin for his car.

He musta called Momma because half an hour later she came stormin in, started slappin at Semelee, callin her a little whore for playin hooky so she could come on to Freddy. Now look what she'd done! Freddy was gone, sayin he wasn't stayin in no house with a freaky piece of jailbait tryin to get him in trouble.

Momma wouldn't listen to her, and Semelee'd been hurt that her own momma was takin Freddy's side over hers. But then Momma crushed her, sayin she wished Semelee'd never been born, wished she'd died like all the other girls been born to the lagoon folk round that time, that she'd been a weight around her neck ever since, draggin her down, her white hair scarin off the men interested in Momma.

That did it. Semelee busted out through the door with no direction in mind and kept goin. She wound up on the beach where she collapsed on the sand. Her momma, who she'd thought of as her best friend, her only true friend, hated her, had always hated her. She wanted to die.

She thought about drowning herself but didn't have the energy to jump in the water. The tide was out so she decided to just lie here on the sand and let the water come to her, wash her out to sea, and that would be the end of it. No more hassles, no more names like "Granny," no more heartbreak, no nothin.

She lay there on her back in the sand with her eyes closed. The sun was so bright it blazed through her lids, botherin her. She didn't have her sunglasses on her but she did have those two shells around her neck. They was just the right size to go over her eyes. It'd be like layin in a tannin booth.

As she sat up to untie the thong, she saw the gulls glidin overhead and wished she had wings like them so she could fly away.

She lay back on the sand and fitted a shell over each eye—
What?

She snatched the shells away from her eyes and levered back up to sittin.

What just happened?

She'd put the shells over her eyes expectin to see black. But she'd seen white instead . . . white sand . . . and she'd been above it, lookin down on a girl lyin in the sand . . . a girl with shells over her eyes.

Semelee put those shells over her eyes again and suddenly she was lookin down on a girl sitting in the stand—a girl with fire-engine hair.

That's me!

She pulled off the shells again and looked up. A seagull

hovered above, looking down at her, probably wondering if she had a sandwich and might throw it a crust or two.

She started experimentin and found she could look through the eyes of any bird on the beach. She could soar, she could hover, she could spot a fish near the surface of the water and dive for it. Then she discovered she could see through fishes' eyes, swim around the rocks and coral and stay underwater as long as she pleased without comin up for air.

It was wonderful. She spent the rest of the day testin her powers. Finally, after the sun had set, she headed home. She didn't want to go there, didn't want to see her momma's face, but she had no place else to go.

When Semelee opened the door to the trailer Momma was all tears and apologies, sayin she hadn't really meant what she'd said, that she was just upset and talkin crazy. But Semelee knew the truth when she heard it. Momma had said what was deep in her heart and meant every word of it.

But Semelee didn't care now. She'd thought her world had ended but now she knew it was just beginnin. She knew she was special. She could do somethin no one else could do. They could make fun of her, call her names, but no one could hurt her now.

She was special.

But now she'd lost one of her shells. She'd lose all her specialness without them. She'd be a nobody again.

Semelee gripped the edges of the canoe in white-knuckled panic. "I just had a terrible thought, Luke. What if I dropped it back in that hospital room?"

6

When Jack returned to his father's room, almost an hour after he'd left, he was in a foul mood. He could have called the rental agency to come and change the tire, but had canned that course of action. He'd had no idea where he was, so how could he tell them where to find him?

So he'd changed the tire himself. No biggee. He'd changed a lot of tires in his day, but usually on pavement. Today the jack had kept slipping in the sand, fraying his patience. Then the clouds wandered off to let the sun out so it could cook him. But all that wouldn't have been so bad if the mosquitoes hadn't declared his skin a picnic ground. Never in all his life had he seen so many mosquitoes. Now his forearms looked like pink bubble wrap and the itching was driving him nuts.

Felt like a jerk for letting those yokels sandbag him like that.

The TV was on and some news head was talking about Tropical Storm Elvis. It had lost a lot of steam crossing northern Florida but was now in the Gulf where it was gaining strength again, stoking itself over the warm waters. Elvis had not entirely left the building.

He went to the bed and checked his father. No change that he could see. He stepped to the window and looked out again at the parking lot. Who were they, the girl and those odd-looking people? From the way the girl had approached the bed—or at least started to—she'd come here with a purpose. But what?

As he turned back to the bed he spotted something on the floor, something glossy black and oblong. He squatted beside it, wondering if it was some sort of Florida bug, a roach maybe. But no, it looked like a shell. He bent closer. It was curved like a mussel but flatter. Some kind of clam, maybe.

As he reached to pick it up, something under the bed caught his eye. Not under the bed exactly—more like behind the headboard. Looked like a slim tree branch standing on its end.

Jack picked up the shell and stepped to the head of the bed. He peeked behind the headboard and found a tin can painted with odd little squiggles sitting atop the branch. He'd seen something like this before, then remembered Anya's yard—it was full of them.

He smiled. The old lady must think they're good luck or something. Probably put it here for him when she visited the other day. Might as well leave it. Sure as hell wasn't doing Dad any harm. And who knew? Maybe it would help him. Jack had seen a lot stranger things these past few months.

As he straightened he noticed a glistening design on the back of the headboard. He slid the bed a few inches away from the wall for a better look. Someone had painted a pattern of black squiggles and circles there. No question as to who, because they were very similar to the squiggles on the can. But how had that skinny old lady moved the bed? It was damn heavy.

Jack decided to ask her later. He pushed the bed back, then placed the shell on the nightstand. Maybe one of the staff had dropped it. If so, they could reclaim it here. At least this way no one would step on it.

Scratching his arms, Jack said goodbye to his father and headed back to the car. He hoped his father had some calamine lotion at home.

7

Back at Gateways Jack found another car parked in the cul-de-sac. Maybe Anya had company. But when he went around to the front of his father's place he found the front door open and heard voices inside.

He stepped into the front room and found a young woman in a jacket and skirt showing an elderly couple through the house.

"Who the hell are you?" Jack said.

The old folks jumped and the young woman clutched her looseleaf notebook defensively against her chest. Jack figured he might have had a little too much edge on his voice, but that was the kind of mood he was in.

"I-I'm with Gateways," the woman said. "I'm showing this couple the house." She squared her shoulders defiantly. "And just who are you?"

"The owner's son. What are you doing here?"

The woman blinked. "Oh. I'm so sorry for your loss, but—"

"Loss? What loss? You talk as if my father's dead."

Another blink—a double this time. "You mean he's not?"

"Damn right, he's not. I just came from the hospital. He's not too healthy at the moment, but he's not dead."

The old couple were looking uncomfortable now. They stared at the ceiling, at the rug, anywhere but at Jack.

"Oh, dear," the younger woman said. "I was told he was."

"Even if he was, so what? What are you doing here?"

"I was showing it to these—"

Fury hit him like a kick in the gut. Vultures!

"Showing it? Where do you get off showing this place to anyone? It's his until he sells it."

Another squaring of the shoulders, this time with a defiant lift of the chin. "Apparently you don't know the arrangement in Gateway communities."

"Apparently I don't. But I'm going to find out. As for now"—he jerked a thumb over his shoulder—"out."

"But—"

"Out!"

She strode out the door with her head high. The old couple shuffled out behind her.

"I'm sorry," the old woman said, pausing as she passed.

"Not your fault," Jack told her.

She put a wrinkled hand on his arm. "I hope your father gets well soon."

"Thank you," he said, feeling suddenly deflated.

He closed the door after them and leaned against it. He'd overreacted. He told himself it was the frustration of all these questions with no answers. Not one goddamn answer.

Bad day. And it was only noon.

He was just turning away from the door when he heard a knock. He counted to three, promised he'd be more genteel this time about telling the sales lady where she could stick her commission, and pulled open the door.

But Anya stood there instead. She held out a familiar taped-over FedEx box.

"This came while you were out," she said. "I signed for it."

Ah. His Glock and his backup. Now he could feel whole again.

"Thanks."

"Heavy," she said. "What've you got in there? Lead?"

"You might say. Come on in where it's cool."

"I can't stay. You were by the hospital already?"

Jack nodded. "No change." He debated whether or not to ask her about the can on the stick behind his father's headboard but decided to save it for later. "Are you going over?"

She nodded. "I thought I'd sit with him for a while."

What a grand old lady. "I'll give you a lift."

She waved him off. "I've already called a cab." She turned to go. "I'll be back later. Cocktails at five, if you're available."

He couldn't turn her down twice. "It's a date." Jack thought of something. "By the way, who's the head honcho around here?"

"You mean Gateways?"

"Yeah. The general manager or acting director or chairman of the board of whatever you call him. Who runs the show?"

"That would be Ramsey Weldon. You can find him at the administration building. You can't miss it. It's mostly glass and right on the golf course. Why?"

"We need to have a little tête-à-tête," Jack said.

8

The administration building was pretty much as Anya had described it: a small, cubical structure sheathed in mirrored glass. As Jack got out of his car he saw a tall, distinguished-looking man unlocking the door to a classic-looking four-door sedan. He looked fiftyish, had longish black hair, graying at the temples, and wore a milk-chocolate brown lightweight silk suit that perfectly matched the color of his beautifully restored car: two-tone—white over brown—with wide whitewall tires.

"Am I dreaming," Jack said, "or is that a 1956 Chrysler Crown Imperial?"

The man's smile was tolerant, and his tone carried a hint of impatience.

"It's a Crown Imperial, all right, but not a Chrysler. Everyone makes that mistake. Chrysler spun off the Imperial into its own division in 1954. This baby came out two years later."

"It's beautiful," Jack said, meaning it.

He ran a hand along the crest of the rear fender to one of the stand-alone taillights, sticking up like a miniature red searchlight. The chrome of the split grille gleamed like a gap-toothed grin; the flawless finish threw back his reflection.

God, he wished he could use something like this for his wheels. But it was too conspicuous. The last thing he wanted was people to notice him as he drove around. That was why he'd finally given up Ralph, his old '63 Corvair convertible. People kept stopping him and asking about it.

"You restore this yourself?"

"Yes, it's a hobby of mine. Took me two years. Fewer than eleven thousand Imperials were made in '56 and only a hundred and seventy were Crowns. This one has the original engine, by the way—a 354-cubic-inch Hemi V-8."

"So it cranks."

"Yes, indeed. It cranks." He looked at Jack. "Visiting, I assume?"

"Yeah, in a way. My father's in the hospital in a coma and—"

"You're Tom's son? Poor man. How is he?"

Jack was surprised at the instant recognition. "Not great. You know him?"

He stuck out his hand. "Ramsey Weldon. I'm director of Gateways South."

"Isn't that something," Jack said, shaking his hand. "I came here looking for you."

"I bet I know why, too. I got a call from one of our sales team. It seems she was given false information about your father. The initial word from the hospital was that he was DOA. I'm terribly sorry about the misunderstanding."

"Okay," Jack said. "I can see somebody getting the wrong information, but where did she get off showing the place to prospective buyers?"

"Because she thought—erroneously—that the place belonged to Gateways."

"Where would she get an idea like that?"

Weldon's eyebrows rose. "Upon the death of the owner—or owners—the house reverts to Gateways."

"You're kidding."

He shook his head. "That's the arrangement. It's not unique. Plenty of graduated-care senior communities have similar arrangements."

"I can't believe my father signed on for that."

"Why not? His purchase of the home and the bond guarantees him not only a place to live, but quality care from the moment he signs to the moment he goes to meet his maker, no matter how long it takes. Members of a Gateways community will never be a burden on their families. 'What do we do with Papa?' or 'Who's going to take care of Mom?' are questions that will never arise in their families."

A smooth pitch, delivered with the timing and conviction of a lifelong salesman. Jack could see how powerful that pitch could be to someone like his father who had a lot of pride and had always been an independent sort.

"At no point," Weldon went on, "will your father be a burden on his children. And at no point will you have to feel guilty about him, because you can rest assured that he's being well cared for."

"Maybe it's not so much guilt I'm feeling as—pardon me if I sound paranoid, but it seems to be to your advantage to have a quick turnover in housing."

Weldon laughed. "Please, please, we're asked that all the time. But you have to remember, this isn't a Robin Cook novel. This is real life. Trust me, it's all been amortized and insured and reinsured. You can check our financials. Gateways is a public company that posts an excellent bottom line every year."

He noticed that Weldon was starting to sweat. But then, so was Jack. It was like a steam bath out here on the macadam.

"Then I'm not the first to raise the question."

"Of course not. Our society is conspiracy crazy, seeing dark plots wherever it looks. I assure you, Gateways takes excellent care of its citizens. We *do* care. And our caring is what makes our citizens recommend Gateways to their friends and relatives. That's why we have waiting lists all over the country and can't build these communities fast enough. Just one example is the availability of free annual exams I instituted last year to catch medical problems early when they're most treatable."

"Really? Where are they done?"

"Right there in the clinic." He pointed to a one-story structure a hundred yards away across a dead lawn. "It's attached to the skilled nursing facility."

Jack guessed that was Gateways-speak for nursing home.

"Do you think I could speak to the doctor about my father?"

"Please. Go right ahead." He glanced at his watch. "Oops. Going to be late for my meeting." He thrust out his hand again. "Nice meeting you, and good luck to your father. We're all pulling for him."

He slipped into his car and started it up. Jack listened to the throaty roar of its V-8 and, again, wanted one.

He watched him drive away. During all that talk he'd tried to get a bead on Ramsey Weldon but couldn't get past the smooth all-business, all-for-the-company exterior. If his father's accident hadn't been hit and run, he wouldn't have bothered. But since it was . . .

He shook his head. Maybe he was just looking for something that wasn't there. He knew there was plenty going on out there where no one could see. He didn't need to be inventing a conspiracy around here.

9

The doctor working the clinic today was named Charles Harris. He wasn't too busy at the moment so Jack got to see him after only a short wait.

A nurse led him into a walnut-paneled consultation room with a cherry wood desk and lots of framed diplomas on the walls. Harris wasn't the only name Jack saw, so he assumed other doctors rotated through the clinic. Dr. Harris turned out to be a young, dark, curly-haired fellow with bright blue eyes. Jack introduced himself by his real surname—a name he hadn't used in so long it tasted foreign on his lips—and then added: "Tom's son."

Dr. Harris hadn't heard about the accident but offered his wishes for a speedy recovery. Then he wanted to know what he could do for Jack.

"First off I'd like to know if my father had a physical here recently."

Dr. Harris nodded. "Yes, just a couple of months ago."

"Great. Dr. Huerta is his neurologist at the hospital—"

"I know Inez. Your father's in good hands."

"That's comforting. But I'm wondering about his medical condition before the accident."

Jack thought he sensed Dr. Harris recede about half a dozen feet. "Such as?"

"Well, anything that might have contributed to the accident, or might explain what he was doing driving around at that hour."

Dr. Harris leaned forward and thrust his hand across the desk, palm up.

"Could I see some ID?"

"What?" Jack hadn't seen this coming. "What for?"

"To prove you're who you say you are."

Jack knew he couldn't. All his ID was in the name of John Tyleski. He owned nothing with his own surname.

"I've got to prove I'm my father's son? Why on earth—?"

"Patient privilege. Normally I wouldn't under any circumstances discuss a medical file without the patient's permission, even with a spouse. But since this particular patient is incapable of giving permission, I'm willing to make an exception for a close relative—*if* that's what you are."

Since Jack couldn't show ID, maybe he could talk his way around this.

"If I wasn't his son, why would I care?"

"You could be a lawyer or someone hired by a lawyer looking for an angle to sue."

"Sue? What the hell for?"

"On behalf of someone injured in the accident."

"But my father was the only one injured."

Dr. Harris shrugged. "I don't know that. I know nothing about the accident. I do know that people in these parts sue at the drop of a hat. They're caught up in some sort of lottery mentality. Malpractice insurance is through the roof. People may not be able to figure out a presidential ballot but they damn sure know what lawyer to call if they stub a toe."

He could see Dr. Harris was getting steamed just talking about it.

"Look, I assure you I'm not a lawyer. I can't even remember the last time I spoke to one—that is, if you don't count my brother who's a judge in Philadelphia."

Maybe that'll mollify him, Jack thought.

It didn't.

"On the other hand," Dr. Harris said, "you could be a con man looking to pull some kind of slimy scam."

"Like what?" Jack was interested in hearing this.

He shrugged. "I don't know, but Florida's got more con men per square mile than any other state in the union."

"I'm not a con man"—at least not today—"and I'm concerned about my father. In fact, you've got me worried now. What's wrong with him that you won't tell me? What are you hiding?"

"Not a thing." Dr. Harris wiggled the fingers on his still outstretched hand. "We're wasting time. Just show me some ID and I'll tell you what I know."

Shit.

"I don't have it with me. I left it at my father's place."

Dr. Harris's features hardened. He shook his head and stood up. "Then I'm afraid I can't do anything for you." He hit a buzzer. "I'll have the nurse show you out."

"All right," Jack said, rising. "But will you at least call Dr. Huerta and tell her what you know?"

Dr. Harris obviously hadn't expected that one.

"I . . . well, of course. I can do that. I'll call her this afternoon."

As frustrated and worried as he was, Jack had to respect this guy's ethics. He forced a smile and thrust out his hand.

"Thanks. Nice to meet you, doc. You could be classified as a real pain in the ass, but I'm glad my dad has someone like you looking after his privacy. My doc at home is the same way."

Of course, Doc Hargus was a different case. His license to practice had been pulled, so no one was supposed to know he even *had* patients.

Jack didn't wait for the nurse. He left the thoroughly befuddled Charles Harris, MD behind and headed for the clinic exit.

Along the way he paid close attention to the windows and the walls—especially the upper corners near the ceiling—and the door frame as he stepped through it. No alarm contacts or release buttons, no motion detectors.

Good.

10

"Is it workin?" Luke said. "Can you see?"

Semelee sat on a bench in the galley of the *Bull-ship*. Some of the clan was in town, beggin, while others was ashore, dozin in the shade. She and Luke were the only ones aboard. She wished he'd get away and stop hangin over her shoulder and leave her be. But his heart was in the right place and so she bit her lip and kept her voice low.

"Just give me a minute here, Luke," she said as she adjusted her one remaining shell over her right eye. "Just give me a little space so's I can see if I can get this to work."

It was so different with only one shell. With two she could focus right in. With one . . .

With only one eye-shell she could still get into the heads of higher forms like Dora, but the lower forms . . . they were hard even with two. They didn't have much goin for them brainwise, and that meant she had to concentrate all the harder. If only she had that other shell.

"I could take a few of the guys and hop the fence and watch him ourselfs. We—"

"Just hesh up, will you? I think I'm gettin it."

"Yeah?"

She could hear the hope, the excitement in his voice.

She didn't see any way she or one of her clansmen could sneak into the hospital to hunt down that other eye-shell, but if she could keep an eye on the old guy's son, the special one who'd been sent to her, maybe she'd find out if he had it.

But she had to get control here.

Control . . . back in her teens she'd thought her power was limited to only seein through a critter's eyes, but she soon learned that was just part of the story. She found out in her junior year when Suzie Lefferts paid her a visit on the beach.

Semelee had been comin down to the ocean almost every day, except for the rainy ones, to put on her eye-shells and fly, soar, and dive with the flocks, or swim and dart through the depths with the schools. She could even get into a crab and crawl along the sandy bottom. These was the only times she felt truly alive . . . truly free . . . like she belonged.

The sudden sound of a too-familiar voice behind her jarred her back to the beach.

"So this is where you spend all your time."

Suzie must have realized that she was no longer getting to Semelee, that her taunts and tiny tortures weren't having their usual effect. So she'd followed her to see why.

"I thought you might've had a new boyfriend or some-thing," Suzie said, "but all you do is sit here with those stu-pid shells over your eyes. You were always a loser, Semelee, but now you've totally lost it."

When Semelee didn't even remove the shells from her eyes or bother to reply, Suzie flew into a rage. She grabbed the shells and put them over her own eyes.

"What is it with these things anyway?"

Oh, no! She'd see! She'd know!

But Suzie mustn't've seen anything. She called them junk and tossed them toward the surf.

Terrified they might wash out to sea, Semelee screamed and ran down to the tide's edge. She found what she thought was them—they were freshwater clamshells after all—but wasn't sure. As Suzie walked up the dune laugh-ing, Semelee wanted to choke her, but she couldn't go after her, not until she made sure she had the right shells . . . to see if they still worked . . .

They did. She put them on and there she was, glidin high over the beach, watching Suzie strutting toward her car. The bitch!

Suddenly she was divin toward Suzie, beak open, screechin. She plowed into the back of her neck, staggerin the bitch. And then she was peckin at her head, cuttin her scalp and tearin out her teased blond hair in chunks.

Semelee was so surprised she dropped her shells. She watched the squawkin gull leave Suzie's head and flap away while Suzie ran screamin for her car. The truth smacked Semelee right between the eyes then: She couldn't just get inside things and look through their eyes, she could control them, make them do what she wanted.

This cool feelin of power surged through her. She wasn't just a tiny bit special, she was *really* special.

But was she all that special with only one shell?

She clapped a hand over her left eye and focused all her

will, all her concentration through her right. Something
was coming into focus. A blade of grass, dry and brown,
loomed huge in her vision, like the trunk of a tree.

"I'm there!" she cried. "I got one. Now I got to get another."

And another after that, and another, and another . . .

This was going to take time and effort. Lots of effort.

"I got to spread myself around the old guy's house and
get in if I can."

"You really think he has it?"

"Don't know. But I'm gonna do my damnedest to find
out."

"And if he got it, then what?"

"We ain't come to that bridge yet, Luke. When we do,
we'll figure somethin out."

And maybe in the meantime I'll just test this guy's inner
stuff, she thought. See if he's worthy of me.

11

Jack's head was spinning. Not from the wine he'd been
drinking but from this damn game he was trying to learn.

He'd spent the latter part of the afternoon in his father's
hospital room with Anya—and Oyv, of course. No change
in Dad's condition—still the same random, involuntary
movements and incomprehensible sounds. He'd been hoping to see Dr. Huerta and find out if Dr. Harris had con-
tacted her. He figured he might be able to get her to tell
him what the doc was hiding about his father's pre-
accident condition.

But she didn't show, and finally he drove Anya and Oyv back to Gateways. She didn't let up on his joining her for a drink, so after a shower and a call to Gia to reassure himself that she, Vicky, and the baby were fine, he ambled next door.

He found Anya outside on her front lawn, cigarette in one hand, wine-glass in the other, reclining face up on a chaise lounge next to a big liter-and-a-half bottle of red wine chilling in an ice bucket. She wore huge sunglasses with turquoise frames. Her flat breasts were encased in a pink halter top over skimpy black shorts. She'd coated the exposed areas of her wrinkled, leathery brown skin with some sort of sun-tanning oil and lay marinating in the sun.

Oyv was curled up next to her. He barked once when Jack stepped across the line of dry brown grass onto Anya's lush green lawn, then settled down again.

"I started without you, hon," she said. "Pull up a chair and pour yourself a glass."

"Chilled red wine," Jack said. "I don't think I've ever had that."

"Don't tell me you're a wine snob."

Jack shook his head. "A bit of a beer snob, maybe, but I wouldn't know a cabernet from a merlot without the label."

"Glad to hear it. You've probably had people tell you that the only wine you should drink cold is white or blush or rosé. Trust me, kiddo, they're talking out their *tuchuses*. This is a Côtes du Rhone. That's French, by the way."

"Really?"

"You probably expect an old broad like me to be a whiskey sour or Manhattan drinker, but as far as I'm concerned, on a hot summer day like this, a glass of chilled Côtes du Rhone or Beaujolais hits the spot. Try it and see if you like it. If you don't, sorry, but that's what we serve at Casa Mundy. You want beer, you'll have to bring your own. I'm not into that fizzy hops-and-malt drek."

So Jack poured himself a glass and damn if it didn't, as Anya had said, hit the spot.

"Not bad."

He pulled up a chaise lounge on the other side of the table with the ice bucket.

"How come you're the only one visiting my father? Doesn't he have any other friends?"

"He has lots. But they probably don't know. I think I'm the only one who knows, and I don't talk to many people."

"How did you find out?"

"When I saw his car was missing Tuesday morning, I called the police and asked if there'd been any serious accidents. They sounded pretty suspicious until I told them why I was calling. They told me about your father so I went right over to the hospital to see."

"Shouldn't you let people know?"

"Why? So they can send dead flowers and come in and stare at him? Tom wouldn't want that."

No, he wouldn't. Jack guessed she did know his father after all.

Together they sat and sipped and watched the sun settle in the west.

"Maybe we'd better go in," Jack said as it sank below the distant treetops. He checked his watch. 7:10. "The Wehrmacht mosquito squadrons will be launching soon."

"So?"

"You like mosquito bites?"

"You like to deny those poor females their sustenance?"

"Females?"

"Only the female mosquito bites. The males suck nectar."

"Male or female, I'm not keen on being a mosquito buffet."

She waved a hand at him. "Not to worry. They won't bother you here."

"Why not?"

"Because I won't let them."

Ooookay, lady, Jack thought. If that's what you want to believe.

But damn if they didn't sit there well into the dusk without a single mosquito bite.

When the magnum of Côtes du Rhone was done, Anya draped a fuchsia blouse over her shoulders, rose, and faced him.

"Come on inside, hon. I'll fix you dinner."

Not having a better offer, Jack accepted.

He stopped short as he crossed the threshold. He'd thought the outside was lush, but inside was a mini jungle of potted plants and trees lining the perimeter and clustered here and there on the floor, with vines growing among them and climbing the walls. He could identify a ficus here, a bird of paradise and a rubber plant there, but the rest were a mystery: potted palms of all sorts—were those baby bananas on the big one in the corner?—and smaller plants with leaves mixing reds and yellows and even silver on a couple. Reminded Jack of one of the plant shops on Sixth Avenue.

Anya turned to him and said, "I'm going to change into something more appropriate for dinner."

"What's wrong with what you're wearing?"

"I want something more *haute couture*," she said with a wink.

"Not necessary, but this is your party . . ."

As she threaded her way through the plants toward the master bedroom, Jack decided to take a look around. Oyv, curled like a cat on a worn yellow easy chair, watched him with his big dark eyes as he wandered the front room.

He realized that her layout was the mirror image of his father's—whatever was on the right here, was on the left there. But where his father's walls sported some artwork—

mostly south Florida beachscapes—and some photos, Anya's walls were bare except for the vines. Not a shell, not a fishnet, not a knick knack. Nada.

She'd said she had no family. Jack guessed she was right. But how about a painting of *something*? Even Elvis or a tiger on black velvet would say something about her.

And the furniture . . . a nondescript mishmash. Jack knew his talents for interior décor were on a par with his ability to fly a 747, but this stuff looked like secondhand junk. Fine if Anya didn't care, but he was struck by the lack of personality. He'd been in motel rooms with more personal touches than this. It was as if she lived in a vacuum.

Except for the plants. Maybe they were her personal statement. Her family. Her children.

Anya reentered and struck a pose with one arm held aloft. "What do you think?"

She'd wrapped herself in some sort of psychedelic kimono which made her skinny figure seem even thinner. She looked like a Rainbow Pop that had been left out in the sun too long.

"Woo-woo," Jack said.

It was the best he could do on such short notice.

Dinner turned out to be as idiosyncratic as the chef. She mixed up a wok of walnuts, peanuts, peas, jalapeño peppers, and corn seasoned with, among other things, ashes falling from her ever-present cigarette, all rolled up in big flour tortillas. Despite Jack's initial reservations, the mélange proved very tasty.

"Can I hazard a guess that you're a vegetarian?" he said.

They were into their second magnum of Côtes du Rhone. Anya kept refilling his glass, and Jack noticed that she was putting away two or three glasses to every one he had, but showing no effects.

Anya shook her head. "Heavens, no. I don't eat vegetables at all. Only fruits and seeds."

"There's corn in this," Jack said around a mouthful. "Corn's a vegetable."

"Sorry, no. It's a fruit, just like the tomato."

"Oh. Right." He remembered hearing that somewhere. "Well, how about the peas?"

"Peas are seeds—legumes. Nuts are seeds too."

"No lettuce, no broccoli—?"

"No. Those require killing the plant. I don't approve of killing. I eat only what a plant intends to discard."

"What about Oyv?" He glanced at the little Chihuahua chowing down on something in his bowl. "He needs meat."

"He does perfectly well on soy burgers. Loves them, in fact."

Poor puppy.

"So I guess if I stop by with a craving for a bacon cheeseburger—"

"You can just keep on going, hon. There's a Wendy's not too far down the road toward town."

Gia would be right at home here, Jack thought. She wasn't a vegan or anything, but she'd stopped eating meat.

Whatever. This dish was delicious. Jack wound up having four burritofuls.

He helped clear the dishes, then Anya brought out the mahjongg tiles, saying, "Come, I'll teach you."

"Oh, I don't know . . ."

"Don't be afraid. It's easy."

She lied.

Mahjongg was a four-person game played with illustrated tiles, but Anya was teaching him a two-player variant. The images on the tiles swam before his eyes—circles, bamboo stalks, ideograms that were supposed to represent dragons or the four winds—while terms such as *chow* and *pong* and *chong* searched for purchase in his brain. He didn't have any references for this stuff. Why couldn't the tiles have spades and hearts or jacks and queens and kings?

The constant stream of smoke from the chimney that was Anya didn't help. Neither did her plants. They seemed to be watching the game, like a gaggle of curious spectators crowding around a high-stakes poker table in Las Vegas. One strand of vine with broad green and yellow leaves kept falling off a palm frond and draping across his shoulder. Jack would put it back, but it wouldn't stay up.

"That's Esmeralda," Anya said.

"Who?" Jack replied, thinking she was referring to some new tile or rule in the game.

"The gold-net honeysuckle behind you." She smiled. "I think she likes you."

"I'm not fond of clingy women," he said, reaching once again to remove the vine from his shoulder. But when he saw Anya's frown he changed his mind and let it stay where it was. "But in this case I'll make an exception."

She smiled and Jack thought, Sweet lady, but nutso, nutso, nutso.

In addition to the green, leafy distractions, all the wine he'd consumed wasn't exactly helping his learning curve. Anya lifted the bottle—she'd opened a third magnum—to give him a refill. Jack put his hand over his glass.

"I'm flagging myself."

"Don't be silly, hon. It's not as if you have to drive home."

"I have something I want to do tonight."

"Oh? And that would be . . . ?"

"Just getting some answers to a few questions."

"Answers are a good thing," she said. Her voice was clear, her hand steady as she refilled her glass almost to the rim. No doubt about it: The woman had a hollow leg. "Just make sure you're asking the right questions."

12

Even in his slightly inebriated state, Jack had no trouble entering the clinic. All it took was a flat-head screwdriver from his father's toolbox to pop the window lock and he was in.

He'd managed to extricate himself gracefully from the mahjongg lesson with a promise to return for another real soon. He wasn't big into board games, although he'd played *Risk* a lot as a kid. He liked video games, though. Not so much the first-person shooters that were mostly reflexes; he did well in those but preferred role-playing games that involved strategy. He liked trying to outwit the designers.

After leaving Anya's he'd gone back to his father's place and doused himself with a mosquito repellent spray he'd found on a shelf with the tennis racquets and balls. Then he'd walked around some to clear his head and get the lay of the land. Here it was 9:30 and no one was out. This was good. An occasional car drove by but he'd duck into the bushes as soon as he saw its lights. One set of lights had turned out to be a cruising security patrol jeep.

A couple of times he'd stayed in the bushes longer than he had to because of the faint feeling that he was being watched. He couldn't find a trace of anyone following him, though, and wrote it off to his being on unfamiliar ground.

He'd approached the clinic building from the rear, where there was less light, and held his breath as he lifted the window, ready to run in case it was armed with an alarm system he hadn't spotted. But nothing sounded.

Made sense when he thought about it. Why spring for the extra expense of alarming all the buildings when you had a real live security force manning the gates and patrolling the streets?

He crawled through, closed the window behind him, and began searching about. He used the penlight he'd found in his father's top drawer, flicking it on and off as he moved. He found the small file room to the right of the receptionist area. He'd been hoping it would be windowless, but it wasn't, so he had to search the files with his penlight.

Again that feeling of being watched, but he was the only one here. He sneaked to the window but saw no one outside.

A few minutes later he found his father's slim chart. Holding it in his hand, he hesitated before opening it. What was the bad news Dr. Harris had been hiding? He knew the question—did he want the answer?

Again, the matter of his father's privacy. The information inside could be pretty intimate. Did he have a right to peek this far into the man's life?

Probably not. But the guy was in a coma, and Jack needed answers.

Taking a breath, he opened the file and flipped through it. He found two pages of lab test results. He didn't know what all these numbers meant but noted that the "Abnormal" column was blank on both sheets. Good enough. An EKG had a typewritten reading at its top: "Normal resting EKG." Even better.

But hadn't Dr. Huerta said something about his father developing an abnormal rhythm in the hospital? Maybe from the stress of the injuries. Everyone had heard of the patient with the normal EKG who has a heart attack on the way out of the doctor's office.

He checked the handwritten notes but couldn't read

much of Dr. Harris's scribbling. The last entry was fairly legible though.

Reviewed labs w pt. All WNL. Final assess: excellent health.

Excellent health. Well, that was a relief.

But damn it, doc, why couldn't you have just said so in the first place? Would have saved me a whole lot of trouble.

13

Jack fished the house key out of his pocket as he walked down the slope toward his father's place. The good news was that the man was in excellent health. The bad news was that Jack didn't know one damn thing more than he had when he woke up this morning.

Nearing the house, he passed a beat-up old rustbucket Honda Civic parked in the deep shadows on the grass adjacent to the cul-de-sac. Hadn't been there when he passed by before.

On alert now, Jack slowed his pace. Before rounding the rear corner of the house, he peeked first. He froze when he saw the silhouette of someone squatting beside one of the trees between his house and Anya's. Was this who'd been watching him?

Dropping into a crouch he hugged the jalousied back porch and crept toward the figure. The wash of light from the parking area of the cul-de-sac cast long shadows across the space, but not enough light for Jack to make out his features. Could be one of those weird-looking characters from the pickup truck this morning.

Then the figure flicked a flashlight off and on—only for a second, but that was enough for Jack to identify him.

He straightened and walked up behind him.

"What's up, Carl?"

The man jumped and let out a little yelp. He wore a lightweight, long-sleeved camouflage suit—if nothing else, it protected him from mosquitoes—but a screwdriver instead of a hand protruded from the right cuff. He looked up at Jack and held his left hand over his heart.

"Oh, it's you. Tom's son . . ." He seemed to be fumbling for the name.

"Jack."

"Right. Jack. Boy, I gotta tell you, Jack, you shouldn't come up on a body like that. You just bout scared the life outta me."

Jack noticed something metallic with a silver finish on the grass before Carl. He couldn't tell what it was, but he knew it was too bulky to be a gun.

"I've found that people tend to get jumpy when they're doing something they shouldn't. You doing something you shouldn't, Carl?"

Still in a squat, Carl looked away. "Well, yeah, I guess so. Sorta. But not really."

Now there's a clear-cut answer, Jack thought.

"And what would that be?" When Carl hesitated Jack said, "Share, Carl. It's good to share."

"Oh, all right. Might as well tell you since you caught me in the act." He looked up at Jack. "I'm doin a job for Dr. Dengrove."

"Who's he? Your therapist?"

"Naw. He lives three houses back, near the beginnin of the cul-de-sac. He wants me to catch Miss Mundy in the act of waterin her stuff and all."

"Why would he want to do that?"

"Because it's makin him crazy that his grass and his

flowers is all dead and wilty while Miss Mundy's is all green and growin like a jungle."

"So you're supposed to hang out here all night and catch her in the act?"

Carl nodded. "Sorta. He's been after me for weeks, offering me money to do it, but I keep tellin him no."

"Because you don't want to get Miss Mundy in any trouble, right?"

"Well, yeah, there's that, but also on account of how I gotta be up bright an early ever mornin for my job. That don't stop him from offerin me more money, though. But I just kept on tellin him no."

" 'Kept'?" Jack said. "I guess your being here tonight means he made you an offer you couldn't refuse."

"In a way, yeah." He motioned Jack down. "Here. Take a look at this."

Jack glanced around to see if anyone else was lurking about. He sensed Carl was exactly what he seemed to be: just a cracker working as a groundsman. But still . . . after having one of his tires slashed by another cracker this morning, he wasn't taking any chances.

It looked like they were alone out here, so Jack squatted beside Carl.

"What've you got?"

"Somethin really cool." He picked up the metal object and held it toward Jack. "Dr. Dengrove lent it to me. Ain't it somethin?"

Jack took it and turned it over in his hands. A digital minicam. He noticed two slim wires trailing from the casing.

"What do you think you're going to do with this?"

"Get pictures. Dr. Dengrove wants me to get a movie of Miss Mundy waterin her stuff."

Jack shook his head. "In this light, Carl, I'm afraid all you're going to get is a dark screen."

"Nuh-uh. Nuh-*uh*." Jack detected a certain note of nyah-

nyah glee in Carl's tone as he reached over and pressed a button above the camera's pistol-grip handle. "Take a look."

Jack raised the viewfinder to his eye and blinked as the walls of Anya's house and the grass and plants surrounding it leaped into view.

"Whoa," he said. "A night-vision camera."

He could make out the palms and the larger flowers—not the colors, of course, because everything was either green or black, just the shapes—along with her array of crazy lawn ornaments. As he swung the view past a lighted window the image flared, losing all detail. As he kept moving, the light from the window left a wavering smear across the tiny screen that quickly faded, allowing him to make out details again.

"Yeah," Carl said. "Almost like I'm runnin a *Big Brother* show, dontcha think?"

"I suppose."

Jack had never watched a single episode. His own life was more interesting than any reality-TV show. He'd tuned into *The Anna Nicole Show* now and again, but that couldn't be classified as reality. At least he hoped not.

"These don't come cheap," he said as he lowered the camera and turned it over in his hands. "What's this Dr. Dengrove doing with it?"

"Ask me, I think he bought it just so's he can catch Miss Mundy in the act. He don't seem to be hurtin none for bucks, but he's sure hurtin bad for a green lawn." He snorted a laugh at this little turn of phrase. "Hurtin so bad he's near about crazy."

"Crazy enough to drop a bundle on a night-vision video camera and hire you to run it?"

Carl grinned. "You betcha."

Jack shook his head. Some people. "I think Dr. Dengrove should get a life."

"Mostly I think he eats. You should see the gut and butt on him—real pan-o-ramic."

"Pano—?"

"You know." He spread his arms. "Like you told me: wide."

A panoramic butt . . . Jack opened his mouth, then shut it again. Let it ride.

"He's like most of the folks here, I guess. They got too much time on their hands so they worry about all the wrong things. That's why I liked your daddy so much—"

"*Like*, Carl. He's still alive, so you can still like him."

"Oh, yeah. Right. Well, anyway, he didn't just sit around and complain. He kept busy. Always seemed to have somethin to do, someplace to go."

"Speaking of going places . . . the accident happened out on a swamp road in the dead of night. You have any idea what he was doing out there?"

Jack couldn't make out Carl's expression but saw him shake his head.

"Nope. I go home at night and I stay there."

"Where's home?"

"Got me a real nice little trailer in a park just south of town. Me and the guy next door share a satellite dish. For bout thirty bucks a month each we got us a zillion channels. No reason to go out. And even if there was, you wouldn't catch me out in the Glades at night. I told you: It's angry these days."

"Right. You did. But you're out tonight—nice camo suit, by the way."

"These here are my jammies."

"They're you, Carl. So the plan is, you're going to sit out here all night and wait for Miss Mundy to show?"

"Nup. Don't hafta. At first I figured I'd just set the camera up and let her run, but that wasn't going to work. Even if the battery would last, the memory wouldn't. But then I came up with this real smart idea to solve all my problems. Lookit here."

He held up a little circuit board.

"What's that do?"

"It's a motion detector."

This Carl was full of surprises. "Did Dr. Dengrove give you that too?"

"Nup. Got it myself. Took it out of a singin fish."

"I'm sorry," Jack said, poking a finger in his right ear. "I thought you just said you took it out of a singing fish."

"That's right. That's what I did. Actually, I took it out of the board the fish sits on."

"You're losing me."

"Big Mouth Billy Bass . . . the singin fish. He bends out from the board and sings 'Don't Worry, Be Happy,' and some other song I never heard before."

"Oh, right. I know what you're talking about."

Jack had seen one in a store once and couldn't imagine why anyone would want one. But a clerk had told him he couldn't keep them in stock.

"Course you do. I bought mine years ago. Was one of the first around here to get one. Hung it by my front door and anytime someone came in it started singin. Pretty soon everyone in the trailer park had one, but I was first." He shook his head. "Haven't used it much lately, though. Got pretty tired of havin to listen to those same two songs every time I walked by. So I let the batteries run out. But just the other night I remembered that it had a motion detector inside that set it off every time you passed." He waved the circuit board. "And here it is."

"I get it," Jack said. "You're going to attach the motion detector to the camera, and when Anya comes out to water, you'll catch her."

"That's the plan. I made sure I popped off the speaker, though." He chuckled. "Wouldn't do to have that fish voice start singin 'Don't Worry, Be Happy' in the middle of the night, now would it."

"I guess not. You think this'll work?"

"Oh, it works. I checked it out at home."

"You really think you'll catch her?" Jack didn't like the idea of Anya getting in trouble.

"Nup. But don't tell Dr. Dengrove that, and don't you go tellin her I'm doin this. I don't want her mad at me."

"And you also don't want her tipped off that she's being watched." He nudged Carl with his elbow. "Won't you feel bad if you get her in trouble?"

"I would, cept that's not gonna happen. Like I told Dr. Dengrove, all this work's gonna be for nothin. We ain't never gonna catch Miss Mundy waterin."

"Why not?"

"Because she don't. All she does is sit and watch TV all night. Just like everbody else. Reruns of either *Matlock* or *Golden Girls*. That and the Weather Channel's all anybody round here ever seems to watch." He licked his lips. "But there's somethin else."

"What?"

"She looks dead when she's watchin TV."

"How do you know?"

"I peeked in last night while I was settin up, and I thought she was dead. I seen my share of dead folks—I'm the one found Mr. Bass dead in a chair on his front porch awhile back, and Miss Mundy looked just like him. Boy, was I glad to see her up and about this mornin."

"Didn't you call anyone?"

"Hey, I wasn't supposed to be there. And if she was as gone as she looked, there wasn't nothin nobody could do anyhow. Tonight I looked in again, just a few minutes ago, and it was the same thing. Gwon. Look for yourself."

Jack shook his head. "I don't think so."

"Gwon. See if I ain't lyin. It's creepy, I tell you."

The last thing Jack needed was to get caught acting like a Peeping Tom, but his curiosity was piqued. He crept up to the lighted window that looked in on the front room and peeked through the lower right corner.

Still in her kimono, Anya lay back in her recliner, mouth slack, eyes half open and staring straight ahead. A *Law and Order* episode was playing—Jack recognized the music—but Anya wasn't watching it. Her gaze was fixed on a spot somewhere above the TV. Oyv was stretched across her lap, looking equally dead.

Jack watched her for signs of breathing but she was still as, well, death. His comatose father showed more signs of life. Jack straightened and was about to head around front to knock on her door, when he saw her chest move. She took a breath. Oyv took a breath too, at exactly the same time. Just one each. Then they went dead still again.

Okay. So she was alive. Maybe it was all that wine—she must have put away three liters—that put her into such a deep sleep.

Shaking his head, he returned to where Carl waited.

"You weren't kidding," he said. "But I saw her breathe. She's okay." He put a hand on Carl's shoulder. "But you haven't explained how she can have such a healthy lawn without watering."

"Magic," Carl said, looking around as if someone besides Jack might be close enough to hear. "You may think I'm loco, but that's the only explanation."

Jack remembered Abe telling him about Occam's razor earlier in the year. It went something like: the simplest, most direct explanation—the one that requires the fewest assumptions—is usually the right one. Magic required a lot of assumptions. Water didn't.

"I like water better as an explanation."

"Nuh-uh. Not when you look at where her green grass ends and the brown begins. It runs in a perfect line twenty feet from her house all the way around in a big circle. And when I say line, I mean it's got sharp edges. I know, cause I cut it. I may not know much about lotsa things, but I know you can't water like that."

Jack couldn't see the line in the low light. He figured Carl was exaggerating. Had to be.

"I think it's them doohickies she's got all over her yard," Carl said. "And that writin on her walls."

"Writing?" Jack didn't remember seeing anything on Anya's walls.

"Yup. You can't see it lookin at it reglar, but—here." He handed Jack the camera again. "You look through that while I put my flashlight on. Now I'm only goin to put it on for a second so you look real hard."

Jack peered through the viewfinder at the blank wall, avoiding the glare of the lighted window. A section of the wall lit as Carl's flashbeam hit it. And there, flaring to life, a collection of arcs and angles and squiggles, very much like the symbols on the homemade ornaments dotting her lawn.

And like the symbols he'd found behind his father's headboard.

"Y'see em? Didja see em?"

"Yeah, Carl. I saw them." But what did they mean? He'd never seen anything like them. On a hunch, Jack did a one-eighty turn. "Flash that on my father's place, will you?"

When Carl complied, the same symbols appeared.

Dumfounded, Jack lowered the camera. "He's got them too."

"Hmmm," Carl said. "They sure ain't doin nothin for his lawn. Wonder what they's for?"

"Let's do a little research," Jack said.

With Carl in tow, Jack used the same procedure to check out three other nearby houses, but their walls were blank.

Returning to Carl's original spot, he handed back the

camera. That feeling of being watched was back and stronger than ever. He scanned the area and spotted a bunch of dead leaves scattered across the remains of his father's lawn. Hadn't noticed them before. Not unexpected, though. He'd seen trees drop leaves in a hot dry spell.

While Carl attached the motion detector to the camera—still no sign of a right hand, just a screwdriver poking from the cuff—Jack turned toward Anya's house.

He had to admit he was baffled. That strange old lady was the common factor here: She lived next door to his father . . . visited him in the hospital . . . the symbols on her house were also on his dad's place. Jack knew his father hadn't painted them on his hospital bed. Not while comatose. So that left Anya.

She must have painted them with some sort of clear lacquer so they'd be invisible. But what did they mean? And what did she think she was accomplishing with them?

Maybe he should just ask her. But then he'd have to explain how he knew.

He glanced around again and noticed even more leaves on the lawn. Their number had doubled or tripled since his last look. Where the hell were they coming from? They were small, maybe three inches long; light from the parking area glinted off their shiny, reddish brown surfaces. Odd . . . dead leaves usually lost their gloss.

Jack looked around for the source but couldn't see any trees in the vicinity with that kind of leaf.

"There," Carl said. Jack turned and saw him on his feet, dusting off his knees. He'd duct taped the camera to the slender trunk of a young palm. "All set."

"Tell me something, Carl," Jack said, jerking a thumb over his shoulder. "Where'd all those leaves come from?"

Carl was facing the light when he glanced past Jack. Jack saw his expression change from curiosity, to puzzlement, to shock. He turned and looked and knew his expression must be mirroring Carl's.

No grass was visible. The leaves had multiplied till they now covered every square inch of the lawn.

"Those ain't leaves," Carl said in a hushed, awed tone. "Them's palmettos!"

"What's a palmetto?"

"A bug! A Florida roach!"

"You mean like a cockroach?"

"Yeah. But I can't remember ever seein more'n half a dozen palmettos in one spot at the same time."

Jack had encountered his share of cockroaches—couldn't live in New York without seeing them—but never this size. These were cockroaches on steroids. His skin crawled. He wasn't the squeamish type, but these were big, and there had to be thousands of them, all just a few feet away. If they started scuttling his way . . .

"What're they doing here?" Jack said.

"Dunno. There ain't nothin for them to eat on that lawn, that's for sure." He looked over his shoulder. "Tell you what I'm gonna do. My car's parked in the shadows on the other side of your daddy's place. I'm gonna head around the front of the house and get to it that way."

"Why don't you just shine your flashlight at them. Cockroaches hate light. Turn one on and they disappear."

"Not Palmettos. Light don't bother them ay-tall. They actually *like* the light." He turned and took a step away. "Be back tomorrow."

That step seemed to trigger the bugs. With a chittering whir of wings they took to the air in a cloud.

"They *fly?*" Jack shouted as he started backing away. "Cockroaches don't fly!"

"Palmettos do!" Carl broke into a run.

Jack felt a surge of fear and didn't know why. They were just roaches; not as if they were going to eat him alive or anything. But his adrenaline was kicking in, pushing his heart rate up a few notches. He quickened his backpedal.

At that instant the churning mass of bugs turned as one and swept toward him in a swirling cloud. Jack whirled and dashed after Carl.

"Here they come!" he shouted.

Carl didn't even turn his head; instead he put it down and upped his speed.

But neither stood a chance of outrunning the bugs. The palmettos were too fast. They swirled around Jack, engulfing him, clinging to his face, his arms, his hair, buzzing in his ears, scratching at his eyelids, wiggling their antennaed heads into his nostrils, digging at his lips. The clatter of their wings sounded like a million tiny hands applauding. He felt countless little nips all over his exposed skin. Were they biting him? Did they have teeth?

He swept a mass of them from his face but they poured back in on him. He couldn't see and he was afraid to open his mouth to breathe—they might crawl down his throat. He tore them again from his face and stole a quick look ahead. The last thing he needed now was to run into a wall or tree trunk and knock himself silly.

He saw that he'd reached the corner of the house. Carl was still ahead, waving his arms wildly about, all but unrecognizable under a swarming mass of palmettos, but still maintaining a stumbling run. Jack cupped a hand over his mouth, took a quick, bug-free breath, and shouted.

"Carl! Forget the car! Go into the house!"

But Carl either didn't hear the muffled advice or chose to ignore it. Jack had to close his eyes again against the storm of palmettos. He angled to his right—the front door was somewhere in that direction—and hoped he wouldn't trip over one of the front porch chairs.

He slammed into a wall and heard some of the bugs

crunch against the siding. He felt to his left, found the handle to the screen door, and pulled it open.

The front door—had he locked it? He hoped to hell not. This being a gated community and all, why would he bother? But he was a New Yorker, and New Yorkers never—

He fumbled around, found the knob, turned it, pushed it open, and leaped inside. As he moved he was trying to think of ways to kill the bugs that made it through the door with him, but then he realized that wouldn't be necessary. They were peeling off of him at the threshold line, like vacuum wrap being stripped from a piece of meat. Jack stopped two feet inside the door and looked down at his arms, his clothes—not a single bug had made it in with him.

He turned and stared through the door as the screen banged shut. The palmettos were buzzing off in all directions, scattering like . . . like the leaves he'd first mistaken them for.

What the hell was going on here?

14

"Semelee! Semelee, answer me! Are you all right?"

Semelee opened her eyes and saw Luke's big face and hulking form hangin before her. No . . . hangin above her. She shook her head, propped herself up on her elbows, and looked around.

"What happened?"

"You was usin the shell, had it over your eye, and you was smilin and laughin and then all of a sudden you yelled and fell back on the floor. What happened?"

Good question. Real good question. But it was startin to come back to her now.

She'd spotted the old man's kid, the special one, outside his daddy's house and followed him through palmetto eyes to one of the buildings in the old folks' village. She'd been hopin he'd show her that he had her other eye-shell but he surprised her by breakin into the building. She tried to follow him inside but he closed the window too quick. She peeked through the windows and saw him lookin at some papers. She had no idea what they were and didn't care. She was lookin for her eye-shell.

Pretty soon he was out again. She followed him back to the house where he met someone outside. She thought there was somethin familiar about the stranger but couldn't place him.

It was about then that she'd started feelin the strain of controllin mindless little creatures like palmettos with just one eye-shell. She had to make somethin happen, get the special one into the house where she could have a look around for her eye-shell.

So she'd gathered as many as she could and attacked. She'd been havin a good time chasin him and seein what he was made of, and was gonna follow him into the house and give him a good scare—maybe have the bugs gather in the air and spell out somethin spooky—so he'd leave and let her search the place. But as she approached the front door she started feelin strange, a little sick even. And then when she tried to follow him inside it was like runnin into a wall. She was slammed back and things got a little fuzzy after that.

"It's him," she told Luke. "It's him made me sick in the hospital room this mornin."

"How you know that?"

"Cause I felt the same way just now tryin to follow him into his daddy's house."

She'd sensed he was special, but she hadn't known just how special.

"You think he's got your other eye-shell then?"

"I'm willin to bet on it."

"What're we gonna do?"

"I don't know." She rolled over and buried her face in her arms. "Let me think on it."

She had no experience in this sort of thing. Sometimes she wished she didn't have to make all the decisions. She was only twenty-three. Wasn't being special and having a destiny enough? Did she have to lead too?

And worse was realizing that the man, the special one, might not be here *for* her . . . the way she'd been stopped dead at his doorstep tonight made her suspect he might be *against* her.

People against her paid a price, a high one, for treatin her bad.

Suzie Lefferts found that out. In spades.

After Semelee had experimented with her control powers for a while, she decided to put them to the test. She chose prom night. No one had asked her to go, of course. Like, big surprise. And guess who Jesse Buckler asked: big-haired Suzie Lefferts.

So Semelee had sat in her bedroom—another thing she'd discovered was she didn't have to be on the beach to fly with her birds—and got together a flock of big fat seagulls and followed Jesse's car from Suzie's house to the prom. When they was both out of the car, she arranged the gulls into a low circle. As each one got near them it let loose with a big load of bird shit. Suzie started screamin as the big white globs landed in her hair, on her dress. Same with Jesse. They both jumped back in the car and drove away. Toward home, most likely. Semelee was sure Suzie wasn't goin into the prom lookin like that.

Semelee lay on her bed and near split her sides laugh-ing. But she realized how a few of her gulls hadn't done their thing yet, so she chased after the car, droppin big white splotches all over Jesse's nice new wax job. He kept goin faster, trying to outrun them, but that wasn't gonna happen. Then a particularly big glob landed on his windshield. She saw the wipers come on but they just smeared it all over the glass. That was when Jesse missed the curve and smashed into the utility pole. The two of them'd been in such a rush to get away from the bombardment that they never buckled up. Jesse wound up dead; Suzie survived but with a broke neck. Doctors said she'd never walk again.

Semelee had been shook up somethin terrible. She put her shells away, but only for a little while . . . she couldn't stay away from them too long. But she used them only for flyin and swimmin. She didn't try to control no more critters.

Leastways not while she was still in Jacksonville.

But that was then. The now Semelee thought the then Semelee was a dork. Don't make no sense to waste a special power. You don't use it, you ain't special no more. You're just like everybody else.

Besides, people tend to get what they deserve.

Semelee lay on the deck a moment longer, till the stink of the floorboards—the spilled drink and bits of old food rubbed into them over the years—became too much. She climbed to her feet.

"Well?" Luke said. "You gotta plan?"

She told him the truth. "No. Not yet, anyways. I'll figure something out." She turned to him. "There was somebody with him tonight. Somebody I think I seen before."

"Who?"

"If I knew that, I'd tell you his name. But I know I seen him. It'll come to me."

"Well, in the meantime we got unfinished business. That old man—"

"Yeah. We're gonna have to finish him. That's number one on the list."

But how? She wished she knew.

"If his kid is standin in the way, I can take care of that. Me and Corley can go out and catch him alone and—"

"No! Don't you touch him!"

"Why the hell not? He's in the way, and he's even makin you sick. He . . ." Luke squinted at her. "Hey. You ain't sweet on him, are you?"

"Course not." She couldn't let on about the connection she felt between her and the special one. Luke might go off and do somethin really stupid. "But like I told you before, we ain't killers. We do what needs to be done but we don't go past that. This guy's only protectin his kin. Can't blame a body for that."

. . . protectin his kin . . .

Of course. It wasn't a matter of him fightin against her, he was simply doin a son's duty. That thought gave Semelee a surge of hope. Suddenly she felt better.

"I can too blame him if he's gettin in our way and makin you sick and knockin you to the floor!"

"Just don't do anything unless I tell you, okay? Are you listenin to me, Luke? Nothin until I say so."

Luke looked away. "Awright."

Semelee didn't know whether she could believe him or not. She knew Luke would do anything to protect her, whether she needed protectin or not. And that worried her.

15

After watching the cloud of palmettos disperse into the night, Jack slammed the door and ducked into the rear bedroom. He peered through the window in time to see a bug-free Carl getting into his old Honda and roaring off. Obviously the bugs had lost interest in Carl as well.

Jack rubbed his arms and face as he returned to the front room. He could still feel them crawling on him. What had made them attack like that? And what had made them quit just as suddenly?

What was happening around here? Odd ornaments on lawns and behind beds, invisible symbols painted on walls, flying killer cockroaches . . . what had he stepped into? It didn't smell of the Otherness, but that didn't mean the Otherness wasn't lurking behind these weird goings on.

Bigger question: Where did Anya fit in? She was involved, no way around it. Whether peripherally or centrally, he couldn't say. But she seemed to be on his father's side, and that gave him a little comfort. Very little. If she weren't dead to the world in her recliner, he might go over and ask her for an explanation.

And say what? *I was just attacked by palmetto bugs. Know anything about that?*

Maybe she did, maybe she didn't. He was pretty sure she didn't cause it. But at the very least she could explain the symbols on her house and his father's, and how they'd got there.

Jack decided to let it go until tomorrow.

He paced the front room a couple of times. He was still feeling the after-buzz of the bug-induced adrenaline surge. It had burned away the alcohol from the wine and he was thirsty. Right now he needed a beer.

He grabbed a couple from the fridge—getting low; he'd have to pick up some tomorrow—and settled himself in front of the TV. After listening to the latest on T.S. Elvis, now drifting south in the Gulf and threatening to become a hurricane, he surfed around until he chanced upon his favorite Woody Allen film, *Zelig*, playing on TCM. He always envied Zelig's talent for blending in with any group; it would be so handy in Jack's fix-it business back home.

He sat and watched with the lights on. He wasn't about to let any bugs sneak up on him.

THURSDAY

1

A soft clattering noise woke Jack. He lifted his head from the pillow on the guest room bed and squinted at the clock. The red LED numbers swam for a second, then came into sharp focus: 8:02.

He rolled out of bed and went to the window for a peek outside. There he was: Carl, dressed in the same shirt and work pants as yesterday, but this morning a set of electric hedge clippers protruded from his right sleeve as he trimmed away at dry-looking bushes that didn't need it.

Jack pulled on a pair of shorts from his open gym bag on the floor and went outside.

Carl Scissorhands looked up and jumped at Jack's approach. He shook his head and stopped the clippers.

"Mornin," he said. "Man, that gang of palmettos was somethin last night, wasn't it. Never seen nothin like that in all my born days. Never heard of it neither. How'd you finally do with them?"

"Soon as I got inside the house they just flew off. How about you?"

"Same. I was halfway to my car when they suddenly lost interest. Pretty weird, huh?"

"Very weird."

"I had trouble sleepin. I kept feelin like they was still on me." He shivered inside his flannel shirt. "Gives me the willies just thinkin about it. And then my car wouldn't start this mornin. My luck's runnin pretty bad and pan-o-ramic these days."

Jack glanced over to where Carl had set up his camera last night. The spot was empty now.

"How did the video surveillance go?"

Carl shook his head. "Nada. I come by real early this mornin to pick it up, you know, before anyone else found it." He winked and jerked his thumb at a tattered backpack sitting among his gardening tools. "I quick-checked the playback but the only thing on it was me bendin over it and picking it up. Least ways I know the motion detector's workin. Told Dr. Dengrove and he wasn't too happy, but wants me to try again tonight."

"You going to?"

"Sure." He grinned. "He wants to keep payin me, I'll keep settin up the camera. It's his money, and I could sure use some of it."

"Fine, as long as you don't catch Miss Mundy doing anything that'll cause her trouble."

"Told you: no worry bout that."

"Speaking of Miss Mundy . . ." Jack turned and looked at Anya's place. No signs of life there. Considering how she looked last night . . . "maybe I should go over and see how she's doing."

"Oh, she's doin fine. She was up bright and early this mornin, waitin for a cab. It picked her up a little before seven."

"Oh? Well, it's good to know she's all right."

Jack wondered where she'd be going at that hour. Hardly anything open then except the convenience stores.

The idea of a convenience store got him thinking about coffee. He needed a couple of cups, but he didn't feature the idea of winding all through Gateways twice, then back and forth through the security gates, and hunting down a store in between. Oh, for the Upper West Side where he could walk around the corner and have his choice of coffee spots.

He remembered his father had always been a big coffee drinker. He'd seen a can in the refrigerator.

"I'm going to make some coffee," he told Carl. "Want some?"

Carl shook his head. "Had some at home. Besides, I gotta keep lookin busy otherwise they'll lay me off. Not a lotta gardenin to do when nothin's growin."

As Jack turned away he glanced again at the clippers protruding from Carl's right sleeve. What was holding them? Maybe he didn't want to know.

2

Back inside Jack pulled the can of coffee from the fridge. Brown Gold—"100% Colombian Coffee." Sounded good. But he couldn't find a coffee pot. Just a miniature French press. Jack remembered seeing a big version of this in a restaurant where he once waited tables, but had never worked one.

And he needed coffee. Now.

He flipped on his father's computer, did a Google search for "French press," sifted through sites about French news-papers and other sites wanting to sell him a press until he found one telling how to use one: two scoops of coffee into a small press, followed by near-boiling water at about 195–200 degrees—were they kidding? Stir after one minute. After a total of three minutes, put on the cap and push the plunger to the bottom.

Jack followed the directions using boiling water—like he was going to check the temperature, right?—and finally had his coffee. A damn good cup of coffee, he admitted, but who had time for all this rigamarole every time you wanted some?

Retired people, that's who. And his father was one of them.

He flipped on the Weather Channel while he was waiting the required three minutes and learned that Elvis was still drifting south in the Gulf. Its sustained winds had reached seventy-eight miles per hour. That meant it had graduated from a tropical storm to a Category I hurricane. Whoopee.

Coffee in hand, he searched through the front-room desk until he found a couple of Florida maps. One was a roadmap of the state, but the other was Dade County only. That was the one he needed.

He found Pemberton Road and followed it till it intersected with South Road . . . the site of the accident. Out in the boonies. Way out.

Time for a road trip.

He was halfway through refolding the map—these things never wanted to go back to their original state—when a knock on the front door interrupted him. He found Anya, dressed in a bright red-and-yellow house dress, standing outside with Oyv cradled in her arms.

"Good morning," she said. Hot, steamy air flowed around her.

Jack motioned her inside. "Come on in where it's cool. If you've got half an hour, I can make you a cup of coffee."

She shook her head as she stepped in. "No thanks, hon."

"Sure? It's made from beans." He winked at her. "And on the label it says that no plants were killed during the making of Brown Gold coffee."

She winked back. "I'll have to try some another time." She gestured to the map in Jack's hand. "Planning a trip?"

"Yeah. Out to where my father got hurt."

"I'll come with you."

"That's not necessary." Jack had planned to do a little aimless reconnoitering after checking out the intersection and didn't know if he wanted an old lady and a yip-yip dog along.

"No trouble at all," she told him. "Besides, you're a newcomer and I've lived around here awhile. I can keep you from getting lost."

Well . . . on that score, maybe she'd be more of a help than a hindrance.

"Okay. Thanks. But I want to stop at the hospital and check up on my father before we head out to the swamps."

"That can wait till you get back," she told him. "I was just there."

"You were?" He was touched by her devotion. "That's awfully nice of you. How was he?"

"When I left he was just the same as yesterday and the day before."

"No progress?" Bummer. "How long can this go on?"

"Not much longer, hon," Anya said with a smile. "I have a feeling he'll be taking a turn for the better soon. Just give it a little time. But as for exploring the hinterlands, we should get started before it gets too hot."

She had a point. "Okay. Just let me throw a few things together and I'll be right out."

"Oyv and I will meet you at the car."

Jack figured he'd bring his backup .38 along—just in case. And mosquito repellent. Lots of mosquito repellent.

3

A voice had called him from his long dream of the war and he'd responded. He was glad to leave the dream . . . so many dead men, with pierced skulls and ruptured chests . . . staring at him with mournful eyes . . .

And then he was out of the dream and awake. He sat up. He was in a bed, in a barrack. But where were the other beds, the other soldiers? No one here but him.

Then he saw a little woman, a thin bird of a woman in some sort of uniform, mopping the floor. He spoke to her. Not volitionally. The words seemed to pop out of his mouth. He didn't even hear them. But the woman did. Her head snapped up. Her eyes widened. Then she hurried from the room.

Where am I? he wondered.

Was this still part of the dream? If not, how did he get here?

4

Jack tried to draw Anya out during the trip but she wasn't very responsive. He told her about the palmetto attack last night but she didn't seem horrified or even concerned. Her only remark was that it was "very unusual."

"How about you?" he said, shifting the subject from him to her. He wanted to know more about her. "Where are you from?"

"I moved here from Queens," she said.

"I'd have thought you came from Long Island."

"Well, I've lived there too."

"What about your childhood? Where'd you grow up?"

"Just about everywhere, it seems." She sighed. "It was so long ago it seems like a dream."

This was getting nowhere. "Where *haven't* you lived?"

"On the moon." She smiled at him. "So what's with all the questions?"

"Just curious. You seem to know a lot about me and my father, and you two seem close, so don't you think it's natural for me to want to know a little about you?"

"Not to worry. We're not involved. We never will be. We're just friends. Isn't that enough?"

"I suppose it is," Jack said.

He supposed it would have to be.

He took Pemberton Road southwest with Anya following on the map and acting as navigator. Oyv lay stretched out in the sun on the deck under the rear window. A drainage ditch paralleled the road, sometimes on the left, other times on the right. Probably served as a canal of some sort in normal times, but now it was mostly a succession of intermittent pools of stagnant water.

"They're called borrow pits," Anya said, as if reading his mind. "They're where the dirt and limestone came from when they were building up these roads. This time of year they should be filled with water, with turtles and little alligators and jumping fish. Now . . ."

He could see what filled them now: beer cans, Snapple bottles, old tires, and hunks of algae-encrusted Styrofoam.

Coarse brown grass stretched away to either side. He spotted three white-tailed deer—a doe and two fawns—grazing near a stand of trees. As the car approached they leaped over a bush and disappeared.

He saw a sign that read PANTHER CROSSING.

"Panthers?"

Anya nodded. "They still have some around here."

The idea of wild panthers about was a little unsettling even when in a car. Imagine seeing that sign while on foot.

"I've driven through here with your father a couple of times. Every time we pass that sign he says some rhyme about a 'panther' and 'anther.' "

Jack had to laugh. "Ogden Nash!"

"Who?"

"He was a very clever, down-to-earth poet. No airs about his stuff. Wrote a lot for kids. Dad loved him."

Jack remembered his father's nightly ritual of doling out a few of Nash's animal poems at bedtime.

He'd forgotten about those times. He made a mental note to check the bookstores when he got home and see what was still in print. Vicky would love Nash's wordplay.

He was jarred back to the present as they passed a burnt-out area where some asshole probably had flicked a cigarette out the window. Up ahead, a sign displaying a goofy-looking alligator informed them that this was a "South Florida Water Management District."

"Not much water to manage at the moment," Jack said as the pavement ran out and became a dusty, rutted dirt road bed.

"Even when there is they *mis*manage it. All the development north of here, it's screwed up the Everglades—screwed it royally."

Jack sensed anger in Anya's voice. And something else . . .

"You sound as if you're taking it personally."

"I am, kiddo. I am. No decent person can feel otherwise."

"Pardon my saying so, but isn't it really just a big swamp?"

"Not a swamp at all. Swamps are stagnant; there's constant flow through the Everglades. It's a prairie—a wet, saw grass prairie. This whole part of the state runs downhill from Lake Okeechobee to the sea. The overflow from the lake travels all those miles in sloughs—"

"Whose?"

"Slough. It's spelled S-L-O-U-G-H but pronounced like it's S-L-E-W. The sloughs are flows of water through these prairies that keep things wet. We're near the Taylor Slough here. The Miccosukee Indians call the Everglades *Pa-hay-okee*: river of grass or grassy waters. But look what's been done in the past fifty years: Canals have been cut and farms have been put in the way, leaking all their chemicals into the water—or should I say, whatever water reaches here. What the farms don't take is 'managed' by so many canals and dikes and dams and levies and flood gates that you've got to wonder how any of it gets where it naturally wants to go. It's amazing anything at all has survived here. Just pure dumb luck that the whole area's not a complete wasteland." She glanced at him. "Sorry, kiddo. End of lecture."

"Hey, no. I learned something. But I'd think that since

Florida is just an overgrown sandbar, all of the water in the sloughs would just seep into the ground."

"Sandbar? Where'd you get that idea?"

"I heard somebody describe it that way, so—"

She wagged a finger at him. "He was talking out his *tuchus*. Florida is mostly limestone. It's not an overgrown sandbar; if anything, it's a huge reef. There's sand, sure, but dig down and you hit the calcified corpses of countless little organisms who built up this mound back in the days when all this was under water. That's why the water runs downhill to the Everglades: Because it must."

"How'd you manage to learn so much about these problems?"

"It's no secret. You just have to read the papers. Supposedly the government is going to spend billions to correct the mess. We'll see. Shouldn't have let it happen in the first place." She glanced down at the map. "We should be coming up on it soon."

"On what?"

"The intersection." She pointed through the windshield. "There. That must be it."

Jack saw a stop sign ahead. He slowed the car to a stop a dozen feet before the intersection. The crossing road was unmarked. Jack took the map from Anya and stared at the intersection he'd circled.

"How do we know this is the place?"

"It is," Anya said.

"But nothing says that's South Road."

"Trust me, kiddo. It is."

Jack looked at the map again. Not too many crossroads out here. This had to be it.

Leaving the engine running to keep the AC going, he got out and walked to the stop sign. It sported a couple of bullet holes—.45 caliber, maybe—but the rime of rust along their ragged edges said they were old. A sour breeze limped from the west. He stepped into the intersection and looked left and right. He checked the ground. Little pieces of glass glittered in the dust. This was where it had happened.

"What are you hoping to find?"

He turned and found Anya approaching. Oyv trotted behind her, weaving back and forth as he sniffed the ground.

"Don't know," he said. "It's just that a lot of things don't add up, especially with the timing and the assumption that my father ran a stop sign."

"I imagine a lot of people do that out here. Look around. Here we are, midmorning on a Thursday and not a car in sight. You think maybe there were more in the early A.M. Tuesday?"

"No. I guess not. But he was—*is*—such a by-the-book guy, and not a risk taker, that I can't see him doing it. And I can't see what he was doing out here in the first place."

"Oh, I can tell you that: He was driving."

Jack tried not to show his irritation. "I know he was driving. But where to?"

"To nowhere. Many nights he had trouble sleeping, so he'd go out for a drive."

"How do you know?"

"He told me. Asked me if I wanted to come along some night. I said he should include me out. I don't know from insomnia. Like the dead I sleep."

So I noticed, Jack thought.

"Where did he go?"

"Out here. He said he always took the same route. He'd drive with his windows open. He said he liked the silence, liked to stop and look at the stars—you can see so many out here—or watch an approaching storm. That would have been back when we had storms, of course." She sighed. "Such a long while since we've heard thunder around here."

"All right. So he's out here on his nightly drive and—"

"Not nightly. Two, maybe three times a week."

"Okay, so Monday night or early Tuesday morning, he's out here and somehow he winds up in the middle of an intersection when something else is coming along. Something big enough to total his car and keep on rolling."

"A truck then. Sounds as if he pulled out in front of a truck."

Jack looked up and down the road. His father's Marquis had been hit on the right front fender. That meant . . .

"A truck? It would have to have been coming from the west . . . from the Everglades. Maybe he had a little stroke or something."

"Dr. Huerta said his brain scans showed no damage."

"Then it's a mystery."

"I don't like mysteries, especially when they involve someone I know. And speaking of mysteries, I'm still trying to find out how someone reported the accident from downtown Novaton—"

Anya shook her head. "You call that a downtown?"

"Okay, from the local supermarket—before it happened."

Anya peered at him through her huge sunglasses. "How do you know when it happened?"

"From my father's watch. It's cracked and broken, and the time on the face is something like twenty minutes after the accident call. How is that possible?"

"Clocks," Anya said with a shrug. "Who can trust them? One's set too fast, one's set too slow—"

"My father was always a tightass about having the right time."

" 'Was,' " Anya said. She *tsk*ed and pointed a gnarled finger at him. "What do you know about his watch lately?"

Jack looked away. She had him there.

"Not much."

"Right. And—"

Oyv started barking. He was standing at the edge of the ditch with his head down and his ears drawn back flat against his head.

"What is it, my sweet doggie?" Anya said. "What have you found?"

Jack followed Anya over to where Oyv was still making his racket.

"Oh, my!" she said.

Jack came up beside her. "What?"

"Look at these tracks."

Jack saw five-toed impressions in the damp mud at the bottom of the ditch. They spanned about a foot across. Whatever had made them was big. And pigeon-toed.

"Got to be a crocodile."

Anya looked at him and made a face. "Crocodile? The Florida crocodile likes brackish water. These are alligator tracks. See that wavy line running between them? That was left by his tail. Look at the size of those feet. This is a *big* alligator."

Jack did a slow turn. With all the reeds and saw grass around, it could be hiding anywhere.

Now he knew how Captain Hook felt.

"How big?"

"Judging from the size of these prints, I'd say twenty feet long, maybe more."

Jack couldn't imagine how she'd know that, but wasn't going to call her on it. This lady knew an awful lot about Florida.

"Twenty-plus, huh? Why don't we get back in the car."

"Not to worry. These look old. See how the mud is dry? They were probably made days ago."

"That doesn't mean the maker isn't still nearby."

The tiny Chihuahua was down in the canal sniffing at the tracks. He showed no fear. Jack half expected him to start cooing, *Heeere, leezard, leezard, leezard . . .*

His right hand drifted to the small of his back where his little AMT backup rested in its holster under his T-shirt. He wondered if a .38 caliber frangible would stop a gator that size. Probably break up on its head. But he alternated them with FMJs in the magazine. They might do some damage.

"Anyway, I've seen what I came to see."

"Which was?"

"Nothing in particular. I just thought I should come out and see where it happened."

What had he been hoping for? A mystery-solving clue, like in the movies? It hadn't happened. Wasn't going to happen. The whole thing was just a stupid accident.

But still . . . he wished he knew who'd been barreling along South Road out of the swamp in something big and heavy early Tuesday morning.

Back at the car, Jack played the gentleman and held the door for Anya—and Oyv—as she settled herself in the passenger seat, then he walked around to the other side. Physically he was heading for the driver seat; mentally he was miles away, thinking about giant gators and heavy rolling equipment. He was reaching for the door handle when Oyv started barking again. He looked up and saw a red truck racing toward him—*for* him.

No time to get in the car so he back-rolled onto the hood and got his feet up and out of the way just as the truck side-swiped the Buick.

Jack's heart pounded. That son of a bitch almost—

The truck . . . an old red pickup he'd seen before. Jack couldn't make out who was driving but he'd bet he wasn't pretty. Coughing in the trailing dust cloud, he slid off the hood, pulled open the door, and jumped inside.

"What was that?" Anya said as Oyv kept barking.

Thanks little guy, Jack thought. Bark all you want.

"That was an attempted hit and run."

He slammed the car into gear and spun the tires as he started pursuit.

Anya looked worried. "What do you think you're doing?"

"Going after them."

"And if you catch them, then what?"

"As the saying goes, I'm going to kick ass and take names—in a very literal sense."

The bogus nurse in his father's room yesterday had driven away from the hospital in that truck, and now that truck had tried to drive into him. It wasn't big enough to cause the damage that had befallen his father's Grand Marquis without totaling itself, but it was connected. Oh, yes. Definitely connected.

Jack followed the pickup's dust cloud along Pemberton. He was gaining on it when it suddenly braked and hung a hard right. Jack skidded to a halt, almost missing the turn. He nosed onto a pair of sandy ruts that curved to the right. He accelerated but the dust was so thick that he missed the path and slid off into the brush. It took a few back-and-forth maneuvers to get moving again, and by the time he made it back to the road—that pair of ruts was nothing more than an arc that curved back to South Road—the truck was nowhere to be seen.

Jack drove to the intersection and got out. He scanned the roads up and down in search of a tell-tale dust cloud, but saw nothing. The truck had either slowed or pulled off the road to hide in the brush.

Frustration set his teeth on edge as he swung back into the driver seat. He pounded once on the steering wheel.

"Not to worry," Anya said. "I have a feeling you'll be seeing that truck again."

"So do I," Jack said. "That's the problem."

5

Jack needed to pick up some beer and a few munchies. Anya said she needed to do some food shopping as well. So, following her directions, he drove them to the Publix in downtown Novaton. On the way he saw a number of homeless types begging on the sidewalks. He hadn't noticed them on past trips through.

A fellow with a cauliflower nose and a lumpy face that looked like he'd stuffed his cheeks with marbles stood near the door. He held a Styrofoam cup and shook the change within, looking for more.

As Jack slowed, trying not to stare but wondering if this guy was related to the two in the pickup, Anya grabbed his arm and pulled him through the automatic door.

"Give him nothing. His type are up to no good."

Inside, he and Anya split, she rolling her cart toward the produce section while he headed for the snack aisle. There he found more varieties of fried pork rinds and pork cracklins than he'd ever imagined possible. He'd heard of them but never tried any. He passed them by and stocked up on healthier fare—tubes of cheese Pringles, one of his household staples. On his way back past the pork rinds he gave in to an impulse and picked up a bag. He'd try anything once. Couldn't tell Gia, though. She'd be grossed out.

He found the beer section on the left side of the store where it took up the whole wall. But nowhere on that wall could he find Ybor Gold. He saw a stock boy who didn't look old enough to drink stacking twelve-packs of Bud Light in the cooler; he had late acne and an early goatee. His brown hair was gelled into shiny spikes. Jack asked him where they hid the Ybor Gold.

"I don't think we carry that one anymore," he said.

Damn. He'd enjoyed those two he'd had on the way down.

"Why not? It's a local beer."

"That's not local. It's made in Tampa."

Exasperated, Jack started waving his arms. "If you can stock Sapporo Draft from the other side of the world, how come you can't stock something from the other side of the state?"

"Wait a minute," the kid said. "Come to think of it . . ."

He went over to the imported section, shuffled some stock around, and pulled out a six pack of Ybor Gold. He held it up, grinning.

"Knew I'd seen this somewhere."

"My hero," Jack said.

"There's one more back there. Do you—?"

"Sold!"

As the kid put the two six packs in the cart, Jack handed him a five-dollar bill.

"Naw, that's okay," he said. "Just doing my job."

Jack shoved it into the breast pocket of the kid's shirt. "Yeah, but you deserve a raise."

He hunted up Anya and followed her around as she picked out what she wanted. This involved playing touchy-feely with almost every piece of fruit in the store. Finally she was done and they checked out. Jack qualified for an Express Lane and cooled his heels by the door as her order was rung up.

Out in the parking lot, he was loading everything into the trunk when he spotted a battered red pickup parked against the far curb half a block down. Anya and Oyv were already in the car; it was running with the AC on. Jack leaned in the driver door.

"Can you spare a few minutes?" he said. "I want to check something out."

She glanced at her watch. "Don't be too long. I'd like to stop in on your father before we head home."

That was on Jack's to-do list as well. But first . . .

He angled across the parking lot, then crossed the street. As he approached the truck—no question now that it was the same one—he noticed a slim young woman with a dark complexion and wild hair a startling silver white. She leaned against a nearby wall. She wore white Levis and a tight black vest over a long-sleeved white shirt buttoned up to the collar.

He stared at her. Something familiar about her. Not the hair, but that face, those black eyes . . .

And then he knew. Stuff that hair under a black wig, put her in a nurse's uniform, and she'd be the mystery woman who'd fled his father's room yesterday.

First she's a brunette in the hospital, now she's white haired and hanging out on the street. What the hell?

Next to her stood a hulking man Jack recognized as the one who'd ferried the mystery nurse away yesterday.

The woman's eyes met his and he saw an instant of recognition there. She hid it immediately and slid her gaze off him, but he'd caught it.

Jack stepped back and edged toward the truck. The guy with the bulging forehead was leaning against it. Couldn't forget him. He'd been driving when Jack's tire was slashed. Had he been driving an hour ago?

Time to find out. Time to see if he could provoke a little something out of this clown.

Jack lidded his anger and sidled up to him. The man's misaligned eyes were fixed on the crowd. Jack got his attention by giving his right shoulder a none-too-gentle shove. The guy bumped against the truck's passenger door and whirled on Jack.

"Hey! What—?"

Whatever he was going to say never got out. Jack saw his eyes widen with recognition and knew he had his man.

"Almost nailed me out there, didn't you," Jack said, stepping closer and getting in his face.

"Luke?" the guy said in a high, quavering voice.

Jack gave him another shove. "Whose bright idea was that? Yours? Or somebody else's?"

"Luke?" he said again, louder this time, his eyes darting back and forth. "Luke!"

Jack was about to give him another shove when the big burly guy who'd been next to the woman came up. His little pig eyes fixed on Jack.

"What's goin on?"

"This your truck?"

"What if it is?"

"It sideswiped me out in the boonies a little while ago."

Luke shook his head. "No way. It's been sittin here all day. Ain't that right, Corley?"

Corley missed a beat, then nodded his misshapen head. "Yeah. That's right. Here all day."

"Really?" Jack stepped over to the right front fender and ran his hand along the beige-streaked dent there. "I bet if the police compare the paint on these scrapes to the paint on my car they'll come up with a perfect match."

He had no intention of getting the cops involved, but they didn't know that.

Luke's eyes shifted from the scrapes, to Corley, to Jack. "What if it does? Don't prove nothin."

"I think the cops will see it differently, and then I won't be the only one wanting to know why you tried to run me down."

"Somebody tried to run you down?" said a woman's voice behind him.

It was the girl.

"Do I know you?" Jack said.

She stuck out her hand. "My name's Semelee. What's yours?" Her dark eyes were alive with interest as she looked at him.

"Jack," he said as he shook her hand. Her skin was soft, like a baby's. He nodded his head toward Luke and Corley. "You connected to them?" He knew the answer but wanted to see how she'd respond.

"They're kin. You think they tried to run you down?"

"I don't know who was driving, but I know it was that truck."

Her expression darkened. "Oh, it was, was it?" She turned and glared at her "kin." "Get in the truck."

Luke spread his hands. "But Semelee . . ."

"In the truck," she said through her teeth. "*Now!*"

The two of them moved off like whipped dogs. If nothing else, Jack had learned who ruled the roost.

She was all smiles when she turned back to him. A nice smile. The first he'd seen. It lit up her face and made her almost pretty.

"I'm sure it was just an accident. Those boys drive a little crazy sometimes. Why don't I buy you a drink and we can talk it over. Maybe—"

"What were you doing in my father's room?"

"Your father?" Her brow furrowed. "I don't think I—"

"His hospital room. You were in it yesterday, wearing a wig and dressed like a nurse."

She snapped her fingers. "I *knew* I seen you before."

Yeah, right. She'd known him the instant she saw him.

"What were you doing there?"

"Oh, that. I been thinkin bout becomin a nurse, so I dressed up like one and went to the hospital to see what it was like. It didn't work out. Made me feel kinda sickish. I guess nursin ain't for me."

"I guess it ain't."

Good story. It fit nicely with what he'd seen, but Jack wasn't buying a word.

She smiled again. "Now, about that drink . . . ?"

He hesitated. A little face time with her and he might get a handle on what was going on between his father and Semelee and her "kin." But he had Anya back in the car and he hadn't seen his father yet today. But maybe he could catch her later.

"Have to take a rain check," he told her. "Got to get to the hospital."

"Oh, yeah. Your daddy. Is he bad sick?"

"He's been better."

Another battered pickup, this one blue, pulled up beside the first. For a moment he thought it was filled with migrant workers, but then Jack saw their misshapen heads and bodies. If they were any sort of workers, they looked like they might be extras for Wes Craven if he was doing a new sequel to *The Hills Have Eyes*. He recognized the marble-cheeked guy from the Publix. All the funny-looking street people he'd seen begging on his trip through town were gathered in these two trucks.

"Well," Semelee said, "we'll try for that drink some other time."

Jack tore his eyes away from the blue truck. "We sure will. When?"

"Whenever you want."

"How do I reach you?"

"Don't worry." Her smile broadened as she opened the passenger door of the pickup and climbed in. "Just say the word and I'll know."

Something in her tone sent an icy trickle down Jack's spine.

6

Jack walked into the hospital room and froze just inside the door. His father, dressed in an open-back hospital gown with little booties on his feet, was sitting up on the edge of the bed eating a plate of green Jell-O.

"Christ! Dad . . . you're awake!"

His father looked up. He looked fresh and rested. He might have been sitting on his front porch having a gimlet.

"Jack? You're here? You?"

His blue eyes were clear and bright through his steel-rimmed glasses. His hair was damp and combed, his face looked freshly scrubbed. If not for the facial bruises and the bandage on the side of his head, there was no evidence that he'd been seriously hurt.

"Yeah. Me." He shook his head. "I can't believe this. Last night you were still level-seven coma and today . . ."

"They told me one of my sons had been visiting. I assumed it was Tom. But come to think of it, I seem to remember hearing your voice."

"I was talking to you a lot."

"You were? Maybe that's what brought me out. I couldn't believe you were here so I had to see for myself." He sighed and looked at Jack. "Is this what I have to do to get you to visit?"

"Such a thing to say!" Anya said, bustling around Jack and heading for the bed. She'd hung back at the doorway, making Oyv comfortable, she'd said, and had waved Jack ahead. "Be nice, Thomas."

"Anya!" his father said, eyes lighting at the sight of her. "What are you doing here?"

"Jack brought me. We've become fast friends." She took his right hand in both of hers. "How are you?"

"I'm fine. Better every minute, especially since they took that catheter out of me." He shuddered. "That's not something—"

"There she is!" said a heavily accented woman's voice. Jack turned and saw a thin little Hispanic woman, dressed like a nurse's aide, standing next to the hulking form of Nurse Schoch, pointing at Anya. "She's the one I told you about."

Nurse Schoch, looking as stern as ever, glanced down at the aide and spoke in a rumbling voice. "You want to tell me again what you saw?"

"I was in the bathroom, washing the sink, when she come in and hold his hand and say, 'Okay, Tom. You've been asleep long enough. Today's the day you get up.' That's what she say."

Anya laughed and waved a hand at her. "How do you know I don't say that to him every day?"

The little woman shook her head. "Right after she leave, he sit up in bed and ask me if he miss breakfast."

"Did I?" his father said, smiling. "I don't remember. I was a little groggy after I first woke up, but I'm fine now." The smile faded. "So many things I don't remember. They tell me I had an accident but I don't remember a thing about it."

The aide was still pointing at Anya. "*Bruja!*"

Jack knew enough Spanish to know she was calling Anya a witch.

"Enough of that," Schoch said. "Go clean something. Git."

After one last fearful look at Anya, the little woman scurried off. Nurse Schoch stepped over to his father's side and took his blood pressure. She nodded and wrote on a clipboard.

"How am I doing?" he said.

"Fine." Schoch smiled and, surprisingly, it didn't break her face. "Amazingly fine. Dr. Huerta's coming up to see you."

"Who's he?"

"*She*. She's been taking care of you since you were brought in to the ED."

"Well, she'd better get here fast, because as soon as I finish this Jell-O, I'm going home."

Jack and Schoch began talking at the same time, telling him he couldn't, that he'd just had a serious injury, and so on and so on. Didn't faze him.

"I don't like hospitals. I feel fine. I'm going home."

Jack recognized the note of finality in his father's voice. He'd heard it as a kid. It meant Dad had made up his mind and that was that.

"You can't," Schoch told him.

He peered at her through his glasses. "I guess I'm a little confused. When did I become the hospital's property?"

Schoch blinked and Jack guessed no one had ever asked her that.

"You're certainly not the hospital's property, but you became its *responsibility* when you were wheeled through the doors."

"I appreciate that," he said. "Really, I do. And from the way I feel right now, you've all done a wonderful job. But I no longer need a hospital, so I'm going home. Where's the problem?"

"The problem, Dad . . . ," Jack said, feeling his patience slipping. His father was acting dumb. "The problem is that you had a serious accident—"

"So I'm told. Can't remember a thing about it so I guess I'll have to take people's word for it."

"It happened," Jack told him. "I've seen the car. Totaled."

He winced. "Not even a year old." He shook his head. "I wish I could remember."

Jack watched his father's expression. Was that fear in his eyes? Was he afraid? Of what?

"That's not the point," he told him. "The point is you've been in a coma for three days and how do we know you won't lapse back into one in the next minute or hour or day?"

His smile was thin. "We don't. But if I do, you can bring me back here." He held out his arm—the one with the IV running into it—to Schoch. "Would you remove that, please?"

She shook her head. "Not without doctor's orders."

"Okay, then. I'll do it myself."

"Christ, Dad," Jack said as his father began peeling off the tape that held the line in place.

"All right, all right," Schoch said. "I'll take it out for you. Just let me get a tray."

As she lumbered out, Jack looked at Anya. She hadn't said a word through all this. He looked at his father who had lowered the top of his hospital gown and was peeling off the cardiac monitor leads.

"Can't you convince him?" he said to her. "I obviously can't."

Oyv popped his head out of her big straw bag as Anya shook hers. "I should be making his decisions? He's not crazy."

"He's acting crazy."

"He wants to leave the hospital because he feels fine. What's so crazy about that?"

Thanks for the help, he thought. He'd feel a lot better if his father would stay just one more day, to make sure his condition was stable. He had to find a way around his reckless stubbornness.

Anya was staring at him. "Switch places. What would you do in his situation?"

I'd get the hell out of here and go home, he thought. But he couldn't say that.

"I'm lots younger and—"

Oyv dropped back down into the bag as an anxious looking Nurse Schoch came charging into the room, carrying a tray. She stopped at the foot of the bed and shook her head as she stared at the cardiac leads scattered across the sheet.

"I figured that was what you were doing when the monitor flatlined, but I had to be sure."

A few minutes later, Dad had a gauze patch taped over the spot where the IV had been. He stood and looked around.

"All I need now are my clothes."

"They had to throw them out." Here was the angle Jack had been looking for. "They were too bloody to keep. You know what? Why don't you hang out here one more night and I'll come back first thing in the morning with some of your clothes. How does that sound?"

"Terrible. I'll wear this if I have to."

Jack thought of refusing to drive him home, but what would that accomplish? All he had to do was call a cab.

He caught a glimpse of his father's skinny white buttocks through the back of the hospital gown as he walked to the tiny closet.

"Well, will you look at this!" he said as he opened the door. He held up a white golf shirt and tan Bermuda shorts. "Just what the doctor ordered."

"Somehow I doubt that," Jack said. He looked at Anya. "Where'd they come from? You were here this morning. Did you—?"

"You think I go snooping in closets?"

His father headed for the bathroom. "I'll be out in a minute."

"Dad, those aren't your clothes."

"I'm claiming them for the moment. I'll bring them back tomorrow."

I give up, Jack thought. I'm licked. He's going home.

While he was changing, Anya puttered around the room, opening and closing drawers, filling a little plastic bag with the soaps, mouthwash, toothpaste, and other necessities the hospital had supplied.

"No sense in letting any of this go to waste," she said. "He's paid for it, after all—probably through the nose, if I know hospitals."

Jack watched as her hand darted behind the headboard. She pulled something out and quickly shoved it into the plastic bag. He didn't see it, but he could guess what it was. She was taking back her painted tin can totem.

Dad, still wearing his hospital booties, stepped out of the bathroom and spread his arms to show off his new duds.

"Would you believe it? A perfect fit."

"Imagine that."

Jack looked at Anya but she wouldn't make eye contact. What was her part in all this? Was that nurse's aide right? Could Anya have had something to do with his father's miraculous recovery? That would be strange, but he was becoming used to strange.

"Are we ready?" his father said. "Then let's go!"

7

On the ride back to Gateways—Jack driving, his father in the passenger seat, Anya and Oyv in the back—he told his father what he knew about the accident, including the anonymous call to the police that appeared to have been made before the crash.

"I wish I could remember," he said. "The last thing I recall is leaving the house and driving out the front gate. And that's it. What happened during the drive? Why can't I remember?"

"It's called retrograde amnesia," Jack told him. "You can't retrieve memories of events right before you got hit. There's a good chance over time your brain will sort them out, but then again, it may never."

His father stared at him. "How do you know so much about it?"

Oops. "A sort of lecture I listened to once. Very interesting."

The speaker had been Doc Hargus. Jack had been knocked cold in a fall from a fire escape. After coming to he'd known enough to get to Hargus to have his scalp sewn up, but couldn't remember why he'd been on the fire escape in the first place. The doc had explained about post-traumatic memory loss, both antegrade and retrograde. It had taken a few days, but Jack finally remembered how he'd got there. And who'd shoved him off.

"Well, I hope mine comes back soon. As for the accident being reported before it happened . . ." He shook his head. "Impossible. So we can forget that. Somebody's watch was way off. That's the only explanation. Wasn't it Sherlock Holmes who said, 'When you eliminate the impossible, whatever remains, however improbable, must be the truth'?"

Jack was sure he'd heard Basil Rathbone state that a hundred times.

"Yeah, I think so."

Except, considering the course of Jack's life these past months, the impossible was not as easy to eliminate as he'd once assumed.

After Jack parked the car in the cul-de-sac, his father insisted—over his son's protests—on helping carry Anya's groceries into her house. They left her there with a promise to return for cocktail hour.

As he preceded Jack into the front room of his house, he said, "I guess I should be saying, Boy, it's great to be home. But I can't. I may have been in that hospital bed for days, but I feel as if I left here only a few hours ago."

He lowered himself into the recliner and stared into space. Jack watched him and realized he was scared. He'd never seen his father scared, or imagined he could be. He knew he couldn't leave him like this.

"I'm going to stay a few days," he told him. "If that's all right with you."

His father looked up at him. "You? Acting like you're a member of a family? What gives?"

The remark stung, and that must have shown in Jack's face because his father's voice abruptly softened.

"I'm sorry. I shouldn't have said that. I'm glad you're here. You don't know how glad. It's just . . ."

"Just what?"

"Kate's funeral. Why weren't you there? I still can't believe you didn't show up."

"I couldn't."

"Like hell. A hundred, maybe two hundred people showed up. Mothers bringing the children she'd treated, people she'd treated as kids bringing their own children. All those strangers made it to her funeral, but not her own brother. She touched a lot of lives in her life, Jack, but yours most of all. She practically raised you. You brought out the nurturer in her. When you needed changing or needed to be sung to sleep, she'd take over, she'd say she'd do it. She'd all but fight with your mother to take care of you."

"I know," Jack whispered through a constricting throat. "Don't you think I'd have been there if it had been possible—any way possible?"

"Then why weren't you?"

How could he tell him it was because BATF and FBI people were there too? Taking pictures. Because of the way Kate died, and the events leading up to and connected to her death, they'd camped outside the funeral home and cemetery with their telefoto lenses. Jack had spotted them just as he was about to turn into the funeral home parking lot. He'd driven on. He couldn't let them take his picture and have it end up pinned to a corkboard wall with a question mark beneath it. Who he was a question he didn't want them even asking, let alone answering.

"It wasn't . . . it just wasn't possible."

"Why not? Were you in jail? In a hospital in a coma? Those reasons I'll accept. Anything less . . ."

"I was there. I couldn't make it to the ceremonies, but I visited her grave after the funeral."

"If you could show up then, why couldn't you show up before?"

Jack remembered the anger he'd felt at spotting the feds outside the funeral home. But it had been an anger tinged with guilty relief. Their presence meant he wouldn't have to face Kate's kids, her ex-husband, and his father. Because there'd be too many questions about Kate's last days and he couldn't tell them anything because there was so much she hadn't wanted them to know. But most of all because he felt in some ways responsible for her death. In her last moments he'd soothed her while she bled, held her cooling hand after she died.

"Through the whole ordeal," his father said, "everyone kept asking if the long-lost Jack would show, and I said of course you would, especially since she'd just been taking care of you while you were sick."

"You know about that?"

"She called Ron the night she died . . . told him. She was still looking after you, even after you'd grown up." Tears filled his eyes. "She brought Kevin and Lizzie down for Easter week last spring. I didn't know it would be the last time I'd see her alive. I was supposed to go up and stay with her awhile in July. Instead I went up for her funeral." His voice hovered on the edge of a sob. "I miss her, Jack. Even though I moved down here we still talked. We phoned each other two or three times a week."

Jack took a step closer. He reached out a hand to put on the old man's shoulder, hesitated halfway there—would he shrug it off?—then pushed past the doubt. He gave his father's bony shoulder a gentle squeeze.

"Kate was a wonderful person, Dad. You can always be proud of her. You and Mom deserve a lot of credit for that."

He looked up at Jack. "I wonder. Kate turned out great, but you and Tom . . . where is he, anyway?"

That reminded him: He should call Tom and let him know Dad was out of the coma. Not that he seemed too worried. He'd yet to call for an update.

"He couldn't make it. He told me he's tied up with some legal thing in Philly."

He shook his head. "Figures. Tom's always got something else to do; we all know who's number one in his life. And then there's you . . . the vanished son. I suppose your mom and I deserve credit for the two of you as well as Kate, don't we."

He sounded so bitter. Maybe he had a right to be. Jack started to slide his hand off the shoulder but his father grabbed it and squeezed.

"I'm sorry, Jack. I had to let this out. It's been eating at me since the funeral. And since you never returned my calls . . ."

"Yeah, sorry about that." Again, he hadn't known what he could say.

". . . I never had a chance to get this off my chest. I still don't understand, and I guess I never will. You're holding back on me. I don't know why but I hope someday you'll tell me the real story." He released Jack's hand and slapped his palms against his thighs. "Until then, I'm through with this kind of talk. It's putting me in a funk."

He sat in silence for a moment, Jack standing beside the chair, trying to come up with something to say. But he didn't have to. His father broke the silence by rising from the chair and heading for the kitchen.

"I'm going to have a beer. Want one?"

"Do you think you should? I mean, you were in a coma this morning and—"

"Do you want one or not?" he snapped.

If you can't beat him, Jack thought, join him.

"Yeah, okay. Pop me one."

His father opened the refrigerator door and pulled out an amber bottle. "What's this?"

"Oh, that's an Ybor. It's a Florida brew I discovered."

His father gave him a hard look. "What did you do? Move in while I was out cold?"

"Well, Anya said you'd want it that way."

"She did, did she?"

These mood swings between friendly and hostile were getting to be a bit too much. "Look, if you want me to move out—"

"I wouldn't hear of it."

He popped the caps off a pair and handed one to Jack. They clinked the bottles.

Jack said, "To letting bygones be bygones?" At least for now.

"Not always as easy as it sounds, but I'll drink to that." His father took a sip and then studied the label. "Ybor Gold, ay? I like it."

Jack took a long pull. "Yeah. But they should have named it Y*gor* Gold. Then they could have had this sneaky-looking hunchback on the label. Would have been very cool."

His father stared at him. "Now why on earth would you think of that? Why would anyone think of that? You know, I used to worry that all those monster movies you watched as a kid would warp you. Now I can see they did. I swear they did."

"Hey, I've watched lots of romantic films too, Dad, but they didn't make me romantic. And I know I must have seen hundreds, maybe a thousand comedies, but they didn't make me funny. I haven't committed stand-up yet and, trust me, I'm *not* the life of the party."

His father laughed for the first time since he'd come out of the coma. That was a good thing.

8

They hung around the front room for about twenty minutes or so, sipping their brews and making small talk, then his father dozed off in his recliner. At first Jack worried that he'd lapsed back into coma, but he responded when Jack shook his shoulder. He left him sleeping in his chair and went outside.

Through the late afternoon haze he spotted Carl working three houses down. When he saw Jack he hurried toward him across the dry grass. A small garden spade protruded from his right sleeve.

"I heard about your daddy," he said, flashing a yellow grin. "Real glad he's okay. That's pan-o-ramic!"

"Sorry?"

He shrugged. "I just like the word. Anyways, I'm glad he's back."

"Thanks, Carl. He's napping now."

"Good. Real good. Looks like the list don't get more pan-o-ramic."

Wishing he'd never uttered that word, Jack said, "What list?"

"The list of Gateways folks who've gone before their time—not that 'before their time' means a whole helluva lot round a place like this. Funeral home waiting rooms is what they is."

"I'm not following you."

"Had a bunch of strange deaths real recent like."

Jack felt a crawly sensation in his gut. "Like what? Hit and runs?"

"Nup. Nothin like that. I mean strange. Like Mrs. Borger bein attacked by about a dozen pelicans last year—right before Christmas, it was. Pecked her to death. I hear tell one of them bit into her neck and there was blood shootin everwhere. Been in Florida all my life and I ain't never heard of no one bein attacked by no pelicans. Then back in March there was Mr. Leo, all bitten up by a bunch of spiders. Brown recluses, they say." He shuddered. "If I was ever on *Fear Factor*, that's what would set me to runnin. Anyways, Doc Harris said he's never heard of someone gettin bit more'n once, but there you go. Poor old guy died in the hospital."

"Jeez."

"Then just last June, Mr. Neusner trips and falls into a whole nest of coral snakes. He was DOA like the others. Come to think of it, your daddy was the only accident that made it to the hospital alive. I guess that's a good sign."

"Let's hope so."

"Funny thing about Mr. Neusner and the coral snakes. We got a sayin down here: 'red touch yellow—kill a fellow.'"

"What's that mean?"

"Well, there's coral snakes, which got red, yellow, and black stripes, and they's poisonous as all get out. And then there's the scarlet snake and the scarlet king snake which got similar stripes but they're harmless. The way you tell 'em apart is by the order of their stripes."

"You mean people hang around long enough to check out the stripe order?"

"Sure. If it's got a red stripe next to a yellow stripe, it's a coral snake. If it don't, then you're okay. You may get bit, but you won't get poisoned." He pronounced it "pie-zund."

Jack said, "I'm a city boy. I see any snake, striped or plaid, I'm gone."

He much preferred dealing with human snakes than the legless kind.

"But the thing is," Carl added, "I seen one of them snakes, the one Mr. Neusner stomped on before he keeled over. Don't know bout the other ones that bit him, but this one didn't have no red touchin yellow. It shouldn't have been poisonous, but it was." He shook his head. "Kinda scary when somethin you always depended on turns out not to be true anymore."

Tell me about it, Jack thought. He'd seen the pins kicked from under more than one Cherished Truth lately.

"You said there was a nest of them? Right here at Gateways? How? The place looks so . . . manicured."

"I can't figure that one neither. I run the mower over that

spot every week and I ain't never seen no snake nest. I think a buncha them just coiled theirselfs all together durin the night and was still there when Mr. Neusner come by like he did every mornin." Carl looked away, toward the Everglades. "Almost like . . ."

"Almost like what?"

"Like they was waitin for him."

Jack's gut crawled again. "You don't really believe that, do you?"

A shrug. "Just a thought."

"I'm having a thought too," Jack said as the crawling sensation increased. "December, March, June . . . every three months someone buys it. And three months from June is—"

"September," Carl said. "You're thinkin of your daddy, right? But the others was done in right here at Gateways by things like birds and spiders and snakes—all natural like. Your daddy had a car accident and he wasn't here at Gateways like the others."

But the regularity of the fatal mishaps to Gateways residents, the steady three-month intervals between them, bothered Jack. Especially since his father had almost bought it at the end of another three-month cycle.

Something might be going on, but it sure as hell wasn't the Everglades seeking revenge.

Jack feared something less substantial but far more real might be behind it.

9

Tom awoke from his nap and looked around. Where was Jack? Or had he only dreamed he was here? That might mean that the whole coma thing was a dream too.

Then Jack walked in the front door and he felt a strange mix of emotions: up that his prodigal son had come home, even if only for a few days, and down because it meant the accident and coma were all real.

"Oh," Jack said. "You're awake. Short nap."

"The short ones are the best. They don't leave you groggy."

Jack headed toward the kitchen. "I'm going to have another beer. Want one?"

"No, thanks. But you go ahead."

Tom watched him twist off the top of an Ybor Gold and thought how much he looked like his mother. He had Jane's brown hair and brown eyes. And he moved with her grace, her economy of motion.

Tom hadn't seen his younger son in over a year, not since that father-son tennis match he'd roped him into last summer. He'd changed in that time. He didn't look older, but his eyes held a different look. He couldn't call it a hunted look. Maybe haunted? Haunted by Kate's death? Or was it something else? Guilt, maybe. Well, he *should* feel guilty about missing Kate's funeral. Damn guilty.

He didn't know what to make of his younger son. He'd thought they'd been close. He'd made a special effort to spend time with Jack while he was growing up. An unplanned baby. He and Jane had their boy and their girl and were content with that. But Jack showed up eight years after Kate, and neither Tom nor Jane had quite the energy they'd had with the first two. But Tom hadn't wanted to shortchange the little guy, thus the special effort.

But then Jane was killed; and less than a year later Jack disappeared. He'd called home once to say he was okay and not to worry, but wouldn't say any more. In the space of less than a year Tom lost his wife and one of his sons. He'd never imagined he could hurt so much. He thought his world had come apart.

He blamed himself at first—what had he done, where had he gone wrong? But then he came to realize that disappearing was in keeping with Jack's character as he'd come to know it.

He'd realized early on how bright Jack was, brighter than either Tommy or Kate, but he was also something of a loner. Okay, more than something of a loner. He did well enough gradewise, but all his teachers said he'd do better if he applied himself. That and "Does not play well with others" were constants during his early schooling.

Although a natural athlete, he never seemed to care for sports. At least not team sports. It was his father's urging rather than any desire to compete that drove him to sign up for a couple of the high school teams. He joined the track team, but as a cross-country runner where he was competing with the terrain and himself as much as the opposing school's team. He also spent two years on the swim team. Both loner sports.

Even his first summer job—cutting lawns in the neighborhood—was a solitary enterprise. He borrowed the family lawnmower and went into business for himself. As a college student he needed more cash so he went to work for one of the local landscapers.

But what he really seemed to enjoy most was reading far-out fiction—if it had a monster or a spaceship on the cover he bought it—and watching old sci-fi and monster movies.

He'd worried about Jack, urging him into more social activities. *It's a beautiful Saturday. Go down to the park and get into one of the ball games!* Jack would reluctantly get on his bike and pedal off. Later, as Tom was riding through town, he'd spot Jack's bike chained to a standpipe outside the local theater that was showing a Saturday afternoon monster double feature.

He'd worried then, he worried now. Jack earned his living, at least as far as Tom could tell, as an appliance repairman. In the few times during the past fifteen years that he'd seen his son—times he could number on the fingers of one hand—and had a chance to ask him about it, he'd always seemed evasive. Maybe because he sensed his father's disappointment. Nothing wrong in being a repairman in and of itself; the world needed people who could fix the mechanical and electronic conveniences of modern life. Fine. But he wanted more for his son. Jack had three and a half years of college behind him that he wasn't using. What was he going to do when his eyes got bad and his fingers got arthritic? Did he think he was going to get by on that Ponzi scheme called Social Security? Tom hoped not.

But what bothered him more was that Jack seemed rootless, disconnected, adrift. Not exactly a ne'er-do-well, but . . .

But what? Why was he so secretive about his life? Tom was a believer in everyone's right to privacy, but really . . . it was almost as if Jack were hiding something.

Earlier this year Tom had gathered the courage to ask if he was gay. Jack had denied it, and his easy laugh as he'd assured him that he was attracted only to women had convinced him he was telling the truth. Tom wouldn't deny that that had been a relief. But if Jack had said yes, well, Tom would have tried to find a way to accept it. He was glad that wouldn't be necessary.

So if it wasn't that, what? Was he using drugs? Or worse, dealing them? He prayed not. And for some reason, thought not.

He supposed Jack's unused education rankled him the most. Education wasn't something Tom took lightly. He'd fought and killed to get his.

He slid back along the lines of his life to his childhood. He'd been born during the Great Depression, the son of a truck farmer outside Camden who'd been scraping by before the economy crashed, and continued to scrape by after. At least they always had food on the table, even if it was only vegetables they picked or pulled from the ground themselves.

Tom's father had been just old enough to see a little action in the First World War, and just a little bit too old to fight in the Second, although that hadn't stopped him from trying to enlist after hearing news of what the Japs did to Pearl Harbor. Tom remembered being afraid that they'd soon see hordes of yellow men running wild through the streets of America. He'd read numerous scenarios describing just that during the late thirties in the pages of the *Operator 5* magazines he borrowed from a kid in school.

But his father was rejected and the Japs never set foot one on North America. So much for that worry.

But when Tom hit eighteen there was no money for college. He'd done well in high school but not well enough for a scholarship. So he enlisted in the Army. It was peacetime so it seemed a safe place to be: earn a little money, save what he could, and maybe see some of the world in the bargain. But most importantly, it offered a chance to get off that farm.

A year after he enlisted he was seeing the world, all right. Shipped to Japan and then to South Korea to fight in a UN "police action." Even now, he ground his teeth every time he heard that phrase. It had been a full-blown war. He'd fought from sunny Seoul to the frozen hills of North Korea where he witnessed firsthand the Red Chinese human-wave assaults. For years after, he awoke sweating and shaking with the memory. At least he was alive to have nightmares, unlike too many in his unit who came back in boxes.

When he returned to the States he found a day job and used the GI Bill to put himself through night school. He graduated with an accounting degree and soon qualified as a CPA. He was able to provide his wife and children with all the things his own father had been unable to give him. To Tom, the most important of those was a higher education. Tom Jr. had made good use of it, so had dear Kate. The result was a lawyer and a doctor in the family.

And then there was Jack . . .

The man in question dropped into a chair opposite Tom.

"Can I ask you something, Dad?"

"Sure."

"What were you doing out on those back roads at that hour?"

Tom almost told him it was none of his business but bit it back. He had to put this anger behind him, forget what happened before and be glad for the now.

Could he do that? He had to try.

"Just driving. I have trouble sleeping lately. I lie there in bed and I close my eyes but it won't come. They tell you not to stay in bed if you can't get to sleep, so I go out for a drive."

"And do what?"

"Not much. Lots of times I stop the car and sit on the hood and watch the sky. Jack, you wouldn't believe it. You can cruise those back roads at night and not see another soul. You stop the car and turn off the headlights and get out and above you are stars like you've never seen, stars like I haven't seen since I was a kid in the Jersey sticks, when the air was still clean enough to see the Milky Way smeared across the top of the sky. It's breathtaking."

"You always drive the same route?"

"Pretty much. There aren't many roads to choose from out there."

"So you have a pretty set pattern?"

"I guess so. Why are you asking?"

Jack took a sip from his bottle. "Just trying to put some pieces together. Since there's no one out there, do you bother to stop at stop signs?"

"Well, yes. Of course I do. It may not make sense but . . . I guess it's just habit. And it's not as if I'm going anywhere, or in a hurry to get there."

"The cops think you might have blown through a stop sign and got tagged by something speeding along South Road. Something big."

Tom shook his head. "I wish I could remember."

It disturbed him no end that a piece of his life was missing—an important piece, one that had put him in a coma for days. It scared him a little . . . no, it scared him a lot not knowing any of the details. That was why he couldn't stay in the hospital. If he had to be in the dark as to what had happened to him, he'd rather be in the dark here, in familiar surroundings . . . where he felt he was in control. Or felt he had at least some modicum of control, even if illusory.

"Do you remember a woman attacked by pelicans last year?"

"Sure. Adele Borger. Terrible thing. I heard she was walking with two other women whom the pelicans ignored. They attacked just her. They say she was a terrible mess."

"And the guy bitten by the snakes?"

"Ed Neusner. Where'd you hear about him and Adele?"

"From Carl."

Tom had to smile. "Telephone, telegraph, tell Carl. He's the Gateways gossipmonger. Not the brightest bulb in the box, but a good man. Hard worker. He's got some wild ideas, though. Has he told you his theory about the angry Everglades yet?"

Jack nodded. "Yeah. Maybe it's not so far-out. What about the guy killed by spiders?"

"Joe Leo? What about him?"

"Hasn't anyone noticed a pattern to these deaths—like every three months?"

"No." Was he right? Every three months? "No one's ever mentioned it. But why would they? It can't be anything other than coincidence."

"Do you realize your accident falls right into the pattern?"

Good Lord, Jack was right. The muscles along the back of his neck tightened, but only for a second. Coincidence. That was all it was, all it could be.

Tom forced a smile. "Is this what you do in your spare time—invent conspiracies?"

Jack looked at him. "As a matter of fact, yes."

"Don't tell me you believe in UFOs. Please don't."

"The kind with aliens inside? Hardly. But I've had to stop believing in coincidences."

Tom wondered at the bleakness in his son's tone. "What does that mean?"

"Nothing." Jack shook his head. "Maybe I'm reading too much into this. For a minute I had this wild idea that the Gateways honchos might be offing some of their healthier residents in order to have their houses revert to them."

"That *is* a wild idea."

He sighed. "I know. Especially when I realized that the houses would stay with the spouses. So there goes the motive for that scenario."

"Except . . . ," Tom said as that tightening sensation crept again into the back of his neck, stronger this time. "Except that Adele was a widow and Joe and Ed were widowers."

"Oh, Jeez," Jack said as they stared at each other.

10

In Semelee's vision, at least in the eye covered by the shell, she moved at a height varyin from one foot to almost two foot above the ground. Clumps of saw grass whipped past at eye level. Then she was splashin through a shallow pond, and now back up into the grass again. The goin was tougher than it shoulda been. In September of any other year, she—or rather, Devil—woulda been able to stay in the wet for the whole trip. This year, though, was different. Still, the drought wasn't gonna keep Devil from goin where she wanted him to.

The goin was rougher for another reason: She had to stay on course and find her landmarks with only one eye.

At last she came to the pond she'd been searchin for. The level was down, but not as much as most others. She slid into the water and dove deep. Devil's underwater vision was good, better than any human could claim, and soon enough she found the mouth of the tunnel.

She entered a dark place, so dark that even Devil's eyes was no good here. Sometime long ago, when all this land was formed, something happened hereabouts that left a channel through the limestone. Its width was enough to allow Devil to swim through, but just barely. She had to go mostly by feel.

The channel branched and Semelee guided Devil to the left. It seemed to go on forever, but eventually she saw a glimmer of light ahead. Devil surged forward. She could feel his hunger, but she held him back, slowin him to a stop a few feet below the surface. She made him hover there for a few heartbeats, then started a slow float toward the surface. She let only his eyes and the top of his snout break the surface. An egret wading at the pond edge saw him and took flight. Smart bird. As Devil took a breath through the nostrils atop his snout, Semelee focused on the old man's house.

She'd been watchin the place through a frog's eyes, waitin for the son to come home. After bein so close to him in town this afternoon, she had to see him again. She'd felt somethin click between them. Like magic. She sensed destiny there. No doubt about it.

But as she'd been watchin she saw him arrive with that old crone from next door *and* his daddy! Semelee was so shocked she almost dropped her eye-shell. She thought this was bad at first, but then changed her mind. She realized that somethin must be helpin her, somethin big and powerful, maybe even the Glades itself must be guidin events. Because now that the old man was out of the hospital, he was closer to her. Comin home put him within strikin distance.

And strikin was just why she'd guided Devil here. She had to get this finished. And it had to be this old man. He'd been offered, and had to go before the time of the lights.

As a bonus, after the old man was gone, there'd be nothin standin between her and the son. They could get together, just like they was meant to.

She watched the front door. She wondered when the old man would come out . . . or if he'd come out. Might be a long wait.

She heard voices. Good thing a gator's ears was atop his head, just behind the eyes, otherwise she woulda missed it. A swish of Devil's tail angled him around so she could see who was talkin and . . .

Semelee blinked—her own eyes, not Devil's—and stared. There he was: the old man—wearing one of the ugliest Hawaiian shirts she'd ever seen—and his son sittin in the neighbor lady's front yard. This was too good to be true.

She made Devil sink toward the bottom of the pond, and then had him back up to the far end. When she and Devil made their strike, he had to be movin fast. He had to come out of the water at full speed and charge right at the old man. The big gator was hungry so she couldn't let him get distracted and go for anyone else—not that skinny old lady and especially not the son. She had to keep him on course. Not such an easy thing because when a gator opened his mouth, it blocked his straight-ahead vision. To make up for that, nature made it so that if anything touches the lower jaw, the upper snaps down like a bear trap. That meant she had to aim just right so that nothin—not furniture and not the wrong people—got in Devil's way.

Once he got his teeth set in the old man, nothin was gonna break his hold. Semelee would have Devil drag him into the pond and take him to the bottom. The tunnel was too narrow to fit both gator and prey, so once the old man was drowned, she'd let Devil chow down a little before hightailin it back to the lagoon.

Back at the far end of the pond now, she surfaced for another look. Yes . . . there he was, talkin and drinkin . . . if she angled herself just right, she'd have a clear shot at the old buzzard. She'd sink, use Devil's powerful tail to propel them through the water, then hit the land a-runnin. The old man wouldn't know what hit him. And finally she'd finish off what she, Luke, and Devil had begun the other night.

11

Tom watched the sunset. He and Anya did this a lot. Not every afternoon, but often enough to approach the status of a tradition. He was wearing one of his favorite shirts, the one with Mauna Loa in full eruption on the back with bright orange lava flows trailing around to the front. As usual, Anya was sipping her wine. He'd brought over a few beers. Often he'd supply a stainless-steel shaker of gimlets that he put in the ice bucket, but the Sapphire supply seemed lower than he remembered. Had Jack been nipping at it?

Jack had called his brother to tell him their father was up and about, then handed him the phone. His older son had made a stab at sounding overjoyed, but what he really sounded was distracted. He said everything was fine but Tom sensed that something was bothering him.

Did this mean he now had two secretive sons?

Jack had come along for the sunset tonight, and Tom learned that he and Anya had done the watch last night.

They really seemed to have hit it off, those two. He felt a twinge of . . . what? Jealousy? No, that was ridiculous. He liked Anya—loved her, in fact—but in a brotherly way. He felt no sexual attraction to her. She was a friend, a confidante, a drinking buddy. He could talk to her, confide in her. She'd lent him an ear when he'd talked about his self doubts and his wayward children, she'd held him when he'd cried after receiving word about Kate's death. What sexual urges he had—and they seemed to be diminishing—were more than satisfied by a couple of the horny widows populating Gateways South. They weren't looking for long-term relationships—what an alien concept in this environment—and neither was he. The couplings were Viagra fueled, but a lot of the pleasure was in the snuggling and cuddling and having someone else in bed with you.

He turned on the battery-powered CD-player-radio he always brought along. But instead of the usual gentle music from the AM station he kept it tuned to, rap burst from the speakers.

"What the hell?" He checked the dial and, sure enough, it was tuned to the right band. "What's going on here?"

"They changed the format while you were in the hospital, hon," Anya said.

"No!"

"Afraid so. Sorry."

He jabbed at the off switch. "What's happening to the world? Used to be I'd drive behind women and they'd be doing eye makeup and fixing their hair in the rearview mirror. Now it's men who can't take their eyes off themselves—staring at themselves and primping. Christ, everything's going to hell in a hand basket."

"Yeah," Jack said, "and you can bet it's got a Fendi or Gucci logo on it."

"Very funny." He pointed at his son's T-shirt. "Look at that. 'Hilfiger' all across the front of your shirt. They sell you the shirt, then turn you into a free walking advertisement for their product. You should be charging *them* to wear it."

"It's the way of the world, Dad," Jack said. "Everybody does it."

"And that makes it right? Since when do you of all people want to look like everybody else?"

"Long story, Dad."

"I'll bet."

What's the matter with me? he thought. Why am I so cross? I sound like a crotchety old man.

He smiled to himself. Hell, I *am* a crotchety old man. But not without reason, not—

Anya's dog started yipping. The little Chihuahua was standing at the edge of the pond barking at the water. Crazy little dog. Tom had noticed a snowy egret there a few moments ago but it was gone now. Probably scared off by the pooch. Nothing in sight but placid water.

He noticed another sound. A chorus of clanking rattles from all around him. The homemade ornaments—the painted cans on sticks salted in among the leprechauns, bunnies, turtles, and flamingoes—were shaking and rattling on their sticks. Funny . . . he didn't feel a breeze.

The dog increased the pitch and volume of his yipping.

Tom turned to Anya. "What's wrong with him? He hardly ever barks."

"He must sense something out of the ordinary," she said. "Oyv! Get away from there and stop that racket. A migraine I'm getting already. Go back to—"

Suddenly the water erupted and something huge and bellowing exploded from the pond. Tom dropped his beer and his mind blanked in shock for an instant. What the hell was it? All he saw at first was a wide-open set of jaws bordered with daggerlike teeth, the delicate pink membranes lining the maw, and the long, tapered, slightly darker tongue waggling within. Then he saw the dark green scaly legs and the thick undulating tail behind.

An alligator, bigger than any he'd ever seen in all the gator parks he'd visited. And it was racing right for him.

The only thing between Tom and those jaws was Anya's

Chihuahua. The little dog held its ground for a second, then charged the gator, leaping at it with a high-pitched growl. The onrushing jaws scooped up the dog and snapped closed.

"Oyv!" Anya cried.

"Holy shit!" Jack was out of his chair and reaching for the small of his back.

Without breaking stride, the alligator made one convulsive swallow and the dog was gone, devoured like a canapé.

The monster gator was still lunging forward. Tom started to leap up but his foot slipped on the grass and suddenly he was falling backward in his chair. Before the gator opened its jaws again, Tom got a look at its head. He caught a flash of two scaly protrusions, gray-green like the rest of its hide, each about six inches long, on either side just behind and below the large brown eyes with their vertical-slit pupils. They looked like horns.

Something twisted in his chest . . . something familiar about this alligator. But what? How could he ever forget a creature like this?

As he and his chair hit the ground, Tom rolled to the side and started to scramble to his feet. He heard Jack mutter a curse and saw his hand coming out from under his shirt at the small of his back. Jack moved quickly, like a pouncing cat, grabbing the back of his chair and holding it out legs first, like a shield. To Tom's shock, he leaped between him and the gator.

"Dad! Get back!"

Tom regained his feet and backed away, but Jack hung in there, facing the big gator down.

"Jack! Anya!" Tom cried. "Into the house!"

"Not to worry," Anya said.

Tom looked her way and saw that she was still on her recliner. She'd straightened so that she was off the back rest, but she still held her wine-glass.

"Anya!" he said. "Get up! It's—"

She glanced at him. Her eyes and expression were unreadable, but her voice was calm, almost serene.

"No creature on earth will harm you here."

"Tell that to Oyv!" Jack said, backing away from the onrushing gator, but keeping himself between it and Tom and Anya.

His son's courage and protective stance amazed Tom. He'd known guys like that in the service—most of them long gone, sadly—but had seen little of it in today's everyman-for-himself world.

And then, incredibly, the gator halted its charge. One second it was roaring toward them, the next it stopped as if it had run into a wall. It stood on the border of Anya's emerald sward and the brown grass that typified the rest of Gateways. It closed its jaws and shook its head as if confused. It tried again to cross the line but then quickly retreated.

It turned left and stalked along the margin of green, thrashing its huge tail as it looked for a way in, and that was when Tom saw something dangling from its right flank. He squinted in the failing light and saw that it was an extra leg. But it looked vestigial. It didn't move and didn't touch the ground. It simply hung there.

The gator then turned and stalked the other way. Tom saw another vestigial limb on its left flank. But far more puzzling was its inability to cross onto Anya's lawn. It made no sense.

And then it occurred to him that the situation might be only temporary. If only he had a gun!

"Call the cops!" he cried. "Call security! Get someone here to either drive this thing off or kill it before it kills someone!"

"No need," Anya said from her recliner. "It will be leaving soon."

The alligator stopped its stalking and bellowed. It shook

its head and whipped its tail back and forth. It seemed confused. It bellowed again, and this time it sounded as if it was in pain. Then it rolled onto its side, and from there onto its back, swinging its head back and forth, thrashing its tail and clawing at the air with its taloned feet.

With another throaty bellow it rolled back onto its feet but didn't charge. Instead it made a slow turn and began a limping retreat toward the pond. As it moved away Tom noticed a fist-sized bulge in its left flank, just ahead of the vestigial limb. Not so much a bulge as a pulsation.

The gator roared again as the bulge ruptured, spewing blood along the hide, a crimson splash along the gray-green scales. Something moved within that opening, something red and snouted. The hide split further and—

"Holy shit!" Jack shouted. "It's Oyv!"

Dear God, he was right! The little Chihuahua was chewing its way out of the gator. It squeezed through the ragged opening like a baby being born. Once the upper half of his body was clear, the rest of him slid out. He landed on all fours and shook himself, then started barking at the retreating gator, chasing after it, nipping at its tail until it slid into the water and disappeared below the surface.

The dog dove into the water, repeatedly dipping its head under as it paddled in a small circle, then emerged with the blood washed away. He shook off the water with an almost epileptic shudder, then trotted back toward Anya with his tail wagging, his little head held high, and his black eyes shining. Proud, and very pleased with himself.

"Good boy," Anya said, patting her lap. "Come to Momma."

"What?" Jack started to laugh and Tom thought he heard an hysterical edge to his voice. "What the—? This is impossible! Just plain. . . ." his voice trailed off to a whisper ". . . impossible."

Jack turned and stared at Anya and she stared right back.

Tom would have asked what was going on between them, but he couldn't speak. He had to sit down. He quickly righted his chair and dropped into it, panting for air as his chest tightened.

He remembered now where he'd seen that horned alligator before.

12

Semelee dropped the eye-shell and fell to the floor, clutchin her left side. She felt as if someone had shoved a spear halfway through her. Never in her life had she felt pain like this.

"It hurts, Luke. Oh, God, it hurts!"

He hovered over her, hands reachin toward her, then pullin back. "What happened? What's wrong?"

"Not sure." The pain was easin off now. "Don't know how, but Devil got hurt. Hurt bad."

"Did you finish the old man?"

"No. I couldn't get to him."

"That old guy?" Luke's tone said he didn't believe a word of it. "He hurt Devil?"

"No-no. It was the same like in the hospital, only ten times worse. There was this line I couldn't cross without feelin like I was gonna be sick or explode or both. I couldn't push Devil past it." Truth was, she couldn't push herself past it. "And then this pain in Devil's side that I felt too. Like he was bein stabbed, but from the inside."

"The old guy's kid?"

"I don't think so. This wasn't even at the old man's

house. It was at the old lady's next door. It's her. Gotta be her. She's the one that's been messin us up."

"Whatta we do?"

"I don't know. I'll worry about that later. First thing I gotta do is get Devil home. He's hurt bad, and he won't know where he is. I gotta bring him in."

She looked down at her eye-shell. She knew that if she put it on she'd feel that pain again. But she had to. She couldn't leave Devil hangin. Had to bring him back to his gator hole where he could wallow and heal up.

How'd that skinny old hag do it? How'd she hurt Devil whose hide was like armor plate?

Semelee didn't know but she was gonna find out. And when she did, that old lady was gonna pay for what she'd done to Devil. That bitch was gonna hurt like Devil. Maybe even worse.

13

"Dad? Are you okay?"

Tom looked up from his chair and found Jack staring at him, a worried look on his face.

I must look like hell, he thought. He tried to respond but all he could do was shake his head and sweat.

"Is it your heart?"

"No." Finally he could speak. "Not my heart. It's my head. I remember what happened Monday night."

"You mean, Tuesday morning?"

"Whenever I had the accident. That . . . that alligator was there."

"That same one?" Jack said.

"You think I could forget those horns and those extra legs?"

Anya was watching him from her recliner. "Don't go out at night like you do—how many times did I tell you that?"

"Countless times." He shook his head. "I should have listened."

Jack dropped into his own chair, opposite. "But how does that alligator figure into your accident? Or doesn't it?"

"Oh, it does. I remember it now. I was driving south along Pemberton, taking my time . . ."

No hurry, no place to go, no timetable to hew to on that warm yet unseasonably cool night. Cool enough to drive with the windows open, not worrying about the mosquitoes because even that easy pace was too fast for them. He remembered the hum of his tires on the pavement, the soft feel of the wind swirling through the car and the mix of fragrances riding it: the sour smell of the saw grass yearning for water, the sweetness of the flowering roadside bushes.

". . . and as I came to the stop sign on South Road, I slowed to a stop—well, maybe not a complete stop, but a sort of rolling stop. I was taking my foot off the brake as the car eased into the intersection, but before I could give it gas again I saw something crawl onto the road ahead of me. I hit the brakes hard and came to a dead stop maybe three-quarters of the way through the intersection."

"An alligator?" Jack said. "The one we just saw?"

Tom nodded. "No question. I couldn't keep going. Something that size—I mean it must be twenty feet long— doesn't leave you any room to go around it. And truth be known, I didn't want to go around it. I felt safe in the car— especially after I put the windows up. It wasn't threatening me, just staring at me. I put on the high beams for a better look at it, and I must have been so fascinated by the sight of this horned gator that I didn't hear the truck until it was practically on top of me. My closed windows and its off headlights didn't help either."

"Wait," Jack said. "The guy was driving out there in the dark with no lights? Not even running lights?"

"Nothing. I heard a rumble to my right and looked and saw this dark shape roaring down at me from the west. It was practically on top of me. I didn't have time to react—or maybe I froze in shock. Whatever the reason, I couldn't move out of its way and it rammed me hard. I saw a big bumper smash into my right front fender and then the car was jerked around like . . . like I don't know . . . like it had been punched by God. My head hit something and everything went dark for a while, I don't know how long, and then I was back again, but the world was blurry and full of steam. My ruptured radiator, maybe."

"Did you see any part of the truck? I mean, was it an old red pickup, by chance?"

Tom shook his head. "No. This was a big rig, and seemed to be in good shape. At least its bumper was. I remember seeing what looked like a wall of shiny chrome slamming into me. Why did you think it was a pickup?"

"Just a thought." Somehow Jack looked disappointed.

"Getting hit wasn't the worst part. The really frightening part came after the impact. I was lying there, feeling sick, hurt, bleeding, barely able to move, but alive and so thankful I'd worn my seat belt, when I heard these voices, growing louder as they got closer. I remember hearing someone sounding mad, cursing, saying something about hitting me too hard and what if they'd killed me. And then the door was pulled open and I almost fell out of the car. That was when I heard someone say, 'Look! He's moving! You damn well better thank your lucky stars he's still alive!' "

"That sounds like they meant to hit your car."

"They did." Tom repressed a shudder. He glanced at Anya who was watching him impassively, her expression neutral. "It didn't click then, but now I'm sure they did."

"Sure?" Jack said. "What makes—?"

"By what came next. They unbuckled my seat belt and pulled me out and laid me on the road. I thought they were being awful rough with a man who might have a spine injury. As I was lying there I saw the big truck pulled over down along the side of South Road."

"Wait," Jack said. "The truck pulled over? But the police said it was a hit and run."

"In a very real way, it was. It's just that the run part was delayed a bit. Let me finish, will you?"

"Okay," Jack said. "Just trying to keep all this straight in my head."

"Forget about the truck for now. I know I did as soon as I saw that big alligator start to waddle toward me. I couldn't be sure, but I thought the men who'd pulled me from the car were waving it forward. Like they wanted it to maul me . . . kill me . . . eat me." This time he couldn't repress the shudder. "It was within ten feet of me when I heard a siren. I couldn't see any flashing lights but I could hear the two men start cursing about a cop car and what was he doing out here. That sort of thing."

"Officer Hernandez," Jack said.

"You know him?"

"Met him. Remember I told you that a call about your accident came in twenty minutes before it happened?" He glanced at Anya but she didn't react. "He's the one who went out to investigate. Sounds like that call saved your life."

But that didn't make sense, Tom thought. How could anyone have known about the accident before it happened? Yet *something* with a siren had been coming down the road.

"I don't know who or what was heading my way. All I know is that it scared off the two men who'd pulled me from the car, because they started calling to the alligator as if it was human, as if it could understand. I heard one yell, 'There's a cop on the way! Get out of sight. We'll meet you back at the lagoon!' And then they started running back toward the truck."

"Did you notice anything about them?" Jack said. "Like did one have a funny-shaped head?"

"Funny-shaped head? Why—?"

"*Anything* distinguishing," Jack added quickly.

"No. Not that I could tell. I didn't take my eyes off that alligator until it slithered off the road and into the grass, and by then they were almost to the truck."

"Do you remember anything at all about the truck? Like what kind? Was it a semi or a big van or what?"

"A semi, maybe, but it didn't have the usual big rectangular trailer. This had an odd shape, like those trucks that carry gravel or something."

"What about a name or a sign?"

"None that I could see. I had only moonlight and starlight to go by and . . ." Something flashed in his memory.

Jack leaned closer. "What?"

"On its rear panel . . . I think I saw something that looked like a flower, but all black. At least it looked black in the moonlight. After that, I remember flashing lights and then I didn't see anything until I woke up this morning."

A sudden realization hit him like . . . like an onrushing truck. He looked at Jack and then at Anya.

"Someone tried to kill me."

"Not necessarily," Jack said. "From what you heard them say . . . 'thank your lucky stars he's still alive . . . that sounds like they *didn't* want to kill you."

He sensed that Jack didn't believe a word of it, that he

was just trying to make him feel better. But it wasn't
working.

"They *wanted* to hit my car. And I have a feeling they
were going to feed me to that alligator."

"Maybe you were just in the wrong place at the wrong
time."

No . . . that didn't wash. No question in Tom's mind:
Someone wanted him dead.

The thought sickened him. When he'd been in Korea,
the NKs and the Chinese Reds had wanted him dead, but
that was war, that was to be expected. This was Florida.
He'd been here just a little over a year. He'd made a number of new friends but couldn't imagine how he could have
made an enemy.

Yet someone had tried to kill him.

Suddenly Tom felt exposed out here on Anya's lawn. He
wanted walls around him. He rose unsteadily from the
chair.

"I think I'll head home."

"You okay?" Jack said.

"Yeah. Sure. I'll just go inside and lie down. Excuse me,
Anya."

"Go, Tom," she said. She was still in her recliner, the
wet dog curled up on her lap. "You should rest."

"I'll come with you," Jack said.

"That's okay. I can find my own way."

"That's not the point," his son said, rising and gripping his
arm. "Come on. I'll walk you back. I know how you feel."

No, you don't, Tom thought. And I hope you never do.

A good kid, Jack. No, not a kid. A man, and a pretty
gutsy one at that, placing himself between a ferocious
gator and the old folks with only a lightweight resin chair
as a weapon. But Jack couldn't know what it was like to
fear for his life, to have someone wanting him dead. That
took a war. It had been Tom's great hope for his sons that

neither would have to go to war as he did and know that kind of fear. And it had worked out. Both boys had been too young for Vietnam, and a volunteer army had been in place by the time the Gulf Wars rolled around.

"Wait," he said, turning. "We should call the cops or the wildlife control or something, shouldn't we?"

"Why?" Anya said.

"To let them know there's a monster gator in our pond."

"Not to worry," Anya said with a wave of her hand. "He's gone. And after such a reception as he got here today, I doubt he'll be back."

"Where'd he go?" Jack said.

"There's an underground tunnel that leads from the pond back into the Everglades."

"Really?" Tom said. "I didn't know that."

Jack stared at her. "How do you know, Anya?"

She shrugged. "I've been around here a long time. I shouldn't know things?"

He saw Jack stare at her again for a moment, then point a finger her way. "We need to talk."

She raised her wineglass. "I'll be here."

Tom wondered at that exchange. As soon as they were in the house he turned to Jack. "Why did you say that to Anya?"

"What?"

" 'We need to talk.' About what? What does that mean?"

"I've got some questions for her."

"About what?"

"Things. Tell you about it later."

Why didn't Tom believe that? What was going on between those two? He was about to press him when Jack grabbed the pen and notepad from the counter by the phone.

"Just thought of something. Give me the names again of those three people who were killed."

"Why?" And then he knew. "Oh, no. You don't think—"

"I don't know what to think, Dad. When Carl told me about the others he said you didn't fit the pattern because the others were killed by birds and spiders and snakes. You were different because you were hurt in a car accident. But if what you remember is correct, you weren't going to be the victim of a hit-and-run accident, you were going to be a meal for that alligator. And that *does* fit the pattern."

Tom shook his head. "A few hours ago you were implicating Gateways in a scheme to get properties reverted. Now you think it's . . . what? How, just how, do you get birds and snakes to attack someone?"

Jack stared at him. "How do you get an alligator to attack someone? Twice. Because, Dad, that gator was coming for you. He was aimed at you like an arrow shot from a bow."

Tom wanted to deny it—tried to deny it—but couldn't. Jack was right. Those open jaws had been coming straight at him.

"But it's crazy," he said. Even crazier was how the gator had stopped at the edge of Anya's lawn. He was suddenly too tired to think about that now. Another question was far more pressing. "Why me?"

"That's what I intend to find out," Jack said.

Tom noticed a fierce look in his eyes. There was fire in Jack, a heat and a resolve he'd never expected in his appliance-repairman son.

And something else. He had a sense that Jack already knew the answer, or at least where to look. But how was that possible? He'd been here barely two days.

"Give me those three names," Jack said with the pencil poised over the pad.

14

His father had said good night and retreated to his bedroom. Jack heard the shower run, then the mutter of the TV through the closed door. Maybe Dad was watching it, maybe just zoned out in front of it.

Jack was grateful for the solitude. It gave him time to think. He grabbed a beer from the fridge and paced the front room, mulling what had happened, and what had almost happened. He'd been unarmed. Well, why not? Just visiting a neighbor lady for some conversation and a few sundown drinks. Who needs to be armed?

He'd know better next time. If there was going to be a next time. A few rounds into that gator's eyes or its open mouth . . . that would have stopped it. Or at least he was pretty sure it would have.

But a gun would have been superfluous because the gator hadn't been able to cross the line into Anya's yard.

Jack was getting used to the surreal, but still . . .

Could someone or—worse—some*thing* be controlling the wildlife around here? This whole situation had *Otherness* written all over it. He was convinced the Otherness had taken Kate from him, then it had made an attempt at Gia and Vicky and the unborn baby. Was it after his father now?

Gia and Vicky . . .

He pulled out his Tracfone and punched in Gia's number. She was delighted to hear that his father was out of his coma. Jack left out the other details, like attempted murder

by alligator—twice—and told her he'd be hanging around
a few days more, just to make sure he was okay.

Then Vickie got on the phone. She wanted him to bring
her back a pet alligator. Jack shuddered at the thought but
told her he'd see if he could catch one for her. A little one.
Right.

Then Gia again. She was feeling good; she thought
she'd felt the baby move but wasn't sure. All quiet on Sutton Square.

After I-love-yous and goodnights, he hung up and made
another call to Manhattan. This time to Abe.

When Abe picked up, Jack said, "Hey. It's me."

Jack's Tracfone was untraceable, but he could never rule
out that the BATF had taken an interest in Abe—linked
him to an illegal weapon, perhaps—and were eavesdrop-
ping. So for his own sake and for Abe's, he never mentioned his name or anyone else's, even Abe's.

"Good evening, Me. How's the vacation going?"

"Could be better. You know how I thought I'd have an
easy time at the tournament? It's not turning out that way.
The competition is a lot stiffer than I dreamed possible."

"Is that so? As I recall, you weren't expecting any
competition."

"Turned out I was wrong. Imagine that. But here's the
thing. I need bigger and better equipment. Some new tennis clothes, for sure. Large size."

"How large? X? Double-X? Triple-X?"

"Big as you've got. Think *elephant* when you pick it out."

"Elephant?"

"Mastodon. Oh, and maybe some new racquets."

"Any particular model?"

"You pick them out. I need something with a nice sweet
spot and lots more power than what I've got."

"So it's a power player you're up against?"

"Yeah. Back court all the way until today's round. That

was when he started coming to the net. I don't think I've seen his best stuff yet, so I want to be prepared."

"I should say so. I'll send you a nice selection of racquets that you should be able to adjust to your needs. You want I should include extra strings in case you break some?"

"Definitely. The more the better. You know how I break strings."

"Do I. Anything else?"

"Some tennis balls."

"Balls? I'm not following you here. Surely they have tennis balls where you are?"

"Not like the brand you carry. Yours always seem fresher. And make sure they're yellow. A pale yellow."

"Pale yellow . . ."

Jack detected a note of uncertainty in Abe's voice. "Yeah, pale yellow. Like the color of my favorite fruit."

"A lemon?"

"No! Pineapple, my man. Pineapple. You know how I love pineapple."

"Oy, of course. How could I have forgotten? Yes, well, I'll check to see if I have any of that shade in stock. I should send you how many?"

"Let's see . . . I don't want to run short. How about a dozen?"

"A dozen. Sounds to me like you'll be playing a lot of tennis."

"I hope not. The longer you play, the greater the chance of injury. As you know, I like to rip right through the matches without much wear and tear, but you never know. Best to be prepared, don't you think?"

"Definitely. You want I should send them to that address you left with me?"

"That's the place. And make it quick, okay? Who knows what I'll be facing tomorrow."

"I'll pack it up right away and get it out tonight. I'll use my special carrier. If all goes well you should have them by tomorrow afternoon."

"Swell. Put it on my tab and we'll settle up when I get back. I owe you one."

"I'll add this to the 'owe' list."

"Do that. Oh, and by the way. Have I got a girl for you. She's an older woman, but she could be a soul mate."

"Now you're a matchmaker?"

"Just trying to enrich your life, my friend."

"Okay. I'll humor you. First question: Is she on the thin side or the heavy side?"

"She makes Olive Oyl look like a sumo wrestler."

"Sorry. Not interested. I need a woman with some meat on her, enough bulk so that we don't look like Mr. and Mrs. Sprat when we go out together. Someone who won't frown when I put extra cream cheese on my bagel. Someone, in fact, who'll ask me if I want seconds, or even thirds. An anorexic woman is the last thing I need."

"Okay. Just thought I'd ask."

"Find a Sophie Tucker for me and then we'll talk. But back to the tennis matches: Listen, be careful. Watch your footwork. Sounds like even a minor misstep could take you out of the game."

"Ain't that the truth. Talk to you later."

"Stay in touch. Let me know the scores."

"Will do."

Jack smiled as he cut the connection, but it faded as he turned toward his father's bedroom. He knocked softly on the door. When he received no answer, he pushed it open and peeked in. His father lay in bed, snoring softly, the remote in his hand, the Weather Channel playing on the TV.

Jack turned and headed for the front door. Time to visit Ms. Mundy. He had a few questions he wanted answered. Hell, he had lots of questions, and he knew she had answers to some of them.

15

Anya's front yard was deserted. The furniture was as he'd left it but she and Oyv were gone. So were the glasses, the wine, and the beer Jack and his father had brought over.

Jack knocked on the door. Anya, wearing another garish kimono with bright red sampans sailing across her flat chest, answered almost immediately.

"You're back. That must mean your father's okay."

"Shaken up but he's all right, I think. We need to talk."

"As you wish," she said, moving away from the door. "Come in."

Jack stepped into the greenhouse interior.

"I put your beer in the refrigerator so it wouldn't get warm," she said on her way to the kitchen. "Do you want one?"

"Thanks, no. I'm not here to drink."

She stopped at the kitchen counter where the wine bottle waited. An empty glass stood next to one half filled. Not dainty little claret glasses but big glass balloons that held eight to ten ounces if they held a drop. She topped off both and held out the fresh one to Jack.

"Here. Try this. It's Italian. Valpolicella."

"No, really. I—"

She locked eyes with him. "I don't like to talk to people who won't share a glass with me."

Jack shrugged and took the glass. He'd done worse things to get someone to talk. He took a sip.

"It's good." There. Was she happy? "Now, can I ask you a few questions?"

"If you wish." She seated herself on the sofa overhung with plants and vines. She lit a cigarette and began shuffling a deck of cards. She pointed him toward the recliner. "Sit. You want to ask me about a Russian woman with a malamute, don't you."

Jack felt his jaw drop. "I—I—"

"And an Indian woman with a German shepherd. The one who told you to stay away from that house in Astoria. The one you foolishly ignored."

"How did you know?" Jack said, finding his voice.

She blew smoke and shrugged as she began laying out the cards in a classic solitaire tableau. "Lucky guess."

"Since June I've been running into women who know too much—women with dogs. You're the third. Two isn't a trend. But three . . ."

"Not to worry. You have nothing to fear from them. Or me."

Jack took a deep breath and let it out. He'd expected denials or, at the very least, evasions. To have her come right out and confirm his suspicions . . . it knocked him off balance.

He took a gulp of his wine. Maybe this was why she'd insisted he take a glass.

"Who are you people?"

She finished laying out the cards and began to play, flipping them over with sharp little snaps. "No one in particular."

"I don't buy that. You know too much. Back in June, when I was sick, the Russian lady came to my room"—he saw her in his mind, salt-and-pepper hair, gray jogging suit, big white malamute—"and told me things about a war I'd been drafted into. 'Is war and you are warrior,' she said. I don't know if she mentioned it directly or not, but I'm pretty sure she was going on about something called the Otherness and—"

Anya stopped her card play and looked up at him. "You'd already heard of the Otherness by then."

"Yeah."

Although he wished he hadn't. The first mention had been earlier in the year, in the spring at a—surprise—conspiracy convention. Since then his life hadn't seemed quite his own.

According to what he'd been told, two vast, unimaginably complex cosmic forces have been at war forever. The prize in the war is all existence—all the dimensions, all the realities, all the parallel dimensions up for grabs. Earth and humanity's corner of reality is a minor piece on the game board, of no special importance. But if one is going to declare itself winner, one has to take all the pieces. Even the inconsequential ones.

One side—a force, a state of being, whatever—is inimical to humankind. It has no name but through the ages came to be called the Otherness by people aware of its existence. If the Otherness takes over, it will transform Earth's reality into a place toxic to all known life. Fortunately, Earth and its attendant reality are currently in the portfolio of the other side, the force known only as the Ally. From what Jack had learned, "Ally" was a misnomer. This force was not a friend, merely an enemy of humanity's enemy. The most Earth could expect from it was benign neglect.

"At the time I thought the Russian lady was some sort of fever dream, but then she showed up again and told me . . ."

"That there would be no more coincidences in your life."

Jack nodded. The words still chilled him. The implications were devastating.

"Was she right?"

Anya went back to her game, flipping and arranging the cards in the tableau, moving some aces and deuces up to the foundation.

"I'm afraid so, hon."

"Then it means that my life is being manipulated. Why?"

"Because you are involved."

"Not by choice."

"Choice means nothing in these matters."

"Well, if someone or something thinks I'm its standard bearer, it had better think again."

"You are not the standard bearer. Not yet."

If true, that was a relief. A small one.

"Then who is?"

Anya was dealing to herself from the stock now, and Jack couldn't help but notice that the cards were falling her way, more and more finding places in the tableau or the foundation.

"One who preceded you," she said. "He preceded the twins as well. You remember the twins, don't you."

Jack had a flash of two men in identical black suits and dark glasses, with identical pale, expressionless faces.

"How could I forget?"

"They were meant to replace their predecessor. But when you dispatched them—"

"They didn't leave me much choice. It was them or me. And I tried to help them at the end, but they refused."

"They did what they had to do, but their passing left a void. One that you were tapped to fill."

"But you said there's someone else."

Anya nodded as she laid the final card from her stock on the solitaire tableau. All the cards were face up. She'd won. Without bothering to shift all the tableau cards to the foundation, she gathered them up and began shuffling.

"There is. A *mensch* of *mensches*, that one. But he's old now, and may die before he's needed again."

" 'Again'?"

"He was the Ally's champion for a long time."

"How long?"

"*Very* long. So long you wouldn't believe. But now his days are numbered. After ages in the Ally's service—too long, I think, but who listens to an old woman—he was freed. But it seems his liberation was premature. Even though he has aged, he may be needed again. But if he doesn't live till that day . . ." Her eyes met Jack's.

"Then it'll be me?"

"You."

Against all reason, Jack believed her. With an effort, he shelved his dismay. Maybe that day would never come. Or maybe *he'd* have died of old age when it did.

But he hadn't come here about himself. He'd come about his father.

"Is the Otherness involved in what's been happening to my father?"

She nodded as she finished shuffling and began to lay out another solitaire tableau.

"The Ally is involved here as well, though tenuously."

"But I can assume, at least from what I've seen, that you and your ladies are on the Ally's side, right?"

She shook her head. "No. I oppose the Otherness, but I've no connection to the Ally."

"Then whose side *are* you on?"

"Yours."

"But I'm stuck with the Ally, so that means—"

Anya grimaced with irritation and stopped her card play.

"I didn't say the Ally's side, did I? No. I said, *yours*. That means *you*, separate and distinct from the Ally."

"But why?"

"Because the Ally can be as ruthless as the Otherness. It opposes the Otherness for its own reasons, none of which involves our health and happiness. It will use you and any-one else it can to fend off the Otherness, and not care a whit what happens to you. Humanity's well-being is not on its agenda. It is, however, on mine."

"Why? What's your stake in this?"

She began rearranging the cards in the tableau.

"My stake is your stake. Everyone here on this planet is in the same boat—Earth *is* a boat, when you think of it—and we all deserve to be free of both these meddling pow-ers. This planet, in this subdivision of reality, is inhabited by sentient beings, which makes it all the more valuable in the struggle. But it's more than mere property that can be won or lost or traded at will. If it must belong to one of them, then I'd far prefer the Ally over the Otherness. But why belong to either? Why not be shut of both of them?"

"Sounds good to me," Jack said. He leaned back, trying to get a handle on what she was saying, and what it meant. "But what I'm getting here . . . what you're telling me . . . is that there's a third force involved in all this."

"I suppose you could put it that way."

"And you . . . you and those other women . . . you're part of that?"

"So it would appear."

"But how can you hope to compete with the other two players?"

"Because I must."

"But who are you? *What* are you? Where do you come from?"

"We come from everywhere. We're all around you. You simply never see us."

Jack shook his head to clear it. He didn't want to deal with this now. He'd had trouble enough buying into the cosmic tug-of-war scenario. But now Anya was telling him that a third party had entered the fray—or maybe had al-ways been in the fray but no one had told him. Whatever the case, he'd get to that later. Right now he had to stay focused on his father.

"Why my father? Why would—?"

And then he had a chilling thought. What had she said to him that first day in the hospital room?

Trust me, hon, there's more to your father than you ever dreamed.

"Oh, no! You're not telling me that this 'predecessor champion' you've been telling me about is my father!"

"Tom?" Anya laughed. "Oy! Such a thought! You think you're living in a fairy tale? How can you even consider such a thing!"

"That's not a exactly a 'no.'"

"All right then. You want a 'no'? Here's a 'no.' Your father has *no* direct connection to the Ally or the Otherness. Never did, never will."

She laughed again and continued her card play.

Jack too had to smile. All right, yeah, it was a ridiculous thought. The pen might be mightier than the sword, but an accountant as defender of humanity against the Otherness? Crazy.

Yet . . . for a moment there . . .

"Wait. You said no direct connection. Does he have an *indirect* connection?"

"Of course. Isn't it obvious?"

"Because he's my father?"

Anya nodded. "A blood relative."

Jack closed his eyes. This was what he'd suspected, what he'd feared.

"That alligator, then . . . it was sent by the Otherness."

"Sent? No, that was someone else's idea. I can tell you that the creature was created by the Otherness, but whether intentionally or accidentally is hard to say."

"Why? You seem to know everything else. Why don't you know that?"

"I don't know everything, kiddo. If I did, maybe the two of us could send the Otherness and the Ally packing."

"Why do I get this feeling you're holding back? You don't know everything? Fine. Nobody does. But why don't you just come out and tell everything you *do* know?"

"Because sometimes it's best that you learn things on your own. But I can tell you about the connection between the Otherness and that alligator."

Jack leaned back and took another slug of wine. "I'm all ears."

"It was born near a nexus point."

"And that is . . . ?"

"A place. A very special place. In various locales around the globe there are spots where the veil between our world and the Otherness is thin. Occasionally the veil attenuates to the point where a little of the Otherness can enter our sphere. But only briefly. Rarely do beings from the other side pass through. But influence . . . ah, that's another matter."

"Let me guess a location," Jack said. "Washington, DC, maybe? Say, near the Capitol Hill or the White House?"

Anya smiled as she gathered up her cards. She'd won again.

"I'm afraid those *gonifs* have no such excuses for their behavior, hon. But one is near here, and another near where you live."

"Where?" Somehow Jack wasn't surprised.

"In the New Jersey Pine Barrens. At a place called Razorback Hill."

Jack had gone into the Barrens last spring, and almost hadn't come out.

"It must be pretty well hidden. I mean, don't you think someone would have stumbled across it by now?"

"There are places in the Pine Barrens that no human eyes have seen. But even so, the nexus points manifest themselves directly only twice a year—at the equinoxes. But their indirect effects can be viewed every day."

"Like what?"

"Mutations. Something leaks through from the other side around the time of the equinox; whatever it is changes the cells of the living things around it—plants, animals, trees . . . and people."

"You'd think someone would have noticed *that* by now."

Anya shook her head. "The nexus points are located in unpopulated areas."

"How convenient."

"Not so. When you consider that these leaks have been occurring for ages, and that most people experience a sense of uneasiness when they near a nexus point, it makes sense. Nexus points don't occur in places that people avoid. Just the opposite: People—most people, that is— instinctively avoid nexus points."

Jack was thinking, *nexus point . . . mutations . . . a humongous horned alligator . . .*

"There's a nexus point out there in the swamp, isn't there."

"I told you, it's not a swamp, it's—"

"A river of grass. Right. Okay. But am I right that there's a nexus point nearby in the Everglades?"

Anya nodded. "In a lagoon within one of the hardwood hummocks."

"How do you know all this?"

Anya shrugged. "Like I said before, hon, I've been around here longer than you."

"How long?"

"Long enough."

"All right, then." He sensed a certain timelessness about Anya, and was convinced she was more than she pretended to be. He took a chance and asked her flat out: "How long have you and these other women been around?"

"I should tell you my age?"

She lit another cigarette and gathered up her cards. She'd won another game. That made three in a row. More than luck there. Had to be. She was either cheating or . . .

Let it go.

"All right, don't tell me. Maybe if I see that Indian woman again"—he remembered her orange sari and long braid, and her German shepherd—"maybe I'll ask her. She looked young."

Anya laughed. "*Never* ask a woman her age!"

Thinking of the other women with dogs reminded Jack of something one of them had said.

"The Russian woman mentioned someone called the Adversary. Who's that? She said I'd met him."

Anya leaned back and stared at him.

"You have. Remember my telling you about the aging one who once spearheaded the Ally's cause? Well, the Otherness has its own champion. He's very dangerous. He's ancient. He's been killed more than once but each time he's been reborn."

"And I've met him? I—"

And then Jack knew. The strange, strange man who'd first explained the Otherness to him, the man he suspected of being ultimately responsible for Kate's death . . .

"Roma," he whispered. "Sal Roma. At least that was what he told me his name was. I later learned that was a lie."

"Always you must expect lies where he is concerned—unless the truth will hurt you. He feeds on pain."

"Yeah. That was what your Russian friend told me: human misery, discord, and chaos. But who is he, really?"

"More like *what* is he. He used to be a man just like you, but now he is more. He is destined to become something else, but he hasn't reached that state yet. He can do things that humans can only dream of, but he is still in the process of becoming. He's known as 'the Adversary' to those who oppose the Otherness, and 'the One' to those aligned with it."

"Why would people work for the Otherness when they know it means the end of everything?"

Anya shrugged. "Who can explain people? Some are so filled with hate that they want to see everything destroyed, some believe their efforts toward bringing the Otherness apocalypse will be rewarded afterward, some believe packages of lies they've been fed, and some are simply mad. The Adversary orchestrates their movements from afar."

"But what's his *name*?"

"He uses many. He has many identities, many different looks, but he never uses his True Name."

"Do you know it?"

Anya nodded. "But I will not tell you."

"Why the hell not?"

"Because he would hear you. And you do not want to attract his attention."

"Says who?" Jack said, feeling the heat of the rage he'd been carrying around for months now. "I've got a score to settle with him and—"

"No!" Anya was leaning forward in her seat, eyes ablaze. "You stay away from him! Whatever you do, you must not antagonize him. He will snuff you out like a match if it suits him."

"We'll see about that. Just tell me his name and let me worry about the rest."

Anya shook her head. "Speaking his name would lead him here—and he's looking for me."

"You? Why?"

"To kill me."

Her words shocked Jack. And the matter-of-fact way she said it, as if she'd been dealing with this threat for so long she'd grown used to it, made it all the more believable.

But could it be true? If so, he'd lay off pressing her for Roma's real name.

"Because you oppose the Otherness?"

"More than that. I stand in its way—in *his* way."

Jack wanted to say, You're a little old lady . . . how can you stand in anyone's way? But he hadn't forgotten how that alligator had been unable to enter her yard. Perhaps she and the others were keeping out the Otherness just as she'd kept out the gator, but on a far greater scale.

This little old lady was a lot more than she seemed. She had power . . . but from where?

Jack wasn't going to waste his time asking. She'd already made it damn clear there were things about her and her friends she didn't want known.

"You stand in his way to . . . what?"

"To opening the gates to the Otherness. The Adversary will remain in a state of becoming until he succeeds. If he does, he will be transformed and life, reality, existence as we know it will end. He thought he'd found a shortcut earlier this year. You were there and—"

"How do you *know* this stuff? Or was one of your ladies watching?"

"You might say that."

Jack remembered gazing down into a bottomless hole . . . into an abyss glowing with strange lights . . . a steadily enlarging hole that he feared might devour him and the rest of the world.

Anya said, "The Adversary failed then because he acted prematurely. That shows me he's anxious to finish his becoming. Since then he and those he has manipulated have doubled and redoubled their efforts to open those gates. But to achieve final success he must kill me or hurt me so severely that I can no longer oppose them."

Apprehension tightened his shoulders. If the Adversary or the One or Roma or whatever the hell he was called was as dangerous as Anya said, she could be in big trouble. Jack hadn't known her long, but he'd taken a real liking to this old broad.

"But if he doesn't know where you are, he can't hurt you, right?"

She shook her head. "No. He can hurt me. He hurts me all the time."

"But how—?"

Anya stiffened and grimaced with pain as she sucked air through her teeth with a hiss. She arched her back and reached around to touch her right shoulder blade. Oyv jumped up and started barking.

"See?" she gasped. "Even now he does it! He's hurting me again!"

Jack was up and around the chair, looking at her back.

"What? What's happening?"

"Oh!" She was taking quick, shallow, panting breaths. "He stabs me! It hurts!"

"What can I do?"

"Nothing. It will pass."

Jack thought he saw a small spot of red—blood red—appear on the back of her kimono, but couldn't be sure because it was within the hull of one of the bright red sampans.

"Are you bleeding?"

She leaned back against the chair, hiding her back from view.

"I'll be all right."

Her color was better and her breathing, though not normal yet, was easing in the right direction.

"Should I get a doctor?"

She shook her head. "No doctor can help with this. I'll be fine. This isn't the first time he's hurt me, and it won't be the last. He's moving closer and closer to his goal. A strange season is upon us, and it will grow stranger."

"Damn it, Anya, tell me his name. I'll put an end to this."

She shook her head. "No, Jack. He's immune to your methods. He's more than you can handle."

"Then how do we stop him?"

Anya looked up at him and Jack saw fear in her eyes. "I don't know. We can only hope that he makes a fatal mistake—he's not perfect you know—or that the Ally steps in on our side. Otherwise, I don't know if he *can* be stopped."

16

After Anya's pain had subsided, she shooed Jack out of the house. He felt he should stay but he could see that she wanted to be alone.

He stood in her front yard among the ornaments, staring at the rising moon, and wondering at how his life had changed since a year ago last summer when he'd accepted the seemingly simple, straightforward job of finding a stolen necklace. Now it seemed that every time he turned around, a new revelation leaped at him, tearing a jagged rent in the fabric of the snug, familiar worldview he'd been wrapped in for the first thirty-five years of his life.

A year ago he'd have written Anya off as a loon. But no more.

He popped into his father's house and peeked again into his bedroom. The old guy was still sleeping peacefully with the TV going. Jack found the screwdriver and flashlight he'd used last night, then stepped outside and headed for the clinic.

Although he'd broken in once before, he didn't take for

granted that it would be as easy the second time. He was just as careful about approaching the building, keeping to the bushes and watching for the security patrols. About halfway there he realized he'd forgotten the mosquito repellent. They'd declared his arms and neck an all-night deli and were ordering takeout.

Slapping and scratching, he picked up his pace and made it to the clinic faster than last night. He popped the window latch again and slid inside. After reclosing the window, he killed a couple of mosquitoes that were still drilling into his skin, then got to work.

Straight to the record room where he began flipping through the charts. He had the list of names his father had given him and though it was a long shot that they'd all had recent physicals, he had to check.

He started at the top of the alphabet and worked his way down, pulling the charts as he came across them: *Adele Borger . . . Joseph Leo . . . Edward Neusner. . . .*

All here.

No second guessing the ethics of invading privacy this time. These folks weren't his father, and they were dead.

Inside the charts, Jack knew where to look. He went to the bottom of the final page of the complete physical. Each one read the same: *Final assess: excellent health.*

A prickling sensation ran along the back of his neck. Seemed like being single at Gateways South and passing your free physical with flying colors was not a good thing. In their cases, it appeared to be a death sentence.

The pattern was obvious: The healthiest single members of Gateways South were dying by mishap. An early demise meant that, instead of having to wait many years for these healthy folk to go, the management was able to resell their homes immediately.

Jack had a pretty good idea as to the *why* and the *who*, and a wild idea as to the *how*.

He wondered if the doc was in on it. Probably not. He seemed like too much of a straight shooter.

Besides, you didn't need the doc to get a look at the files. Jack's presence here proved that. But there was an even easier way. If you were someone with an official position at Gateways South, and if you had a key to the clinic, you could stroll in here at night, check out the names of those who'd had a complete physical lately, and peruse their files to your heart's content.

Jack decided that he and Gateways South director Ramsey Weldon were going to have a little heart-to-heart chat tomorrow.

FRIDAY

1

Jack jogged along the asphalt walking/bicycle path that wound through the pines lining the eastern limits of Gateways South. A thin morning mist wound between the trunks; brown needles, shedding early due to the drought, littered the path. The scent of pine lay thick in the air.

He'd awakened to silence for a change. Carl must have been trimming someone else's hedges this morning. His father was just starting to stir, so Jack had come out for a run. He'd been too sedentary the past few days. Needed to get the blood flowing. He'd thought about checking on Anya but it was too early. He'd swing by on the way back.

He chugged along in a Boneless T-shirt and gym shorts, building a sweat; he wore his leather belt under the loose shirt to hold the small-of-the-back holster for his Glock 19; the way it bounced against the base of his spine as he ran was annoying, but no way he was going unarmed around this place.

An eight-foot chain-link fence ran along the Gateways border to his right. The links of the par-3 golf course lay to his left. He noticed a lone, vaguely familiar figure hunched over a putter on a rise ahead. As he neared he recognized him: Carl.

Jack veered to his left and found Carl on a putting green, working with a club that protruded from his right sleeve.

Jack had thought he was a righty, but he was using a lefty stance.

He waited until Carl had hit the ball—he just missed, rimming the cup—before speaking.

"When did you join the community?"

Carl jumped and spun. "Oh, it's you! You scared me again! You gotta learn to make more noise when you come up on people."

"Sorry," Jack said. "I'll work on it. Say, did your video camera catch any signs of Ms. Mundy watering her lawn?"

"Zilch again." He grinned. "And I hope it don't. Wouldn't mind keepin this up the rest of the year, long as old Doc Dengrove keeps payin me."

Jack glanced down at the balls Carl had arranged on the grass before him, sitting in a line, waiting for the putter. "Is a golfing membership one of the perks of your job?"

He shook his head. "Only on weekdays, and only on my day off, and only if I stay out of everbody's way. I ain't much with the drivers—I mean, my scores for eighteen holes are pretty pan-o-ramic—but I like to putt. I ain't a bad miniature golf player."

"No kidding." This was fascinating, simply fascinating. Jack waved and turned away. "Got to keep moving. Good luck. Sink those putts. Make those birdies."

But he never got restarted. The sight of a beat-up red pickup cruising the dirt road on the far side of the fence stopped him cold. It slowed as a pair of mismatched eyes peered at him from under the brim of a dirty John Deere cap, then picked up speed again.

A thought struck Jack. He turned back to Carl, intending to ask him if he knew them, but the half-sick look on his face as he watched the pickup bounce away into the trees said it all.

"You know those guys, don't you."

Carl swallowed. His left eye was already looking away; the right followed. "Why you say something like that?"

"Because I think you do. Who are they?"

"Nobody to mess with. You don't want to know em."

"Yeah, I do." Especially after what his father had told him last night about the accident. Jack gave him a hard stare. "Who are they, Carl?"

Carl looked like he was going to try to float some bull-shit, then his shoulders sagged and he shook his head.

"They live out in the Glades. On a lagoon in one of the hardwood hummocks."

"I thought no one was supposed to live out there except maybe some local Indians."

"Well, I think you know that what's upposed to be and what is ain't necessarily the same thing."

Yeah. Jack knew that.

"You know where this lagoon is?"

Carl nodded. "I guess so."

"How do I get there?"

"You don't, not unless you know the way."

"Can you show me on a map?"

Another shake of his head. "It ain't marked on no maps. It's pretty well hid."

"Then how come you know where it is?"

Carl looked away. "I was born there."

This didn't surprise Jack. He'd seen what the folks connected to the red pickup looked like, and figured there had to be something wicked strange about Carl's right arm. Add that to what Anya had said about the mutating effects of the Otherness leak at the nexus point in the Glades, and the connection looked obvious.

He remembered other misshapen people he'd met earlier in the year . . . Melanie Ehler and Frayne Canfield . . .

both had attributed their deformities to "a burst of Otherness" during their gestations. Carl's story was most likely the same.

"All right then," Jack said, "take me there."

Carl backed away a step, holding up his hand. "Nuh-uh. No way. I left there years ago and I ain't goin back."

"Well, if it's not on a map, and you can't tell me how to get there, and you won't take me there, how am I supposed to find it?"

"You ain't. That's the whole point."

As if to say he was through talking, Carl bent over his putter and lined up a shot. He tapped the ball and it went wide.

"I've good reason to believe they caused my father's accident and were setting him up to be eaten by an alligator when the police interrupted them."

Carl straightened and looked at him. "Alligator? That woulda meant your daddy'd go the same way as the others, killed by a swamp critter."

"Well, this wasn't no ordinary swamp critter." Jeez, Jack thought. A couple of conversations with this guy and I'm starting to talk like him. "This gator was huge, with what looked like horns sticking out of its head."

Carl visibly shuddered. "Devil. That could only be Devil."

"Who's Devil?"

"Big freaky bull gator that hangs around the lagoon. But how on earth did they get him out of the swamp?"

"Couldn't say. But it seems Devil gets around. He visited Gateways last night."

"No way!"

"Way."

Jack gave him a Reader's Digest version of the attack, leaving out Oyv's amazing feat and the gator's inability to cross into Anya's yard. He remembered what his father had said about Carl being the community gossip.

"I want to get a look at this lagoon, Carl. I've already met the people, now I want to see where they live."

"You met them?"

"In town yesterday. Met that woman, too. The one with the white hair."

"Semelee."

"Right. What do you know about her? Is she as spooky as she looks?"

"Can't rightly say. I left the clan about—"

"Whoa! Are we talking Kluxers here?"

"Naw. That's just what we call ourselfs. We're all kinda related in a way."

"Yeah? How?"

Carl's good eye shifted away again. "Not by blood or anything like that. More like we was all in the same situation. Anyway, it was just us guys, maybe twenty of us, when she showed up a couple years ago. I'd been kinda plannin on leavin anyway, but when she showed up I took it as a sign and skeedaddled outta there."

"A sign of what?"

"That things in the clan was gonna head south real soon. I mean, you got eighteen-twenty guys and one woman, that's trouble."

"They seemed pretty tight when I saw them in town yesterday."

"Yeah, well, maybe. I seen em from a distance a couple times. We always done some panhandlin, but now they's become like professionals. I stay away from em cause we ain't exactly on good terms."

"Why not?"

"They was kinda pissed I left. Luke—he was sorta kinda like the leader—he called me a traitor and all sortsa stuff like that. But that don't matter to me. I'm glad I got out. I didn't wanta live like them no more. Y'know, like gypsies. They live on the boats or in what's left of a bunch of old

Indian huts on the shore. No runnin water, no lectricity, no TV." He shook his head. "Man, I sure do love TV. Anyways, I wanted my own place where I didn't have to sleep next to nobody cept myself."

"A room of one's own," Jack murmured. He knew the feeling.

Carl grinned. "Hell, I got more than just a room, I got me a whole trailer."

"But do you have any money in the bank?" Jack said as an idea hit him.

"Naw. Pretty much everthing gets spent just for livin."

"Okay, then. What say I pay you a thousand bucks to take me to this lagoon?"

"A thousand?" Carl laughed. "You're shittin me, right?"

"Nope. Five hundred when we leave, and another five when we get back. That sound fair to you?"

Carl licked his lips. "Yeah, but . . ."

"But what?"

"But they's gonna be awful mad if they find I brung an outsider to the lagoon."

"Don't worry about that." Jack flipped up the back of his shirt to show Carl the Glock. "I'll get you back home. I promise. And anyway, if we go in the afternoon, won't they all be in town, begging?"

"Come to think of it, yeah. Specially this bein Friday."

"What's so special about Friday?"

He shrugged. "Lotsa people round here get paid on Thursdays, and on Fridays they're happy the work week's over, so they're looser with their change. Saturday's pretty much the same. But Sunday's usually a bust."

"Spent too much on Saturday night, right?"

"Yeah. Or they just come from church and did some givin there. Monday's even worse." He scratched his jaw. "So yeah. We should have the lagoon pretty much to ourselfs this afternoon."

"Then that's when we'll go. A quick trip for a quick look-see. In and out. Easiest thousand you ever made."

Carl took a breath. "Okay. But since my car ain't workin, you gotta drive me down to the waterside." He began picking up his golf balls. "Guess I better get movin. Gotta get home, gotta find us a boat."

"How'd you get here without a car?"

"Bike. How else?"

More power to you, pal, Jack thought. Maybe the thousand would let Carl repair his junker Honda.

He got directions to Carl's trailer park—it was the one Jack had seen between the auto body place and the limestone quarry—and continued his jog.

2

Semelee stood with Luke a couple dozen feet from Devil's gator hole and watched. The big gator lay half sunk in the water at the shady end, his eyes closed. The water around his left flank wound was tinged red. At first she thought he was dead, but then she saw his sides pull in a little as he took a breath.

"He's still bleeding," Luke said.

"I know," she said through her clenched teeth. "I got eyes."

She felt so on edge this morning she wanted to take a bite out of somebody.

Devil was the biggest gator anybody'd ever seen, so it made sense he'd have the biggest gator hole in the Glades. Like all gators, as the winter dry season began, he'd scrape out all the vegetation from this low spot in the limestone floor and create a big wallowing hole. Fish would work their way into it, turtles and frogs too, and even some birds would come around to see if they could snag a quick meal. Sometimes those birds and turtles became gator snacks.

In the wet summers gators left their holes and spread out through the Glades, but not this year. The dry spell made gator holes more important than ever.

The edges of Devil's hole were piled high with muck he'd scraped out. This provided rootin soil for things like cattails, swamp lilies, ferns and arrowleaf. Yellow-flowered spatter-dock lilies floated on the surface of the blood-tinged water.

Devil lifted his head and let out a hoarse, rumbling bellow, then let it flop back down into the water as if it was too heavy to hold up.

"He's hurtin, Luke. Hurtin bad."

Because of me, she thought.

Guilt scalded her. She'd considered Devil indestructible, invincible, almost supernatural. But he wasn't. He was just a big, misshapen gator who would have been happy spendin his days doin what gators do: lolling in his hole, eatin this and that, waitin for the rains.

But no. Semelee couldn't let him be. She had to roust him out of his comfy hole and lead him out of the Glades into the outer world where he didn't belong. The result was he got hurt. Hurt bad.

"He can't die," she said. "He just can't."

She had this terrible feeling that if Devil died, part of the spirit of the Glades would die with him. And it would be all her fault.

"It was that guy," Luke said. "That city guy you been takin a shine to. He done this."

"No, he didn't. I already told you that. He didn't have nothin to do with hurtin Devil. It was the old lady. She's the one. She's some sorta witch. So's her dog."

In a way Semelee was secretly glad that the old witch's spell, or whatever it was, had kept Devil out of her yard. Because she'd seen her man, the special one, place himself between Devil and his father. She'd've had to go through him to get to the old man, and that would've meant hurtin him, maybe even killin him, somethin she definitely didn't want to do. But it had showed her that he was made of good stuff. That was important.

"I say we do all three of them—old lady, father, and son—and have done with it."

"No. I told you: The son ain't to be touched."

Luke grumbled. "All right. We'll have another go at the old guy, but the lady . . . what're you gonna do about her?"

"Don't know yet. We can't *do* her unless we can get to her. I'll think of somethin. But it'll have to wait till the lights is done. I ain't lettin nothin get between me and the lights."

"Awright. But what do we do till the lights come? We goin panhandlin as usual?"

"Not durin the lights. We'll just hang out. Besides, we don't need to go beggin cause we'll be gettin a hunk of cash from those dredgin guys when they finish at noon."

"What if they try to stiff us?"

"They won't. They ain't gettin out of the lagoon less'n they pay up."

But Semelee didn't want to think about dredgin or money or nothin cept the lights. Anticipation thrummed through her like she was a plucked guitar string. The lights-'d start tonight and run for three days. But this year would be like no other. This time they wouldn't be underwater, which meant they'd be bigger and brighter and better than ever before.

Starting tonight, everything in her life would change. She sensed it, she knew it.

3

Tom had been watching the Weather Channel's reports on Hurricane Elvis. It continued to move south off Florida's west coast; although its winds had increased to 90 miles an hour, it was still a Category I. And no threat to Florida at this point.

He was just finishing his cup of coffee when Jack came through the door, dripping with sweat.

"I was wondering where you were." He'd been a little anxious after awakening to finding the house empty and Jack's car still parked outside. Obviously he'd been out jogging. "I don't suppose you'd care for a cup of hot coffee right now."

"After my shower I'd love one. Never turn down coffee."

As Jack ducked into the bathroom, Tom rinsed out the French press and began to make another serving. He noticed his hand shaking a little as he spooned the ground coffee. He touched the fresh bandage on his head. The stitches were still a little tender under there. He'd been shocked at the sight of his bruised, black-eyed face in the mirror this morning. He felt so good he'd almost forgotten about the accident.

Now he couldn't get it out of his head. Someone wanted him dead. Why?

Last week his life had been safe and sane, prosaic, maybe even a little dull. Now . . .

What was happening? He didn't live the sort of life where he got on people's wrong side. Was it a mistake?

Had he been mistaken for somebody else? Who on earth would want to kill him?

He pondered those imponderables until Jack returned, in fresh shorts and T-shirt, his wet hair combed straight back.

"Hey, good coffee," he said after sipping the cup Tom had made for him.

"Colombian. I was thinking of scrambling some eggs. Want some?"

"Sure. And some hash browns and toast, and maybe some grits with extra butter. Oh, and while you're at it, a side of biscuits and gravy."

Tom gave him a dour look.

Jack shrugged and smiled. "Hey, we're in the south so I figured one of their traditional, artery-clogging breakfasts would be in order."

"What do you know about southern cooking?"

"There's a place called Down Home a few blocks from where I live. In New York you can eat any style you want."

"Right now," Tom said, "I don't feel like eating at all. Hard to be hungry when there's someone out to get you. If I knew who or why, maybe it wouldn't be so bad. I'd still be scared, but . . ."

"Maybe I can help there," Jack said softly.

"You? How?"

The phone rang. It was the front gate, wanting to know if he was expecting any packages.

"Not that I know of. Wait." He turned to Jack. "Are you expecting a delivery of some sort?"

"Yeah!" He grinned. "It's here already? Great. Good old Abe."

Tom told the gate to send the truck through, then turned back to Jack.

"You were saying something . . . ?"

Jack cleared his throat. "I checked out the medical records on Borger, Leo, and Neusner last night and—"

"How on earth did you do that?"

"I got in through one of the clinic's windows."

"What?"

"No biggee. I popped the lock on one and crawled through. Don't worry. You'd have to look pretty close to the underside of the sash to even suspect someone was there."

Tom couldn't believe this. His own son breaking and entering—and the clinic of all places.

"Dear God, why?"

"Stay calm. I wanted to see if any of them had had physicals recently—the answer turned out to be yes to all three, by the way—and to see how they did."

"What if it had an alarm, or what if you were caught on camera? You could go to jail for something like that!"

"Only if I got caught, which I didn't. No alarm, no surveillance cameras. I checked that out first. But I found what I was looking for: Each one of them passed their physical with flying colors."

"A lot of good it did them. They're all dead."

"I think they died *because* they passed with flying colors."

"Oh, you're not going back to that Gateways conspiracy thing you were talking about yesterday, are you?"

"Follow the money, Dad. Whenever you wonder if something funny might be going on, follow the money. And the money leads to Gateways."

Had he gone completely paranoid?

"Jack—"

"Think about it: It's only younger, healthy widows and widowers being attacked—the ones who stand the best chance for holding on to their houses the longest. Coincidence?"

"You're talking about a billion-dollar corporation, Jack. This is penny-ante stuff. Imagine the impact of four extra resales in a year on a nine-digit bottom line. Meaningless!"

"It may be meaningless globally, but what about locally? What if someone in Gateways South needs to boost his bottom line and this is a way—just one of a number of ways, say—to do it?"

Tom didn't know what to say. Breaking into offices, digging up "clues" . . . he had to admire Jack's initiative, and was touched that he'd go to all that trouble for him, but . . . Jack seemed to think he was Philip Marlowe or Sam Spade. And he wasn't. He was an appliance repairman, and he was going to get in over his head and in deep trouble if he kept this up.

"I suppose you can make a circumstantial case for it, but it just doesn't add up. You're implying that Ramsey Weldon or someone at his level of management went out and hired those men to smash up my car and then have me eaten by an alligator. It's preposterous."

Jack scratched his head. "I know it seems that way, but so far he and Gateways South are the only ones I can see benefiting from your passing. I'll have to go with Weldon for the time being."

Tom felt a surge of acid in his stomach. " 'Go with'? What does that mean?"

"Oh, I don't know," Jack said with a smile that did nothing to relieve Tom's anxiety. "Have a little tête-à-tête or something like that."

"Don't. Please, don't. You're just going to get yourself in trouble."

"Don't worry. I'll be discreet. The very soul of discretion."

Somehow Tom doubted that. But before he could say anything else, the doorbell rang.

"I'll get it," Jack said.

A delivery man stood at the door holding a cardboard carton.

"I've got four packages for 'Jack.' "

"That's me." Jack took the box and placed it on the floor. "I'll help you with the others."

As Jack followed the man outside to his truck, Tom stepped over and looked at the return address: *Bammo Toy Co.*

Toys?

He noticed too that the shipping label was addressed to "Jack" at this address. No last name, just "Jack." Odd.

When all four cartons were inside the door, Jack tipped the driver, then lifted one of the boxes.

"I'm going to put these in the spare bedroom, if you don't mind."

"Sure. Go ahead."

As Jack headed for the bedroom, Tom lifted one of the packages to help. He hefted it . . . heavier than he'd expected.

Jack had already relocated the first box and almost ran into Tom in the bedroom doorway. He took the package from him—rather quickly, Tom thought.

"Hey, no, Dad. Thanks, but that's okay. I don't want you hurting your back."

"Don't be silly. They're not that heavy."

He returned to the living room and picked up another package. Jack was right behind him, hovering like a mother hen.

"Dad, really—"

Tom ignored him and carried the carton into the bedroom.

When all four were piled against the wall, he said, "It says they're from a toy company. What kind of toys are we talking about? Toy robots? I mean, they're heavy enough."

"Just toys." Jack seemed tense.

"Do you mind showing me one?"

A heartbeat's hesitation, then Jack said, "I guess not. But we'll need a knife to cut the tape."

"I'll get one."

Tom found an old serrated steak knife in the kitchen drawer, but by the time he'd returned, Jack had the smallest box already open.

He held up a folder with a curved blade. "I forgot I had one in my pocket."

Inside, Tom saw an odd-looking stuffed toy, some unidentifiable little animal a little bigger than a football. "What's that?"

"It's a Pokemon. This one's Pikachu. They were all the rage with kids a few years ago."

"But why are you buying them?"

"I'll probably wind up giving them to a local kids' charity."

Tom shook his head. What an odd man his son had turned out to be.

Jack found Carl waiting on the street outside his trailer park in knee-high green rubber boots; a short wooden paddle protruded from his right sleeve.

"Where's the boat?" Jack said as Carl slid into the passenger seat.

"It's waitin. A guy I know's lettin me borrow it." He stuck out his hand. "My money?"

Jack handed him an envelope. "As promised."

He'd come down with about a thousand in cash. His deal with Carl was going to leave him short, so he'd stopped at an ATM for an advance on the John L. Tyleski Visa card.

Another envelope with the balance of the fee was tucked into a back pocket.

Carl checked the contents. Didn't take long to count five bills. The reverent way he touched them made Jack wonder if Carl had ever seen that much money at once.

"I hope I ain't makin a big mistake," he said, still staring into the envelope.

"Don't worry. A few hours from now you'll be sitting in front of your TV with another one of those in your pocket."

He sighed and folded the envelope. "Okay. Let's go."

As they pulled away, Jack noticed high chain-link fencing disappearing into the foliage; a rusted length of chain with a beat-up NO TRESPASSING sign spanned a gap that looked like an entrance.

"That the quarry I've heard about?" Jack said.

Carl nodded. "Some company carved a mess of limestone blocks outta there, then went outta business."

"What's it like down there?"

Carl shrugged. "Just a big hole in the ground. Used to have a big pool of water in its bottom, but not this year."

"Much security?"

"None I ever seen. You can't steal a hole in the ground. Kids sneak in there at night to drink, smoke dope, and screw. Never seen anyone kick em out. Why you so interested?"

"Just curious."

Jack hoped it wouldn't be necessary, but if worse came to worst, he might have use for the quarry.

He followed Carl's directions, turning this way and that, heading in a generally northwest direction. Along the way he saw a black bird with a red head pecking at something on the side of the road.

"Christ, that's an ugly bird."

"That's a turkey vulture—'TV,' for short. Right homely, aren't they. Good thing about them is they clean up roadkill. They do such a good job that round here we call road-kill 'TV dinners.' " He snickered. " 'TV dinners.' Get it?"

"I get it, Carl."

The vegetation became reedier as they rolled along. Finally Carl pointed to a small building with a big AIR BOATS sign. Another, smaller sign—not much more than a slim board with a handwritten message—had been tacked to the bottom.

CLOSED DO TO DROWT.

Jack wondered what the owners were doing with all this extra spare time. Playing Scrabble maybe?

"We're going on an air boat?" He'd seen them whizzing across the Everglades in movies and nature shows and had always wanted to ride one. "Cool."

"Can't use no air boats when it's this dry. There's enough water in the big channels, but the little ones—forget it."

Jack followed Carl around to the rear of the shack where a beached canoe waited on the mud.

"That's our boat?"

"That's her," Carl said with a grin. "She ain't too pan-o-ramic, but she's got a motor."

Jack looked at the tiny, odd-shaped hunk of steel clamped to the right rear stern.

"You call that a motor? I've seen bigger eggbeaters."

"Don't knock it. It's better'n paddlin the whole way."

Carl stepped into the water and pulled the canoe off the mud. He hopped into the stern seat and used the paddle jutting from his right sleeve to steady the boat. Jack had no choice but to wade in, sneakers and all, after him.

"Didn't you bring no boots?"

"Ain't got no boots." There I go, talking like him again.

Jack was calf high in water before he reached the canoe and eased himself onto the forward bench. Carl primed the motor, then: a couple of quick pulls on the cord, a

cloud of smoke, a bubbling clatter, and—hi-yo, Silver—
they were off.

Jack looked down at the sodden legs of his jeans, and his
once white sneakers, now tinted brown with mud. His feet
squished and squeaked inside them.

Swell.

"This channel's usually so much deeper and wider this
time of year. And most of this saw grass is half underwater." He shook his head. "Man, we really need us some
rain."

Jack looked up. A lid of clouds had moved in, hiding the
sun and the sky, but none of them looked like rain clouds.

"What you need down here, Carl, is a big storm, a hurricane to dump a load of water. Maybe Elvis will take care
of your drought."

"I'd go for a tropical storm, okay. You know—thirty-
five- or forty-mile-an-hour winds and a ton of rain. I could
handle that. But no hurricane, thank you. I was here when
Andrew came through and I don't never want to see the
likes of that again."

As they slid along, Jack heard a call and response of
throaty roars from either side.

"Those alligators?"

"Yep. Bulls callin from their gator holes."

"What are those grunting sounds? The females?"

Carl laughed. "Naw. Them's pig frogs. Got the name
cause they grunt like pigs."

Jack noticed lots of snails, with shells maybe an inch to
an inch and a half across, floating near the surface. The
tops of some of their shells broke the surface as they clung
to underwater growths. He saw little pristine white beads
lined up on blades of saw grass and asked Carl about them.

"Those're snail eggs. Cormorants love the snails. Use
the hook on the end of their beak to yank them from their
shells."

A goose-necked turtle with a smooth brown shell and an uncircumcised nose stuck its head above the water and looked at him.

"Hello," Jack said.

The turtle ducked away.

"That's a soft-shelled turtle. Gators just *love* to catch those. Gobble them up like crunchy tacos."

Jack slapped at his neck. He didn't have a long-sleeved shirt so he'd sprayed on lots of repellent, but it didn't seem to be helping much.

"How can you stand all these mosquitoes?"

"*All?* You kidding? This is a good year, a *great* year for mosquitoes. The drought dried up most of their little breedin pools."

If this is a good year, Jack thought, remind me to stay far away in a bad one.

He reached out a hand to grab a few of the long thin blades of grass brushing the side of the canoe. A sharp sting made him snatch it back. He looked and found long scratches across his palm.

Carl laughed. "Now you know why they call it saw grass." He swept his paddle around in a wide arc. "Pa-hay-okee."

Jack remembered Anya using that word.

"Indian, right? Means 'river of grass' or something?"

Carl grinned. "Hey, you been studyin."

A river of grass . . . *sea* of grass was more like it. An ocean of browned saw grass swept away in all directions, dotted here and there by islandlike hummocks of cypress, oak, and pine that looked like giant green mushrooms sprouting from a dead lawn. He hoped it wasn't dead. Just sleeping.

So flat, so like he'd envisioned Kansas might be. Too open for Jack. He was used to living in steel-, concrete-, and glass-lined canyons. The horizon seemed so far away here. Who needed a horizon anyway? Horizons gave him the creeps. He could live very well without one. In fact, back home he did.

Why on earth would anyone want to live out here? No deli, no pizza delivery, no electricity to keep beer cold. Like living in the Dark Ages.

Carl said, "I got Miccosukee blood in me, you know. At least that's what my momma told me. They've got a reservation north of here off Route 41, and even a casino, but I ain't never been to neither. The Miccosukee's on my momma's side. Don't know bout my dad. My momma met him at the lagoon. I hear he didn't hang around after he seen me. Just took off and we never heard from him again."

Jack flicked a glance at Carl's covered right arm. Should he ask about it?

Maybe some other time.

Instead he said, "So there's been people living around this lagoon for generations?"

"Yeah and no," Carl said. "The only people livin there now are the kids of the ones who used to live there. Everybody moved away when we was itty-bitty babies because they thought the lagoon was makin us all strange. But we kids came back."

"Why?"

"Cause I guess we didn't seem to fit no other place."

Jack tried to think of a delicate way to say this. "Because of the way you all looked?"

Carl shrugged. "Some of that, maybe. But mostly because the lagoon seemed right for us. It felt like . . . home."

"You moved out, though."

"Yeah. But not far. That's why I wasn't too excited bout goin back. I'm afraid I might get sucked in again."

"So how many live there?"

"Bout twenty. We're all bout the same age too, give or take a couple years."

Jack ducked as a big bird with an enormous wingspan swooped above them.

"What the hell is that?"

"Just a big ol' heron."

"Oh."

For a moment there Jack had thought it was a pterodactyl. Or maybe a pteranodon. Whatever. The one with the tail.

They began to pass alligators of various sizes sunning themselves on the banks, but none came even close in size to the monster from yesterday.

Jack heard a scraping sound from the bottom of the canoe.

"That's all for the motor for a while," Carl said.

They used their paddles until the channel grew too shallow even for that.

"What do we do now?"

Carl rose and stepped out of the boat. "We carry her till the water gets deeper."

Easy for you to say, Jack thought. You've got boots.

The hauling itself wasn't so bad—only about thirty yards before the water deepened again—but the knowledge that a gator might step out of the surrounding greenery at any second upped Jack's pace until he was fairly dragging Carl behind him.

"Too bad they don't do a *Survivor* down here," Carl said. "*Survivor: Everglades* . . . they'd never let me on, but I know I could win that million."

Another reality show. Carl did like his TV.

Jack looked over his shoulder. "If you did win, what's the first thing you'd do?"

"Get me a new TV." He grinned. "One of them big sixty-inch models. Oh, and a new easy chair, an electric one that massages your back while you're sittin in it. And get my car fixed."

"How about travel?"

"What for? I've already been all over the world watchin *Survivor* and *Celebrity Mole* and the Travel Channel."

"But it's not the same as being there."

Listen to me, Jack thought. The guy who never leaves New York.

"Is for me," Carl said. "Oh, yeah, and I'd probably give some money to Mrs. Hansen. She's havin a hard time. Might lose her trailer."

"That's a nice thought, Carl."

He shrugged. "Just bein neighborly."

Back in the water and putt-putting along again, Jack saw larger plants starting to crowd the saw grass off the banks. Ferns and trees fought for space. Jack spotted a fruit-bearing tree.

"What's that?"

"Pond apple. Don't even think about eatin one less you're partial to the taste of kerosene."

He went on to point out willows that didn't look like willows, live oaks that didn't look like oaks, and trees with exotic names like cocoa plum and Brazilian pepper.

Jack pointed to the tall, scraggly, droopy-needled, cedarlike pines that loomed ahead.

"What are those?"

Carl looked at him as if he'd asked if the sun rose in the east or the west.

"Them's cypresses."

"They look like pines."

"Yeah, I guess they do. But they drop their needles come winter. Pines don't do that."

Jack noticed that the leaves on some of the live oaks were turning red or orange, as if it were fall. The drought, he guessed.

As they glided nearer the cypresses, Jack saw long, gray-brown Merlin beards of moss hanging from the limbs and swaying in the breeze.

He spotted other trees. He knew a Nelson pine when he saw one; royal palms had that distinctive smooth sleeve of green at the upper end of the trunk, and of course coconut palms and banana palms were identifiable by their fruit. But the rest were mysteries.

Carl pointed to a couple of dragonflies, one riding on the back of another.

"Looky there. Makin baby dragonflies."

"And in public," Jack said. "Have they no shame?"

Carl laughed. "Hey, don't knock it. Dragonflies eats up tons of mosquito babies."

"Yeah?" Jack raised a fist in salute. "Go for it, you two!"

Carl shut off the motor.

"What's up?" Jack said. "More shallows?"

Carl shook his head and pointed. "We're getting close now. See that big hardwood hummock dead ahead?"

Jack saw a rise studded with trees of all different sizes and shapes that blocked most of the western horizon.

"The lagoon's in there," Carl said. "So we got to go real quiet now."

"I thought the place was going to be deserted."

"Y'never know. Sometimes somebody's feelin poorly and they don't go to town."

Jack pulled the Glock from its SOB holster, worked the slide to chamber a round, then tucked it away again.

They paddled ahead to where the channel ran into a dense green tunnel of vegetation. Speaking softly, Carl pointed out gumbo limbo trees, aerial plants, orchids, ferns, banyan trees with their dangling aerial roots, coffee plants, vines trailing from tree to tree, and every imaginable variety of palm.

"Looks like a rain forest," Jack whispered.

Carl nodded. "Yeah. Even now, when there ain't no rain. It stays wetter here cause the sun can't get through."

As they paddled around a few more bends in the channel Jack started noticing subtle changes in the greenery, most obvious in the royal palms. Every one Jack had seen till now had had a ramrod-straight trunk. These were bent here and there at odd intervals along their lengths.

Was this the first evidence of the mutation effects of Anya's so-called nexus point?

Then Carl turned to him and put a finger to his lips. He nodded and made a hooking motion with his arm.

Jack got the message: almost there . . . around the next bend.

And then they rounded that bend and the right bank fell away, opening into a wide pond, 150, maybe 200 feet across. The surface lay smooth and placid, but the surrounding vegetation was anything but.

The willows, oaks, cypresses, and palms lining the banks had been twisted into grotesque, unnatural shapes, as if they'd been frozen mid-step in some epileptic ballet. And in one area they all appeared to be leaning away from an opening on the edge of the bank, as if trying to escape it.

That had to be it—the nexus point, where a little of the Otherness slipped through a couple of times a year. Anya hadn't been exaggerating about the mutations. The vegetation looked like it had been designed by someone with PCP for blood.

All we need to make this scene complete, Jack thought, is the Creature from the Black Lagoon rearing its ugly head.

A large, skiff-style boat, *Bull-ship* across its stern, rocked gently against the far bank. Its crude, ramshackle superstructure looked like it had been built by someone with only rudimentary carpentry skills. Another smaller, equally rundown skiff, the *Horse-ship*—cute—lay directly to their right. They looked like floating tenements.

As he and Carl glided toward the center of the lagoon,

Jack searched the banks for stray members of Carl's clan. Just as predicted, the place was deserted.

Well, it *looked* deserted. Somehow it didn't *feel* deserted.

"That's funny," Carl whispered, pointing to a small fleet of canoes beached on the far bank. "All the boats is here. If they went into town—"

"Well, well, well," said a gruff voice from behind and to the right. "Look who's here."

Jack started at the sound and swiveled to see half a dozen men standing on the deck of the *Horse-ship*. As he watched, the snow-haired Semelee emerged from the superstructure and smiled at him.

"Hi, Jack," she said.

Jack noticed the color draining from Carl's face. "Oh, shit!"

Jack faced front again and saw another dozen or so men gathering on the deck of the bigger *Bull-ship*.

"Paddle!" Carl cried as he began yanking on the little motor's starter cord. "We gotta get outta here!"

Jack thought that might not be a bad idea. He reversed his oar stroke to turn the canoe around, but then noticed that the men in the *Horse-ship* were poling it across the lagoon entrance, blocking their escape route.

He laid a hand on Carl's shoulder. "Forget it, Carl. Looks like we're staying awhile."

"Long time, no see, Carl," said the big guy Jack had run into in town. His grin was feral. "I knew you'd be back someday."

"Hey, Luke," Carl said in a faint voice. His shoulders slumped. He looked defeated.

Jack checked the comforting weight of the Glock at the small of his back. Not the right time to reveal what he was carrying, especially when they were such sitting ducks out here on the water. Better to wait and see what happened, wait till these guys got closer, or things got ugly.

Who knew? Maybe he wouldn't need artillery. Maybe he'd even come away with some answers. Like, what do you have against my father? Or, who hired you to kill him?

"Knew I shouldn'ta come," Carl muttered. His good eye veered right and left like a frightened rabbit on the run.

"Easy," Jack whispered. "I promised I'd get you back to your trailer, and I will. Let's just go with the flow here for a bit."

"Don't see's we got much choice."

Luke pointed to the row of canoes on the bank. "Why dontcha beach it over there with the others," he called, "and we'll all get real friendly like."

Jack started paddling. "Let's do like the man says."

Carl hesitated a few heartbeats—he seemed frozen in place—then shook himself and joined in.

5

When they reached the far bank, some of the men from the *Bull-ship* helped pull its nose onto the dirt. Jack recognized the flat-bottomed motorboat he'd seen Semelee ride away in—the *Chicken-ship*. Next to it was a canoe labeled *No-ship*. Someone in the clan was a regular Shecky Green.

He managed to step ashore without resoaking his sneakers, but Carl got out and waded.

They all seemed to know Carl. A few acted genuinely glad to see him but most were standoffish, some even hostile.

As Jack and Carl stood together and waited for the *Horse-ship* to be poled over, Jack looked around. Close up, the vegetation looked even more demented. Back from the banks, maybe a hundred feet, stood half a dozen hutlike structures with open sides. Each seemed to be little more than half a dozen wobbly poles, three to a side, topped by a pitched roof of dried palm fronds. A small fire smoldered between two of the nearest. When they weren't on the boats, Jack guessed they lived there.

Crooked men in crooked houses. He had little doubt that each contained at least one crooked mouse.

"Old Indian huts," Carl said, following his gaze. "Been there forever."

When the smaller boat arrived, Semelee was the first to step off, followed by Luke, bulge-browed Corley, and the rest. Soon the whole clan was assembled behind her, facing Jack and Carl in a semicircle.

Circe and her pigs.

A single woman with—Jack had made a quick count—eighteen men.

One scary looking bunch, Jack thought, eyeing their misshapen heads, mismatched limbs, and twisted bodies. Looked like they'd suffered an algae bloom in their gene pool. But he knew that, just like the trees, it must be due to the nexus point. The trees had no choice about where they grew, but these folks . . . why did they stay?

Only Semelee and Luke looked reasonably normal . . . if you discounted her wild white Medusa hair. Storm from the X-Men had nothing on Semelee in the hair department. She wore the same Levi's and tight black vest as yesterday, but her long-sleeved shirt was red this time, with the top two buttons left open.

"Who's this one?" she said, pointing to Carl. "He's one of us, ain't he."

Luke flashed his nasty grin at Carl. "He sure is. He just don't act like it."

"How come I ain't never seen him before?"

"You probably did but just don't remember. Carl decided to leave right after you showed up. I don't think we're good enough for him no more." He stepped closer. "Ain't that right, Carl? Ain't that right? But that was okay. This ain't no prison. You can come and go as you please." He got into Carl's face. "But that don't mean you can bring outsiders. You know the rule about outsiders."

He reached to grab the front of Carl's shirt and Jack laid a hand on his arm—gently but firmly. He wasn't looking for a fight, not against these impossible odds, but he was not about to let Carl be manhandled.

"Don't," Jack said.

Luke's fingers stopped inches from Carl's shirtfront. "What?"

Jack kept his voice low but gave Luke a hard look, hoping he'd think twice. He didn't have a plan—he'd been expecting an empty lagoon—but he was willing to ad lib, maybe do something quick and very nasty to make a point and throw the crowd off balance.

"Just . . . don't."

Luke glared at him, then glanced toward the water. "Back off or you'll be goin for a swim."

"Doesn't sound so bad to me."

"Yeah?" He grinned. "Look who you'll be swimmin with."

Jack turned and saw what appeared to be a giant turtle gliding toward shore. Its head was down but its mossy, four-foot long shell looked like a relief map of the Himalayas.

Then it raised its head—and then its other head. Christ, it had two—big, ugly, rough-hewn things—both of which were now angled up, their beaked, sharp-edged jaws agape, showing huge mouths that could fit a regulation NFL football with room to spare. Its four beady black eyes were fixed on Semelee as it reached the bank and waited with its long, snakelike tail thrashing back and forth in the water behind it.

Luke grabbed a fallen tree branch and shouted, "Show time!" He stepped closer and lowered the branch toward the waiting jaws. "This here's a alligator snapper. When you take your swim—and we'll see that you do—here's what's gonna happen to your arms and legs."

The branch came to within a foot of the left head and in a flash the neck telescoped out and the jaws chomped, breaking it in half with a loud crunching *crack*, as easily as Jack might snap a toothpick. One of the halves tumbled into the right head's strike zone and suffered a similar fate. Three pieces of branch floated on the water.

Jack's tongue tasted dusty.

" 'When'?" Jack said, knowing this many guys would have no trouble tossing him into the water. But he couldn't back down. "You mean 'if,' don't you?"

Luke stepped toward him. "No, I mean—"

"Just hold on there," Semelee said, wedging herself between them. "Ease up. This ain't no way to treat company." She turned to Jack. Her eyes locked on his, displaying none of the animosity radiating from Luke. "What're you doing here?"

Jack had his reply ready. "You suggested we have a drink together. Well, here I am."

"Bullshit!" Luke said.

This guy had one helluva chip on his shoulder.

Semelee ignored him and smiled. "Yeah. I can see you're here. But I meant back in town."

"I guess I misunderstood. I happened to mention you to Carl and—"

"You did?" Her face lit as her smile broadened. "You were talking about me?"

Jack realized with a start that she was infatuated with him. He couldn't fathom why. She'd had a couple of glimpses of him and they'd exchanged a few sentences; she didn't know anything about him.

Or did she?

Jack debated playing to her infatuation, then discarded the idea. It could backfire too easily, especially with the jealousy he sensed seething in Luke. It was plain that he wanted Semelee looking at him like she was looking at Jack.

"Yeah, sort of," Jack said, keeping it neutral. "When Carl said he knew where you lived, I convinced him to take me there."

"And here you are."

"Right. But I wasn't expecting such an unfriendly reception."

"Oh, don't take Luke too serious. He's been right cranky lately." She patted his arm. "Ain't that right, Luke."

The big guy only glowered at Jack.

"Hey," said Carl, pointing along the bank with his oar. "Don't tell me that's the lights hole!"

"It sure is," Semelee said. "Want to see?"

Lights hole? Jack wondered. What's a lights hole?

Semelee led the way toward a patch of ground completely bare of vegetation. Jack followed Carl. The crowd parted to let them pass. The center of the bald area was pierced by a roughly oval opening, maybe eight feet across. It ran straight down into the limestone like a well. Jack even knew what it was called: a cenote.

He stopped next to Carl at the edge and peered down. Deep. Deeper than he'd expected. He could just barely make out the pool at the bottom.

Carl gasped. "It wasn't never this deep. What happened to the sand?"

Luke grunted. "Semelee sold it. Some guys came here and sucked a whole lot of it out. You just missed them."

"Got a pretty penny for it too," she said.

Carl looked from Luke to Semelee. "Looks like I ain't the first to break the no-outsiders rule."

Score one for you, Carl, Jack thought.

"That was different," Semelee said.

Carl didn't seem to hear. His eyes were fixed on the hole.

"I was a-fearin this," he said, "what with the drought'n all. The lights hole ain't never been above water before. That's bad enough. But then you went'n had sand sucked out."

"Why's that bad?" Semelee said. "I think that's good."

"Good? How can it be good? The light used to have to come up through the sand and the water, and even then, look what it did to us. Now there ain't hardly nothin in the way."

Semelee grinned. "Ain't it cool?"

"Nuh-uh. That ain't cool. That's scary."

Jack knelt at the edge and peered into the depths. He didn't like deep holes, at least not since the spring when he'd had a bad experience with one out on Long Island. But that one hadn't had a bottom. This one . . .

He found a thumb-size stone and dropped it. He heard a satisfying *plop*, saw ripples on the water far below.

. . . this one definitely had a bottom.

But for how long?

"What are these lights like?" he asked.

Semelee squatted close beside him. He glanced up briefly and noticed the others wandering off. The two of them had the hole to themselves.

"Like nothin you ever seen in your life." Her voice was full of hushed wonder as she spoke. "I mean, whoever heard of lights comin outta the ground?"

Jack had seen light shooting up from a hole in the earth . . . just last spring.

"What color are these lights?"

"Sorta like pinkish orange, but that ain't right. Every time you think you got the color pinned, it melts into somethin else just a teeny bit different. I can't describe it. You gotta see it to believe it."

Jack believed. He'd seen a light just like she described.

"How often do they come?" Jack asked, knowing the answer.

"Twice a year."

"No kidding. When's the next show?"

"Tonight."

"But—" Jack caught himself. Anya had said the nexus points opened during the equinoxes, but that wasn't until tomorrow night. He knew; he'd checked. But if he admitted that, Semelee would realize that he knew way more than he should.

She frowned at him. "But what?"

What to say? "But that's too soon!" he blurted. "I won't be able to get my cameras set up for—"

"Who said anything bout cameras?"

"Well, it's obvious, isn't it? I take some pictures of the lights and we sell them to the papers, to National Geographic, to—"

"Wait-wait-wait," she said, waving her hands in front of his face. "What makes you think you're gonna take pictures? Nobody takes no pictures of the lights."

"No exceptions?"

"No way, no how. As a matter of fact, I can't even let you see them, cause then you'd talk about them."

"No, I wouldn't."

Jack had no desire to see these lights, but he didn't want to appear anxious to leave. Maybe the way to get out of here was to pretend to want to stay.

Semelee shook her head. "Maybe you wouldn't, but I can't risk it. Not yet, anyways. But maybe when I get to know you better . . ."

Jack noted how she said "when" instead of "if."

"What's wrong with getting to know each other now? We could go back to town, have that drink, maybe two or three, and do some serious talking."

"Not tonight, or tomorrow or the next night, for that matter."

"Why not?"

"The lights run for three nights. I gotta be here for that. But after Sunday . . ." She leaned closer and he caught her pleasant, musky scent. ". . . . We got all the time in the world."

That's what you think, sister.

But he had to be careful here . . . hell hath no fury and all that.

Then he noticed the black shell dangling from the thong around her neck. The same size and shape as the one he'd found in his father's hospital room. Even had a hole drilled at the hinge end. Had to be the same.

He pointed to the shell. "How'd you get that back?"

Semelee started and clutched the shell. Jack figured from the sudden widening of her eyes that she hadn't wanted him to see it. Because that meant she'd visited the room a second time—and he didn't like that one bit.

But if that were the case, why had she worn it around her neck and left the collar loose?

"What do you mean?" she said.

"I found it by my father's bed in the hospital, right after you were there. When did you go back for it?"

"I . . . I didn't." She kept the shell wrapped in her fist. "I had two."

"Oh." That made Jack feel a little better—if she was telling the truth. "I guess I saw the other one then."

"Where?" She grabbed his wrist. "Where'd you see it last?"

Jack was about to shrug and say he'd left it on the bedside table and assumed the housekeeping staff had chucked it out, but her tight grip on his arm and the intensity in her eyes made him hold off.

"I'm not sure. Let me think . . ."

Why was a damn shell so important?

He glanced around and noticed Carl was missing.

"Carl?" Jack broke Semelee's grip on his arm as he rose to his feet and scanned the lagoon banks. "Hey, Carl! Where are you?"

"Never mind him," Semelee said, rising with him. "What about that shell?"

Jack left her behind. He skirted the edge of the cenote and headed in the direction of the huts where he saw a number of the men sitting around the little fire, smoking, drinking, but Carl wasn't among them.

Shit! Where was he?

He called his name a few more times but got no response. He asked the group by the fire where he was but they ignored him.

Jack's gut began a little crawl. If they'd done anything to Carl it would be Jack's fault for inducing him to come back here.

Luke strolled up to the fire. The men around it looked up, their mismatched eyes questioning, and he nodded to them.

"Where is he, Luke?" Jack said.

Luke didn't look up, didn't turn, didn't acknowledge Jack's existence.

Jack's concern boiled over into anger. He pulled the Glock and sent a round into the fire. The mini-explosion of ash and flaming embers scattered the men, sending them rolling and tumbling. Luke ducked away and faced him.

Now he had their attention.

"I'm going to say it once more, and this time I'd better get an answer: Where . . . is . . . Carl?"

"Right where he belongs," Luke said. "With us."

"He doesn't want to be with you. He left, remember?"

"Maybe. But he's had a change of heart. He's gonna stay."

Jack sensed movement around him. His peripheral vision caught about a dozen clan members scurrying toward him, armed with rifles and shotguns. Should have figured they'd be armed—couldn't live out here and not do some hunting.

The newcomers didn't seem to give Luke much of a boost in confidence, especially when Jack pointed the Glock at the center of his chest. "I want to hear that from him."

Luke's eyes darted left and right. He seemed about to say something when Semelee spoke up.

"Don't worry, Luke. He ain't gonna kill you."

Jack glanced left and saw her standing a few feet away, smiling at him.

"Right, mister," Luke said, licking his lips. "That's because you'll be full of holes if you do."

"That won't make you any less dead."

"You won't," Semelee said to Jack. "I know it, and you know it."

She was right. This wasn't a killing situation. He lowered the pistol a few inches.

"Maybe not. But one of these hollowpoints can mess up a knee like you wouldn't believe."

Luke was sweating now. Taking one in the knee seemed to bother him more than one in the chest.

"Semelee . . . ?"

"You won't do that neither. Because we ain't hurt Carl and we ain't keepin him here but for a few days."

"You've got no right to keep him a minute."

"Yeah, we do," Luke said, emboldened by the fact that Jack hadn't pulled the trigger again. "He's kin. He's blood."

"I promised I'd get him back home. I intend to keep that promise."

"It's only gonna be three days," Semelee said. "We

want him to stay for the lights. But I tell you what: You find my other shell and we'll do a trade . . . the shell for Carl."

"Semelee," Luke said. "You got no right. Carl belongs here."

She turned on him, eyes flashing. "What's more important—givin Carl a light show or gettin my eye-shell back?"

Luke looked away and said nothin.

Semelee turned to Jack. "So that's the deal. How's it set with you?"

"Lady, I don't know where this shell of yours is. If I'd known it was going to matter, I'd have kept track of it."

She pointed to Carl's borrowed canoe. "Maybe you'd better start lookin."

Keeping his pistol trained on Luke, Jack considered his options. He had a few, but didn't like any of them.

He could do a little shooting, but he could see how that could turn counterproductive. He could do his own search for Carl, but he'd be a stranger looking for someone who'd been stashed away by folks who knew every nook and cranny of the terrain. He could head back and take one of these guys with him, then trade him back for Carl; but Jack had no place to stash him.

Or he could go back and find the shell, which was one tall order.

Going back . . . there was another challenge. He wasn't Woodsman Jack. The closest he ever wanted to get to out-door life was a copy of *Field & Stream*.

"I don't know the Everglades," he said. "I'll get lost out there."

Semelee laughed, a musical sound, void of harshness or derision.

"No, you won't. The drought ain't left too many wet

channels. Every time you come to a fork, just take the east-most. It ain't all that far."

"And if I do find this shell, how will I let you know?"

"Easy. Just stand outside you daddy's house and say, 'I found the shell.' I'll hear you."

Jack didn't think she was lying, and that gave him the creeps.

"All right," he said. "I'll go." He hated to leave without Carl, but he'd be back. He also hated leaving without satisfying the reason he'd come here in the first place. "But I want to know something before I go: What have you got against my father?"

Semelee looked away, then back to him. "Nothin."

"Like hell. You folks tried to kill him the other night, and somehow sicced that freaky alligator on him yesterday. Let me ask you: What did he ever do to you?"

"We ain't after him," she said.

Jack caught Luke giving her a sharp look, but she didn't see it.

"Why don't I believe that?" Jack said.

She shrugged. "That's up to you. But I tell you true, your daddy ain't got nothin to fear from us."

"How about me?" Jack said. "What happens when I turn my back on you and your clan?"

"Nothin. You can't find me my shell if you're dead, now, can you." She turned to the clan. "Ain't that right, fellers." They looked at one another but didn't say much. Semelee's expression turned fierce. "Ain't that *right*? Cause I hate to think what would happen to anybody who stopped this man from doin what I need him to do."

Jack saw a lot of uneasy, fearful expressions as the men nodded and lowered their weapons.

What kind of hold did she have on them? What could that slim little woman threaten them with?

Taking a breath and hoping he wasn't making a mistake, Jack holstered the Glock and walked back to the canoe. He stepped into the water, pushed off, and slid in. A couple of pulls got the engine going. He putted away, propelled by the weight of dozens of eyes on his back.

6

"Why'd you let him go?" Luke said.

Semelee stood on the bank and watched Jack's retreating form as he turned the canoe left and disappeared around the bend.

"Told you why."

"You believe him?"

She could hear lots of anger in his voice. She knew he was jealous, but she figgered his pride had got hurt bein on the wrong end of Jack's gun.

"Yeah, I do."

She wasn't sure why, but she had the feeling that he'd thought there was only one shell until she told him otherwise.

"You're actin like a fool, Semelee. We coulda gone lookin for that eye-shell ourselfs."

"Yeah? Like where? Like how? We can't go to the hospital and ask about it when I wasn't supposed to be there in the first place. We can't search his daddy's place like he can."

"We coulda tried. Way it stands now we ain't never gonna see him or your other eye-shell again."

"Oh, we'll see him again . . . one way or the other."

"What's that supposed to mean?"

"Didn't you hear him? He said he promised Carl he'd get him back home. If he finds the shell he'll be back to make the trade. But even if he don't find it he'll be comin for Carl. He'll take him home again or spread a whole lotta hurt tryin."

Luke snorted. "What makes you think you know so much about him? You ain't spoke to him but twice."

She turned to him. "Let me tell you somethin, Luke. That's a man who keeps his promises."

She'd seen that in his eyes. Not a lick of fear, just stubborn as all get out. And that made him all the more special. Brave and loyal, two traits any woman wanted in a man. But Jack wasn't just any woman's man. He was destined to be hers.

The way things was fallin into place . . . it was like it was all part of a plan. His daddy gets chosen to die, but he don't. He lives and that brings Jack down here where he and Semelee can meet and be together. She lost an eye-shell, but now Jack was gonna find it, and that was gonna bring them even closer together.

"What do you need that other eye-shell so bad for anyway?" Luke said. "You been doin all right with just the one."

"No, I ain't. Ain't the same. Much harder to keep control and see where I'm goin. I need the two of them."

"Awright awright. But you was kiddin bout layin off his daddy, right?"

"Wrong. We ain't interested in his daddy no more."

"But Seme—"

"We got us a new target."

She didn't know how, but Jack had somehow connected her and the clan to what had happened to his daddy. If his daddy got killed, he'd blame her, and that might keep them apart and wreck their destiny. No, she had a better victim, someone who *needed* killin.

Luke was starin at her. "Who?"

"The old lady. She'll be takin daddy's place."

7

How was he going to find that damn shell?

The question plagued Jack as he drove toward Novaton.

Semelee had been right: It hadn't been all that hard to find his way back to the real world. He'd left the canoe beached by the air-boat dock and headed toward town. The clouds persisted but hadn't dumped drop one of rain.

Where to start? The hospital was the obvious place, but Dad had checked himself out almost twenty-four hours ago. Jack was sure the room had been stripped and scrubbed by now. Probably even had a new occupant. That meant he might have to go pawing through the hospital's Dumpsters.

He shook his head. Maybe if he had half a dozen people helping him they might—just *might*—come up with that shell. He doubted it.

He decided that before he gave the hospital another thought, he'd check out his dad's place. Maybe by some freaky turn of good luck the shell had wound up there. But again, the chances—

If nothing else, he could get out of these sodden sneakers.

He'd stopped at a red light. A dump truck was turning in front of him, going the opposite way. He wouldn't have given it a second thought except for the insignia on the door of the cab. It looked like a black sun . . . a shape that might be mistaken for the head of a black flower.

Jack would have hung a U right there if he'd been in the left lane. Instead he had to cut through two parking lots to turn himself around. By the time he was heading north, the truck was out of sight. Racing along as best he could in the Friday afternoon traffic, trying to catch up, he almost missed the truck parked in a Burger King lot.

Jack pulled in next to it and got out. It had been backed diagonally across two spaces at the rear of the lot where it was out of the way. The cab was empty but the big diesel engine was running. He checked out the logo—definitely a black sun. And beneath it: *Wm. Blagden & Sons, Inc.*

He walked around it. It sure as hell looked big enough to inflict heavy damage on any car, even a Grand Marquis. He wondered what the left end of the front bumper looked like.

Jack stopped and stared at the dent in the fender . . . and the streaks of silver paint ground into its black surface.

"Can I help you with something?" said a voice behind him.

Jack turned to find a prototypical truck driver—big cowboy hat, big gut, big belt buckle, big boots—walking his way with a bag of burgers in one hand and a travel mug of coffee in the other.

"Yeah," Jack said. "Just admiring the ding in your fender here." A euphemism; the "ding" was a deep dent. "Looks pretty fresh."

"It is. Best I can figure it must've happened Monday night when the truck was stolen."

"Stolen? No kidding? By who?"

The driver unlocked the door to the cab, put the burgers and coffee inside, then shrugged.

"Damned if I know." He rubbed his weather-beaten face. "Never happened to me before. After she got the first part of her load Monday evening, I locked her up and hit the hay. I got up the next morning and she was gone. Couple hours after I reported her missing the cops found her in a liquor store parking lot. I was so glad to get her back—I mean, you don't know what kind of shit was gonna come down on me if she was gone for good—that I didn't notice the ding till later."

"You report it to the cops?"

"No. Why?"

"Because your rig might have been involved in a hit and run."

His eyes narrowed. "You a cop or something?"

"Nope. Just an interested party." He saw the questioning look on the trucker's face. "My dad's car took a wallop early Tuesday morning."

"He okay?"

"Luckily, yeah."

"Good." He hauled himself into the cab. "Because I can't hang around for no investigation. I ain't running or nothing, but I got a schedule to keep."

"I hear you," Jack said.

He thought about stopping him but decided against it. If his story was true—and Jack sensed it was—what good would it do? If he hadn't reported his truck stolen, Jack could call Hernandez and the Novaton cops would pick him up.

Of course, the reported theft could have been a cover, but Jack doubted that.

As the cab door slammed shut, Jack said, "What're you hauling?"

"Sand."

"Where to?"

"North Jersey."

Jersey? Jersey was loaded with sand.

"What the hell for?"

The driver shrugged. "I don't set up the jobs or choose the loads; I just get it where it wants to go."

Then Jack remembered Luke saying something about Semelee sucking all the sand out of the cenote and selling it. Could this be . . . ?

"Where'd you get the sand?"

Another shrug. "It got boated in from somewheres in the swamp. That's all I know."

With that he threw the truck into first and headed for the exit.

Jack watched him go. He made a mental note of the company name. Wm. Blagden & Sons. He might look them up when he got back north, maybe find out who'd hired them. Shipping sand from a Florida nexus point to New Jersey . . . he couldn't imagine the reason, but it couldn't be good.

He started back toward his car. At least now he knew what had hit his father's Marquis. And he had a pretty good idea who had been driving it.

But he still didn't know why. Had a pretty good idea about that too, and hoped to nail that down this afternoon.

8

By the time Jack reached Gateways South he'd stopped at a local hardware store for a roll of duct tape, then called the Novaton Police where he reached Anita Nesbitt. After a quick check she told him that, yes, on Tuesday morning a dump truck had been reported stolen during the night and was found shortly thereafter.

Okay. So Wm. Blagden & Sons, Inc., was covered.

Jack parked in the cul-de-sac and hurried into his father's place.

His father was watching TV. Classic ESPN was running the 1980 Wimbledon slugfest between Borg and McEnroe.

McEnroe was screaming at himself for missing a bullet passing shot.

He looked up at Jack and grinned. "Right about now I bet McEnroe wishes Borg had never been Bjorn."

Normally Jack would have groaned, but a bad pun was a good sign. His father loved puns. He was getting back to normal.

He looked down at Jack's muddy sneakers and still-wet jeans. "What happened to you?"

"Took a little boat trip."

"You went boating? Why didn't you tell me? I would have—"

"It wasn't exactly a pleasure trip. Look, Dad, do you remember seeing a little black shell in your hospital room?"

He frowned. "No. When would this have been?"

"I found it the day before you woke up. It was black, oblong, had a little hole drilled in the hinge."

Please remember. *Please . . .*

Dad was shaking his head. "Sorry. Never saw anything like that."

Jack suppressed a groan. He'd have to try the hospital next.

Hospital . . . Jack remembered the plastic bag of sundries that Anya had thrown together as his father was signing himself out. He knew it wasn't in his car. Had he brought it in?

"Did you see a bag of goodies from the hospital? You know, toothpaste, mouthwash—"

"Oh, that. I threw it out."

"You didn't see a shell in there?"

"I didn't really look. I mean, I glanced inside but I don't use any of those brands so I tossed it out."

Maybe . . . maybe . . . Jack didn't want to get his hopes up.

"Where? In the kitchen?"

"Well, yes, at first. But this morning I tossed the kitchen bag into the can out back. Look, what's so important—?"

Jack didn't wait for him to finish. He dashed outside and around to the back porch. The green plastic garbage can sat to the left on a small concrete slab. Just his luck, Friday would be garbage pickup day and the shell—if it was in there—was on its way to the county dump.

But no. The can was empty except for one white plastic bag. Jack untied the top and poked around until he found the bag from the hospital. He yanked it out and pawed through the sample-size toiletries. He sent out a silent prayer to the patron saint of garbage that he'd find the shell within, but it wasn't looking good . . .

And then he reached the bottom and felt something hard and rough edged. He pulled it out—

"Yes!"

He had it. Now Carl could come home. But first Jack had to arrange an exchange. He shook his head. A shell for a human being . . . what kind of a deal was that?

What had Semelee told him to do? Stand outside his father's house and announce that he'd found it. Riiiight. But she'd said she'd hear him, and she probably could. Jack's Doubting Thomas days were over. Anything goes.

"Okay," he said aloud, feeling foolish but forcing himself to go on. "I've found the shell. Did you catch that? I've found it. Tell me how we make the trade."

Now what? He supposed he'd have to wait until Semelee got in touch with him.

Pocketing the shell, he turned and found Dad staring at him through the back porch jalousies. He wore the same perplexed expression as when Jack had unpacked those stuffed animals from Abe. Maybe more perplexed this time.

Probably thinks I'm doing drugs.

"Hi, Dad."

"Are you okay, Jack?"

No, he thought. I'm not. Someday I'd like to be, but at the moment . . .

"I'm fine."

His father pushed open the porch door. "Come back in this way. It's shorter."

Jack took a step toward the porch, then remembered again that it was Anya who'd packed up the bag. Had she known . . . ?

He glanced toward her place and noticed a figure stretched out on a lounge in the front yard.

"Be with you in a minute," he said. "I want to say hello to Anya."

As Jack crossed onto the green grass, Oyv trotted up to meet him, wagging his tail in welcome. The dog escorted him toward Anya, but Jack slowed, letting Oyv pull ahead as he noticed that Anya was topless.

She lay face down on a towel on the lounge cushion, dressed only in lime-colored Bermuda shorts, baking her bare back in the afternoon sun. He was about to turn away when he noticed a pattern of red marks on her exposed skin. He took a step closer and . . .

Jack bit his upper lip. They looked like burn marks . . . and crisscrossing her skin between them were thin, angry red lines, as if someone had been stubbing out cigarettes on her back and then whipping her with a fine lash.

Jack wanted to turn away, but couldn't. He had to stay and stare, horrified, yet fascinated.

Anya's voice startled him.

"A map of my pain," she said without looking up. "See what he does to me?"

"Who?"

"You know. The Adversary. The One."

Oh, yeah. The One . . . whose True Name Jack wasn't supposed to know.

"But how? Why?"

"I've told you the why: Because I hinder his path. As to the how . . . he has many ways, and they are all written here, on my back."

"But how do those burns, those cuts get there?"

"They simply appear. They map his efforts to destroy me."

Jack shook his head to clear it. "I'm not following. *What* is he doing to destroy you?"

"Help me with this towel," she said. "Fold the ends over my back."

Jack did as she asked, allowing her to wrap the towel around her upper torso as she rose to a sitting position.

"Talk to me," Jack said.

Anya shook her gray head. "You have your own concerns. Those you should be worrying about. And besides, what can you do to help? Nothing. This I must face on my own."

"Try me."

He liked this old lady. He wanted to help her, do something to lighten her load.

"It's all right, Jack. The sun makes it feel better. The rays don't heal me, but they lessen the pain." She rose to her feet. "I'm going in to lie down."

"Are you okay?"

"I'm better than I was this morning and I'll be even better by tonight."

"Will you be up for drinks later? We'll do it at my father's place this time."

She shook her head. "Not tonight. But tomorrow definitely."

Jack watched her and Oyv enter the leafy interior of her house, then, feeling sad and angry and helpless, he turned away.

9

Jack had lounged around with his father, dodging questions about the toys and the shell until his father nodded off in his recliner. An afternoon nap—one of the great pleasures in life. But Jack couldn't indulge today. He had to wait for word from Semelee.

But that wasn't the only matter on his afternoon schedule.

He stepped into his father's bedroom and dialed Ramsey Weldon's office. He learned from the receptionist that Mr. Weldon was on another line. Would he care to leave a message?

"No. When can I call back?"

"Well, he'll probably be leaving in a half hour or so."

Jack thanked her, hung up, then went out to his car.

The duct tape he'd bought earlier sat on the front seat in a flimsy white plastic bag emblazoned with the Novaton Hardware logo. He snatched it up, bag and all. As he was closing the door he spotted an envelope on the floor by the passenger seat. He picked it up and checked the contents.

Carl's five hundred dollars.

He'd trusted Jack enough to leave it in the car for safe-keeping. He'd also trusted Jack to bring him back.

"I've got your damn shell," Jack said aloud. "I'm ready to trade."

He glanced at his watch. Couldn't wait around here any longer. He set off on a stroll toward the administration building.

This time he could walk in the open and say hello to

passers-by instead of ducking into the bushes every time someone approached. When he reached the parking lot, his heart gave a kick when he didn't see Weldon's Crown Imperial, but eased back when he spotted a '57 DeSoto in Weldon's space. This guy had some neat cars.

Jack strolled over to it. A four-door Firedome with a glossy turquoise body, white roof and side panels, big chrome bumpers, white-wall tires, and those fins— humongous wedge-shaped projections, each fitted with a vertical row of three rocketlike red lights that made the car look like a spaceship. Jack peered inside. White-and-turquoise upholstery and a dash-mounted rearview mirror.

What was wrong with Detroit—or Japan or Germany, for that matter? Why the hell didn't they make cars like this anymore?

He hung around the DeSoto, studying it from every angle for what seemed like forever before Weldon showed up. He wore a pale beige silk suit today, so pale it was almost white.

"Another beauty, Mr. Weldon," he said.

Weldon grinned. "Tom's son, right? Jack?"

"You've got a good memory."

"And you've got excellent taste in cars. How's your father?"

"Doing great. He came home yesterday."

Weldon's cheek twitched. "Really? I had no idea. Why didn't anyone tell me?"

"I don't think anyone else knows." Jack ran his fingers lightly along the DeSoto's right front fender. "Say, would you mind giving me a little ride in this baby?"

Weldon shook his head. "I'd love to, but I've got to get straight home."

Jack opened the door and slipped into the passenger seat. "That's okay. Just drive me to the front gate and I'll walk back. I need the exercise."

Weldon didn't look happy about it, but Jack hadn't left him much choice.

The interior was like a furnace. Jack cranked down his window as Weldon fired her up and backed out of his space.

"Smooth ride," Jack said once they were rolling.

"Torsion-Air suspension."

Jack watched him closely as he asked the next question. "You ever hear of a woman named Semelee?"

Weldon's hands tightened on the steering wheel, whitening the knuckles. His right cheek twitched as it had before.

"No, can't say as I have. Is she one of our residents?"

"Nope. Too young for Gateways. Lives out in the Glades with a bunch of funny looking guys. She's got this snow white hair. You'd remember her if you ever met her. You *sure* you don't know her?"

Weldon looked ready to jump out of his skin and his forehead was beaded with sweat. It was hot in the car, but not that hot.

"Quite sure," he said.

"You're sure you're sure?"

"Yes! How many times do I have to tell you that?" He began to brake. "Well, here's the gate. I hope you enjoyed—"

"Keep driving."

"I told you. I have to—"

Jack pulled out the Glock and held it in his lap, pointed in the general direction of Weldon's gut.

"You'll be in a world of gut-shot hurt if this happens to go off. Think *Reservoir Dogs*. So keep driving. We haven't finished our chat. Smile and wave to the nice guard. That's right. Now . . . let's head out to where my father had his accident."

"Where's that?" Now Weldon was really sweating.

"You don't know? Pemberton and South Road."

"But there's nothing out there."

"I know."

"This is illegal, this is carjacking, it's kidnapping, it's—"

"It's happening. Relax. Don't fight it and we'll have a nice ride."

"If you want the car, take it."

"I don't want the car."

"Then . . . then why are you doing this?"

Jack let him stew in his juices for a while before responding.

"Just wanted to ask you what you know about people who've been dying at Gateways South." Weldon opened his mouth to reply but Jack held up a hand to stop him. "I don't want to hear any bullshit about them being elderly and what can you expect. I'm talking about three spouseless people in excellent health—your own doctor said so—who've suffered death by mishap over the past nine months. At a rate of one every three months. I'm sure you know their names: Adele Borger, Joseph Leo, and Edward Neusner."

Weldon had turned pale. He looked as if he might be getting sick.

"Of course I know their names. Those were terrible tragedies."

"My father would have made number four, and right on schedule. Know anything about that, Mr. Weldon?"

"No, of course not. How could I?"

That did it. Jack looked around, saw no other cars in sight. This was as good a place as any.

He made Weldon pull over, then he got out and made him slide to the passenger side—easy with the bench seat.

"Now, put your hands behind your back."

"W-w-what are you going to do?"

"I'm g-g-gonna tape your wrists together."

"No!"

Jack grabbed a handful of Weldon's longish dark hair. "Look. We can do this the easy way—which is you doing what I tell you—or the hard way, which means I have to shoot you in the hip or through the thigh or something equally messy and bloody and keep on doing that until you cooperate. Me, I don't like getting splattered with blood. The stains are almost impossible to get out. So I prefer neat and easy to messy and bloody. How about you?"

Weldon sobbed and put his hands behind his back.

Jack duct taped his wrists together, then his knees, then his ankles. That done, he took over the driver seat and put the DeSoto back in motion. He pointed it toward town and kept hammering at Weldon about the three dead folks, his father, and Semelee. Weldon kept stonewalling him. Finally Jack pulled up before the locked gates to the limestone quarry.

"So," he said. "You don't know nuttin' 'bout nuttin', is that it?"

"Please. I don't. Really. You've got to believe me."

Jack didn't.

"This is going to hurt me almost as much as it hurts you."

With that he gunned the DeSoto and rammed it against the gates. Weldon cried out as the chain snapped and the gates flew back.

"The bumpers! The chrome!"

Jack turned the car left onto the steep grade of the narrow road that ran down into the pit. A rough limestone wall loomed to his left. He didn't want to do it—he hated himself for doing it—but forced his hands to turn the steering wheel and drag the left side of the car against the stone.

"My God, no!" Weldon cried.

"Sorry." And he was.

As they reached the bottom of the quarry Jack didn't quite make the turn, ramming the front end into an outcropping of stone. The impact stopped the car short, hurling Weldon off the seat and into the dashboard. Without a seat belt or his hands to protect him, he hit hard, then flopped back against the seat.

"Whoa," Jack said. "That must have hurt. But probably just a fraction of what my father felt when that truck clocked his car out on South Road." He looked around. "Let's see. We've remodeled the left side, let's see what we can do with the right."

Between getting a taste of what his dad had gone through that night and realizing what he was doing to this beautiful, classic, innocent car, Jack was having trouble keeping his tone light.

"No, please!" Weldon screamed.

Jack accelerated and rammed the right front end against another outcropping. Once again Weldon went flying forward, this time hard enough to catch his chest on the dashboard and his head against the windshield. He wound up on the floor instead of the seat.

Weldon was sobbing now. "Okay, okay. I'll tell you about it, but you're not going to believe it."

"Try me." Jack threw the on-the-column automatic shift into neutral and set the emergency brake. "You'd be amazed at what I can believe."

Weldon struggled back into his seat. A blue-black goose egg was swelling under the hair that hung over on his forehead. He held his back-tied hands toward Jack.

"Please?"

Jack pulled out his Spyderco folder and slit the tape. He left the knife open and in hand.

"Don't get any ideas. Now talk."

Weldon sagged back. His neck bowed against the top of the backrest as he looked at the ceiling.

"It was just about this time last year that the white-haired woman you mentioned, Semelee, called me with this crazy story, a demand that Gateways make sacrifices to the Everglades. Figuring this was some clumsy sort of local shakedown I asked her what kind of sacrifices. She said . . . human."

He glanced at Jack. If he was expecting to see shock or incredulity, he was disappointed. Jack had half expected something like this.

"And you laughed her off."

"Of course. Wouldn't you? It was ridiculous. Or so I thought then. But she wouldn't quit. She kept calling me, at the office, at home, on my cell phone, going on about how Gateways South had encroached too near the 'lagoon'—I still don't know what lagoon she was talking about—and that the Everglades was angry and demanded sacrificial victims. Four a year. Ridiculous, right? But she kept after me, saying that I, as head of Gateways, must make the offering. By that she meant, choose the victim. All I had to do was point out a resident and the lagoon would do the rest. If I didn't, the lagoon would choose one for me—from my own family."

"And so you caved."

"No. At least not yet. As soon as she threatened my family, I went to the police. Since I had only a voice on the phone, and couldn't tell them what she looked like or where she lived, all they could do was keep an eye out for her and do regular patrols past my house."

"And I take it that didn't work."

Weldon shook his head. "That same night, my son was bitten by a brown recluse spider and had to be rushed to the hospital—he was only three and almost lost his arm. And right there, in Kevin's hospital room, the woman calls me on my cell phone and says this was just a warning. Had I changed my mind? I hung up but she called right back and asked me if my daughter was afraid of snakes. And if not, she should be." Weldon rubbed a hand over his face. "I've got to tell you, that spooked me. I don't know how she knew about the spider bite, I don't know how she got a brown recluse close enough to my son to bite him, but I was really spooked."

Jack couldn't blame him. He knew how he'd felt when Vicky had been threatened.

"Did you go back to the cops?"

"What for? I couldn't tell them any more then than before. So I took matters into my own hands. I packed up my wife and both kids and sent them to stay with my in-laws in Woodstock, right outside Atlanta. I figured putting them hundreds of miles away in a different town, a different state, would keep them safe." He shook his head. "The very first day there Laurie was bitten by a copperhead and almost died. After spending a week up north, waiting for Laurie to be released from the hospital, I finally returned home—alone, because I couldn't bear the thought of bringing them back here until I'd dealt with this woman."

"Obviously you didn't succeed."

"Not for lack of trying. When I got home I found this young woman with white hair waiting in my backyard. She was sitting with her back to me, holding her hands up to her face, and in an instant I knew who she was. I grabbed the revolver I keep in the top of our bedroom closet and went out to her. I was going to shoot her, so help me, I was, but as soon as I raised the pistol I was attacked by a swarm of bees and—"

"Killer bees?"

Weldon nodded. "Only they didn't sting me enough to kill me. They concentrated on my face and my gun hand and didn't let up until I'd dropped it. Then she turned and I saw her face for the first time. I was surprised that she was so young. From her white hair I'd assumed she'd be some old witch, but she was young and—"

"Not bad looking. I know."

"You've met her then. How did you—?"

"Let's stick to you. What did you do then?"

"What could I do? She told me I already had two strikes against me. I still remember her words: 'Strike three and your wife is out.' What else could I do? Tell me you would have done any different."

"My approach to settling problems differs a bit from the average."

"I don't know how, but this woman somehow controls snakes, insects, birds, and who knows what else? Don't you see the position I was in?"

Jack stared at Weldon. No question, the guy had been thrust into an appalling situation: Finger a relative stranger for death or lose a family member. A no-brainer, but also a no-win.

"I see that a man has to put his family before strangers, which is regrettably acceptable. But when one of those strangers is my father, we have a problem." Jack jabbed the knife blade at Weldon's face, stopping the point an inch from his nose. "We have even more of a problem when it becomes clear that you took an awful predicament and used it to turn a quick buck."

"I did no such thing!"

Weldon cowered back, pressing himself against the door as the knife point touched the tip of his nose.

"Now's not the time for lies, bozo." Jack was doing his best to check his flaring rage. "I could go along with you doing what you had to if you'd picked out the sickest Gateways folks, the ones with the shortest life expectancy. But you didn't do that. Instead you picked ones who were not only the healthiest, but were unattached, guaranteeing that their homes would go back on the market years, maybe even a decade or two before their natural time."

"No!"

"Yes!" The word hissed through Jack's teeth. "Yes, you son of a bitch! You fingered people whose deaths would turn you a profit! And one of them was my father!"

Weldon's face crumpled. His eyes squeezed shut and he began to sob.

"I'm sorry, I'm sorry . . ."

"Three innocent people are dead and my father was put in a coma, and that's all you can say?" He wanted to drop the knife and throttle him. "Get out!"

Weldon looked at him. "What?"

"Get out, you pathetic bastard. Out before I cut you."

Weldon fumbled behind him for the latch. As the door swung open, Jack raised his right leg and kicked him. Hard.

"Out!"

Weldon fell out the door and landed on his back in the limestone powder and rubble. Without bothering to close the door, Jack threw the DeSoto into gear and hit the gas. He gunned the car into a tire-spinning turn, then raced back toward where Weldon was staggering to his feet. He let him scramble out of the way. Despite Jack's dark urge to maim, maybe even kill the man, Weldon wasn't worth the hassle.

He tore up the steep roadway out of the pit and onto the street. He knew Weldon wouldn't be going to the police about this; he'd fear it would draw a loot of unwanted attention to the deaths at Gateways. Let him find his own way home.

As he passed the trailer park he pulled in. An impulse. He spotted Carl's junker parked by a mildewed trailer. He got out and checked the door. Locked. He lifted the lid of a garbage can by the steps and found takeout containers—

KFC, Chinese, Domino's. He pulled out his wallet as he
scoped the area. No one about so he slipped the door latch
with his MasterCard. Inside he closed the door behind him
and looked around. He wasn't sure why he was here. Just
an urge to know a little more about Carl.

The air conditioner was off and the trailer smelled
faintly of old food and sweat. The kitchen, bathroom, and
bedroom lay to the left, the main room to the right. He noticed the disassembled remnants of Big Mouth Billy Bass,
the singing fish, on the kitchen counter, neatly stored in a
little box. Jack was struck by how clean the place was. Carl
had said he loved his little trailer, and it showed.

In the main room sat a good-size TV. It looked like at
least a twenty-seven-incher—pan-o-ramic, one might say.
A battered Naugahyde recliner sat before it. The thick Direct TV program guide for September lay open on the seat,
marked up with a yellow pen. Jack picked it up and saw
that Carl had highlighted *Survivor*, *Fear Factor*, *Boot
Camp*, *Big Brother* . . . secondhand living.

But that seemed good enough for Carl.

Jack shrugged. Whatever gets you through the night . . .

But nowhere in the trailer was there a sign of who Carl
was. No family pictures, no sign that he had a past. Maybe
his past wasn't anything he wanted to remember.

Jack stepped out, locked the door, and drove back toward Gateways. He turned off the road and parked in the
trees next to the security fence. He noticed other tire tracks
nearby. After wiping down the steering wheel, gearshift,
door and window handles, he stepped up on the hood and
went over the fence.

Easy. Too easy. Semelee's clan could do the same with
their pickup.

Semelee . . . As he walked back to his father's house he
ran the Semelee situation back and forth and sideways
through his head, looking for a solution.

He agreed with Weldon on one point: Semelee seemed to be able to control the swamp creatures. How, Jack didn't know, but he'd bet it had something to do with the nexus point at the lagoon. She'd used that power to commit perfect murders—"sacrifices," as she'd put it to Weldon—in plain view without anyone suspecting that a human agent lay behind the attacks. No question in Jack's mind that she was behind the palmetto swarm and the alligator attack as well.

She had to be stopped, that much was clear. He had no idea how, but he'd worry about that later. The first thing he had to do was put Carl back in his trailer . . . his home.

10

"There you are," Dad said as Jack stepped through the door. He'd obviously awakened from his nap. Looked like he'd showered and shaved too. "Where have you been?"

"Here and there. Did anyone call or come by while I was out?"

He shook his head. "No. All quiet. You're expecting someone?"

Jack hid his frustration. "Yeah. Sort of."

"Well, I need to do some grocery shopping. How about driving me down to the Publix so I can stock up?"

"How about I give you the keys and stay here? In case that call comes, or someone shows up."

"Are you in some sort of trouble, Jack? Because if you are, maybe I can help."

Jack laughed and hoped it didn't sound as forced as it

felt. "Trouble? No, not me. But someone I know might be in a little."

"What kind?"

Jack knew he'd been acting strange—at least in his father's eyes—but he wasn't used to all these questions, or having his comings and goings noted and commented on.

This is why I live alone.

"You might say it's a kind of family thing."

"Do those toys have anything to do with it?"

"It might come down to that."

Dad sighed and dropped into his recliner. "You are the hardest person to talk to, Jack. You were a great kid, but now you're a stranger. It's like you don't want to know me or me to know you. You've got this wall around you. Is that my fault? Did I do something . . . ?"

This was painful. Jack could see the hurt in his father's troubled eyes.

"Absolutely not. It's me. It's just the way I am."

"But it's not the way you were."

Jack shrugged. "People change. You must know that."

"No. I don't. Most people don't change. Kate didn't change. And Tom didn't—although it might not be such a bad thing if he had. But you—you're a completely different person."

Jack could only shrug again. He wanted off this uncomfortable topic.

"Enough about me. How about you, Dad? How are you getting on down here?"

His father gave him a long, baffled stare, then shook his head.

"Me? I guess I'm doing pretty well. I like the climate enough, but . . ."

"But?"

"I don't know. Sometimes I think I made a mistake moving down here. Sometimes I wonder why I ever left Jersey."

"I'd wondered the same thing. So did Kate."

"I've never been the impulsive sort, but this was an impulse. A Gateways South brochure came in the mail one day and that was it. I took one look and had to be here. The graduated care aspect and the idea of never being a burden appealed to me . . . appealed to me so much it became an obsession that took hold and wouldn't let go. I couldn't get it out of my head that this was the place for me. I sold the old house and reinvested some of the money in this place and . . ." He spread his hands. "Here I am."

"From what Anya told me while you were in your coma, it sounds as if you've gotten into the swing of things down here."

"I have. I've had to. I had it in my head that Kate and Tom would jump at the chance to gather up the grandkids and come down to Florida to visit. But only Kate did that. And only once. Everyone's so busy these days. So I made a choice: I can sit before the TV and ossify, or get up and about and do things while I still can. I figure I'd rather be a moving target than a stationary one."

Target, Jack thought. Helluva word choice, Dad. If you only knew . . .

Dad was shaking his head. "But as nice as it is, I still can't believe I sold the family home and left my kids and grandkids up north to move down here. I know not being a burden was a big part of it, but really . . . what was I thinking?"

Something in the words sent a chill through Jack. His father had done something he didn't quite understand . . . developed a compulsion to move down here, to this particular development, right outside the Everglades, close to the lagoon where Semelee and her clan lived . . .

. . . close to a nexus point.

Hadn't Carl told him that he'd developed a yearning—

an "ache," as he put it—to get back to the place where he'd
been born, back to the lagoon . . . ?

Back to that same nexus point.

Coincidence?

He'd been told there'd be no more coincidences in his
life.

Was someone or some *thing* moving pieces around the
board—Jack's board?

But wait . . . Anya had said she'd done part time work
addressing brochures. Had she sent one to his father? Had
she influenced him to come down here? So she could—
what?—protect him?

Jack's head spun. One thing he knew was he wanted his
father out of here, out of Gateways, out of the whole damn
state.

"Nothing says you can't go back. In fact, I think you
should. I'm sure Jersey's got a load of graduated care
places, if that's what you want."

Dad stood silent a moment, then, "I don't know. I'd feel
like an old fool."

"Which is more foolish: admitting you made a mistake
and rectifying it, or hanging around a place you don't
like?"

"When you put it that way . . ." He shook his head. "I'll
have to think about it." He clapped his hands. "But no matter what I decide, we have to eat tonight. I'll run out and
get eggs and cheese and some ham. I make a mean omelet.
How's that sound for dinner?"

"Perfect."

With a pang of reluctance, Jack gave him the keys to his
rental. He had an urge to go with him, to not let him out on
his own unprotected, but Semelee had said he wasn't a target, and he believed her. She'd had Jack at her mercy—
outnumbered and outgunned—when she'd said it, so she'd
had no reason to lie.

11

As soon as he was alone, Jack pulled out the toys. He inspected them for repaired seams, found one on each, and slit it open. He removed the sundry weapons Abe had sent him and, armed with a screwdriver and an adjustable wrench, hid them around the house.

Then he called Gia. She and Vicky and the baby were doing fine.

"When are you coming home, Jack?" Vicky asked. "I miss you."

"I miss you too, Vicks, and I'll be home as soon as I can. As soon as I know my dad's okay."

He seemed okay now, but it would take a little doing to make sure he stayed that way.

Still no word from the clan. Jack stepped outside and looked around. The sun lay low over the Everglades, brushing the fringe of the far-off hardwood hummock. He wondered if that was the same hummock that housed the lagoon and his nexus point. If so, he might see these mysterious lights tonight.

"I've got your damn shell!" he shouted into the fading light. "Let's do this!"

Then he waited, not really expecting anything, but hoping. After a moment of listening to frogs and crickets, he turned to go back inside. He noticed a light on at Anya's. Maybe she'd like to come over for dinner.

His knocks went unanswered, even by Oyv, so Jack stepped around to the side window. There he saw her and

Oyv sleeping in front of the TV, in the same positions they'd been in Wednesday night. Again, they looked dead. But he kept watching until he caught Anya taking a breath.

He was halfway back to the house when he saw his rental car pull into the parking area. He angled that way and arrived in time to carry a couple of the grocery sacks.

"I picked up some scallions," Dad said as they were unpacking. "I figured that would add a little extra flavor."

"You've become a regular Chef Boyardee."

"Had to learn *some* cooking. When you live alone, you can get awful tired of frozen dinners and fast food. And it gives me something to do at night." He looked at Jack. "Nights are always the hardest."

Jack wasn't sure what to say. He wanted to tell him he was sorry about that but sensed his father wasn't looking for pity. He'd merely been stating a fact.

So Jack ducked it. "Hey, want me to slice those scallions?"

"Sure," Dad said with a grin. "Think you can slice them nice and fine?"

He washed them off, then handed Jack a slim knife and a cutting board. Jack positioned himself on the other side of the counter and began slicing.

"Hey," Dad said. "You're pretty handy with that blade."

"I'm a super sous chef." He'd picked up a lot from helping Gia cook.

"While you're doing that, I'll open this bottle of Chardonnay I've had in the fridge. Been saving it for a special occasion."

"Omelets are a special occasion?"

"Company is a special occasion, especially when it's one of my sons."

Jack realized then with a pang how lonely his father was.

"Can I ask you something, Dad?"

"Sure." He'd pulled a pale bottle from the refrigerator and was twisting a corkscrew into its top. "Go ahead."

"Why didn't you ever remarry?"

"Good question. Kate always asked me that, always encouraged me to get into a new relationship. But . . ." He grabbed two glasses and half filled them. "There's more where this came from, by the way."

Jack got the feeling he was trying to stall, or maybe even evade an answer. He wasn't going to let that happen.

"You were saying about not remarrying?"

He sighed. "Having your mother taken away like that—one moment she's sitting next to me in the car, next moment there's blood all over her and no one can save her. She's . . . gone. You were there. You knew what it was like."

Jack nodded. His knife picked up speed, slicing the scallions faster, harder, thinner.

Dad shook his head. "I never got over it. Your mother was special, Jack. We were a team. We did everything together. The bond was more than love, it was . . ." He shook his head. "I don't know how to describe it. 'Soul mate' is such a hackneyed term, but that pretty well describes what she was to me."

He pulled a carving knife from a drawer and started dicing the thick slice of cured ham he'd bought.

"And let me tell you, Jack, the grief over losing someone that close to you, it doesn't just go away, you know. At least it didn't for me. Something like that happens and people pepper you with all sorts of platitudes—it got to the point where I wanted to punch out the next person who said, 'She's in a better place.' I almost committed murder on that one. Then there was, 'At least you had her for a little while.' I didn't want her for a little while. I wanted her forever."

Jack was moved by the depth of his feeling. This was a side his father kept hidden.

"If I can use an equally hackneyed phrase: She wouldn't have wanted you to spend the rest of your life alone."

"I haven't been completely alone. I've allowed myself short-term relationships, and I've taken comfort in them. But a long-term relationship . . . that would be like telling your mother she can be replaced. And she can't."

Heavy going here. Jack tossed off the rest of his wine and poured them both some more, all the while trying to think of an adequate response.

His Dad saved him by pointing the carving knife at Jack's chest.

"Your mother," he said. "That's it, isn't it. I've always suspected that it made you a little crazy, but now I want to hear it from you. I remember you at the wake and the funeral. Like a zombie, hardly speaking to anyone. You were never a momma's boy. Far from it. You were closest to Kate. But to see your mother killed by violence, to have her bleeding and dying in your arms . . . there's no shame in having a breakdown after what happened. No one should have to go through that. No one."

Jack gulped more of his wine. He could feel it hitting him. He'd had nothing to eat since breakfast and the alcohol was jumping directly into his bloodstream. So what? And why not?

"I agree that no one should have to go through that. But it wasn't Mom's death that put me on the road."

"What then? It's driven me crazy for the past fifteen years. What made you disappear?"

"Not her death. Another death."

"Whose?"

"I was pissed at everyone back then for not finding the guy who'd dropped that cinder block. The state cops were going on about keeping an eye on the overpasses, but it takes a lot of effort to track down someone who commits a random act of violence. And they had better things to do—

like ticketing speeders on the Turnpike. God forbid we drive above the limit. And you, you weren't doing anything but talking about what should happen to the murdering bastard when they caught him. Only it wasn't a 'when,' it was an 'if'—an 'if' that was never going to happen."

Jack finished the glass and poured himself some more, killing the bottle.

Dad looked up from the ham. "What the hell was I supposed to do?"

"Something. Anything."

"Like what? Go out and track him down myself?"

"Why not?" Jack said. "I did."

Oh, shit, he thought. Did I just say that?

"You *what*?"

Jack raced through his options here. Say never mind and stonewall it? Or go ahead and tell all. Abe was the only other person on earth who knew.

But now the wine and a cranky, don't-give-a-shit mood pushed him to let it roll. He sucked in a deep breath.

Here goes.

"I tracked him down and took care of him."

Jack thought he saw Dad's hand tremble as he put down the carving knife. His expression was tight, his eyes bright and wide behind his glasses.

"Just how . . . I'm not sure I want to hear this but . . . just how did you take care of him?"

"I saw to it that he never did anything like that again."

Dad closed his eyes. "Tell me you broke his arms, or smashed his elbows."

Jack said nothing.

Dad opened his eyes and stared at him. His voice dropped to a whisper.

"Jack . . . Jack, you didn't . . ."

Jack nodded.

Dad sidled left to one of the counter stools and slumped

on it. He cradled his head in his hands, staring down at the pile of sliced scallions.

"Oh, my God." His voice was a moan. "Oh, my God."

Here it comes, Jack thought. The shock, the outrage, the revulsion, the moral repugnance. He wished now he could take it back, but he couldn't, so . . .

He walked around the counter, past his father's bent back, opened the refrigerator, and took out another bottle of wine.

"How did you know it was him?" Dad said. "I mean, how could you be sure?"

Without bothering to remove the black lead foil, Jack wound the screw through it and into the cork.

"He told me. Name was Ed, and he bragged about it."

"Ed . . . so, the shit had a name."

Jack blinked. Other than hell and damn, his father had always been scrupulous about four-letter words. At least when Jack was a kid.

He lifted his head but didn't look at Jack. "How?" He licked his lips. "How did you do it?"

"Tied him up and dangled him by his feet off the same overpass. Made him a human piñata for the big trucks going by below."

The cork popped from the bottle as Jack remembered seeing Ed swinging over the road, the meaty *thunk!* as the first truck hit him, then the second.

Music. Heavy metal.

Dad was finally looking at him. "That's why you left, isn't it. Because you'd committed murder. You should have stayed, Jack. You should have come to me. I would have helped you. You didn't have to spend all those years dealing with that guilt alone."

"Guilt?" Jack said, pouring more wine for both of them. "No guilt. What did I have to feel guilty about? No guilt, no remorse. Send me back in time to relive that night and I'd do the same thing."

"Then why on earth did you just take off like that?"

Jack shrugged. "You want an eloquent, thoughtful, soul-searching answer? I don't have one. It seemed to make sense at the time. From that moment on the world looked different, seemed like another place, and I didn't belong. Plus I was disgusted with just about everything. I wanted out. So I got out. End of story."

"And this creep, this Ed . . . why didn't you call the police?"

"That's not the way I work."

Dad squinted at him. "Work? What does that mean?"

Jack didn't want to go there.

"Because they'd have carted him off and then let him out on bail, and then let him plead down to a malicious mischief charge."

"You're exaggerating. He'd have done hard time."

"Hard time wouldn't cut it. He needed killing."

"So you killed him."

Jack nodded and sipped his wine.

Dad started waving his arms. "Jack, do you have any idea what could have happened to you? The chance you took? What if somebody saw you? What if you'd been caught?"

Jack opened his mouth to reply, but something in his father's words and tone stopped him. He was going on about . . . he seemed more concerned about the possible consequences of the killing rather than the killing itself. Where was the outrage, the middle-class repugnance for deliberate murder?

"Dad? Tell me you wish I hadn't killed him."

His father pressed a hand over his eyes. Jack saw his lips tremble and thought he was going to sob.

Jack put a hand on his shoulder. "I never should have told you."

Dad looked at him with wet eyes. "Never? I wish you'd

told me back then! I've spent the last fifteen years thinking he was still out there, unnamed, unknown, some kind of wraith I'd never get my hands on. You don't know how many nights I've lain awake and imagined my hands around his throat, squeezing the life out of him."

Jack couldn't hide his shock. "I thought you'd be horrified if you knew what I'd done."

"No, Jack. The real horror was losing you all those years. Even if you'd been caught, you could have pled temporary insanity or something like that and got off with a short sentence. At least then I'd have known where you were and could have visited you."

"Better for you, maybe."

A jolt in the joint, even a short one . . . unthinkable.

"I'm sorry. I'm not thinking straight."

Jack still couldn't believe it. "I killed a man and you're okay with that?"

"With killing *that* man, yes, I'm okay. I'm more than okay, I'm—" He threw his arms around Jack. "I'm proud of you."

Whoa.

Jack wasn't into hugs, but he did manage to give his dad a squeeze, all the while thinking, Proud? *Proud?* Christ, how could I have read him so wrong?

Once again Anya's words from that first day came back to him.

Trust me, kiddo, there's more to your father than you ever dreamed.

They broke the clinch and backed off a couple of feet.

Jack said, "If I'd have known you felt that way, I might have asked you for help. I could have used some. And you would have been *doing* something instead of waiting for the police to do it for you."

Dad looked offended. "How do you know I wasn't doing something? How do you know I didn't take a rifle and sit in the bushes, watching that overpass, waiting to see if someone would try again."

Jack managed to suppress a laugh but not a smile. "Dad, you don't own a rifle. Not even a pistol."

"Maybe not now, but I could have back then."

"Yeah, right."

They stood facing each other, his father staring at him as if seeing a new person. Finally he thrust out his hand. Jack shook it.

Dad looked around and said, "I don't know about you, but I'm starving. Let's get going on these omelets."

"You start the eggs," Jack said, "and I'll finish dicing the ham."

A good night. A surprising, shocking, revelatory night. Like nothing he could have anticipated.

He might have enjoyed it even more if he'd managed to bring Carl home. He wondered how the poor guy was doing.

12

Carl looked up at the starry sky, at the misshapen shadows of the surroundin trees, at the water in the lagoon, anywhere but at the lights. Least-ways he tried not to look. But as much as he wanted to stop it, his gaze kept driftin back to the sinkhole . . . and the lights.

They'd set him here on the ground, his back against one of the Indian hut support posts. They'd been ready to tie his hands behind him when they remembered that he only had one, so they lashed him to the post with coils of thick rope around his arms and body.

He'd overheard Semelee mention that Jack had found her shell but how's it would have to wait till tomorrow. Tonight was too important.

The air was warm and wet and thick enough to choke a frog—maybe that was why they weren't peepin. Even the crickets had shut up. The lagoon and its surroundins was quiet as a grave.

The lights had started flashin a little after dark, strange colors and mixes of colors he never seen nowheres else. That was when it really got crowded around the hole. But there'd been lots goin on before that. Luke and Corley and Udall and Erik had been settin up some sort of steel tripod over the mouth. It had a pulley danglin from the top center where the three legs came together. They threaded a good, long length of half-inch rope through it, then tied that to some sorta chair.

He kept telling himself, Naw, she ain't really gonna do that. She ain't that crazy.

But come full dark, when the crazy flashin colors was lightin up the trees and the water, sure enough, Semelee put herself into the chair. She was danglin over the hole, with the lights reflectin even stranger colors off that silver hair of hers, and then Luke and a couple other guys Carl couldn't recognize cause their pan-o-ramic backs was to him started lowerin her down into the hole.

After she disappeared he could hear her voice echoin up from below.

"What're you stoppin for? Keep me goin!"

Luke called out, "You're deeper'n you should be already. How much to go till you hit the water?"

"Can't see no water. Looks like it all dried up."

"Then where's the bottom?"

"Can't see no bottom, just the lights."

"That's it," Luke said. "I'm haulin you up now."

"Luke, you do that and I ain't never gonna speak to you

again! You hear that? Never! It's like nothin I could ever
dream down here. The lights . . . so bright . . . all around
me . . . feels like they're goin *through* me. This is so cool.
You keep on lettin out that rope. I want to see where they
come from."

Carl wasn't sure of a whole lotta things in life, but he
was damn sure that was a real bad idea. He was glad he
was back here, away from the lights. He would've liked to
be even farther, like in his trailer watchin TV. He was
missin all his Friday night shows. But he couldn't worry
about that now. He had to get outta here.

He'd been usin his hand, workin at the knot behind his
back, but this was one good knot. When you lived out here
in the wilds, specially on the water, you learned how to tie
a good knot. But that didn't keep him from tryin to loosen
it up.

"Keep a-goin!" he heard Semelee call up from the hole,
her voice faint and all echoey like.

Luke shouted, "We're almost outta rope!"

"Take me down to the end! As much as you got!"

Good, Carl thought. They's all concentrated on her.

If he could just get this knot loose, he could sneak down
to the water and steal a canoe and slip away real quiet like.
He could be long gone before anyone noticed. Then he'd—

He jumped at the sound of a scream, a long tortured
sound like someone havin their skin tore off—not just a
piece, but the whole thing.

Everbody around the hole started shoutin and callin and
movin this way and that. Four-five guys was haulin on that
rope as fast as they could. Finally they got to the end. Carl
caught a peek between the shufflin bodies and saw
Semelee still in the chair. But she was all slumped over like
a piece of fish bait and not movin a muscle.

She looked dead.

SATURDAY

1

Semelee heard herself scream and woke up all sweaty and thrashin.

Where am I?

"Semelee! Semelee, are you okay?"

Luke's voice . . . and then his face appeared, hovering over her.

She sat up, recognized her corner of the *Bull-ship*, then flopped back.

"Here," Luke told her. "Drink this."

He tipped a bottle over her mouth and she gulped. Water. Lord, that tasted good.

She looked around again. "How'd I get here? I don't remember going to bed. I—"

"You was down in the lights," he said.

The lights! Of course.

She remembered now. She'd been down in the hole, baskin in them strange weird lights like a sun worshipper. But she hadn't felt strange. She'd felt welcome, more welcome than she'd ever felt in her own home. She remembered wantin to tear off her clothes so the rays could go straight to her skin. But she didn't get the chance . . .

Because that was when the voices began.

Whispers at first, so soft she could barely make them out. Not sounds, really. More like voices in her head, like she was a mental case or somethin. She wasn't even sure they was talkin to her. Maybe they was jawin at each other and their words was passin through her head, but she had a feelin they was talkin to her. She *wanted* them to be talkin to her.

"What happened to you down there?" Luke said. "You screamed like I ain't never heard nobody scream, and when we pulled you up you was out cold. I thought you was a goner."

Out cold . . . she jammed her hands against her temples. Damn, she wished she could remember what had happened, and remember more of what them voices had said. She did know she kept hearin about 'the One.' All sorts of yammerin about the One, repeatin it over and over again. The One what?

Suddenly she realized they was talkin about a person. The One was preparing the way, everything depended on the One because the One was special.

Wait, she thought, stiffening as a thrill ran through her. *I'm* special. I got a power like no one else. And then there's my name . . .

She levered up to a sittin position and crossed her legs, Indian style. "Yes!"

"What is it?"

"Luke, do you know what my name means?"

"Y'mean Semelee? It means . . . it means 'Semelee.' Just like Luke means 'Luke.'"

"All names mean somethin. I ain't got no idea what Luke means, but my momma told me that Semelee means 'one and only.' She said she named me that because I was her first and I was a real hard birth, and she wasn't goin through that again. She said I was her first and last kid, her one and only."

Luke frowned. "Okay. So?"

"I heard voices down in that hole and they was talkin about 'the One.' That has to be me. They was talking about *me*." She closed her eyes. Excitement flashed like lectric shocks through her body. "And they kept on sayin somethin else too."

What was it? It was right there, just out of reach . . . started with an *R* . . . but what was the rest?

And then she had it! The name popped into her head like she'd known it all along.

A strange name. She'd never heard nothin like it before. But then she'd never heard nothin like those voices before neither. Was that strange word their name for her, their name for the One? Had to be.

But who were the voices and what did they mean about "preparing the way"? What was the "everything" that depended on her, the One?

She had to find out. Maybe she'd learn tonight. But she had to do a couple of things before then. One of them was gettin her other eye-shell back. But first . . .

"I'm changin my name, Luke."

He laughed. "That's crazy! You can't just change your name anytime you feel like it."

"No. I got to. That's why I was called back here. I thought the lagoon was talking to me when it said it wanted sacrifices, but it wasn't. It was the lights—or at least the things that live in the lights."

"Lay back down, Semelee. You're talkin outta your head."

"No." She pushed him away. "Don't you see? It was all to bring me here, to this place, at this time—to teach me my True Name. And now that I know it, I'm gonna use it." She rose to her feet and looked out at the lights still flickering up from the hole into the early morning darkness. "Big changes comin, Luke, and I'm gonna be part of them, I'm gonna be right at their heart. And if you and the rest of the clan stick by me, we'll have our day. Oh, yes, Luke, we'll have our day."

"Semelee—"

"Told you: I ain't Semelee no more. From this moment on you call me—"

The name died on her lips. She realized that she mustn't tell no one her True Name. It was only for her and those closest to her. Luke was close, but not close enough. The man called Jack, the special one . . . she could tell him maybe, but not right away. He'd have to prove himself worthy first.

"Call you what?" Luke said.

"Semelee."

Luke stared at her. "Wasn't you just tellin me—?"

"Changed my mind. I'm goin to change my name inside, but outside you can keep callin me Semelee." She rubbed her stomach. "We got anything to eat round here?"

Luke straightened. "I'll go check by the fire."

As soon as he was gone, Semelee stepped out onto the deck and looked up at the stars wheelin above her.

"Rasalom," she whispered, lovin the way it rolled off her tongue. That was her new name. "Rasalom."

2

The man who was something more than a man opened his eyes in the darkness.

His name . . . someone had spoken his name. Not one of the many he used in the varied identities he assumed for various purposes. No, this had been his True Name.

He'd been reveling in the continued corporal mutilation of a teenage girl named Suzanne and the spiritual ruination of the family that tortured her.

Poor Suzanne had been chained to the other side of the wall of this Connecticut home for eleven days now. She had been raped and defiled and tortured and mutilated beyond the point of her endurance. Her mind had snapped. She had no more to give. She was dying. Her brain had shut down all but the most basic functions. She barely felt the corkscrew being wound into the flesh of her thigh.

But what was so delicious here was the nature of the one twisting the corkscrew: an eight-year-old boy. For it was not simply the pains of the tortured that nourished this man who was something more than a man; the depravity and self-degradation of the torturers were equally delicious.

He'd returned to this house to bask in the dying embers of a young life's untimely end.

But now that was ruined, the delicious glow fading, cooled by a growing anger and—he admitted it—concern.

Someone had spoken his True Name.

But who? Only two beings in this sphere knew that name: one was listening for it, and the other dared not speak it. They—

There! There it was again!

Why? Was someone calling him? No. This time he sensed that the speaker was not merely saying his True Name, but trying to usurp it.

Rage bloomed in his brain like a blood-red rose. This was intolerable!

Where was it coming from? He rose to his feet and turned in a slow circle—once, twice—then stopped. The source of the outrage . . . it came from there . . . to the south. He would find the misbegotten pretender there.

All his plans were progressing smoothly now. After all these centuries, millennia, epochs, he was close, closer than he'd ever been. Less than two years from now— barring interference from those who knew he was the One—his hour, his moment, his time would be at hand.

But now this. Someone usurping his True Name . . .

Never!

The man who was something more than a man strode away from the house through the dissipating darkness. He had no time to waste. He must head south immediately, trace his True Name to the lips that were speaking it, and silence them.

He paused at the curb. But what if that was just what someone wanted him to do?

This could be a trap, set by the one man he feared in this sphere, the only man he must hide from until the Time of Change.

Back in the days of his first life, when he was closer to the source, he had enormous power; he could move clouds, call down lightning. Even in his second life he could control disease, make the dead walk. But here in this third life his powers were attenuated. Yet he wasn't helpless. Oh, no. Far from that. And he could not allow anyone to use his True Name.

He must proceed with caution. But he must proceed. This could not go on.

Jack stepped into the front room and found his father fiddling with the French press.

"Don't bother, Dad," Jack told him. "I'll pick up some coffee and donuts in town."

He'd seen a Dunkin' Donuts the other day and had awakened with a yen for some of their glazed crullers.

"Donuts? That sounds good. But I don't mind making coffee. After all, the job has its perks."

Jack groaned. "What kind do you like?"

"A couple of chocolate glazed would be great."

Jack headed outside, trying to concentrate on donuts in the hope that would help take his mind off Carl and how he was going to bring him back. The air seemed less humid. Felt like a cool front had come through.

About time. The relentless heat day after day had been wearing him out. Maybe this was Elvis's doing. If so, thank you, Big E.

A mist lay over the saw grass sea stretching away to the distant hummock. The egret was back in the pond, black legs shin deep in the water by the edge, waiting like a snowy statue for breakfast to move and give itself away.

He headed around the side of his house toward the car. He stopped when he rounded the corner. A woman was seated on the hood of his car. She wore cutoffs and a green tank top. Her white hair had been wound into a single braid. The companion to the shell Jack had found hung at her throat.

Semelee.

"About time you showed up," he said, moving toward her, wary, eyes scanning the surroundings. Had she come alone? "I've been standing out here like some kind of nut announcing to the air that I've found your shell. I thought you said you'd know."

She smiled. "I did know. That's why I'm here."

Jack couldn't pin it down but she looked different. Her hair was just as white as ever, but her eyes held a strange look, as if she'd peeked through someone's window and seen something she wasn't supposed to know.

That was it. She looked like she'd discovered some sort of secret no one else knew. Or thought she had.

"Took you long enough."

Her smile remained. "I had other things to do."

Jack tensed. "Like what? You better not have hurt Carl."

"Carl's fine." She held out her hand, palm up. "My shell, please."

Now it was Jack's turn to smile. "You're kidding, right?"

"No. You give me the shell and I'll send Carl back."

"Not likely."

The smile vanished. "You don't trust me?"

"Tell you what: You send Carl back, and I'll give you the shell."

"No way."

"What? You don't trust me?"

Semelee glared at him. "The One don't lie."

Jack stiffened. The One? She'd just mentioned the One.

"What did you say?"

"Nothin."

"You called yourself the One. What did you mean by that?"

"Told you: nothing. Now leave it be."

Anya had talked about the One, but she'd indicated that Sal Roma was the One. Was he involved in what was going down here?

"Do you know a guy named Roma?"

She shook her head. "Ain't never heard of him."

"Is he the one who got you started on this sacrifice-to-the-swamp kick?"

Semelee's eyes widened. She slid off the hood and stepped toward him. "How do you know about that?"

"Not important. Just tell me: Was it Roma?"

"Told you: Don't know no Roma."

Jack believed her. "Then who? Who gave you such a crazy idea?"

"Wasn't no 'who.' It came from the lagoon its own self. If you listen, the lagoon'll talk to you. Leastways, it talks to me. Told me in a dream that it was pissed off and that

Gateways had to pay. Said it would exact a price of four Gateways lives a year and—"

"Wait-wait. That's what it said? 'Exact'?"

That didn't sound like it belonged in Semelee's vocabulary—at least not as a verb.

"Yeah. 'Exact.' Pretty weird kind of talk, doncha think?"

Jack wondered if it had been a dream at all. It sounded as if someone or something had been influencing her, and he doubted very much it was her lagoon. Much more likely it was an influence from that nexus point within the cenote.

He said, "You ever hear of something called the Otherness?"

"Don't reckon I have," she said, shaking her head. "Should I?"

"Never mind." Just because she hadn't heard of the Otherness didn't mean she wasn't working for it, knowingly or unknowingly. "But why Gateways people? There must be other folks living even closer to your lagoon."

"There is, but the lagoon wants Gateways folks. Don't ask me why, it just does."

Jack jerked a thumb over his shoulder. "There's one Gateways folk in there it's not going to get. We clear on that?"

She nodded. "Absolutely. The lagoon's already done what it set out to do with the sacrifices. There's still maybe a score to settle, but the sacrifice thing is over."

"What score?"

"That's between me and the lagoon, but don't you worry. Your daddy ain't a part of it."

Jack believed her this time, and found relief in the fact that his father was no longer in the clan's crosshairs. But that was tempered by the knowledge that he'd been replaced by someone else.

"He'd better not be. And I'd better see Carl pretty soon or I might just lose that shell. Or it might slip out of my pocket as I'm crossing a street downtown. Wouldn't take long for the traffic to reduce it to powder."

Semelee went pale beneath her tan. "Don't even joke about that."

"What's so important about that shell?"

Her hand went to the one around her neck. "I've had em since I was a kid, is all. I just want it back."

"And I want Carl back."

She sighed. "Looks like we'll have to put together a swap meet. Bring the shell to the lagoon and—"

Jack shook his head. "Uh-uh. Bring Carl here."

Jack watched Semelee's hands open wide, then close into tight fists.

"You're makin this awful hard." She looked up at the hazy sky, then back to him. "Guess we'll have to meet somewheres in the middle. You got any ideas?"

Jack reviewed his trip with Carl and remembered the dry stretch where they'd had to carry their canoe. He mentioned it to Semelee and she knew where it was.

"Okay," she said. "We'll meet there in an hour."

Jack looked out at the Everglades and the clinging haze. Semelee seemed on the level but he didn't know about the rest of the clan. And because of that, he wanted maximum visibility.

"What say we make it noonish?" he said.

"Why're you makin me wait so long?"

"I need the time."

"All right. See you then. And don't be late."

She turned and walked off. Jack watched the sway of her hips as she moved away. He missed Gia.

He was still watching her, wondering how she was going to get out of Gateways, when his father's voice interrupted him.

"I hope you're not really thinking of going through with this."

Jack turned to find Dad standing on the porch, staring at him through the jalousies.

"You heard the whole thing?"

"Just the end. Enough to know that she's connected to what happened to me, and probably to the others who've been killed. But what was that about Carl? Carl the gardener?"

"One and the same."

Jack gave him a quick overview of what had happened—about the trip to the lagoon, and Semelee and her clan.

Dad was shaking his head. "You've only just got here, Jack. How did you manage to get involved in something like this in just a couple of days?"

"Lucky, I guess."

"I'm serious, Jack. You've got to take this to the police and the Park Service."

"That's not the way I do things."

"What's that supposed to mean? This is the second time you've said something like that."

"It's plain and simple, Dad: I promised Carl I'd get him back safely. Me. Not the cops, not the park rangers. Me. So that's how it's going down."

"But you didn't know the odds against you when you made that promise. He can't hold you to it."

"He's not," Jack said. He shook his head. "You wouldn't understand."

Dad rubbed his jaw. "I understand perfectly. And you know, Jack . . . the better I know you, the more I like you. Carl's not holding you to your promise . . . you are. I can respect that. It's damn foolish, but I have to respect that."

"Thanks."

How about that? Dad did understand.

"But you can't go out there alone. You're going to need backup."

"Tell me about it. Know where I can find any?"

"You're looking at him."

Jack laughed. Dad didn't.

"I'm not kidding, Jack."

"Dad, you're not cut out for that."

"Don't be so sure." He pushed open the porch door. "Come inside. I need to tell you some things you don't know."

"About what?"

No matter what he was told, Jack wasn't taking an accountant in his seventies as backup, especially if that accountant in his seventies was his father.

"About me."

Inside, Dad handed him a cup of coffee, then, before Jack could ask him what this was about, disappeared into his bedroom. He returned a minute later carrying the gray metal lockbox Jack had found back on Tuesday. He hadn't expected to see it again, but he was more surprised by what his father was wearing.

"Dad, are you kidding with that sweater?"

His father pulled the front of the ancient brown mohair cardigan closer about him. "It's cold! The thermometer outside my window says sixty-nine degrees."

Jack had to laugh. "The Sasquatch look. It's you, Dad."

"Never mind the sweater." He set the box on the coffee table. "Have a seat."

Jack sat across from him. "What've you got there?" he said, already knowing the answer.

Dad unlocked the box and flipped it open. He pulled out an old photo and passed it to Jack: Dad and six other young guys in fatigues.

Jack pretended to study it, as if seeing it for the first time.

"Hey. From your Army days."

"Army?" His father made a face. "Those clods? These are Marines, Jack. Semper fi and all that."

Jack shrugged. "Army, Marines, what's the diff?"

"You wouldn't say that if you'd ever been in the Corps."

"Hey, you were all fighting the same enemy, weren't you?"

"Yeah, but we fought them better." He tapped the photo. "These were my wartime buddies." His expression softened. "And I'm the only one left."

Jack looked at those young faces. He pointed to the photo. "What are you all smiling about?"

"We'd just graduated Corps-level scout-sniper school."

Jack looked up from the photo. "You were a sniper?" He'd learned to believe in the unbelievable, but this was asking too much. "My father was a sniper?"

"Don't say it like it's a dirty word."

"I didn't. I'm just . . . shocked."

"Lots of people look on sniping with disdain, even in the military. And after that pair of psychos killed all those folks in the DC area a while back, so does just about everybody else. But those two weren't sniping. They were committing random murder, and that's not what sniping is about. A sniper doesn't go out and shoot anything that moves, he goes after specific targets, *strategic* targets."

"And you did that in Korea."

Dad nodded slowly. "I killed a lot of men over there, Jack. I'm sure there's plenty of soldiers walking around today who've killed more of the enemy—Germans, Japs, North Koreans, Chinese, Vietnamese—in their tours of duty than I did, but they were just shooting at the faceless foreign bodies who were trying to kill them. We snipers were different. We positioned ourselves in hiding and took out key personnel. We could have a hundred, a thousand soldiers milling around just five hundred yards away, but we weren't interested in the grunts. We were after the officers, the NCOs, the radio men, anyone whose death would diminish the enemy's ability to mount or sustain an attack."

Jack was watching his dad's face. "Sounds almost . . . personal."

"It does. And that's what makes people uncomfortable. They feel there's something cold-blooded about picking out a specific individual in, say, a bivouac area, sighting down on him, and pulling the trigger." He sighed. "And maybe they're right."

"But if it saves lives . . ."

"Still pretty cold-blooded, though, don't you think. When I started out, if I couldn't nail an officer or NCO, I'd go after radio men and howitzer crews. But I noticed that whenever I took a guy out, another would pick up the radio or jump in and start reloading the howitzer, and then I'd have to take them out as well."

Jack started nodding. "So you began going after their equipment."

"Exactly. Know what a .30 caliber hardball will do to a radio? Or to the sights on a howitzer?"

"I can imagine." Jack had a very good idea of the damage it could do. "Good for the junk pile and nothing else. You guys were using M1s back then, right?"

"A World War Two vet named Nacht trained us on the M1903A1 with an eight-power Unertl scope, and that's what I used. Made a couple of thousand-yard kills with that."

A thousand yards . . . three thousand feet . . . killing someone more than half a mile away. Jack couldn't imagine that. He tried to keep guns out of his fix-its whenever possible, but when the need arose he had no qualms about using them. Usually it was up close and personal, and never more than twenty-five feet.

A thousand yards . . .

"What kind of round were you shooting?"

"I got hold of a cache of Match M72s and I hoarded them."

Jack wasn't familiar with the round. "How many grains?"

Dad's eyes narrowed. "You shoot?"

Jack shrugged. "A little. Mostly range stuff."

"Mostly?"

"Mostly." He didn't want to get into that. "Grains?"

"One-seventy-five point five."

Jack whistled.

"Yeah," Dad said, nodding. "Penetrated eleven inches of oak. Nice little accuracy radius. I loved that round."

"Don't think I'm morbid, but . . . how many did you kill?"

Dad closed his eyes and shook his head. "I don't know. I stopped counting at fifty."

Fifty-plus kills . . . jeez.

"I thought I was hot stuff," Dad said, "really making a difference in the fighting, so I kept count at first. But by the time I reached fifty or so it stopped mattering. I just wanted to go home."

"How long were you there?"

"Not terribly long—most of the latter half of 1950. I was shipped into Pusan in August and what a major screw-up that was, mainly because the Army units didn't do their job. Mid September I was shipped to Inchon where I landed with the Fifth Regiment. By the end of the month we'd fought through to Seoul, recaptured it, and handed it back to the South Koreans. We thought that was it. We'd freed up the country, kicked those NK commies back above the thirty-eighth parallel. Job done, time to go home. But no."

Dad drew out that last word in a way that reminded Jack of John Belushi. He rubbed a hand across his face to hide a smile.

"No, MacArthur had the bright idea of pushing into North Korea so we could reunite the country. And there we found ourselves facing the Red Chinese. What a bunch of crazies they were. No respect for life, their own or anyone else's, just hurling themselves at us in human waves."

"Maybe what was facing them at the rear if they didn't do as ordered was worse than charging you guys."

"Maybe," Dad said softly. "Maybe." He seemed to shiver inside his cardigan. "If there's a colder place on Earth than the mountains of North Korea, I don't want to know about it. It was chilly in October, but when November rolled around . . . temperatures in the days would be in the thirties but at night it would drop to minus-ten with a howling thirty- to forty-mile-an-hour wind. You couldn't get warm. So damn cold the grease that lubricated your gun would freeze up and you couldn't shoot. Fingers and toes and noses were falling off left and right from frostbite." He looked up at Jack. "Maybe that's the deep psychological reason I moved down here: so I'd never be cold again."

Christ, it sounded like a nightmare. Jack could see this talk was disturbing his father, but he needed answers to a few more questions. He pointed to the medal case resting in the bottom of the box.

"What's in there?"

Dad looked embarrassed. "Nothing."

Jack reached in and snatched up the case. "Then you won't mind if I open it." He did, and then held up the two medals. "Where'd you get these?"

Dad sighed. "The same time and place: November 28th, 1950, at the Chosin Reservoir, North Korea. The Chinese commies were knocking the crap out of us. There seemed no end to the men they were throwing our way. I had a good position when what looked like a couple of companies of reds made a flanking move on the fifth. I'd brought lots of ammo and I took out every officer I could spot. Anyone who made an arm motion or looked like he was shouting an order went down. Every radio I spotted took a hit. Pretty soon they were in complete disarray, all but bumping into one another. It might have been funny if it had been warmer and if my whole division wasn't being chopped to pieces. Still, they told me I saved a lot of lives that day."

"By yourself . . . you faced down a couple of Chinese companies by yourself?"

"I had a little help at first from my spotter, but Jimmy took one in the head early on and then it was just me."

Dad didn't seem to take all that much pride in it, but Jack couldn't help being impressed. This soft-spoken, slightly built man he'd known all his life, who he'd thought of as the epitome of prosaic middle-classdom, had been a stone-cold military sniper.

"You were a hero."

"Not really."

Jack held up the Silver Star. "This medal says different. You had to have been scared."

"Of course I was. I was ready to wet my pants. I'd been good friends with Jimmy and he was lying dead beside me. I was trapped. They weren't taking prisoners there, and if I surrendered, God knows what they'd have done to me for killing their officers. So I hung in and figured I'd take as many of them with me as I could." He shrugged. "And you know, I wasn't that scared of dying, not if I could go as quickly as Jimmy. I hadn't met your mother, I had no kids depending on me for support. And at least I wouldn't be cold anymore. At that moment, dying did not seem like the worst thing in the world."

Fates worse than death . . . Jack understood that. But there was still the Purple Heart to be explained. Jack held it up.

"And this one?"

Dad pointed to his lower left abdomen. "Took a piece of shrapnel in the gut."

"You always told me that scar was from appendicitis!"

"No. I told you that's where I had my appendix taken out. And that's what they did. When they went in after the shrapnel they discovered it had nicked my appendix, so they removed it along with the metal fragments. Somehow they got me to Hungnam alive, put me on penicillin for a week, and that was the war for me."

Jack looked at his father. "Why'd you keep all this hidden? Or am I the only one who doesn't know?"

"No, you're the only one who *does* know."

"Why didn't you tell me sooner, like when I was eight, or ten?"

As a kid it would have been so cool to know he had a father who'd been a Marine sniper. And even as an adult, he'd have had a whole different perspective on his Dad.

My father, the sniper . . . my father, the war hero . . . yow.

Dad shrugged. "I don't know. When I was finally sent home, I realized how many of my buddies weren't going with me. Their families would never see them again. And then I got to thinking about all the NKs and Red Chinese I'd killed who wouldn't be going home to *their* families, and it made me a little sick. No, make that a *lot* sick. And the worst of it was, beyond getting a lot of good men killed, we didn't accomplish a goddamn thing by pushing north of the thirty-eighth. So I just put it all behind me and tried not to think about it."

"But you kept the medals."

"You want them? Keep them. Or throw them away. I don't care. It was the photos I kept—I didn't want to forget those guys. Somebody should remember them. The rest just happened to come along for the ride."

Jack dropped the medals into the little case and returned it to the strong box.

"You keep them. They're part of who you were."

"And you might say they're part of who I still am. That's why I'll be backing you up when you go out there to get Carl back."

"No way."

"Jack, you can't go out there alone."

"I'll think of something."

Dad sat silent a moment, then said, "What if I can prove to you that I still have it? Please, Jack. I want to do this with you."

His father was practically begging Jack to take him along. But damn . . . it could turn ugly, and then what? He'd never forgive himself if the old guy got hurt.

Still, he felt he owed him a chance.

"Okay, Dad. You're on—for a test run. How are we going to work this?"

His father's eyes were bright behind his glasses. "I think I know a way."

The sign shouted DON'S GUNS & AMMO in big red letters—peeling red letters—with *Shooting Range* below it in smaller black print.

"This must be the place," Jack said as they pulled into the sandy lot on a rural road in Hendry County.

Only one other car, an old Mercedes diesel sedan, in sight. Probably the owner's. Opening time was 9:00 A.M. and it was after ten now. Jack figured there probably would be lots more activity once hunting season started, but at the moment he and Dad seemed like the only customers.

They went inside. Behind the counter they found a slim guy with salt-and-pepper hair and mustache. His lined face made him look sixtyish, maybe even older.

"Are you Don?" Dad said, extending his hand.

"That's me."

"We called about the M1C."

They'd made a lot of calls to a lot of gun shops—amazing how many there were in Florida—and not one of them had a M1903A1. But this place said it had an old M1C. Close enough, Dad had said. Hendry County was a good ways north of Gateways, but they'd had no other options.

Don smiled as he lifted the rifle leaning against the wall behind him and laid it on its side, bolt handle up.

"One M1C Garand, coming up. Heavy sucker. Gotta weigh a dozen pounds. But it's fully rigged—still has the original scope and flash hider."

"I see that," Dad said.

Jack was seeing a beat-up piece of junk: The dried-out wooden stock was scratched and dinged and gouged, the metal finish worn, and the whole thing looked like it had just received its first dusting in years.

Dad picked up the rifle and hefted it. In one seamless move he raised it to his shoulder and sighted down the scope.

"Never liked the M82 scope. Never liked the way it was mounted, and only two-and-a-half power. The Unertl I used was an eight." He looked at Jack. "This was the Army's sniper rifle for a while. Couldn't hold a candle to the M1903A1, if you ask me."

"If you really want to shoot that thing," Don said, "I can sell you a much better scope."

Dad shook his head. "I qualified on this as well as the 1903. It'll have to do. But will it shoot?"

Don shrugged. "Got me there. I'd forgotten I had it until you called. That thing's been here so long, I can't remember when I bought it or who from."

"What do you want for it?"

Don pursed his lips. "I'll let it go for twenty-five hundred."

"What?" Jack said.

Dad laughed. "Let it go? That's way overpriced for Army surplus junk."

"A fully outfitted M1C like this is a collector's item. If this baby was in better shape it'd go for twice that at auction."

"Hey, Dad, you can get a better rifle for a lot less."

"But not one I'm used to."

"Yeah, but twenty-five hundred bucks . . ."

"Hell, it's only money." He looked at Don. "I tell you what: You can have your asking price on the condition that it still fires. That means you've got to let me clean it and fire a few test rounds. Do you have a bench where I can spruce it up?"

Don pursed his lips again. "Okay. I've got a cleaning set-up in the back you can use. Go ahead. But give me a picture ID and your Social Security Number so I can background you while you're doing that."

"Background?" Jack said.

"Yeah. Instant background check. It's the law. I've got to place a call to the FDLE to make sure he hasn't got a criminal record, a domestic violence conviction, or under a restraining order. If he comes through clean, he gets the rifle. If not, no deal."

"Might as well quit now, Dad," Jack said gravely. "You are so busted."

"Very funny." He looked at Don. "No waiting period?"

He shook his head. "Not for rifles, but there's a mandatory three-day 'cooling-off period' for pistols."

Jack was glad he didn't have to buy his guns through legal channels.

Dad fished out his wallet and handed his Florida driver license to Don, saying, "What about ammo? Have any match grade?"

Don nodded. "Got a box of thirty-ought-six Federals. I'll throw in half a dozen rounds to let you check it out."

Dad smiled. "You're on."

"Jesus, Dad," Jack said as he stared through the field glasses.

"Not bad for an old fart, ay?"

Dad was down on his right knee, left elbow resting on his left thigh, eye glued to his scope.

"Not bad? It's fantastic!"

Earlier he'd watched with amazement as his father's wrinkled old hands disassembled the M1C like it was a tinker toy. He'd inspected the firing pin, wiped the scope lenses, cleaned and oiled all the works, scoured the inside of the barrel with a long-handled brush, then reassembled it with a precision and an efficiency that left Jack in awe.

Dad had explained that it was like riding a bike: Do it enough times and you never forget how. Your hands know what to do.

Then it was time for the test firing. Don had a two-hundred-yard rifle range behind his shop with acres of open country beyond it. Dad's targets—large paper sheets with concentric black circles at their centers—were set against a rickety wooden fence.

His first shots had been grouped wide to the left, but as he made progressive adjustments on the sight, the holes in the target crept inexorably toward the heart of the bull's-eye. He'd punched the last three shots through a one-and-a-half-inch circle.

"Not so fantastic," Dad said. "It's only two hundred yards." He patted the stock. "Definitely worth the price."

"A hundred yards is all we'll need, I hope. And by the way, I'm paying."

The Tyleski Visa had a five-thousand-dollar credit limit. Still plenty of slack there.

"Like hell."

"No, the least a guy can do for his backup is arm him." Jack extended his hand toward his father. "You've still got it, Dad."

The flash of his father's smile as they shook hands warmed him.

7

As Jack beached the motorized canoe on the bank of the channel shallows, he got his sneakers soaked yet again. This was getting to be a habit. The clouds had blown off and the sun was cooking his shoulders.

The shell lay nestled in the right front pocket of his jeans. Now where was Semelee?

"You're late," she said.

Jack looked right and saw her rounding a bend on the far side of the shallows. She stood in the front of a small, flat-bottomed boat and—

What the hell? She held a shell over her left eye and had her hand clapped over her right. As Jack watched, she lowered the shell and the hand and smiled at him.

Carl and Corley sat amidships directly behind her; Luke operated the little outboard motor mounted on the stern and glowered at Jack.

Carl grinned and waved the oar protruding from his sleeve. Jack was relieved that he looked pretty much the same as he'd left him.

"Sorry," Jack said. "Had some things to do and everything down here seems to take longer than it does up north. Ever notice that?"

"I wouldn't know," Semelee said. "I ain't never been up north."

Luke pulled up the motor; the hull of the boat scraped the sandy bottom as he let it run aground in the shallows. All four stepped out. Corley stayed by the boat while the other three approached—Semelee and Luke first, Carl behind them.

Jack gave Corley a quick look, noted a knife in his belt, but no gun. Same with Luke: a hunting knife with a six-inch blade in a leather scabbard strapped to his belt, but again, no gun. Good. Jack wanted to keep an eye on that knife, though.

They stopped in front of him. Luke stood with his arms folded across his barrel chest.

"Well," he said with a belligerent edge to his voice, "you can see plain and simple we got Carl. Time for you to show us the shell."

Jack dug into his pocket, all the while keeping an eye on

Luke's hunting knife. If he made a move toward it, Jack would go for the Glock.

He fished out the shell and handed it to Semelee. As she took it and clutched it between her breasts, Luke's right hand moved, not going for the knife but flicking toward Jack's face. He heard a metallic *click* and found himself face to face with a three-inch, semi-serrated, tanto-style blade. Sunlight gleamed off the stainless steel surface.

Jack cursed himself for not guessing Luke might be palming a folder.

"Luke!" Semelee cried. "What're you doin?"

"Taking care of business."

"I've got the shell! Put that away!"

Luke shook his head. "Uh-uh. We're leavin with Carl *and* the shell. None of this trade shit."

Jack started creeping his free hand around toward his back while they argued, taking his time, moving a few millimeters at a time.

"Luke," Semelee said, "we told him we'd trade and that's what we're gonna do."

Luke shook his head, never taking his eyes off Jack. "I'm callin the shots here, Semelee. This is man's work."

"You better put that knife away, Luke," Semelee told him. "His daddy's over there in that willow thicket with a rifle trained on us."

Jack stiffened. The little stand of trees where he'd stationed his father was about a hundred and fifty yards away. How did she know?

Luke's gaze snapped past Jack's shoulder, then back. He grinned. "That old coot? What's he gonna do?"

"Think about that," Semelee said. "He's got a rifle and he's been watchin this spot since before any of us arrived."

How did she *know*?

"Yeah? So? He ain't gonna hit nothin from that distance. But if he's watchin, maybe he'd like to watch me cut his little boy's face."

As Luke drew back his arm for a slash, Jack reached for his Glock and raised his free arm to block the thrust, but didn't have to.

Everything seemed to happen at once—red sprayed from Luke's head, something whizzed by Jack's ear, a rifle *cracked* from somewhere behind him, though not necessarily in that order.

Semelee screamed as Luke staggered back, spun, and crashed face first into the water. A bright red stain began to drift away from him in the barely existent current.

Jack drew the Glock and turned to stare at the thicket.

Jesus, Dad! You didn't have to go for a kill shot.

This was going to make for big trouble—police, coroner's inquests, the whole legal ball of wax—shit!

"Luke! Luke!" Corley cried as he splashed toward him.

Jack kept the Glock trained on him; to his left, Semelee hadn't moved; she stood with her hands pressed against her mouth. Carl was in a squat, looking around like a cat who'd just heard thunder for the first time.

And then, miraculously, Luke jerked his face out of the water and coughed. He shook his head and sat up. Blood still streamed down his forehead, but Jack could see now that it was from a front-to-back furrow along the center of his scalp.

Jack had to laugh. Dad, you pisser! You *pisser!*

"He only parted your hair, big boy," Jack said. "Next time, he parts your tiny brain." He waved his pistol at Corley. "Get him back to the boat." Jack motioned Carl toward the canoe. "Welcome back, Carl. Get that thing turned around and ready to go."

Carl grinned. "You got it."

"Wait," Semelee said as Jack turned to go.

"Sorry. Gotta go. We're finished with this bullshit."

"No." She reached out and touched his arm. Gently. "I need to talk to you."

"Sorry."

"Please?"

8

Jack waited. Semelee looked around as if checking to make sure Luke was out of earshot.

She lowered her voice. "You gotta believe I didn't know Luke was gonna pull somethin like that."

Jack looked into her eyes and did believe. "Okay. But that wouldn't have made much difference if I was the one bleeding now instead of your pal there."

"Please don't be mad at me."

The plaintive note in her voice, the fawnlike look in her huge dark eyes . . . Jack couldn't fathom what she was up to.

"Lady, you've got to be kidding." He went to jab a finger at her and realized he still had the Glock in his hand. So he pointed with his left. "This is all your doing. We're all here because of you. You kidnapped Carl. You're behind the deaths of three innocent folks, and it was only by luck that my dad didn't wind up the fourth."

"You gonna tell the cops?"

"Maybe."

A slow smile stretched her lips. "No, you ain't. I can tell."

Well, she had that right. Jack couldn't see any point of bringing cops into the picture. The Dade County DA was going to charge Semelee with what? Murder by coral snake? Murder by bird? Yeah, right.

"You can't blame me," she said. "Don't you see? It wasn't really me. It was all part of the plan."

"Plan?" Jack felt the weight of the pistol in his hand. I should put one in her right now, he thought. Who knew how many lives he'd save if she never got back to her lagoon. "Well, you'd better come up with another plan, because I'm declaring this one over, done, *finis*."

"Ain't my plan."

That caught Jack off guard. "Then whose?"

"The lights'."

Oh, boy, Jack thought. Here we go.

"You mean the lights—the ones that supposedly come out of your sinkhole—are behind all this?"

She beamed. "Yeah. I didn't see it before, but then I got the big picture. It's all been part of a plan, one big, beautiful plan."

"Okay. The lights have a plan." The lights . . . if they were connected to the nexus point, then, according to Anya, they were connected to the Otherness. "Tell me about it."

Her smile widened. "Can't tell you all of it, but I can tell you some. I can tell you that the lights drew me back here so's I could find out who I was."

"Really. And who would that be?"

"Oh, I can't tell you that. Leastways not yet. Only someone real close to me can know that."

"Well, I'm only a foot or two away."

"Not *that* kind of close. The other kind of close . . . the way you're gonna be with me real soon."

Oooooh, lady, I wouldn't count on that, Jack thought.

"Really."

"Yeah. Which brings me to another part of the big picture: the sacrifices. They was done for a purpose."

"Like what?"

"To get you down here."

Jack's mouth went dry. All along he'd had a niggling suspicion, a creeping fear that his father hadn't been a random victim; but having it laid out before him like this was unnerving.

I'm responsible.

But he saw a problem.

He licked his lips. "Wait. That doesn't make sense. You say your lights figured if they killed my father I'd come down here. But I might *not* have come. My brother might have come instead. And why the other three deaths before him?"

Semelee shrugged. "Who can explain how the lights think? Maybe they liked the sacrifices, maybe they knew Mr. Weldon would get to your daddy sooner or later and so they just let things happen. Maybe your daddy's name came up when only you could come. Don't much matter none. You're here, ain't you."

Yeah, he thought. *I'm here all right.*

"Why would your lights want me here?"

Semelee smiled. "For me."

"For you? What do you want with me? What do you even know about me?"

"I know you're special. And I know we was meant to be together."

"Yeah? Well, sorry. You and your lights are a little late. I'm taken."

"Don't matter. It's gonna be you and me. Can't stop it. It's like . . . like . . ."

"Kismet?"

"Kiss what?"

"Destiny?"

"Yeah, that's it. Destiny. You and me's destined to be together. You're gonna bring me in, take me back with you, make me belong, and then together we're gonna rule the roost."

Make you belong? he thought. Boy, sister, have you picked the wrong guy.

"Listen, if you're an outsider, the last guy you want to hook up with is me."

"Lemme be the judge of that." She stepped closer until her lips were barely an inch from his. "I'll meet you tonight at—"

"Sorry," Jack said, backing away. "Game over. Hang out with your lights and your buddies here, do whatever floats your boat, but stay away from Gateways, especially from my father." He raised the Glock and held it beside his head, muzzle skyward. "I see you or any of your clan within a hundred yards of my father, you're dead. Not figuratively dead, not virtually dead, not merely dead, but clearly and sincerely dead. Got it?"

She stared at him with her big, suddenly sad eyes. Her lower lip trembled.

"No . . . you can't . . ."

"Got it?"

Jack turned and sloshed over toward where Carl waited with the boat in the deeper water.

"You can't!" she screamed behind him.

Watch me.

9

"He needs killin, Semelee," Luke said. "He needs killin real bad."

They had the deck of the *Horse-ship* all to theirselfs. Semelee sat with her legs danglin over the side, starin at her reflection in the water. Luke crouched next to her.

His head had stopped bleedin. Finally. For a while there she'd thought he was gonna lose every drop of blood in his body. He'd refused to go to the hospital, sayin he'd heal up just fine without no damn fool doctors stickin him with needles. Maybe he was right, but he sure looked stupid with that red bandanna tied across his head and under his chin.

"You're right," Semelee told him. "For once, I ain't got no argument with you."

Luke stared at her with shocked eyes. "You mean it?"

"Damn right I do."

"But I thought you was sweet on him."

"Wasn't never sweet on him. I thought he was special but that don't matter none now. He hurt you and—"

"His daddy did the shootin."

"I know that. But his daddy only pulled the trigger. It was him, it was Jack who put him up to it. Probably told his daddy to blow your head off but the old boy only creased you. Can't have that, Luke. Can't have nobody, no matter how special they are, hurtin someone in the clan."

"So then it's okay with you if I take Corley and a couple—"

Semelee shook her head. "Uh-uh. I'm gonna handle this my own self. For you, Luke. It'll be a present from me to you."

The shock in Luke's eyes melted into something like love.

Don't be gettin no ideas, she thought.

Because this had nothin to do with Luke. She was just lettin him think that. He'd been too far away and too busy with his bleedin head to pay any attention to what had gone on between her and Jack in the shallows. Didn't hurt none though to let him think he was the reason she was gonna go after Jack.

But this was gonna be all for her.

She'd wanted to cry all the way back from the shallows. Her heart still felt like it'd been tore right out of her chest. He'd turned her down, turned his back and walked away. He said it was because he was taken, but that was a lie. Semelee had seen it all through her life and she knew the real truth: Jack thought he was too good for her.

But as she'd returned to the lagoon she realized it was the other way around.

Jack . . . how could she've thought he was special and meant for her? What was she thinking? He obviously wasn't so special and definitely not for her. She saw that now. Her visit to the lights in the sinkhole had changed everything. She knew her True Name now, knew that she'd been brought here for a purpose. She wasn't sure what that was yet, but she would. She just knew she would.

She'd been special before—her powers proved that—but now she was even more special. Much too special for Jack.

Yeah, but if that was true, why was she still hurtin? Why this cold hard lump where her stomach used to be?

She knew of only one way to make it better.

"Leave me be for now," she told Luke. "I gotta work on this. I'm gonna fix a big fat surprise for our friend Jack."

He got up and backed away. "Okay, Semelee. Sure. Sure. Maybe I'll go check on Devil. See how he's doin."

Despite how bad she was feeling, Semelee had to smile. Luke'd always been sorta like her puppy dog, but now he was actin like her slave.

But she was okay with that. Every girl should have a slave.

10

"I think this calls for a drink," Dad said as they stepped into the house.

They'd dropped Carl—with his thousand dollars—off at the trailer park. All the way home he'd been so effusive in his thanks for rescuing him from the clan and the lights that Jack had had to shut him up by getting him to describe what he'd seen last night. He'd found Carl's description of Semelee being lowered into the hole particularly unsettling. If the lights, filtered through sand and water, had caused the clan's deformities, what would direct exposure do? Make you crazy? The cenote must have been where she'd learned—how had she put it? *Who I am.* Who was she if not Semelee?

"That was one hell of a shot, Dad. One *hell* of a shot."

Jack kept reliving the emotional swings of that moment.

"Wasn't it? Wasn't it, though?"

Dad had darted into the kitchen and was searching through the bottles in a cabinet above the sink. His speech came in staccato bursts, his movements were quick, jittery, as if he'd mainlined caffeine.

He's higher than the proverbial kite, Jack thought.

"I wasn't looking to kill him, you know, and prayed I wouldn't, but I was also thinking, if it's his life or Jack's, then I can live just fine with a kill shot. All the skills came back as I was sitting in that tree, Jack. Suddenly I was back at the Chosin Reservoir, and I was on autopilot and really,

really relaxed because no one was shooting at me out in the Glades. It was just me and the rifle, and control of the situation was mine for the taking. I—here it is." He pulled a dark green bottle from the cabinet and held it aloft. "Wait till you taste this."

"Scotch? I think I'll go for a beer."

"No-no. You've got to try this. Remember Uncle Stu?"

Jack nodded. "Sure."

Uncle Stu wasn't a real uncle, just a close friend of the family. Close enough to earn "Uncle" status.

"He belongs to a single malt scotch club. He let me try this once and I had to get a bottle. Aged in old sherry casks—amontillado, I believe."

"And discovered with a skeleton behind a brick wall?" When Dad gave him a questioning look, Jack said, "Never mind."

"You drink this neat." Dad poured two fingers' worth into a couple of short tumblers. "Adding ice, water, or soda is punishable by death." He handed Jack a glass and clinked his own against it. "To the best day of my life in the last fifteen years."

Jack was pierced by an instant of sadness. The best? Really?

Not a Scotch drinker, Jack took a tentative sip and rolled it around on his tongue. It had a sweetness and a body he'd never tasted in any other Scotch. And the finish was . . . fabulous.

"For the love of God, Montresor!" he said. "That is *good!*"

"Isn't it?" Dad said, grinning. "Isn't that the best you ever had?"

"No question. Potent stuff."

"That's what I hear, but I haven't seen any proof."

Jack let that one slide. "Where can I get a bottle?"

"You can't. It's all gone. They produce only so many casks and this batch is long sold out."

Jack lifted his glass for another sip. "Then we'd better nurse this one."

"I don't care if we empty the bottle. This is a special day. It's been a long, long time since I've felt this alive." He looked at Jack. "But I have to ask you something."

"Shoot."

"Where'd that pistol come from, the one you pulled after I parted the big guy's hair?"

Jack felt very close to his father at the moment, closer than he could ever remember. The father-son slope had been leveled. They were eye to eye now. Equals. Friends. He didn't want anything to get in the way of that, but he couldn't very well tell Dad he'd imagined the Glock.

So he pulled it from the small of his back and laid it on the kitchen counter.

"You mean this?"

"Yes. That." His father picked it up and hefted it. Jack noted with approval how he kept the muzzle directed down and away from both of them. "What's it made of? Feels almost like . . ."

"Plastic? That's because most of it is. Not the barrel and firing pin, of course, but pretty much all the rest."

He turned it back and forth in his hand, staring at it. "Amazing." He raised his eyes to Jack. "But what's an appliance repairman doing with something like this?"

How to handle this . . .

"Sometimes I wind up in bad neighborhoods and I feel more comfortable knowing I'm carrying."

"But how did you get it down here? I know you didn't carry it aboard the plane."

Jack shrugged. "There are ways."

Dad continued to stare at him. "Tell me the truth: You're not really a repairman, are you."

"Oh, but I am. That's the truth."

"Okay, but what else are you?" He waggled the Glock.

"I saw how you handled this out there. I saw plenty of people handle guns in the war, and you could always tell the ones who knew what they were doing and were comfortable with them, just as you could tell the ones who weren't. You fall into the first category, Jack."

Despite the closeness he felt to his father at this moment, despite the combat-zone bond they'd formed, Jack couldn't bring himself to tell him.

"You're pretty comfortable too, Dad. Maybe it just runs in the family."

"All right. Keep your secrets. For now. But promise me that someday, before I die, you'll tell me. Promise?"

Jack knew a trap when he heard one. This one was a cousin of "When did you stop beating your wife?" If he promised, he'd be admitting there was something to tell.

"Let's not talk about you dying, Dad."

He sighed. "I'm not going to get anywhere, am I?" He poured more Scotch into Jack's glass. "Maybe this will loosen your tongue."

Jack laughed. "No one's ever tried to ply me with liquor before. Bring it on!"

11

The shadows was gettin long by the time Semelee was ready to make her move. Even usin both eye-shells, it had took her a while to get Dora in place. Like any other alligator snapper, she was slow and kinda clumsy. Nothin like Devil.

Poor Devil. Luke said he was doin right poorly and

looked like he was fixin to die. That made her feel bad.

But she shook off the sadness and fixed on what she aimed to do. Now that she finally had Dora where she wanted her, Semelee was ready for the next step.

She moved away from the lagoon and walked through the hummock until she came to the bees' nest. She didn't get too close. These was killer bees and once they got mad they'd swarm and wouldn't stop stingin. They didn't know how.

She fixed the shells over her eyes and concentrated . . .

. . . and sees the inside of the hive. Her vision's all weird, like she's lookin through dozens of eyes at once . . .

Semelee lowered the shells and picked up the rock she'd brought along. She tossed it at the hive, then put the shells back over her eyes, real quick like.

. . . and once again she's inside the hive with that weird way of looking at things. But the hive's different now. It's filled with angry buzzing—real angry. They're movin toward the opening, hittin the air and the sunlight, and then she's flyin, movin right with them.

She sees herself, standin in the shadows with the shells over her eyes. The swarm homes in on her like she's the absolute worst thing in their world, like they gotta protect the hive from her or die tryin. Sweat breaks out all over her body. Maybe she shouldn't have done this. Maybe she should have thought of another way. Cause if she can't turn them, they're gonna kill her.

She pulls at them, pushes at them, there's somethin worse than her, somethin that's a bigger threat to the hive and they've gotta get him, gotta stop him or the hive'll be destroyed.

It doesn't seem to be working. They're still comin at her. Somethin inside her is screamin to run but she knows that won't do no good. Ain't nobody gonna outrun these bees.

Gotta turn em, gotta turn em, gotta—

There! They're turnin, veerin away from her and turnin east. She did it. She's in control now and her own rage adds fuel to the bees'.

12

With his father noisily engaged in an exploration of the deep, dark recesses of napland, Jack wandered outside. Square-foot-wise, Dad's place was bigger than Jack's apartment back in New York, but it felt smaller. Maybe because he didn't have to share his place with anyone. He needed some fresh air.

With the comforting weight of the Glock at the small of his back, he scanned his surroundings as he yawned and stretched, looking for signs of the clan. Semelee had said Dad was no longer a target, but she'd been acting pretty weird out there in the Glades. What was to prevent her from changing her mind?

He started to circle the house, as much inspecting as trying to walk off the Scotch. He hadn't had all that much but it had made him a little drowsy. Not drowsy enough for a nap, though.

No white-haired girl sitting on his car hood this time. No one at all in sight. As he walked around to the left side he heard a faint buzzing, like a far-off chainsaw, filtering through the air. He looked around for the source but saw nothing. Maybe someone was using one on the far side of one of the houses. One thing he knew, it wasn't Carl. He was taking the rest of the day off—although he'd told

Jack he'd return briefly tonight to set up the Anya-cam again.

The buzzing grew louder and Jack did another slow turn. What—?

Then he saw the man-size cloud sweeping toward him from the Glades and knew with a sick, cold dread what it was and who had sent them. All his instincts urged him to turn and run but he forced himself forward, toward them. Because that was where the front door was. He sprinted with everything he had, but the bees got there first.

He staggered back as they swarmed over him and began stinging. Their angry buzzing and pain like dozens of red-hot ice picks stabbing into his flesh became Jack's world. He needed both hands to bat the bees away from his face but that left the rest of him vulnerable—his neck, his scalp, his bare arms. He could feel them stinging him through his T-shirt. He tried for the door again but they drove him back.

Through the cloud he caught a glint of water—the pond. He stumbled in that direction, picking up speed. When he reached the bank he leaped blindly in a headlong dive. As he knifed through the surface he felt most of the swarm back off—but not all. Some still clung to him, stinging as he—

His outstretched hands hit the rough, hard surface of an underwater rock. He clung to it to keep himself submerged. He was safe for the moment, but he was going to need air soon. Very—

The rock moved, twisting under him. Through the murky water he saw that it had scalloped edges and a tail and he didn't need to see the two big heads rearing up, hooked jaws agape, to know what was sharing the pond with him.

He clung to the edges of the shell as the big alligator snapper surged toward the surface, twisting this way and that as it tried to shake him off. The ridged surface was slimy and his fingers were losing their grip. Jack was running out of air as he raced through his options. The pond was clearly a no-win. Had to get out and take his chances with the bees. With the snapper surfacing, he was going to have to deal with them anyway.

As his lungs screamed for air, he drew his legs up under him, folding them till his sneaker soles were on the shell. As soon as his head broke water, the bees were on him again. He kept his face submerged until the last possible instant, then sprang off the shell, leaping for land. His right sneaker slipped, robbing him of the distance he needed, and the breath he'd taken while airborne was knocked out of him when he belly flopped onto the edge of the bank. His legs were still in the water and, for a panicky instant as he heard the splash of the snapper coming for him, he remembered what those jaws could do to a broomstick. A flashing vision of himself crawling the rest of the way out of the water with a bloody stump where a foot used to be threw him into a twisting roll that left him clear of the water. As he batted at the relentless bee swarm, he glimpsed the two heads stretched to the limits of their thick necks snapping at empty air where his legs had been.

Could an alligator snapper move on land? Jack wasn't waiting around to find out, especially with the bees stinging him again. He realized he'd emerged on Anya's side of the pond, so he scrambled to his feet and raced toward her front door. It was closed but maybe it was unlocked.

Please be unlocked!

But he didn't need the shelter of her house. As soon as he crossed into her circle of green lawn, the killer bees peeled off him the same way the palmettos had the other night when he'd jumped through his father's door.

He heard their enraged buzzing rise in pitch and volume

as they hurled themselves at him, only to be turned back as soon as they crossed the line into Anya's space.

"Go!" he heard a voice cry behind him.

Jack turned and saw Anya crossing the lawn in his direction. She was waving both arms in a shooing motion.

"Go!" she shouted again. "Back where you came from!" She pointed to the snapper's two heads, watching from the pond. "You too! Go!"

The bees swarmed in random confusion, then gathered into an oblong cloud and buzzed away. When Jack looked at the pond again, the snapper was gone.

He dropped to his knees, panting. His skin felt aflame, his stomach threatened to heave.

"Thank you," he gasped. "I don't know how you did that, but thanks."

"Didn't I tell you that nothing on earth can hurt you here?"

"I guess you did." He looked up at her. "Who are you? Really."

Anya smiled. "Your mother."

The familiar words chilled Jack.

"That's what the Russian lady said to me by my sister's grave. And that Indian woman in Astoria said the same thing to Gia. What's it mean?"

Anya shook her head. "Don't worry about it, hon. There's no need for you to know. Not yet. Hopefully not ever."

"Then why say it to me?"

Anya had turned and started walking away. Over her shoulder she said, "Because it's true."

13

Semelee stumbled pantin and sweatin along the path through the palms. She stopped and leaned against a gumbo limbo tree to catch her breath.

That same old lady . . . doin it again . . . causin trouble, gettin in the way . . .

She was stronger than Semelee. Somehow she'd just waved her hand and told the bees and Dora to get home and that was that. Semelee's power got canceled like turnin off a light. Everything went black. When she come to, the sun was pretty much down and she was flat on her back in the ferns with the shells off her eyes but still in her hands.

She had to be stopped. But how? How do you stop someone with that kind of power?

Where did she come from? Who was she that she could protect herself from Dora and a swarm of bees—not only keep them out but give them orders?

Maybe she couldn't be hurt. Maybe she was beyond Semelee's special power.

She stumbled up to the bank of the lagoon and saw Luke sitting on the deck of the *Bull-ship*.

He looked up at her with sad eyes. "Bad news, Semelee. Devil's dead."

A wave of sadness washed over her. Feelin weak, she lowered herself to the ground and rested her back against a palm.

Poor Devil . . . her fault . . . if she hadn't—

No, wait. It was that old bitch and her dog. They were the ones killed Devil. Not her.

She ground her teeth. Had to be a way to get back at her.

She glanced to her left toward the sinkhole and saw the glow of the lights seepin up through the darkenin air. Pullin herself to her feet she walked over. She stopped at the edge, then stretched herself out flat on her belly with her head pokin over the rim. She gazed into the flashin deeps and tried to remember more of what happened down there. But nothin came back to her.

She gave up tryin to remember and was just startin to get to her feet when she had an idea. She still had the eye-shells in her hands and figured, Why not? She put them over her eyes. For an instant they blotted out the lights, then suddenly she was seein them again. But they looked different.

Then Semelee realized she wasn't seein the lights from above, she was seein them from within. She was inside some kinda creature down there and was seein things through its eyes. She looked around and saw wings and jaws and teeth—lots of long, sharp teeth.

An idea crept into her head, an idea so wonderful she started to laugh out loud.

14

"I still say we should take you to the emergency room," Dad said.

Jack shook his head as he shivered under the blanket. "I'll be fine, Dad. No doctors."

At least not yet.

He sat on the sofa and shook despite the dark blue wool blanket wrapped around him. Most of his sting-lumped skin was crusted pink with calamine lotion and he was dopey from the Benadryl his father had picked up for him in town. The stings themselves—he hadn't counted them, but Pinhead had nothing on Jack—itched and burned, and now his muscles were aching. The chills and fever had started about an hour after the attack. He figured he had so much bee venom in his system that he was having a reaction. He felt as if he had the flu.

At least he wasn't vomiting; his stomach was queasy but he was holding down the orange juice Dad kept pushing at him.

He'd shown his father how to break down the Glock and wipe it dry. Here was where its mostly plastic construction was a blessing. Dad didn't have any gun oil, but substituted a little 3-in-1 to lubricate the few metal parts.

And now his father paced back and forth between Jack and the TV as the Weather Channel showed a satellite photo of Hurricane Elvis picking up speed and power as it looped southward through the Gulf of Mexico. It had graduated to Category II and was expected to brush South Florida and the Keys sometime tomorrow, then continue on toward Cuba.

"We've got to call the cops," Dad said.

Dad always seemed to want to call the cops.

"And what—tell them about this woman in the Glades who sent a swarm of bees and a two-headed snapping turtle after me? They'll take you away in a straitjacket."

"We've got to do *something*! We can't just sit here like targets and let her take potshots at us!"

"I can't think right now, Dad."

Jack hauled himself unsteadily to his feet and shuffled toward the guest bedroom.

He'd planned to drop in on Anya tonight. He'd cut her too much slack, let her evade straight answers for too long. He was going to get nose to nose with her and find out exactly who she was, how she could keep giant alligators and bees and mosquitoes from trespassing on her property, and have them obey her when she told them to take off. He wasn't going to leave until he had some answers.

But that was all changed now. Christ, he felt awful. If he'd been sitting on the hood of Dad's car when it got clocked by that truck, he didn't think he'd feel much worse.

"I'm going to hit the rack. In the meantime, don't do anything I wouldn't do."

"That's all fine and dandy," Dad said with a touch of acid in his voice, "except I don't know *what* you wouldn't do."

"Well, for one thing, I wouldn't leave the house tonight, that's what I wouldn't do. As for what I *would* do"—he pointed to the reassembled Glock resting on a section of the Novaton *Express*—"I'd keep that handy. See you in the morning."

15

Jack awoke bathed in sweat. He threw back the covers, sat up, and pulled off his undershirt.

What time was it? The clock's LED display was angled away from him. No light filtered through the curtains. Still night. He ran a hand over a tender, bumpy arm. God, he felt like hell.

As he flopped back and pulled the sheet up over him, he

thought he heard a dog barking—high-pitched yips that could only belong to Oyv. They had an almost hysterical edge. Jack wondered what was bothering him. Not that the little guy couldn't take care of himself—look at what he'd done to that big ugly gator—but he hadn't struck Jack as the kind of pooch to bark at nothing.

Jack was ready to force himself out of bed to go have a look when the barking stopped. Whatever had set off Oyv must have passed.

Jack closed his eyes and drifted back to sleep.

SUNDAY

1

I've *got* to get back to New York, Jack thought.

Not just because he missed Gia and Vicky, but here it was Sunday afternoon and instead of watching the Jets kick Dolphin butt up at Giants Stadium, he was sitting here with his father and staring at the Weather Channel.

Trouble was, he found it mesmerizing.

The Weather Channel as a way of life . . . scary.

I stay much longer I'll be as addicted as everybody else around here.

He excused his present fascination by the fact that the weather was about to have significant personal impact: Hurricane Elvis had reentered the building. In fact he was announcing his presence with a chorus of gusts that hurled sheets of rain against the outside of this little building.

Satellite tracking of Elvis showed how it had made a sharp eastward turn during the night and homed in on the Everglades like a cruise missile. At this moment its eye was making landfall on South Florida's west coast. Elvis wasn't a monster; it was a tight little storm with sustained winds now in the 120-mile-an-hour neighborhood, making it a Category III. Multiple waterspouts had been spotted among the Ten Thousand Islands, wherever they were. But apparently it was a very wet storm and everyone was happy that it was going to dump a lot of much needed rain onto the Everglades.

But how many times could you watch the same graphic and listen to the same *Storm Center* report?

Gia apparently had been watching the weather too. She'd called to tell him to stay inside. Not that he had any intention of venturing out into this mess, but he appreciated her concern. He hadn't told her about the bee stings. They were still swollen; not as much as last night, but still itchy and tender.

He was about to ask his father to switch the channel for half a minute—not a second more than that, God forbid—to check the score of the Jets game, when he heard a frantic knocking on the door. As his father peeled himself away from the tube to see who it was, Jack slipped the Glock from where he'd stowed it under his sofa cushion.

"Better let me get it, Dad."

But before either of them could reach the door, it blew open. Jack had the pistol up and aimed at the figure standing in the doorway, his finger tightening on the trigger, when he recognized Carl.

"Come quick!" he cried as wind swirled around him and scattered sections of the Sunday paper. He wore a dripping, dark green poncho, had a screwdriver sticking out of his right sleeve, and a plastic shopping bag clutched in his left. "Y'gotta see this, y'just gotta!"

"See what?" Dad said.

"Miss Mundy's place! It's all tore up!"

Carl turned and started to lead the way, but once they were outside in the slashing wind and rain, Jack broke into a trot and pulled ahead of him. The sudden memory of Oyv's barking last night sent a cold spike of unease through his chest. It speared down through his gut when he saw her doorway.

"Oh, shit!"

The screen had been shredded; gray, mosslike tatters fluttered within the frame. The wooden door behind it stood open.

"Anya!" Jack shouted as he pulled open what was left of the screen door and stepped inside.

He stopped suddenly, just beyond the threshold, causing Dad to bump into him, pushing him forward.

"Oh, dear God!" he heard his father gasp.

"Didn't I tell you?" Carl said. "Didn't I?"

The place was a shambles. That was the only word for it. The furniture had been torn apart, the carpet gouged up, and the plants . . . they'd been torn from their pots, their roots savaged, and every leaf had been torn from the ravaged branches.

Jack forced himself to move forward, calling Anya's name as he checked both bedrooms and behind the kitchen counter. He found a small spatter of darkening red fluid, and something that looked like a severed finger on the floor.

Jack knelt for a closer look. It was pale, the size of a finger, but it was covered with fur.

What the—?

And then he knew: Oyv's tail.

Christ! The blood . . . Oyv had to be dead—died defending Anya no doubt. A slow wave of sadness settled over him. But what could have killed that preternaturally tough little dog? It had to be something bigger and meaner than a giant alligator. But what? And where was the rest of him?

Jack noticed something glittering on the floor. He bent closer: three little slivers of glass. He looked around for a broken window but didn't see one. Maybe a glass had been knocked off the counter and shattered.

He was pushing himself to his feet when he noticed that all three shards appeared identical. Each about an inch and a half long, with the same curve, and the same taper from thicker base to needle-fine point. He picked one up and rotated it in the light. Its edges were smooth, rounded. If he didn't know better, he'd have said it was a fang of some sort. But he didn't know anything that had glass teeth.

He touched the point with the tip of his finger and it

slipped through the skin like a bird's beak dipping into water.

Damn! He started to toss it back to the floor, then decided not to. Maybe he should find out what it was before he threw it away.

He rose and grabbed a paper towel from the roll suspended from the underside of a cabinet. He rolled the needle within and used it to blot the drop of blood oozing from his fingertip.

He turned to his father and Carl, still standing in the doorway.

"What the hell happened here?"

Dad could give him only a stunned look, but Carl held up his plastic shopping bag.

"It's all here!"

"What's all there?"

"What happened. The camera caught it all. Or at least most of it."

2

"When I picked up the camera this morning," Carl said, "I was in a hurry so it just sat in the bag till after I got home. Long after I got home."

They'd all hurried back to Dad's place to set up the camera for playback.

"You didn't check it right away?"

"Nuh-uh. I figured, what for? I mean, I ain't never seen nothin before and figured this wouldn't be no different. So I just left it be until I was watchin the Dolphins game.

That's when I checked it and found the battery didn't have no charge left. That ain't happened before. So I recharged it and took a look to see if somethin'd set it off."

"What's this camera about?" Dad said.

Jack ran through a quick explanation of Dr. Dengrove's attempts to catch Anya watering her yard.

"Dengrove," Dad said. "Cheats at golf but God forbid anyone sneaks a little water onto their lawn. What an ass."

Jack had the two-inch LCD screen flipped open. He hit PLAY and started to watch. Dad hung over his shoulder, Carl crouched farther back. The screen lit with green and black blobs that quickly stretched and coalesced into recognizable shapes—the side of Anya's house, her plantings, the doo-dads, the lawn furniture in her front yard. And then a set of legs went by. Then more.

"Doesn't this thing have any sound?" Dad said.

"If you hook it up to your TV you can get sound. Want me—?"

"We can do that later if we need to," Jack said. He had a sick cold feeling in his gut that they'd be listening to the high-pitched barking he'd ignored last night. "First let's see what's to see."

Carl jabbed a finger toward the little screen. "There they are! See?"

Jack saw. A crowd was gathering in an irregular semicircle around the edge of Anya's lawn. Light from the front windows lit their faces. His intestines began to writhe as he recognized Luke and Corley and a couple of the others. Looked like the whole gang had shown up.

"The clan," he said.

"All cept Semelee. I didn't see her nowheres when I watched."

Jack stared at the tiny screen. He now wished they'd hooked it to the TV. Probably would have lost some resolution, but maybe he'd have a better view of their faces.

Beyond a few grins, he couldn't make out much in the way of expressions. He could read their postures, though, and they radiated something between revulsion and avid fascination, as if they wanted to press forward for a better look, but fear held them in check.

He kept watching, waiting for the clan to do something. He searched for Semelee but couldn't find her. That white hair of hers would be hard to miss. Why were all the men there? What did they have against—?

Oh, right. The big ugly alligator . . . her dog had chewed a hole in its side. And the bees yesterday . . . Anya had chased them off. Yeah, he could see where Semelee could have a bone or two to pick with Anya. But how was she going to get her if Anya's promise—*Nothing on earth can harm you here*—was true?

Obviously it wasn't. Someone had got to her—and to poor little Oyv. What had Semelee—?

"There!" Carl cried. "Didja see that?"

"No." Jack's attention had been wandering. "What?"

"I saw something too," Dad said, "but I don't know what."

Jack found the reverse button and backed up the recording. Again he watched Luke and the rest of the men standing in their semicircle, eyes fixed on the front of the house. The camera angle didn't include the front door, but they were staring like there was a stripper doing her thing there. And then something—maybe three somethings, two feet long at most—suddenly streaked out of the house and over their heads. The way the men ducked and covered made it pretty obvious that they were afraid of the things, whatever they were. More flew out. Once they were gone, the clan came to life. Luke swung an arm and they all charged toward the house.

For a good five to seven minutes, nothing happened, and then the clan reemerged. A group of them seemed to be

carrying something but the way they were bunched together prevented him from seeing exactly what. He didn't
have to see. He knew.

"They've got Anya."

"The sons of bitches," Dad said, straightening and
reaching for the phone. "I'm calling the cops."

Jack grabbed his arm. "Hold on a sec. I want to see this
again—on the TV."

"Fine. And while you're setting that up, I'll be
calling—"

"Just wait, okay? Just let me see it again before we get
officialdom involved."

Dad reluctantly agreed, grumbling about wasting time
as Jack wired the camera to the audio-visual inputs on the
backside of the TV.

"This happened at least twelve hours ago, Dad. Maybe
more. Another ten minutes isn't going to matter."

He finished plugging in the wires, then reran the movie.
The TV screen offered over one hundred times the viewing
area of the camera's LCD. It offered sound as well. The
movie began with the rattle of the lawn-ornament cans and
Oyv's barking, but that broke off with a high-pitched
squeal just as the last of the clan reached the front of the
house. A couple of minutes later the things streaked away.
Jack was ready with his finger on the PAUSE button.

"Got 'em!" he said. He leaned closer to the screen. "But
what the hell are they?"

The camera's image intensification coupled with the
speed of the things left little more than amorphous, blurry
streaks on the screen, but there was enough resolution to
reveal five shapes instead of three in the first batch. He'd
missed the other two because they were farther from the
camera and hadn't caught as much light. He could see that
the three in front had slightly curved bodies that reflected
light like a shell might; their wings were fuzzy blurs.

"Y'ask me," Carl said. "They look like flyin lobsters."

Not a bad characterization, Jack thought. But lobsters didn't fly, so what on earth were these?

Jack felt his neck muscles tighten. On earth . . .

Nothing on earth can harm you here.

But what if those flying lobsters weren't from anywhere on earth? What if they were somehow from the Otherness? Semelee had gone down into that sinkhole. Maybe she'd found something down there that she could control like she did the creatures in the Glades.

Jack pulled the rolled-up paper towel out of his jeans pocket and unwrapped the little crystal shard.

"What have you got there?" Dad said.

"Not sure." He handed it to him on the towel. "Careful. It's sharp. Ever seen anything like it?"

"I did," Carl said. "Saw one just like it stickin outta the tore-up wood on Miss Mundy's door. I just figgered it was glass."

Dad was holding it up, rotating it back and forth in the light. "You know, it almost looks like some weird sort of fang."

Carl laughed. "Glass teeth! That's funny!"

Dad lifted the beer bottle he'd been sipping at during the endless weather reports and scratched the fang's point along the glass. It gave out a faint, high-pitched squeak as it scored the surface.

Dad frowned. "Not glass. Much harder. The only thing I know that can scratch glass like that is a diamond."

"If it is a tooth," Jack said, "that means that Anya was attacked by things with diamond teeth."

They all sat silent for a moment, then Jack restarted the movie. They watched more of the things fly out, then the clan crowd into the house. When they emerged this time he kept freezing the frames but got no better view of what they were carrying than before. What else could it be but Anya?

But alive or dead?

As the movie ended again, Dad slapped his thighs. "That does it. Time to call 9-1-1."

"Don't bother, Dad."

"Why on earth not?"

Jack pulled the Glock from the SOB holster and checked the magazine: full.

"Because I'm going after her and I don't want them getting in the way."

3

Tom could only stare at his son. He'd sensed that the Jack who had gone into Anya's ruined house was a different Jack from the one who'd come out. But now he'd changed further. His mild brown eyes had turned to stone; he seemed remote, as if he'd left the room without moving his body.

"After her? Are you crazy? We trumped a couple of them once because it was a controlled situation and we had surprise on our side. But all that's changed now. You can't expect to stroll in there alone and—"

"Won't be alone," Carl said. "I'll come along."

Tom noticed Jack's cold eyes warm briefly at this simple man's unadorned courage. And in that moment he wished Jack were looking at him like that.

"Not necessary, Carl," Jack said.

"'Tis. She's a good lady. Lotsa people look at me funny, some don't even want me around. But she always smiled at me and when it was hot she gave me lemonade and cookies and stuff like that. My own mother never treated me that good. And besides, the clan ain't got no right to do that to her. Semelee's gone crazy. Ever since she come up outta those lights she's been different. Scary. Who knows what she's got in mind for Miss Mundy. We gotta get her back."

"But that's what we have police for!" Tom cried.

He'd resisted the urge to chime in and say he'd go along too. Anya was a friend, a good one, and his blood curdled at the thought of her in the hands of a bunch of swampland inbreds. But it was just because he cared about her that he had to stop this craziness. Jack's gung-ho plan might wind up putting Anya in greater danger. Might even get her killed.

"And in case you two would-be vigilantes haven't noticed," he added, "there's a Category-Three hurricane blowing out there."

"Exactly why we've got to take care of this," Jack said. "Who're you going to call? The Novaton police? Their whole department, along with every other cop south of Miami, is going to be tied up with the hurricane emergency. They'll be busy with evacuation, shelters, looting prevention. You know the drill. A missing-person problem will be put on a back burner till the storm's passed. Hell, we don't even have proof she was taken."

"But the movie—"

"—will be great in court. But do you think it will get a bunch of cops running around in boats out in the Everglades looking for a particular hummock in the middle of a hurricane?"

Tom had to admit he doubted it—but only to himself. Under no circumstances did he want Jack going out there— not even with Carl, who Tom couldn't see as much help.

"Carl," Jack said, pointing to the screwdriver protruding from his sleeve. "Do me a favor and use that to take the medicine cabinet out of the wall in the bathroom."

Carl gave him a strange look—imagine that—then shrugged and nodded and said, "Okay."

"Medicine cabinet?" Tom said. "What—?"

Jack turned his back and headed for the hall closet.

"Look, Dad," he said as he knelt by the toolbox and began rummaging through its contents. "I don't know for sure, but I think that taking Anya has something to do with the lights. But the lights only last a couple of days. By tonight or early tomorrow morning they'll be gone for another six months."

"What lights?"

"Oh, yeah. Right. I forgot." He pulled a socket wrench from the toolbox and headed for the dinette table. "You don't know about the lights."

"Care to en*light*en me?" Tom said, following. "And what do you think you're going to do with that wrench?"

"You'll see. As for the lights, forget about them for now. Take too long to explain. What matters is that after the lights go out, Semelee and Company will have no more need to hang around their lagoon. Good chance they'll be gone by sunup tomorrow."

"And take Anya with them?"

Jack gave him a stony look before he crouched under the table and began loosening the nuts that fastened it to its support pillar.

"I doubt it. She's the one whose dog chewed a hole in the side of that big mutant gator, remember? I'm worried they'll feed her to it before they go—if they haven't already."

Tom felt his knees go rubbery. "No . . . they couldn't."

"Let's hope not."

"Hey!" Carl called from the bathroom. "They's only one screw holdin this cabinet in place and that's only halfway in."

"I know," Jack called back. "Just twist it out."

One screw? Tom brushed aside questions about his medicine cabinet. The thought of Anya being hurt overshadowed all that.

"Jack, we've got to call the police. Or the Coast Guard, or the Park Service."

Jack stuck his head out from under the table and gave him a you've-got-to-be-kidding look.

"She's a friend, Dad. A better friend than you know. And I owe her."

"For what?"

"For you being alive."

"What are you talking about?"

"She's the one who reported your accident to the police twenty minutes before it happened."

"That's as crazy as going out in this storm. She told you that?"

"She didn't. But I've no question in my mind that's what happened. She knows things, Dad. All sorts of things. And now she needs help. When a good friend needs help, you don't call on somebody else. You go yourself."

The words struck a chord deep within Tom. Yes, he knew that. He'd been taught that. He'd lived that. But where had Jack come by it?

And yet he couldn't allow himself to bend here, couldn't let Jack go out into that storm against twenty men.

"Where's that written?"

Jack slipped out from under the table and rose to his feet, his face barely a foot away. He tapped a finger on the center of his forehead.

"In here. Right in here."

Yes . . . that was where it would be. But not the only place.

He tapped his son's chest, over the heart. "In there too."

Jack nodded. "Yeah. There too."

And as they stood staring at each other, Tom flashed back to Korea. That had been the Marine code: Nobody gets left behind. At least nobody still breathing. Sometimes you had to leave your dead, but you never left your living. If someone was stranded, or hurt and unable to get out on his own, you went in and got him.

And you didn't call on anyone else because there wasn't anyone better. You were US Marines, the toughest sons of bitches on earth. It was a matter of pride. If you couldn't do it, no one could.

Back at Chosin, when Tom took that piece of shrapnel in the gut, he'd radioed in that he'd been hit and couldn't make it out. He'd expected his buddies to *want* to come and get him, but figured there was no way with all the shit coming down on the Fifth. But damned if three of them hadn't shown up after dark and carried him out.

"Help me lift off this top," Jack said.

"What on earth for?"

"Let's just do it."

Tom grabbed one side, Jack the other. They lifted it, tilted it, and leaned it against the kitchenette counter. Then Jack reached into the hollow interior of the post and came up with a black plastic bag. Its lumpy contents clunked together as he laid it on the counter.

"What the hell? How'd that get in there?"

"I put it in the other day. Let me tell you, I had one hell of a time maneuvering that tabletop around on my own."

"But what've you got in there?"

Jack reached in and came out with a fist-size lump of metal that he flipped over the counter. Tom caught it, saw what it was—a smooth metal sphere the size of a tennis ball, with a key ring at the top attached to a safety clip— and felt his heart trip over a beat.

"A grenade?"

"M-67s. I had a dozen sent down after seeing that gator."

"Sent down when? I never saw any—" And then it hit him. "The toys. They were in the toys, right?"

Jack gave him a tight smile. "Right. I also—"

"Hey!" Carl called from the bathroom. "You got a gun in this wall!"

"What?"

A gun? In his wall? Tom started toward the bathroom but Jack got there first. Carl had pulled the medicine cabinet from the wall, exposing the studs and the unfinished backside of the Sheetrock of the opposite wall. The end of an empty metal tube jutted a couple of inches up from the lower end of the space. It had a blued-steel finish and looked like an open plumbing pipe until Tom spotted the blade sight on the end and realized this was the business end of a shotgun barrel.

Jack fished it out and handed it to Carl. Its black polymer stock barely reflected the overhead lights.

"Ever use a shotgun?"

Carl laughed. "You kiddin? Fed myself mostly by fishin and huntin before I came to work here. If'n I wasn't no good, I'da starved." He took it from Jack and hefted it. "But I ain't never see one like this before."

Neither had Tom. He saw a breechlock, a magazine tube, but where was the slide handle?

"It's a Benelli—an M1 Super 90, to be exact. I think the semi-auto action will work best for you."

"A semi-auto shotgun?" Tom said. "I didn't even know they made such a thing."

"She's a beauty," Carl said. "I like the rubber grip. Kinda like a pistol."

"Very much like a pistol. Will you be able to handle it?"

"Sure. I told you—"

"I mean"—Jack glanced at Carl's right sleeve—"will you need to modify the stock or anything?"

"Nuh-uh. I'll be fine."

"Great. Excuse me, Dad," he said as he turned and edged by Tom into the front room. "Be back in a minute."

Without another word he ran out into the storm. Two minutes later he returned, dripping, carrying an oblong object wrapped in a blanket Tom had last seen in the linen closet. He pulled it off to reveal another shotgun.

"I'll use this one," Jack said.

With its ridged slide handle riding under the barrel, this one was more like how Tom pictured a shotgun. Its polymer stock was done up with standard camouflage greens and browns.

"It looks military," Tom said.

"It is. It's a Mossberg 590, made to military specs. Very reliable." He started across the front room. "Now . . . one last thing and we'll be set to go."

Tom followed Jack around to the guest bedroom where Jack pulled out the bottom drawer on the dresser and laid it on the floor. Tom watched in shock as his son reached into the space beneath and produced one box of shells, then another, then another . . .

"Jesus, Jack! Did you think you were going to war?"

"After I saw that gator, I figured a little old 9mm pistol wasn't going to do the job, so I ordered up some heavy artillery."

"But *two* shotguns?"

"Well, yeah. One for here and one for the car, in case something happened while we were out."

Carl stepped into the doorway, carrying the Benelli. "What you got this loaded with?"

"With what's known as a 'Highway Patrol cocktail'— alternating shells of double-ought buckshot and rifled slugs." He held up one of the boxes. "Here are our reloads."

Tom felt a tightening in his chest. He didn't know if it was his heart or dismay at what was happening here. He slipped past Carl, went to his own bedroom, and pulled the M1C from the closet. He carried it back to Jack and Carl.

"What are you doing with that?" Jack said.

"Well, since I can't talk you out of this insanity, I guess I'll have to come along."

"No way, Dad."

Tom felt his anger flare. "Aren't you the one who just gave me a lecture on going out for a friend in trouble?"

"Yeah, but—"

"And have either of you ever been in a firefight?" He didn't wait for an answer. "No, of course not. Well, I have. And that's what you could very easily wind up in. You're going to need me."

"Dad—"

Tom jabbed a finger at him. "Who put you in charge anyway? Besides, your mother would never forgive me if I let you go out there without backing you up. I'm in."

Jack stared at him a moment, then sighed. "All right." He held out the Mossberg. "But put away that antique and take this."

"But I'm more comfortable with—"

"Dad, it's going to be dark with all sorts of wind and rain. Let's hope we can pull this off without any gunplay, but if it comes to that, we'll be working close—maybe twenty-five feet, fifty max. A sniper rifle's no good in that situation."

Tom had to admit he was right. He reluctantly took the shotgun.

"But what are you going to use?"

"I'll have the grenades. But I'll also have . . ." Jack reached back into the space below the drawer and pulled out a huge revolver. It had a gray finish and was well over a foot in length. The barrel alone looked to be about ten inches long.

"Oh, man!" Carl said. "What's *that*?"

"Took the words right out of my mouth," Tom said.

"A Ruger Super Redhawk chambered for .454 Casull

rounds. I do believe this will stop that gator if he shows up again."

"Looks like it'll stop a elephant," Carl said.

A discomforting thought started worming through Tom's brain.

"Jack . . . you're not in one of these right-wing paramilitary groups, are you?"

He laughed. "You mean like the Posse Comitatus or Aryan Nation? Not a chance. I'm not a joiner, and even if I were, I wouldn't join them."

"Then what are you? Some sort of mercenary?"

"Why are you asking all this?"

"Why do you think? Because of all these guns!"

Jack looked around. "Not so many."

"You didn't answer my question, Jack. Are you a mercenary?"

"If you mean one of those soldiers of fortune, no. But people do hire me to, well, fix things. I guess that might make me a mercenary. But—"

Just then the TV started emitting high-pitched beeps. They all hustled into the front room. A red banner took up the lower quarter of screen, announcing that a hurricane-spawned tornado had set down in Ochopee.

"Where's Ochopee?" Jack said.

"Other side of the state," Carl replied. "Way out Route 41."

Jack looked at Tom. "Anyone wants to back out, now's the time. No explanation required, no questions asked."

Carl grinned. "Hey, I live in a trailer park. You know how tornadoes zero in on them places. I figure I gotta be safer out in the Glades."

Just then, lightning lit the windows, followed by a rumble of thunder.

Tom's gut crawled, but he said, "Let's get moving."

And God help us all.

4

Jack drove his paddle into the water to keep the canoe moving against the wind and driving rain. He had a terrible feeling that it might already be too late for Anya, but if not, then the sooner they reached her, the better.

Carl sat in the stern, working the little motor, steering them along the channel. Dad had the front, Jack the middle seat. When the channel nosed them into the wind, the engine didn't have what it took to keep them moving; that was when he and Dad put their paddles to use.

He'd never seen rain like this. He'd expected it to be cold, but it was almost warm. When it wasn't lashing them with horizontal cascades that would put Niagara Falls to shame, it pelted them with huge, marble-size drops that did drum rolls on the hood of his poncho. The rest of the Glades had gone away; the world had narrowed to a short length of the channel's rippling water with only occasional glimpses of its banks. Everything else, including the sky, had been swallowed by dark gray sheets of wet. Only the ever more frequent flashes of lightning and roars of thunder hinted that there might be a world beyond.

Good thing the hardware store had been open so he and Dad could pick up ponchos—dark green, like Carl's—and a hand pump. He didn't want to imagine what this trek would have been like without the ponchos. Jack had his hood pulled tight around his head, the drawstring knotted at his throat. Still he was getting wet.

And the hand pump—they wouldn't have got even this

far without it. Into the wind, they paddled; when the twisting channel put the wind to their backs, Jack let Dad rest while he worked the pump to rid them of the rainwater that kept accumulating around their feet.

The canoe had been flooded when they found it. They'd flipped it to empty it, then wasted precious time trying to get the little motor to turn over. Carl finally got it going and they were off.

Jack cupped his hands around his mouth and leaned back toward Carl.

"Did we get to the shallows yet?" he shouted above the din of the rain.

Carl nodded. "Just passed them."

And we didn't have to get out and walk, Jack thought. Testament to the amount of water falling out of that sky.

"Let me know when we're almost to the lagoon."

Ahead of him Jack noticed that his father had stopped paddling. His oar rested across his lap as he rubbed his left shoulder.

"You okay?" he said, leaning forward.

Dad turned sideways. All Jack could see was his profile; the rest of his head was tucked into the poncho hood.

"I'm okay. Just not used to this sort of thing. At least I don't have to worry about the lightning."

"Why not?"

"I tried to lead an orchestra once and found out I was a poor conductor."

Jack gave him a gentle shove. "One more of those and we toss you overboard!" He could see Dad was exhausted, but not too exhausted to come up with a rotten pun. He gripped his shoulder. "Take a breather. We're almost there."

Dad gave a silent nod.

Jack bent his back into paddling, forcing the canoe ahead into the wind. And as he sweated, he planned.

They'd reach the lagoon soon. He tried to picture the lay-out . . . the houseboats, the huts on the bank. Would the clan be on the boats or ashore? Would they be at the lagoon at all?

Had to be. The lights would keep them there.

Light . . . it was fading fast. Somewhere on the far side of Elvis the sun was crawling toward the horizon, but the storm swallowed up its light, leaving Jack and company in growing darkness.

Good. The lower the light, the longer it would take the clan to figure out how much backup Jack had brought along.

He felt a tap on his shoulder: Carl.

"We'll be getting to the hummock soon."

The storm seemed to let up as they fought their way into the rain-forestlike tunnel of green at the edge of the hum-mock. The palms, banyans, and gumbo limbo trees seemed to hang lower under the weight of the rain; aerial roots and vines brushed against their ponchos.

"Couple more turns and we'll be in the lagoon," Carl said.

Jack leaned back. "Should we shut off the motor?"

At that moment a bolt of lightning struck close enough for Jack to hear its buzz and sizzle; the almost simultane-ous blast of thunder hit him like a fist.

He could just barely hear Carl through the ringing in his ears: "I don't think that'll be a problem. You?"

"Probably not, but shut down anyway."

No telling what kind of vibrations the little motor might set up in the hulls of those ships. Why risk tipping them off?

Wind and rain blasted them again as the canoe slipped out of the tree tunnel and into the relative open. Straight for a while, then around a bend and they were in the lagoon.

At least he thought it was the lagoon. The water was

wider and he could see only the near bank on his right, but where were the houseboats? He had a bad moment as he looked around and couldn't find them, then a flash of lightning lit up the area and he saw both boats through the rain, floating straight ahead. The *Bull-ship* sat to the left, the *Horse-ship* to the right.

Dad must have spotted them too because he turned and started motioning toward the right bank.

"Put it in over there!" he said.

Jack figured he must have his reasons—and he was, after all, the only one with military training—so he passed the message to Carl.

When the canoe nosed into the bank, Dad hopped out and motioned Jack and Carl ashore. He led them to the lee side of a stand of twisted palms where they could converse without shouting.

"If they're here," Dad said, "they're on those boats. Agreed?"

Jack nodded. "Agreed."

"Okay. Then we need to deploy ourselves around the bank at wide intervals along a hundred-fifty-degree arc, no bigger."

"Why not?" Jack asked.

"Because when you get much closer to one-eighty you run the risk of shooting at each other. Ideally we want all three of us to have line of sight to both boats, but if that doesn't work, then the two flanking guns will concentrate their fire on the nearer boat; the gun in the center can fire on either—wherever it's most needed."

"Dad, I'm looking to get this done without turning the lagoon into the OK Corral."

"Amen to that, but we have to be prepared for a worst-case scenario." Dad patted the Mossberg through his poncho. "To get the most out of shotguns in this rain and low light, we'll need to set up about fifty to seventy-five feet from the boats. That's closer than I'd like, and lots closer than I'm used to, but these conditions don't leave us much choice."

Dad's takeover of the tactics impressed Jack. He seemed to be talking from experience, so Jack deferred to his judgment.

"Just don't set up too near the cenote," Jack warned him. "You might see some lights shining up from it, but don't get curious. Just stay away."

"You mean the sinkhole?" Carl said. "I'll take that spot. The lights've already done what they're gonna do to me."

Dad said, "Speaking of lights, if we do get into a fire-fight, don't stay in one spot. We can hide pretty well in the rain and the dark, but our guns don't have flash suppressers, so once we start firing, the muzzle flash will give away your position. Fire and move, fire and move. Unless of course you can time your shot to a lightning flash, but that's a lot easier said than done."

Jack swung the plastic bag with the grenades and the big Ruger over his shoulder. "Carl, you take the north position, near the cenote; Dad, you set up on the south end, I'll take the middle; that way I can lob a grenade at either boat should the need arise."

Which he hoped wouldn't. He didn't feature being shot at, and liked his father being shot at even less. The old guy had the experience, and he had the skills, but he also had a body that didn't move or react like it did in its heyday.

"Anyone see any problems with that?"

Dad and Carl shook their heads.

"Good. Okay, once we're all in position, I'll fire a couple of shots to get their attention, then tell them I'm from the Novaton Police Department and demand they release Anya or else."

Dad grinned. "Novaton Police Department? You're planning to kill them with laughter . . . is that the plan?

Better off saying you're from the Miami-Dade Sheriff's Department."

"What if they don't buy it?" Carl said. "What if they start shooting?"

"Then we'll have to shoot back—unless of course they bring Anya on deck."

"Then what?" Carl asked.

"Then we improvise."

Lifting his poncho to reveal the Mossberg, Dad spoke to Carl. "Since these are loaded with alternating slugs and double-ought, I suggest we aim the buckshot at the decks and the slugs at the waterline, preferably near the bow. Anywhere but the superstructure. At this range the boat walls will, I hope, stop most of the shot, but the slugs will go through them like paper, and Anya could be in there."

Carl nodded. "Gotcha. Easy. Those boats is too pan-o-ramic to miss."

Dad looked at Carl, then Jack.

"Don't ask, Dad." Jack gestured ahead. "Let's go."

"And look out for that alligator along the way," Dad said.

Carl shook his head. "I heard Semelee and Luke talkin while I was stuck here and they was sayin Devil was hurt bad. The way they was talking, I don't think he'll be up for chasin us."

"Be on the lookout anyway," Jack said. "Even if he's not, there's still that two-headed snapping turtle."

"Oh, yeah," Carl said. His lips tightened. "Dora."

"Two-headed snapping turtle?" Dad said. "What—?"

"Later, Dad. Just don't get too close to the water."

"Haven't you both forgotten about something else to look out for? What about those flying things that gobbled up Anya's dog and made such a mess of her place? I don't want to run into *them*."

"A snootful of double-ought buck will clip their wings, don't you think?" Jack said.

Dad frowned. "If you can hit them. The ones I saw in the movie were moving pretty damn fast."

On that reassuring note, Jack turned and led them away from the canoe. Heads down against the wind and rain, they sloshed through the oaks, palms, and cypresses, keeping a good ten feet from the water's edge, heading toward the cenote. Well before they reached it, even through the driving rain, Jack could see the lights flashing up from its depths.

As they arrived at the rim, now only an inch or so above the waterline, Dad leaned close to Jack and spoke in a low voice, barely audible above the storm. "Now isn't this a helluva thing?" He peered down into the flashing depths. "What on earth is going on down there?"

"Not sure," Jack told him. "But you want to avoid too much exposure to those lights."

Dad took a quick step back. "Why? Radioactive?"

Worse, Jack wanted to say, but that would stimulate a lot of questions he didn't have time to answer. So he settled for, "Could be."

Carl stepped ahead and crouched behind the head of a newly fallen royal palm. "This here looks like a good spot. Gives me a good bead on the *Horse-ship*. I'll park here."

Jack nodded and motioned his father southward. Dad followed, but kept glancing over his shoulder at the lights from the cenote. They seemed to fascinate him.

Along the way they passed the clan's little boats—the *Chicken-ship*, the *No-ship*, and others—pulled up, turned over, and tied down on the bank. Jack spied a spot near the old Indian huts to take cover, but he kept walking. He wanted to see Dad as fully protected as possible.

He found him a spot behind the wide trunk of a cypress where he had a good angle on the *Bull-ship*.

Jack gave the old man's shoulder a gentle squeeze and

leaned in close. "Keep your head down, Dad. And if all hell breaks loose, be careful."

His father patted his hand. "I'm the soldier here, remember? You just take care of yourself and don't worry about me."

Jack had a sudden urge to pull everyone out and head back to Novaton. A dark premonition stole over him, a feelin that something terrible was about to happen, that fewer would be leaving here than arrived. But he couldn't turn back now, and he knew neither his dad nor Carl would go. They'd come too far. And Anya needed them.

One more squeeze of his father's shoulder and then he hurried back to the ruins of the Indian huts. He found himself a spot behind a thick support post. He wouldn't have thought it possible, but it began to rain harder.

Jack squatted and spread his poncho like an umbrella over the plastic bag. He removed a few of the grenades and stuck the safety clips into his belt. He pulled out the big Ruger and checked the cylinder. He didn't have a holster big enough to hold it so he stuck it in his waistband. The nine-plus-inch barrel was cold and not a comfortable fit. If Semelee got a look at him she'd probably think he was *very* glad to see her.

But he wouldn't be. It would be just fine with Jack if he never saw her again.

He rose and started to cup his hands around his mouth when he sensed movement behind him. He whirled, pawing at his poncho, trying to get his hand under its flapping hem, but stopped when he saw what it was: a small towel, tacked to one of the hut posts, was flapping in the wind.

Jack waited to let his racing heart slow—for a second there he'd thought he'd walked into an ambush—then turned back to the water.

He cupped his hands around his mouth and shouted.

"Hello the boats!"

He repeated this three times at top volume before deciding that they weren't going to hear him over the storm. He pulled out the Ruger and pointed it skyward. He'd never fired one of these, and had only heard of the .454 Casull round. He knew it was a monster so he was ready for a loud report and a wrist-jolting kick when he fired two shots in the air. Even so, the boom surprised him.

That ought to wake them up.

He replaced the two rounds as he began calling again.

5

"You'll never guess who's out there," Luke said, grinnin and drippin as he came in from the deck. He wore a yellow slicker and a Devil Rays cap. Corley and a couple of the other men trooped in behind him, shakin the water off theirselfs like dogs.

Semelee didn't feel like guessin—specially if she'd 'never' guess the answer—so she waited for him to tell her.

Everybody in the *Bull-ship* had jumped at the sound of those two shots a moment ago. It'd sounded like a cannon goin off. Luke and the others went out to see what was up. Semelee had heard some shoutin back and forth but couldn't make nothin out of it due to the poundin of the rain on the roof and sides of the boat.

Finally Luke told her: "It's your boyfriend."

Boyfriend? Semelee thought. What's Luke—? Oh, shit.

"You mean that Jack guy? He ain't no boyfriend of mine. I hate him."

She did. Sort of. But that didn't keep her heart from flutterin for a second at the passin thought that he'd come all the way out here in this for her. But that thought flew out the window soon as it came. He'd made it awful clear he wasn't interested in the likes of her.

"Good," Luke said. "Cause I hate him too. I hate anybody who thinks I'm stupid, and he must think we're pretty damn stupid. Know what he said? Said he was from the Miami-Dade Sheriff's office and that he's got a whole passle of cops out there in the dark with him."

"You sure it's him?"

"Sure I'm sure. Recognized his voice, even through the rain. Couldn't see him, but it's him."

"What's he want?"

"Says he wants the old lady back. Callin her 'Anya' or somethin like that."

Semelee felt her stomach plummet. "Then he knows we was there."

She went to one of the little rectangles of glass that served as windows on *Bull-ship*'s deckhouse and looked real hard into the storm. The rain splashin against the glass and runnin down its outside kept her from seein even an inch beyond it.

"He knows somethin," Luke said, "but he don't know everthing, that's for sure."

"But how's he know we was there?" She couldn't imagine Jack just watchin from a window. He and his daddy woulda come out sure, probably with guns a-blazin.

"Don't know, don't care," Luke said.

She turned and saw that Luke had opened a closet and was handin out rifles and shotguns. He pointed to Corley.

"Get below and haul everbody up here."

"What you gonna do?"

He smiled at her again. "Gonna give him a nice warm

lagoon-style welcome and make sure he don't leave the Glades—least not alive."

"That really necessary?"

As Semelee watched the men start pilin up from below decks, grabbin guns, and headin for the deck, she felt a little somethin stir in her chest. Like sadness. Like guilt. She'd taken a change of heart about Jack since yesterday afternoon. She'd tried to make him die then, but afterwards she was a little glad she'd failed. Yeah, he'd turned her down right to her face, but he'd only been tellin the truth: *I'm taken* meant he had someone else he liked better. End of story. He could've lied and then used her like she'd been used before, then dump her like she'd been dumped before. That would've been worse. That didn't make her heart hurt any less, but at least he'd been straight with her.

"I think when he don't get what he's askin for—and he ain't gonna—then I got a feelin there may be some shootin. So I figure we'll shoot first."

"What if you're wrong?" Semelee said. "What if that really is a buncha deputies out there?"

"Ain't wrong. It's him, I tell you."

"All right. Say it is. What if he ain't alone?"

Luke's smile turned real ugly. "I hope he ain't. I hope he brought Daddy along." He lifted his cap and ran a hand over his scabbed-up head. "I got me a score or two to even with that old coot."

Semelee stepped back to the window. Why did he come? This storm's tearin up the place and yet here he comes, loaded for bear, lookin for an old lady he only met a couple days ago. What sort of man does that?

She ducked away from the window as the gunfire started outside.

Whatever sort of man Jack is, she thought with a sting of sadness, he's gonna be a dead one pretty soon.

6

Jack had taken cover behind an old fallen trunk at the first sight of a rifle on the *Bull-ship*'s deck. Good thing too, because they'd opened up without warning. Dad and Carl had responded immediately. The element of surprise allowed them to take down a couple of the clan before the rest of them dropped to the deck to take cover behind the gunwales. The *Horse-ship* crew had their guns out now and the air was filled with wind and water and lightning and bullets and shot.

Most of the fire from the *Bull-ship* seemed concentrated on Jack's position. Semelee's idea, probably . . . or Luke's . . . or both. He'd definitely put himself on the wrong side of those two. When Jack dared raise his head, he fired back with the Ruger. He wanted Luke. If he could take him out, the rest of the clan would lose their steam. But Jack couldn't identify him through the dim light and the rain. And even if he did, he'd be hard to hit. Jack wished he were a better marksman, but knew if by some chance he did hit Luke he'd be a goner. He was firing Cor-Bon .454 Casulls, hardcast, flat-point, 335-grain rounds that jerked the barrel high every time he pulled the trigger. Which was okay in a way. If he missed, he wanted to miss high. He didn't want one of those big rounds to plow through the hull and hit Anya.

The fire on Jack's position became so intense he didn't dare raise his head to return it. These guys were good shots. When a lull came, he belly-crawled back to the old huts and took a position behind a post. Maybe from back here he'd be able to take the time to aim and make his shots count. He glanced back at that towel flapping in the rain, thinking it ought to be one damn clean piece of cloth by the time this storm is done.

Lightning flashed as he turned back to the boat, revealing a design on the fabric that caught the corner of his eye. Something familiar about that pattern of lines and dots . . .

Whatever it was caused a ripple of nausea, and a chill, as if something has crawled under his hood and whispered across his neck on spider legs.

Jack fixed his gaze on the cloth, waiting for the next flash, and when it came he saw the pattern again and knew where he'd seen it before.

On Anya's back.

With his blood sludging in his veins, Jack rose and stepped over to the cloth, ignoring the lead whistling around him, because it had to be a cloth, a cloth someone had drawn on, copying the pattern they'd seen cut and burnt and punctured into Anya's back. He reached out and touched it, and when his fingers flashed the message that this was too thick and entirely the wrong texture for cloth, he slumped to his knees in the mud. Somehow he managed to hold on to the Ruger.

A sob burst from his lips, but the grief that spawned it lasted only a few heartbeats before a black frenzy boiled out of the vault where he stored it and took over. Repressing a howl of rage, he rolled back to the post and found his plastic bag of grenades. Breath hissing through bared teeth, he snatched one from within, pulled the pin, popped the safety clip, and waited, counting . . .

One thousand and one . . .

The note Abe had included with the grenades said the M-67 fuse gave a four-to-five-second delay between release of the clip and detonation.

. . . one thousand and two . . .

It also said each grenade had a kill radius of fifteen feet and a casualty radius of about fifty. Dad and Carl weren't much beyond that but he was only peripherally aware of the risk. His focus was tunneled in on the *Bull-ship* and nothing was going to pull it away.

. . . one thousand and three!

As soon as he hit three, he lobbed the grenade up and out, then ducked behind the pole. If it hit the deck and exploded, great; if it exploded above the deck, even better.

But he didn't wait for it to hit before pulling another from the bag. He was popping the clip when the first went off. He poked his head up as he started counting. His throw had been short by maybe half a dozen feet, but not a complete loss. It had exploded at deck level and the screams of the wounded and frightened shouts of the rest were music.

. . . three!

This one sailed toward *Horse-ship*—no need for them to feel left out—and it too fell short, but not without doing some damage to hull and human alike.

It looked so much easier in movies.

Jack was ready to pop the clip on a third when he heard someone thrashing through the underbrush to his right. The fact that whoever it was made no attempt at stealth left him pretty sure it was his father, but he raised the Ruger anyway. Sure enough, seconds later, Dad burst from a stand of ferns in a crouch and dropped down beside him.

"What the hell are you doing, Jack?" His eyes were wide; rain ran down his face in rivulets. "Anya's in one of those boats!"

"No, she's not, Dad," he said through a constricting throat. "She's dead."

He frowned. "How can you know that?"

"I found a big piece of her skin hanging back there."

"No!" he gasped. Jack couldn't see his complexion but was sure it had gone waxy. "You can't mean it!"

"I wish I was wrong, but I saw her back the other day and the same marks are on that piece of skin. They skinned her, Dad. They fucking skinned her and hung it out to dry."

Dad placed a trembling hand over his eyes and was silent a moment. Then he lowered the hand and thrust it toward Jack's sack of grenades. His voice was taut, strained.

"Give me one of those."

7

Semelee lay tremblin on the floor, head down, hands over her ears. It sounded as if war had broken out. Those weren't just guns firin out there. With the explosions and the way the windows was shatterin, it felt like they was bein bombed.

Luke fell through the door, grabbin onto a bleedin shoulder.

"They got grenades, Semelee! They're killin us out there! Corley's dead and Bobby's leg's bleedin real bad! Y'gotta do somethin!"

"What can I do? Devil's dead and Dora's no good on land."

"The things from the sinkhole, the ones you brought up last night . . . we need em now. We need em bad!"

"I can't! I told you before—they won't come up till after sundown."

No matter how she'd tried yesterday, she couldn't get those awful winged monsters to come out of the hole while the sun was up. But as soon as it went down, they were hers—or so she'd thought.

She'd almost lost it when she first saw them. She hadn't been able to get a good look at them while they was down in the lights, but once they was up in the air, in the twilight, what she saw scared her so much she almost dropped her eye-shells.

The most horrible lookin critters she'd ever seen.

They was the size of lobsters—not the crawdadlike things around these parts; no, these was thick and heavy, like the big-clawed ones from up north. These things had shells and claws too, but that's where the likeness ended. Their bodies was waisted, like a wasp's, and they had wings, two big transparent ones on each side, sproutin from the top of the body like a dragonfly's.

Chew wasps—that was the name that popped into her head, and it seemed to fit them perfect.

Plus they had teeth. Oh God did they have teeth—each had big jaws that opened wide as a cottonmouth's, and they was filled to overflowin with long sharp transparent fangs that looked like slivers of glass. One of the weirdest touches was the rows of little blue dots of lights along their sides that glowed like neon. They looked like they'd been drug up from the bottom of the sea where the sun don't shine, a place so deep and dark that even God's forgot about them.

God . . . he must've been havin a real bad day when he made those things. She had to wonder what kind of a world they came from, and how anything else survived with them roamin free.

"It's dark as night out there now! Give it a try! You gotta! They're putting holes in the hull. They're tryin to sink us!"

"But why're they tryin to do that? Why're they throwin grenades, Luke? If they think we got the old lady and they want her back, ain't they afraid of killin her along with us?"

"Who knows why, damn it!" Luke shouted. "They've gone crazy!"

But Semelee caught a look in his eyes, like he was hidin somethin.

"What is it, Luke? What changed their minds? What makes them think she's not here, or that she's dead? You didn't open your big mouth, did you?"

"No. Course not. What kinda fool you take me for?"

"Well, then what? What, Luke?"

Luke looked away. "I guess they found her skin."

"What? How could they do that? You buried it." Luke still kept lookin away. "You did bury it like I told you to, didn't you, Luke?"

He shook his head. "Nuh-uh. I hung it up to let the rain clean it off, then I was gonna tan it . . . you know, like a hide."

Semelee closed her eyes. If she had a gun right now she'd've shot Luke—right through his stupid, brainless head.

Her thoughts flashed back to last night . . .

She'd been in a frenzy, completely out of control . . . so pissed at that old lady for killin Devil and then ruinin her plans for Jack that she just . . . lost it. All the trouble she had gettin those things to come out of their hole didn't help matters none either. By the time she realized that they wouldn't come out in the day, she was all but frothin at the mouth.

When sunset came, so did the things. She had trouble controllin them from the git-go. Soon as they came out they wanted to run wild, but she managed to gather them into a group and herd them toward the old woman's house. When they got there, they went crazy, rippin through the screen and gnawing through the front door.

Their ferocity frightened the hell outta Semelee, and she remembered thinkin, Oh, God what have I got myself into now? And, bein inside them, she was beginnin to feel some of their bloodlust.

When they got through the door, there was the old lady, standin in the middle of her livin room, all done up in one of them funny Japanese dresses. She just stood there smokin a cigarette. Smokin! It was like she knew she was gonna die. She didn't scream, she didn't cry, she didn't even fight back.

But her plants did. They lashed out at the chew wasps and tried to entangle them with her branches. The wasps splintered them and striped off all their leaves.

But they still couldn't get to the lady because of her little dog. Semelee especially wanted to even the score with that mongrel for killin Devil, but he wasn't going quietly. She'd wondered how such a little thing could've killed the biggest gator she'd ever seen, and last night she found out. That tiny dog fought like a full-grown Rottweiler. He brought down two of the chew wasps before three of them ganged up on him and tore him to pieces.

And then there was nothing between the chews and the old lady. She didn't try to run, she just stood there, like she was acceptin what was comin.

That was when Semelee had second thoughts. She sensed somethin special about this lady—something *extra* special—and had a feeling she'd be losing somethin precious if she killed her.

Maybe it was the way she was just standin there. She had to be scared outta her mind but she wasn't showing it, not one bit.

But the thing that most made Semelee want to hold off was knowin that this lady wasn't just gonna be killed, she was gonna be torn apart. Much as Semelee hated her for messin with her plans, she didn't know if she could go through with that. The other folks she'd sacrificed here at Gateways had been stung or bit or pecked up, and they'd died later . . . not right in front of her.

Semelee was gonna have to watch this and she didn't

have the stomach for it. Maybe gettin her house wrecked and her dog killed would be enough for the old lady. Maybe she'd learn her lesson and stop messin where she didn't belong. Maybe she'd even have a heart attack and die later. A lot better'n bein torn to pieces.

But when Semelee tried to turn the chew wasps around and bring them home, they wouldn't go. They smelled blood and there was no stoppin them. They lit into the old lady. And what did she do? She stood there and raised her arms straight out from her sides and just let them come.

Semelee wasn't sure if it was the bravest or craziest thing she'd ever seen, but she did know it was horrible to watch.

More than watch. Semelee was in close with the wasps, *inside* them as they gouged the old lady's flesh, crunched her bones. She could almost taste it, and gagged now at the memory. They was so fierce they didn't even let her body fall to the ground. They ate her upright, even slurped sprays of blood right out of the air. And no matter what Semelee did she couldn't pull them away. She wanted to drop the eye-shells but was afraid the chew wasps would turn on the clan who'd gone there just to see what these ugly-lookin things could do.

Finally, when they were through, there was nothin left of the old lady but the skin of her back. For some reason, the chew wasps wasn't interested in it. They gobbled her up from head to toe, but left that rectangle of skin.

And when they was finished they started listenin to Semelee again. She quick got them outta there and back to the sinkhole. Soon as they was back where they belonged, Semelee yanked off the eye-shells and got real sick.

Back at the old lady's house, Luke did two things, one smart and one dumb. The smart thing was pickin up the two dead chew wasps and bringin them back to the lagoon.

If people came lookin for the old lady and found those, it'd be in all the papers and everyone'd assume they came from the Glades. Soon there'd be scientists and hunters and cops and thrill seekers all over the place, including the lagoon. The clan's whole way of life'd be messed up.

The dumb thing Luke did was bring back the old lady's skin. He—

The boom of another grenade—sounded like it must've exploded over by *Horse-ship*—yanked Semelee back to the here and now.

"Why, Luke?" She finally opened her eyes and stared real hard at him. "Why'd you do such a fool thing?"

"I wanted to keep it. You know, kinda like a souvenir. I like all those marks. They're almost like a map. But never mind that. Y'gotta try those wasp things again, Semelee! You just gotta!"

She didn't want to tell him that she was afraid to. She hated the way they made her feel . . . like all dark and ugly inside, with this endless hunger. Even with the gunfire, the explosions, the howlin wind, the leakin roof, the thunder and lightnin all around her, this seemed like a better place than where she'd been last night.

But she couldn't just sit around and do nothin while the whole clan got massacred. She had to do somethin . . . and there was only one thing she could do.

Her gorge rose as she pulled the eye-shells out of her pocket.

"You're gonna do it?" Luke said, a grin spreadin cross his face.

She nodded. "Yeah, but you gotta get outta here."

The grin collapsed. "But Semelee . . . there's all sorts of shootin out there."

"Then get out there and shoot back. Just leave me alone so I can save our asses."

"Okay, okay."

He headed for the door in a crouch, then crawled out onto the deck.

Taking a deep breath, Semelee pressed the shells over her eyes and went searchin for some chew wasps . . .

"We're not doing a whole helluva lot of damage with these things," Dad said after they'd watched the latest grenade sail through the air and explode off the bow of the *Bull-ship*.

Jack had to agree. He would have thought that something that small and weighing almost a pound wouldn't get tossed around by the wind. But this was no ordinary wind. He'd tried compensating for it by adjusting his throw but the trouble was you couldn't wing these things like a baseball; you had to lob them, and the wind kept changing direction.

"We've caused some hurt, though."

"Not enough," Dad said, his expression grim. "After what they did to Anya, they . . ." He swallowed and shook his head. "They shouldn't be allowed to live."

"I don't think we'll be able to kill all twenty guys."

Dad gave him a strange look. "I said they shouldn't be allowed to live. I didn't say we should do the killing."

Oops. "Oh. Guess I misunderstood."

"You're scaring me, Jack."

"Sometimes I scare myself."

Just then Jack heard something that sounded like a scream. He looked over toward Carl but couldn't find him in the dark. Then lightning flashed and he saw him rolling on the ground as he fought something that had clamped onto his right shoulder. Jack couldn't get a good look at it, but whatever it was, it wasn't alone. More of them were lifting out of the cenote and weaving toward Carl. The one that had him was too close for Carl to shoot at, so he was using the shotgun as a bat. But Jack could see that he wasn't getting anywhere.

He slapped his father on the back. "Stay here and keep firing at the boats. Keep them pinned down. When you reload, forget the slugs and fill up on shot. I think we're going to need it."

"Where are you going?"

"Carl needs a little help."

Rising to a crouch, Jack pulled the Ruger from under the poncho and ran through the rain. Lightning flashes lit the scene, and as he neared Carl and got a better look at what was attacking him, it almost stopped him in his tracks. The thing clinging to his shoulder had the head and saber-toothed jaws of a viper fish, the shelled body of a lobster on steroids, and two pairs of long, diaphanous wings. Another of its kind was gliding in for its own piece of Carl.

Jack stopped, knelt, took aim with the Ruger and fired. He scored a hit. The big Casull slug tore into the flying thing, leaving only a spray of greenish blood and a pair of still-flapping wings. Then Jack leaped next to Carl, rammed the Ruger's muzzle against the eye of the thing chewing on him, and pulled the trigger. This time, not even the wings remained.

Carl groaned. "It hurts, Jack!" His left hand was covered with blood where it clutched his shoulder through the shredded poncho. "Oh, God, it hurts!"

Jack took only a quick look, wincing at what looked like exposed bone and a dozen crystalline teeth still buried in the ragged flesh, then turned back to the cenote. Three more of the things were up and coming their way. He grabbed the Benelli and started firing. The semiautomatic action let him get off four shots quickly. They weren't all direct hits but the shot tore up the wings of the ones it didn't dismember.

"Where are your shells?" Jack shouted.

Carl jutted his chin toward a box on the ground. His teeth were bared in agony. He seemed in too much pain to speak.

Jack started reloading the Benelli's magazine. If he'd known he'd be facing these things he would have had Abe send down flechette rounds.

"Think you can walk?"

Carl nodded.

"Okay, then. Get over to where my dad is. I'll cover you from the rear."

Spreading out had been a good idea against the clan, but it meant certain death against these things. Time to circle the wagons.

"It's Semelee," Carl gritted as he lurched to his feet. "She's controllin them." Then he staggered off.

Jack turned back to the cenote and found half a dozen more of the things hovering over the opening in a cluster. He ducked behind a palm trunk and fired once into their center, knocking down two. They fell into the abyss but were replaced by four more.

Jack felt his stomach knot. This wasn't good. He hadn't brought enough ammo. But he'd brought his father and Carl. That made him responsible for them.

In the background he heard his father firing methodically, rhythmically, at the boats.

Save some of that ammo, Dad, he thought. We're gonna need it.

And now another four joined the flock. But they didn't swarm his way . . . their movements were sluggish and they didn't seem to know he was there. They milled about, looking confused. What were they waiting for? Reinforcements?

If more were coming up from the cenote, maybe Jack could ambush them along the way. He unclipped a grenade from his belt—only a couple left—pulled the pin, and lofted it toward the cenote. It passed through the swarm and down into the opening. A few seconds later he saw a flash, heard a boom, but that was it. The ones fluttering over the hole didn't even react.

If this were a movie like *Rio Bravo*, he'd stumble onto a crate of dynamite, conveniently left behind by a construction company, and use it to seal the cenote. But this was Jack's world, not Howard Hawks's. Things never seemed to work out that way for him.

He heard a scream behind him and recognized the voice this time: Carl again. He looked around and saw him staggering in a circle at the water's edge. One of those things had its fangs buried in the back of his neck . . . and it was chewing . . .

Where'd that one come from?

Jack leaped to his feet and took off on a run. He couldn't use the shotgun without hitting Carl too, so he pulled the Ruger. But before he could use it, Carl pitched over backward into the water.

That wasn't all bad. The cenote thing didn't seem to like water. It loosed it's grip and buzzed back into the air, banking and gliding toward Jack. He already had the Ruger up. He waited until it was close, then fired at it head on. It dissolved in an explosion of green. As its wings fluttered to the ground, Jack dropped the Benelli and the Ruger and jumped into the water to help Carl, who wasn't doing too well.

The water was waist deep and cool, its surface churning and bubbling from the wind and rain. The muddy bottom was slippery and sloped off on a steady decline. A bullet whizzed by, then another. Someone on the *Horse-ship* had spotted them. Jack heard Dad's Mossberg boom, then a cry from the boat, and the bullets stopped coming.

"Carl!" Jack shouted as he leaned forward and stretched out his arm. "Give me your hand!"

Carl, with his poncho floating around him like a lily pad, thrashed and splashed and kicked his way shoreward. Jack grabbed his outstretched left hand and began hauling him in.

Suddenly Carl was jerked back. He let out a scream of pain and Jack was barely able to hold on to him as something pulled him back toward the center of the lagoon.

"Oh, my leg!" he wailed. "My leg! It's Dora! She's got me! Don't let her have me, Jack!"

"I won't, Carl."

He started sobbing. "I don't wanna die, Jack. Please don't let her—"

And then his head plunged below the surface. Jack tried to dig in his heels but the bottom was too slippery. Another powerful tug pulled Jack forward so hard he went face first into the water. He was only under for a few seconds, but during that time he lost his grip on Carl's hand. His feet found the bottom and he stood again, shaking the water from his face and eyes. He was shoulder deep now.

"Carl!"

Nothing. No reply, nothing but empty, wind- and rain-swept water stretching before him. He shouted the name again and thought he saw a hand break the surface and claw the air maybe fifty feet away. But it was there for only a second—if it was there at all—and then it was gone.

"Oh, Carl," he said softly, staring at the spot. "You poor bastard. I'm sorry. So sorry . . ."

A lump formed in his throat. A good, simple man was gone. Jack had known him just a couple of days, but he'd come to respect him. He still didn't know what had gone wrong with Carl's right arm, but that didn't matter. Carl hadn't let it stop him from leading a useful life. He'd adjusted, with no apologies, no excuses.

A bullet whizzed by Jack and he realized he was a sitting duck out here.

My fault, he thought as he quickly waded ashore. If I hadn't bribed him to take me to the lagoon, if I'd just said no tonight when he wanted to come along, he'd still be alive. Probably be sitting in his trailer right now watching his TV.

My fault. But not all my fault.

It's Semelee . . . she's controllin them.

Right. Semelee.

Jack reached the bank and climbed up onto the mud. He looked toward the cenote and saw maybe twenty of the winged things clustered over the opening. As he watched, they began to fan out and glide toward him.

His blood cooled at the sight. No way he and Dad could bring them all down, even standing back to back with shotguns. Some of them would get through. And once they got you down, you were finished.

Couldn't stop the winged things . . . but maybe he could stop the one controlling them.

With the things trailing him, Jack ran back to where his father was still firing at the boats. He heard cheering from the decks as the clan spotted the winged things on Jack's tail. They didn't shoot. Probably thought it would be more fun to watch him get gobbled up like Anya.

"Behind me, Dad! Incoming!"

Dad was crouched behind a tree, with the trunk between him and the boats. Jack dove for the ground, sliding through the mud on his belly as his father looked around.

"Where?"

"Right behind me!"

Lightning flashed and he saw his father's jaw drop.

"Dear God! What are—?"

"Don't talk, shoot!"

And shoot he did, pumping round after round out of the Mossberg into the air behind Jack. Jack didn't look around to see what effect he was having. He assumed it was about as good as it got. He laid the Benelli across Dad's knees for when the Mossberg ran dry, then seated himself back to back with his father and turned to the *Bull-ship*. If Semelee was anywhere, that would be the place.

He wiped the rain from his eyes and took aim at the superstructure. The big Casulls would rip through it, in one plywood side wall and out the other. He couldn't be sure he'd hit Semelee, but at least he could distract her . . .

This was so hard . . .

Semelee crouched in the dark of the cabin and pressed the shells tighter against her eyes. The chew wasps hadn't wanted to leave the sinkhole until the sun was down, but she'd forced them. She'd tried that yesterday and it hadn't worked, but this time she was able to coax them up. Maybe it was the storm or the nightlike darkness up here. Whatever the reason, they came. But so slowly . . . like only one or two at a time.

Then, once she got them outta the hole, she could barely see. Had to be because of the sun. Even though it was hidden behind mountains of storm clouds, it was still above the horizon; she guessed that whatever was filterin through was enough to affect the eyes of the chew wasps.

But she'd been able to see Carl who was right close to

the hole and shootin at the boats. Traitor to his kin! She set a couple of the wasps on him, then went back to draggin others up.

Suddenly one of the ones on Carl got blowed up. And then the other. She seen it was Jack doin the shootin, and though she didn't hate him like before, she couldn't let this stand. She had to end it between them. One of them had to go. Semelee preferred Jack.

She had a whole bunch of the chew wasps up by then but couldn't get them organized. They wanted to go here and there and it was just about all she could do to keep them together. Jack blasted a couple of them out of the air and then got four more with a grenade in the hole as she was pushin them up.

She had to attack with what she had, but couldn't get the swarm to move. She could control one of them, though, so she sent it after Jack. Somehow it wound up on Carl instead. The wasps seemed attracted to sound and movement, and Carl had been makin plenty of both.

But she didn't have to send Dora after Carl when he went in the water—Dora did that on her own.

Good-bye, Carl.

Finally she'd got the swarm to move. She didn't know why she suddenly had more control. Maybe cause the sun got closer to settin while she was chasin Jack. Didn't know, didn't care, all she knew now was she was on the hunt. And though her stomach turned at the thought of havin to go through another chew-up with these things, it had to be done. The survival of the whole clan depended on her stoppin Jack and whoever was with him—probably his daddy.

As she guided the wasps after the runnin Jack, she heard the guys on the deck start to yellin. She wished they'd shut up. The chew wasps kept wantin to turn toward the noise. The voices pulled at them. She had to keep forcin them to stay on Jack's trail.

Suddenly a piece of the wall exploded and showered her with splinters as something whizzed by her head. She was already crouched on the floor in a corner. Now she dropped flat, and just in time too. Another big bullet smashed through the cabin, low this time, just about singeing her butt.

He's tryin to kill me!

She had to move those chew wasps in on Jack and his daddy. Now!

The old man was shotgunnin them, so Semelee split the swarm into two groups. She veered one left over the water, and the other around back. She'd catch em in the middle and—

A third big slug blasted into the cabin then, but this one didn't go all the way through. It plowed into one of the benches of the picnic table and sent it flyin against her. She cried out as it conked her on the head. She didn't think— she put her hands up to protect herself and dropped the eye-shells.

"Oh no!" She started feelin around on the floorboards, real frantic like. But it was so dark in here. "Where'd they go?"

She couldn't control the chew wasps without em. They'd all go flyin back to the sinkhole if she wasn't there to hold them.

Or maybe they wouldn't.

Semelee wasn't sure which would be worse.

10

"Jack!" Dad shouted. "Look!"

Jack was reloading the Ruger, readying to riddle the *Bull-ship*'s superstructure with a few more Casulls. He'd been leaning against his father's back, getting rocked forward whenever Dad's shotgun went off, rocking back with the recoil from the Ruger.

He half turned, not sure of what he'd heard. His ears were ringing from the thunder and the booms of the weapons.

"What?"

"Those things. They were all clustered together at first, then they started dividing into two groups, and now . . ."

Jack turned further and squinted through the rain. He watched for a moment as the cenote things buzzed around in disarray, practically bumping into one another in midair. It looked like they didn't know where they were, but the men from the boats were still cheering them on.

One of the things veered out over the water; two more followed it; then the whole swarm was making a beeline for the boats. Suddenly the cheering stopped, replaced a couple of heartbeats later by the reports of rifles and shotguns. Jack saw the clan knock a few down, but then the swarm was upon them. The shooting stopped, replaced by screams of pain and panic.

11

Semelee waited for the lightnin to flash again. That was the only time she could see what she was doin. Here! A new flash, coming through the broke windows—where was they? She crouched on her hands and knees, searchin the floor. Where was those damn eye-shells?

At least the big bullets had stopped poundin through the walls. Not for long she bet. Probably just reloadin. In another minute—

Somebody started screamin outside. Then another. She recognized Luke's voice among the hellish choir. He sounded like he was bein tortured. She jumped to the door and peeked out.

The chew wasps! They was attackin the clan. Oh shit oh shit oh shit! What was she gonna do?

Another lightnin flash, this time through the doorway. She looked around just in time to see the shells, lyin on the floor right up against the wall to her right. She jumped on them and clutched them tight in her fists.

Thank God! She had them. Now she could turn the chew wasps away and get them headed back to where they should be—on Jack and his daddy. But as she raised them to her eyes the door burst open and somethin came staggerin into the cabin.

Semelee screamed as it lurched to the left, then the right, then stumbled toward her. Whatever it was, it didn't look human. It let out a muffled screech and then the lightnin flashed and Semelee screamed again. It was a man with three of the chew wasps hangin on him. One on his leg, the other with its head buried in his flank, and the third with its teeth worryin his face. He screeched again, then spun and collapsed onto his belly. He twitched a few times, then lay still.

Another flash of lightnin gave her another look at him. Through the rips in his shirt Semelee saw scales and finny spines on his back and knew who it was.

"Luke!"

Her eye-shells. She could use them to get Luke free of the wasps. But before she could get them up, the one on Luke's leg let go and buzzed straight at Semelee's face. She stumbled back and fell out the door onto the deck and into a hell on earth. Chew wasps and blood-soaked men everywhere—and the men who wasn't screamin wasn't movin.

Semelee's arrival got their instant attention. The chew wasp that chased her out of the cabin was still comin, but so were others from the deck. The only place to go was the water.

She slipped in blood and banged her knee as she tried to get up, then broke into a low run and dove into the water. As she kicked toward shore she knew it would take her right into the sights of Jack and his daddy. She pressed the shells over her eyes. She had to get back control of the chew wasps and give those two somethin else to worry about before she came up for air.

12

During a lightning flash Jack caught a glimpse of someone—someone small and slim with dead white hair—leaping off the *Bull-ship* and diving headfirst into the water. He watched a couple of cenote things chase after her and hover a couple of feet over the water, waiting for her to surface.

He tapped Dad on the arm. His father was watching the strobe-lit carnage on the boat decks in horrid fascination. Jack had to tap him again.

"Hey, Dad. Which one of those is loaded?"

Dad shook himself free of the spectacle. "Both now."

"Give me one, will you?"

Dad handed him the Benelli. Jack took aim at the nearest winged thing, not so much from a desire to protect Semelee—she deserved just about anything that happened to her—but because he wasn't up for watching someone being eaten alive.

The shotgun boomed, rocking his shoulder, and the nearest thing blew apart. But its companion, instead of retreating or continuing to hover, darted straight for Jack.

He fell back, raising the Benelli. Good thing it was semiautomatic—those things could *move*. His shot went a little high, missing the body but dissolving the right pair of wings. It went into a spin and landed on the edge of the bank, vibrating its remaining wings and gnashing its teeth in fury as it made circles in the mud.

Movement on the surface of the lagoon caught Jack's

eye. He saw a white head begin to emerge from the water. He took aim with the Benelli but hesitated. He wasn't sure why. Maybe because he felt responsible. Maybe if he'd let her down a little more easily she wouldn't have attacked him, then Anya. Maybe something about her pathetic desire to fit in touched him. Or maybe he couldn't bring himself to blow holes in a young woman, no matter how sick and twisted she was.

Whatever the reason, he dropped the shotgun, grabbed the cenote thing by the roots of its remaining wings, and lifted it. It looked heavy but he found it surprisingly light. It writhed in his grasp, trying to twist around and gouge him with those diamond teeth, but its carapace limited its agility.

Jack leaped off the bank and into the water.

"Jack!" he heard his father cry. "What in God's name are you doing?"

Jack didn't answer. Holding the cenote thing high, he splashed toward where Semelee was emerging from the water. He noticed she was holding two shells over her eyes.

The shells—that was what she'd wanted them for. Somehow they let her control these things.

And I helped complete her set.

He also noticed the other winged things rising from their feasts on the decks of the two boats and heading his way. He put everything he had into forcing himself through the water.

When he reached her he grabbed the back of her hair. He yanked downward, hard, stretching her throat, and held the crystalline teeth of the cenote thing inches from her skin. The twisting, gnashing jaws reminded him of a wood router.

"Drop the shells! Drop them now, Semelee, or this thing gets a free lunch! Don't think I'm bluffing! You may have been right about me not shooting Luke the other day, but this is different. After what you've pulled in the last twenty-four hours, I'm more than ready for payback."

"Okay, okay," she said, but kept the shells over her eyes. "Just let me send the chew wasps back to the sinkhole."

Chew wasps . . . a perfect name.

"You do that."

The approaching chew wasps veered away and headed for the cenote, its lights faintly visible through the rain. Jack watched them fade into the mist, then, with his free hand, pulled Semelee's hands away from her face. He hadn't forgotten about Dora. He took her by the upper arm and guided her toward the bank.

As Jack pulled her up on land, he heard Dad call his name. He glanced over and saw him pointing toward the lagoon.

"Who or what is *that*?"

Jack turned and stared. He saw nothing at first, then the lightning flashed and he spotted a man in a suit standing at the center of the lagoon. Not *in* the lagoon—*on* it. No, not just standing on the water, walking on it. His stride was long and purposeful, moving him along at a good pace, yet without the slightest hint of hurry.

Jack tossed the partially dewinged chew wasp into the lagoon where it sank like a mob hit. He squinted through the storm. Couldn't make out the man's features, but as he neared, Jack noticed that he seemed to be moving in a bubble—not something with a membrane, simply an area around him, a dry area. The rain driving at him from all directions didn't touch him. And it didn't sluice away, it simply . . . went away.

"Oh, God!" Semelee cried, cringing against Jack. "It's Jesus come to get me for my sins!"

"You've got a lot of things to answer for, but I don't think that's Jesus."

Not unless he's taken to wearing Armani, Jack thought.

Of course he hadn't a clue as to the designer—if an Armani suit introduced itself, he'd have to ask it for ID—but it looked expensive, maybe silk, charcoal gray, perfectly tailored, worn over a black shirt buttoned to the collar. Very Euro, this water strider.

When the man moved close enough for Jack to make out his face, he felt his blood congeal. He knew that face, that supercilious expression. He raised the Benelli and roared.

"Roma!"

Jack held him accountable for Kate's death—at least indirectly—and for a lot of other things that had gone wrong in his life since they'd met at that conspiracy convention last spring. He'd called himself Sal Roma then. Who knew what he was calling himself now. He'd tried to kill Jack then and almost succeeded. Either he or the Otherness or the two in league had tried to kill Gia and their baby just last month. Now it was payback time. No hesitation—he wasn't sighting down on a waifish woman, this was the "Adversary" Anya had mentioned, the One whose True Name she refused to speak.

"Good-bye, whoever you are," he whispered, and pulled the trigger.

Or tried to. It wouldn't budge. Jammed!

And then Roma glanced at him and Jack felt himself lifted through the air and slammed back against a palm trunk. The pain of the impact on his spine blew all the air out of him and blurred his vision for a few heartbeats. His knees turned to jelly and he slid earthward to end up sitting in the mud, propped against the palm.

"Jack!" he heard his father cry from what seemed like the end of a long hallway. "Jack, are you all—?"

Jack's vision cleared in time to see his father tumble back into the brush and disappear from view.

He wanted to shout to him but his voice wouldn't work.

Fear spiked his chest. Was Dad hurt? Was he even alive?

Jack tried to get to his feet but couldn't move. For a panicky instant he thought he was paralyzed from a broken spine, then realized that something was holding him in place, something he couldn't see or feel but powerful enough to press on him so effectively that all he could do was breathe. He tried to shout to Roma but couldn't do even that. He was at Roma's mercy.

But Roma didn't seem interested in him, didn't even glance toward Jack as he casually stepped onto the bank to stand not two feet away, facing Semelee.

Semelee cringed back as he stared at her.

"So," Roma said. Jack heard him clearly. The rain and wind seemed to be easing up, although lightning still flashed all around them. "You're the one who's trying to usurp my name."

"Name? What name?"

"You know . . . the one that doesn't belong to you."

"You mean Rasalom? It does belong to me. *I'm* Rasalom."

He slapped her face. The move was so quick Jack would have wondered what had happened if not for the sound of flesh hitting flesh, and the sight of Semelee staggering back a step as her face jerked to the right. Jack could almost feel the sting.

And then it hit him—Rasalom. That was the fuck's True Name.

"Never," Rasalom said softly, with no show of emotion, "*ever* refer to yourself by my name."

"Who says it's *your* name?" Semelee cried, baring her teeth.

Jack had to hand it to her—she wasn't cowed. And the way she took the blow . . . clearly she'd been slapped around before.

"I do," Roma said softly. "And the only reason I haven't

pulled your limbs and head from your torso is that you somehow—through pure dumb luck, I'm sure—managed to find a way to kill the Lady. For that I am in your debt. But don't press your luck, little girl."

"Ain't luck," she said. "And I ain't no little girl! I was down in that hole, in the lights, and I heard the voices. They told me I was the One and that my name was Rasalom."

He slapped her again, harder, and this time she went down. She lay in the mud, rubbing her reddened cheek. A few minutes ago the rain might have soothed it, but it was clearly easing up.

"This is your last warning," he said. "You are not the One. What you heard was talk about *me*, not you."

"No!" she screamed, struggling to her feet and backing away. "I'm the One, and my name is Rasalom! Rasalom-Rasalom-Rasalom!" She raised the shells and pressed them over her eyes. "And now you're gonna pay. Nobody pushes me around anymore! *Nobody!*"

Jack knew what was coming and found himself rooting for her.

Enemy of my enemy . . .

He looked over toward the cenote and saw half a dozen chew wasps rising from the opening. He guessed they hadn't been too far down.

Oh, yes . . . Rasalom was in for one messy, bloody, and—Jack hoped—painful death. He was glad for a front row seat.

The wasps arranged themselves in V formation and charged, homing in on Rasalom.

Jack braced himself. This was going to be ugly, but he wanted to watch every second of it.

Rasalom remained facing Semelee, his back to the cenote. When the wasps were almost upon him, Rasalom gestured with his left hand—little more than a wrist-flick, like a diner signaling a waiter that the amount in the wine-glass was quite sufficient, thank you—and they stopped, hovering around him like bees guarding a hive.

Jack heard a low-pitched screech from Semelee. Her teeth were clenched and bared as she struggled for control of the chew wasps. Jack could tell by the vaguely amused twist of Rasalom's lips that he was enjoying the struggle and that she didn't have a chance.

Finally he seemed to tire of the game. Another flick of his hand and the wasps were on her like ants on a sugar cube. She dropped her shells and tried to bat them away but they attacked from all sides and she went down in sprays of red, kicking, thrashing, writhing. Her screams as they tore her flesh were awful to hear. Jack couldn't help wonder if Anya had wailed like that.

Jack looked away, toward Rasalom, and almost worse than the screams was the avid look on his face as he stood over her and watched her death agonies.

If he could move an arm, just one arm, he could pull out one of the grenades still clipped to his belt and frag this bastard. But his body wouldn't respond.

As soon as Semelee's screaming died away in a gurgling moan, Rasalom seemed to lose interest. He sauntered to where Jack sat propped against the tree trunk and stood over him.

Now it's my turn, he thought as his bladder clenched.

He hoped he didn't go out screaming like Semelee, but the pain of being eaten alive had to be . . . his imagination failed him.

The rain died to a drizzle and the sky lightened fractionally as Rasalom stared down at him. Again Jack tried to speak but his voice was locked.

Then he gave Jack's foot a dismissive kick.

"My instincts tell me to kill you now, that you'll be a stone upon my path. But I can't see you ever being too much of a stone for me to kick aside any time I wish. Besides, killing you now might be something of a favor. It would spare you so much pain in the months to come. And why should I do you a favor? Why should I spare you that pain? I don't want you to miss one iota of what is coming your way."

The words drove a cold spike through Jack.

. . . so much pain in the months to come . . .

What did that mean? What was going to cause it? And how did he know? Jack wanted to shout the questions but couldn't even whisper.

He struggled to move. He wanted at this smug son of a bitch, wanted to smash his jaw and rip out his tongue.

Rasalom glanced back to where Semelee had been. A partially flayed skull and a twisted mass of blood-matted white hair were all that remained of her. The chew wasps milling above her seemed confused; two of them bumped in midair and started to fight. Was it the increasing light? Was that what was bothering them?

Rasalom made another of his little gestures and the wasps darted for the cenote. He pointed toward what was left of Semelee.

"Physical pain is mere sustenance. But a strong man slowly battered into despair and hopelessness . . . that is a delicacy. In your case, it might even approach ecstasy. I don't want to deprive myself of that." He frowned. "Of course there's always the risk that what's coming will only make you stronger. But it's a gamble I'm willing to take. So for now, you live on. But as soon as you stop amusing me . . ."

He let the words hang as he turned and stepped off the bank onto the water.

As Rasalom strode away, Jack felt the pressure against him ease, but slowly. He wasn't able to regain his feet until Rasalom was out of sight. His first urge was to go after him, but that dissolved in a blast of anxiety about his father. He rushed over to where he'd last seen him and found him sprawled in a clump of ferns, his legs and arms splayed in all directions.

Jack rushed toward him. "Dad!"

Was this the sort of pain Rasalom was talking about? He'd lost Kate, now he was going to lose his father?

But as Jack reached him, he moved.

13

Tom sat up and ran his hands over his arms and legs.

I can move! I can feel!

Dear God, I thought—

He looked up and saw Jack skid to a stop before him.

"Dad—you okay?"

"I thought I'd had a stroke! One moment I was standing by that tree. I saw you fly backwards, then the next thing I knew I was on my back and couldn't speak or move a finger."

Jack reached a hand down to him. "Can you get up?"

Tom let his son help him to his feet. He brushed himself off and looked around. He felt shaky and a little weak. Well, why not? He was seventy-one and had just experienced the firefight of his life. He'd been in battle before, but against other men, other soldiers. This time . . .

"Jack! What happened here? Who was that? Was he really walking on water?"

"That's what it looked like."

Jack's eyes were flat. Not hard and cold like before

when he looked like murder personified, but Tom sensed that he'd put up a wall.

"What's going on, Jack? A girl who can control snakes and birds and even flying things from hell—and I'm sure that sinkhole goes straight to hell—and a guy who walks on water . . . what's happening to the world?"

"Nothing that hasn't been going on for a long, long time. Nothing's changed except you got a peek behind the curtain."

"What curtain?"

What was he talking about? Had Jack snapped under the stress of what he'd been through . . . or had he been through something like this before . . . something even worse?

"It's over, Dad."

"What's over?"

"Semelee, the chew wasps, the guy on the water—"

"But you knew him. You called him by name—Roma, wasn't it?"

"Just let it go, Dad. Tuck it away and forget about it. It's over." He looked up. "Even Hurricane Elvis is over."

Tom realized then that it had stopped raining. He could still hear the rumble of thunder, but the wind had died, leaving the air deathly still. He followed Jack's gaze, and through the partially denuded tree branches he saw clear sky, light blue, tinged with orange from the sinking sun.

Over . . . for a while there he'd thought the storm would never end.

He looked around . . . at the fallen palms and cypresses, at the slowly sinking houseboats canted in the leaf- and debris-strewn water, at their red decks and the mutilated bodies littering them like jackstraws.

Tom's mouth went dry. "Did we do that?"

"Some of it." He didn't seem the least bit fazed. "We can take credit for the holes in the hulls and some of the blood, but Semelee bears the freight for the rest. She's the one who called those chew wasps out of the cenote and lost control of them. Good thing too. Otherwise they'd be standing here looking at what was left of us."

Jack picked up one of the shotguns and hurled it far out into the lagoon.

"What—?"

"Evidence."

The second shotgun followed the first. He saw Jack pull the pistol from his belt, look at it, then tuck it back in.

Tom glanced once more at the carnage on the boat decks, then looked again. Had one of the bodies moved?

"I think someone's still alive out there."

"Probably not for long."

"Do you think we should—?"

Jack turned on him. "You've got to be kidding. A few moments ago they were trying to kill us."

"In the Corps we always treated enemy wounded."

"This isn't the Corps, and this isn't war. This is a street fight that just happened to take place where there aren't any streets." His face twisted, almost into a snarl. "What do you think we're going to do? Paddle a couple of them back and lug them to a hospital? How do you explain their wounds? How do you explain the double-ought buckshot in their hides? In this system, you'll wind up behind bars while they lounge around a hospital. And when they're all fixed up, some ambulance chaser will hook up with them and file civil suits to clean you out of everything you own, every penny you've saved up your whole life."

Tom was seeing another side of Jack and wasn't sure he liked this one.

"But—"

"But nothing!"

He turned and stomped off to one of the old huts and returned a moment later with something dangling from his hand. He stopped before Tom and held it up.

"See this?"

It was rectangular and looked a little like parchment, but it was too supple for that. It was patterned with crisscrossing scars and round, punctate depressions the size of a pencil eraser. When Tom realized what it was he took an involuntary step back.

"Right," Jack said. "This is all they left of Anya, and then they hung it up to cure. Now tell me how much you want to risk to help one of those bastards."

Tom felt a rising fury. Anya . . . what they'd done to Anya . . . a part of him wanted to paddle out there and finish off any survivors. But he couldn't allow himself to step over that line.

He shook his head. "Nothing. They're on they're own."

"Damn right."

Jack stared at the grisly remnant in his hands, then looked around. He didn't seem to know what to do with it. He appeared to come to a decision as he rolled up the skin and tucked it inside his shirt.

"What are you going to do with that?"

"It's all that's left of her. I think she deserves some sort of burial ceremony, don't you?"

Here was still another side of Jack. Tom sensed it could be a living nightmare to be his son's enemy, but a very good thing to be his friend.

He nodded. "Most definitely. Now that the storm's over, we'll take her home and find a place to lay her to rest."

Jack looked up at the sky. "Good thing it ended when it did. I thought we were in for a much longer blow."

"So did I."

Then an awful thought struck him. He turned and started pushing through the ferns and brush.

"Where are you going?" Jack called from behind him.

"To high ground. I want the highest point on this hummock."

It wasn't far—these islands in the saw grass sea weren't all that large. Just a few minutes walk and he was standing atop the crest of the hummock.

But he still didn't have the view he needed. He hurried to a nearby live oak that somehow had weathered the storm intact. He stretched for the lowest branch but couldn't reach it.

"Give me a boost," he said to Jack, who had followed him.

"What do you think you're doing?"

"Just help me up, damn it. I need to see."

He was sorry for the sharp tone, but he was worried. He crawled onto the limb, then, hanging on to a nearby branch, straightened until he was standing. When he saw the wall of cloud and rain less than a mile away to the west, his fears were confirmed.

"Jack, the hurricane isn't over. We're in its eye. It's going to hit us again. Maybe even worse than what we've been through. We've got to—oh, hell!"

"What?" Jack said from below.

Tom watched a pale funnel cloud skating back and forth inside the edge of the onrushing eye wall. Another snaked down a short way north of the first.

"Tornadoes!" He turned and slid down the trunk. "We have to get off this hummock!"

"Tornadoes?" As soon as Tom landed on the ground, Jack started climbing. "I've always wanted to see a tornado." He reached the limb and peered west. "I'll be damned. Three of them."

"Three? There were only two before! Get down from there and get moving!"

Jack stared a few heartbeats longer, then joined Tom on the ground.

Jack led the way back to the lagoon on a run. As they passed the sinkhole, Tom slowed and peered into the depths. The lights had faded to a dim glow and the lagoon had risen to the level where water was beginning to trickle over the edge.

"This thing should be sealed up," he said. "Maybe after all this is over we should come back and—"

Jack spoke over his shoulder. "Don't worry about it. It's closing itself down until the spring. Keep moving."

Closing itself down . . . how could he know that?

Tom was winded, with a dull ache squeezing his chest by the time they reached the bank. He hunched over, hands on knees, panting while Jack inspected the clan's boats. He pointed to a water-filled flat-bottom dinghy at the edge of the lagoon with *Chicken-ship* across its stern.

"This one's got a bigger motor than the canoe. We'll make better time. Help me tip it up to get rid of this water." He stared at him. "You okay?"

"Yeah," Tom said. "Just not conditioned for this."

Tipping a boat was the last thing Tom felt like doing right now, but he didn't think Jack could handle it alone. Jack pulled off his poncho and positioned himself at the aft end of the starboard side. As Tom moved to join him, something splashed near Jack's foot. Tom saw him jump and scramble away from the water.

Tom too backed away when he saw what was crawling up the bank. He'd heard mention of a two-headed snapping turtle, and hadn't quite believed it, but here it was— and much larger than he would have imagined. The shell had to be at least four feet long. It's gaping hooked jaws closed with loud clacks and they snapped at Jack.

Jack yanked a grenade from his belt, pulled the pin, and popped the clip.

"This is for Carl," he said, and lobbed it toward the creature.

Tom stood paralyzed for a moment. Carl . . . dear God, he'd all but forgotten about poor Carl . . .

He saw the right head snatch the grenade on the fly and swallow it, then Jack was rushing him, pushing him to the ground.

"Down!"

Tom hit the mud and covered his head with his hands. The explosion was muffled but he could still feel the impact through the ground. And then bloody turtle meat and bits of shell began to rain around them.

When it stopped, Jack helped him to his feet, then stepped back to the boat. The remains of the snapper were sinking into the water, trailing a red cloud. Jack froze, then hurried to the stern.

"Christ! Can't we get a break here?"

"What's wrong?"

"The explosion sheared off the propeller!" He kicked the side of the boat. "Damn! Okay. Looks like it's the canoe."

They hurried along the bank to where they'd left it. Jack slipped into the rear and started yanking on the little motor's pull cord. After a couple of dozen quick pulls, he spewed a string of curses and gave up. The motor hadn't even coughed.

"Won't start. Who knows what was blown or washed into it during the storm. We'll have to power it ourselves."

"Jack . . ." Tom hated to admit it, but he was all in. "I don't know if I can."

Jack stared at him a moment, then said, "It's okay, Dad. I'll handle it. You take the rear, maybe use the outboard as a rudder while I paddle us out of here."

Feeling unsteady, Tom stepped into the canoe and dropped into the rear seat. His chest felt funny, as if his heart was flailing wildly against his sternum. The chaotic rhythm left him drained. But not too drained to grab the tiller of the motor as Jack began paddling.

The canoe nosed out of the lagoon and soon they were gliding along the swollen channel. They hadn't gone too far before the light began to die as the clouds closed in again. Then the wind and rain returned with a vengeance.

Tom still wore his poncho but Jack had shed his a while back. His T-shirt was plastered to his skin and Tom watched the play of muscles across his son's back as he worked the paddle. Not bulky steroidal clumps, but sleek efficient bands, close to the skin. He hadn't noticed Jack's muscles till now. Where had they come from? He'd been such a skinny kid, even in college. Now . . . well, he reminded Tom of a few guys he'd known in the service, lean, quiet types who didn't look like much until someone tried to push them around. He'd seen a guy built like Jack take down someone twice his size.

He'd been angry with Jack all these years for disappearing, and never more angry than when he didn't show up for Kate's funeral. But all that seemed ancient history now. Despite Jack's secretiveness, his reclusiveness, his quirky behavior, Tom realized he loved, even admired the strange, enigmatic man his son had grown into. He sensed a strength, a resolve, a simple decency about him. He'd worried for so long that he must have made terrible mistakes raising Jack—why else would he turn his back on his family the way he had?—but now he sensed that maybe he'd done all right. Not that anyone should take full credit or full blame for how another person turns out; everyone makes their own choices. But as a parent he had to think he'd had *some* input.

More than anything he wanted Jack to survive this storm. He didn't care about himself so much, though of course he wasn't looking to die, but he sensed somehow that it was important for Jack to live—not simply important to his father, but for other, larger reasons. He couldn't pinpoint what those were; they hovered just out of reach, but they were there. Somewhere along the way, Jack was going to *matter*.

Tom's heart had resumed a more sedate rhythm but it jumped again as a lightning bolt speared the saw grass ahead of them. He looked around in the near-night darkness. They were out in the open, begging to be struck by lightning; but staying among the trees of the hummock, especially with this wind and tornadoes, seemed even riskier.

They rounded a bend in the channel and the canoe kicked ahead as the wind roared from behind. Tom spread his flapping poncho to give the wind something more to blow against. It worked. The canoe picked up speed.

He was feeling pretty proud of himself until another bolt of lightning lit up a funnel cloud reaching for the ground a few hundred yards to his left. It hadn't touched down, which meant it wasn't—

Another flash showed it on the ground, kicking up mud and grass and water. It was now officially a tornado.

He leaned forward and tapped Jack on the shoulder. "Look left!"

Jack did so, and of course the lightning chose just that moment to hold off; but then a double flash lit up the funnel, whiter than before, and closer. It was coming this way.

"Fuck!" Jack shouted and started paddling even harder.

Fuck . . . Tom had rarely if ever used the word since leaving the Marines. He didn't believe it belonged within the walls of a family home, and certainly not in mixed company. But looking at that swirling, swaying mass of wind and debris heading their way . . . fuck.

Yes, fuck indeed.

During storms on trips to the Keys, he'd witness an occasional waterspout—long, pale, wispy, short-lived things more beautiful than threatening. Even though there was plenty of water about, this thing to the left wasn't a waterspout, nor was it one of those quarter-mile-wide monsters

the Weather Channel liked to show. Its base seemed to be
only fifty feet or so across—

Only? Tom thought. What am I thinking? That thing is
plenty big enough to kill us both.

He tried to gauge its intensity. He knew about the Fujita
scale—he'd learned a few things during all those hours in
front of the Weather Channel—and hoped this one didn't
clock in at more than an F2. They wouldn't survive a direct
hit by an F2, but they might handle a close encounter. If
they wound up near anything higher up the scale, that
would be it.

No matter what its scale, Tom prayed it would head in
the other direction.

He pulled a paddle from the sloshing bottom of the canoe and did what he could to speed the boat along. He kept
glancing to his left. He could hear a growing roar—that
was the damn tornado getting closer, running on an erratic
diagonal that was sure to intersect their course. At least
that was how it looked. The way it was weaving back and
forth made avoidance a crap shoot.

The big question: Stay in the boat or get out? In the boat
seemed worse than being in a trailer. They were too exposed; if that funnel came even close, flying debris could
cut them to shreds. But to get out . . .

Jack was looking around too.

"Let's dump the boat!" he shouted over the growing
roar.

"And go where?"

He pointed to the right. "I saw something over there."

Tom squinted through the rain and darkness. A flash revealed the dark splotch of a willow thicket sitting like an
island in the saw grass sea. The willows tended to be small
in these thickets, little more than a dozen feet tall. They'd
provide some shelter, something to hold on to without
worrying it would crush them if it toppled over.

A glance in the opposite direction showed the tornado even closer.

"Let's do it!" Tom shouted.

"What about gators?"

"If they're smart they're on the bottom of the deepest channel they can find."

He didn't mention snakes. He had no idea what snakes did in weather like this. He hoped they didn't head for higher ground . . . like hummocks and thickets . . .

Jack jumped out of the canoe, Tom followed. The water was thigh high in the channel. Tom slipped only once climbing the slope to the saw grass where the water was only ankle deep. Jack pulled the canoe up behind him and left it on its side in the grass.

Lightning lit their way as they sloshed toward the thicket, Jack in the lead, while the roar of the twister grew behind them . . . no, not behind them . . . to the left . . .

A flash revealed the swaying, writhing funnel less than a hundred yards away, flanking them. Tom gasped for breath as his heart writhed like the twister. How had it caught up so fast? Another flash showed it veering this way. Almost seemed as if it was chasing them, homing in on them. But that was ridiculous.

Then again, after all he'd seen today . . .

"Crawl in here!" Jack shouted as they reached the thicket. His voice was barely audible over the roar of the onrushing funnel. Tom saw that he was holding aside a patch of underbrush. "Find a trunk and hang on!"

Tom dropped to his hands and knees as he ducked into the leafy mesh, feeling ahead of him in the dark until he found a sturdy-feeling trunk maybe six inches across.

"You take this one!" he shouted to Jack who was close behind. "I'll take the next."

He heard a garbled protest from Jack but kept moving.

Half a dozen feet farther on he found another, more slender trunk, maybe half the size of the first. He dropped prone and wrapped his arms around it. His lungs struggled for air. God, it was good to lie still. He felt his heart ramming at his chest wall as he lay in the mud.

"You okay, Jack?" he shouted. He could barely hear himself above the tornado's roar. "Jack?"

That roar . . . it had to be at least an F2 . . . any higher, they were goners.

Frantic, he looked around for Jack and saw nothing but darkness. And then the tree began to shake and the ground to tremble; he ducked his head against the wind and the saw grass blades whistling through the underbrush like knives.

Thank God they weren't trying to weather this back at the lagoon. The flying debris from the boats and the huts would be lethal. Here it was only grass and mud and water. Not that any of that would matter if the funnel passed directly over them.

The wind scythed at him from all angles as he clung to the trunk. He could hear the twister grinding through the saw grass on the far edge of the thicket, roaring like a freight train—he'd always heard tornado survivors describe the sound that way, and now he knew it was true . . . like a train . . . in a tunnel . . .

Tom felt the underbrush around him being twisted and yanked from the mud. And then his tree started to tilt, first to the left, then the right, then—

Dear God, it was coming out of the ground, ripping free of the mud, rising into the air!

Tom had to let go or rise with it. As he released his grip the willow ripped free with an agonized *crunch* and sailed off. He tried to cling to the rootlets left in the hole but the deluge of water made them slick and they slipped through his fingers. Then he felt his legs lift as he was pulled backward. He clutched for grass or weeds or ferns—anything!—but they came free in his grasp. His body angled off the ground and he clawed at mud that had no more consistency than beef stew. He was losing his last contact with the ground when he felt a hand grab his right ankle and yank him down.

Jack!

Another set of fingers wound around his left ankle and started hauling him backward. He heard Jack's enraged voice shouting above the storm.

"You got away with this once, but not again. No fucking way!"

Who was he talking to? The twister? But he'd said "again." Tom doubted Jack had ever even seen a twister, let alone dealt with one. Who, then?

He'd worry about that later. Right now he wanted to know how Jack was hanging on. If both hands were holding Tom, who was holding Jack?

He felt one of Jack's hands grab his belt and haul him farther back. Tom craned his neck to look over his shoulder and saw that Jack had locked his legs around a willow trunk. He kept dragging Tom back until he could wrap his arms around the larger tree.

And with that . . . the roaring began to fade. After brushing the thicket, the twister was moving on, probably carving a new channel through the saw grass as it traveled.

Jack rolled away from the tree and lay on his back.

"Thought I was going to lose you there, Dad."

As his heart regained a normal rhythm, Tom watched Jack lie there with closed eyes as rain pounded his face.

"I thought I was a goner too. Thanks."

"*De nada.*"

Nothing? No, it wasn't nothing. It was something . . . something very special. He owed his life to Jack.

He couldn't think of anyone he'd more like to be indebted to.

Tom swallowed the lump in his throat. "Come on. Let's see if we can find that canoe and get to someplace dry."

TUESDAY

1

"I've decided to move back north," Dad said as Jack packed his duffel bag for the trip home.

Jack studied his face, still bruised from the accident, and weathered from the storm. "You're sure about that?"

Dad nodded. "Very. I'll never be able to look at Anya's house without remembering what . . . what we saw there . . . what happened to her. And I can't see me ever looking out my front door at the Everglades without thinking of the other night . . . all that blood spilled, especially Carl's . . . and that sinkhole and the things that came out of it. And the storm, that tornado . . ." He shook his head. "We damn near died out there."

"But we didn't," Jack told him. "That's all that counts."

It hadn't been easy getting back. The canoe had been far enough from the twister to come through in one piece, but the subsequent battle through the storm had been an ordeal. With the smaller channels filling up, and no way to judge east or west, Jack had become disoriented and made a few wrong turns. It took nearly two hours of paddling before they arrived at the air-boat dock and gratefully collapsed in the shelter of the car.

Monday had been spent recuperating. Muscles Jack didn't even know he had protested every time he moved. The groundsmen—sans Carl—were out in force cleaning up the mess left by the storm. They must have seen Anya's shredded screen door but probably attributed it to the storm.

Late in the afternoon, after the crews had finished for the day and no one was about, Jack and his father buried Anya's remains in her garden, among the plants she'd loved. Since she kept pretty much to herself, no one had discovered yet that she was missing.

Jack dug a two-foot hole in the wet soil—deeper than any dog or coon would go—and then Dad reverently placed the quarter-folded skin within. He'd chosen not to wrap it in anything. Better to let it decompose quickly and recycle its nutrients back to her plants.

And then a quiet night of mourning, Dad looking for answers to a long list of questions, Jack doing his best not to answer them. Dad didn't need to know more than he already did and, despite what he'd been through, probably wouldn't accept the truth as Jack understood it. So Jack told him only what he'd gleaned from Anya and let him assume that the rest of the answers had died with her. It never occurred to either of them to turn on the Monday night football game.

"Besides," Dad was saying on this bright morning, "what am I doing down here while my sons and all my grandchildren are up north? It makes no sense. I don't know what I was thinking."

Maybe you weren't thinking, Jack thought. Maybe you were being manipulated. Maybe everything that's happened down here was part of a plan—a plan that, thanks to Anya, didn't go quite the way it was supposed to.

And then again, maybe not.

But with the Otherness so obviously involved, Jack couldn't help but think that his father had been scheduled to die last Tuesday morning.

"Maybe I'll come south for just a month or two a year," Dad went on, "say February and March. Statistics say that an American male who reaches age sixty-five can expect to live another sixteen years. That leaves me ten more.

Makes no sense to spend them fifteen hundred miles from the most important people in my life."

"You're right. It doesn't."

Jack had a feeling he'd better watch over his father. He was sure the Otherness wasn't through with him yet. Rasalom's words kept haunting him:

. . . a strong man slowly battered into despair and hopelessness . . . that is a delicacy. In your case, it might even approach ecstasy . . .

How was this battering into despair and hopelessness going to happen? By destroying everyone he cared about?

He was glad his father would be closer to home, but right now he wanted to get back to Gia and Vicky. Worry for them was a knife point in his back, urging him home. And he had to get working on a way to become a citizen before March, when the baby was due.

Yesterday he'd overnighted the Ruger back to one of his mail drops. He'd pick it up after it was forwarded to another drop. All he had to do now was pack up his clothes and head for the airport.

The phone rang.

"That should be the sales office," Dad said. "I phoned them first thing this morning about putting the place on the market."

As he left, Jack reminded himself to check out Blagden & Sons once he got home. See if he could find out why they wanted that sand from the cenote. He had a feeling it wasn't for mixing concrete for back porches.

He scooped the last of his things out of the bureau and froze: The rectangle of Anya's skin lay in the bottom of the drawer.

His mouth went dry. This couldn't be. They'd buried it yesterday, yet here it was, without a speck of dirt.

Jack walked out to the main room where his father was discussing prices and commissions with the sales office;

he went directly to the back porch and grabbed the shovel he used yesterday. He headed for Anya's garden.

The burial spot was just as they'd left it. Jack dug into the loose soil and quickly reached the two-foot level.

No skin.

He dug down another six inches—he knew he hadn't gone this deep yesterday—and still nothing but dirt.

Anya's skin was gone.

No, wait, not gone. It was lying in a drawer in his Dad's guest bedroom. But how . . . ?

Jack didn't waste time with unanswerable questions— how it had gotten out of the hole and into the house, why it was there. Either he'd find out later or he wouldn't.

He quickly refilled the hole and hurried back to the house. Dad was still on the phone. He looked up with a questioning expression as Jack passed but Jack waved him off. Back in the room he went directly to the bureau and froze again. Now the drawer was empty.

What the hell?

He turned and saw a now familiar pattern through the open top of his duffel bag. He stretched the zippered mouth and stared.

There it lay. Apparently Anya, or at least this piece of her, wanted to go home with him.

Jack sighed. Again, he wouldn't ask why, he'd just go with the flow and trust that sooner or later this would all make sense.

He covered the skin with his remaining clothes and zipped the bag closed.

All right, Anya, he thought. You want to come along, be my guest.

He lifted the bag and headed for the front room. Dad hung up as he entered.

"Well, just a few papers to sign and the place is officially on the market."

"Great. I hear they've got people lined up to get in here, so it shouldn't take long."

"Yeah."

A silence grew between them. Jack knew he had to go, but he was reluctant to leave his father here alone.

Finally Dad said, "It's been wonderful getting to know you, Jack. There's so much about you I still don't know, but what I've learned . . . I'm surprised, but pleasantly so."

"You're pretty full of surprises yourself."

"But you know all mine now. I get the feeling—no, I *know* you've still got quite a few left."

Here we go. "Probably not as many as you think. But who knows what you'll find out once you get back north?"

Dad nodded. "Right. Who knows?"

As if there'd been some unspoken signal, they embraced.

"Good to have you back, son," his father whispered. "Really, really good."

They broke the clinch, but still gripped each other's arms.

"Good to know the real you, Dad. You can take my back any time." He broke free and grabbed his duffel. "See you back home."

"Call me when you get in."

"You're kidding, right?"

"No. I've always worried about you, but after what I've learned about you down here, I'll really, really worry about you."

Jack laughed as he pushed through the door and headed for the car and the airport and the plane home to Gia and Vicky.

www.repairmanjack.com

AFTERWORD

South Floridians will know I played fast and loose with some of the geography in *Gateways*. Joanie's Blue Crab Café is not on US 1, but on the other side of the state, on Route 41 in Ochopee. But the crab cakes and softshell crab sandwiches are just as good as I described. While researching the Glades I'd often drive twenty or thirty miles out of my way to grab a bite and an Ybor Gold at Joanie's.

As for Gator Country FM 101.9, it's hard to pull in if you're on US 1, but travel a little ways west and there it is. A good station for modern country and it kept me company during the drives.

Novaton may seem like Homestead, but it's an amalgam of a number of towns I stayed in during my research sorties.

One thing I did not make up or overstate is the shameful neglect, mismanagement, and outright abuse suffered by the Everglades during the twentieth century. It's a fragile, fascinating environment, sui generis, that's been damn near ruined by rampant overdevelopment. There's lots of talk lately of restoring the Everglades; let's hope the folks talking the talk will walk the walk before it's too late.

F. Paul Wilson
The Jersey Shore
March, 2003
www.repairmanjack.com